Annunciation

Books by David Plante

THE FAMILY

THE COUNTRY

THE WOODS

THE FOREIGNER

THE CATHOLIC

THE NATIVE

THE ACCIDENT

ANNUNCIATION

Annunciation

DAVID PLANTE

TICKNOR & FIELDS
New York

I would like to thank John Herman, my publisher,
for his inspiring support and work on this book.
And I would also like to thank Liz Duvall
for the precision and delicacy
of her editing.

For information about permission to reproduce selections
from this book, write to Permissions, Ticknor & Fields,
215 Park Avenue South, New York, New York 10003.

Library of Congress Cataloging-in-Publication Data

Plante, David.
Annunciation / David Plante.
p.   cm.
ISBN 0-395-68091-3
1. Man-woman relationships—England—London—Fiction.
2. Mothers and daughters—England—London—Fiction.
3. Women art historians—England—London—Fiction.
4. London (England)—Fiction.
I. Title.
PS3566.L257A83   1994
813'.54—dc20   93-44724   CIP

Printed in the United States of America

AGM 10 9 8 7 6 5 4 3 2

Book design by Anne Chalmers

TO JOHN AND HUGH
WITH LOVE

Part

ONE

I

A GLASS of water in a dark room —

II

RAIN FELL against the window of the hotel room. In bed, Claire watched the rain. She didn't mind that she and George wouldn't be able to go out for a walk. George, being English, would say the rain didn't matter. She, being American, would answer that rain always meant to her being able to stay in and play dolls.

The bed was wide, with four pillows, all of which were piled behind her head and back so that she lounged, her nightgown as loose about her body as the sheets and blankets were loose on the bed. The blankets and top sheet and even the bottom sheet had come undone, pulled out from where they'd been tucked in, over the night, and when Claire, feeling that she was herself un-tucked, moved, raising a hip to change her position, all the bed-clothes moved with her. She could have stayed in bed all day, and she hoped that the rain would continue all day, or at least until they left the hotel to go back to London. There was something just a little sluttish about her, in the way a forty-year-old woman could be sluttish and amused by being so. Her movements in the bed, causing equal movements in the air, released a smell of body, and she settled again and watched the rain hit and drip down the window.

George was having a bath. The door to the bathroom was open, and Claire heard the sound of splashing water, then si-lence, deep, then again the sound of water lapping resonantly in the big tub.

The sheets were satiny, blue. When Claire was a girl, all sheets had been white, and colored sheets unthinkable. So much, when she'd been a girl growing up in America, had been unthinkable.

Drowsing a little, she thought, English rain.

She was roused when George came to the bed wearing a short terry-cloth robe supplied by the hotel. The blond hairs on his chest were still matted with damp, as were the hairs on his long legs, and the blond, wavy hair on his head, which he always kept combed as flat as he could possibly make it, was dripping at the sideburns. He had shaved and his face was bright.

He asked, "Shall I order tea?"

Claire stretched and yawned and said, "Yes, please," and, writhing a little, settled more deeply among the tousled bedclothes.

George went to the window to look out, or, it seemed, to try to look out. His upper lip rose over his teeth as he peered.

"How does it look?" Claire asked.

"Difficult to say," he answered.

When there was a knock on the door of the room, he went, barefoot on the carpet, to take the tray. He brought the tray to the bed, and Claire, her breasts shaking in the lacy bodice of her white nightgown, sat up when he handed her a cup. With his cup, he sat on the edge of the bed.

"It doesn't look as though we'll be able to go for a walk," she said.

"Of course we can go out for a walk."

"I knew you'd say that."

"Isn't that why we came to stay the weekend in the country, to take walks?" He smiled.

"That's what you think."

"What," he asked, his face stern, "can one possibly do that would be better than taking a walk in the rain?"

"Staying in bed and playing dolls," she said.

The light through the window cast the shadows of dripping rain.

George took her cup from her, placed it on the tray on the floor by the bed, placed his cup on the tray too, and stood, looked about as if for something that he had forgotten and that he was all at once reminded of but that he decided wasn't important enough for him to pay attention to now, and stretched his arms, his elbows bent and his fists at his ears, and groaned. Then he looked at Claire for a moment before he began, smiling, to untie the belt of his robe. She, smiling too, held out her long, bare arms.

But he had his way about a walk before lunch. She had had her way, he said, and he'd have his way. It was still raining, and he borrowed an umbrella from the hotel. He had brought along gumboots from London.

Now she did want to go out in the rain for a walk with him.

The wet countryside was just coming into early spring, and the paths were muddy. The buds, the branches, the moss-covered trunks of trees, the mulching leaves of last year on the ground, seemed to be so saturated with water they might suddenly, with just the addition of one big, round, full drop of rain, all dissolve, and George and Claire would have to turn their large umbrella upside down and get into it and float over an England that had become all green-brown water.

They walked along a country lane, where the hedgerows were beginning to blossom, small white petals among the still bare branches, some of the branches within the hedge cut to stumps. Birds flew in and out of the hedges. George and Claire had to draw back to the side of the lane when a khaki military van passed.

"What's a military van doing here?" Claire asked.

"Perhaps there's a military base nearby," George said. "Don't you think, perhaps?"

"How would I possibly know?" From time to time, Claire heard herself speak with the English accent she had picked up over the three years she had lived in London. But unlike the English, she wouldn't say "Perhaps" to any question she didn't know the answer to. She'd say she didn't know.

They climbed a hill and at the top stopped, pressed together under the umbrella, to look at the view of rain falling on the downs.

They turned to walk back to the hotel. After lunch they'd return to London, and as if this were the least pressing of what they could talk about of their lives in London, George asked Claire questions about her research on the Italian painter on whom she was supposed to be writing a thesis. He hadn't asked before, and he wasn't, she knew, very interested, but she didn't mind this.

She moaned a little and said, "I have really got to get down to it."

"Haven't you discovered something that would get me interested in him?"

"Well, the more I find out about him," she said, "the more I think my husband must have been like him. Like my artist, Frank was a big, dark man, and like my artist, he had all the big, dark feelings to go with the way he looked."

"Frank was big and dark, was he?"

"Yes."

George was big and blond.

Whenever Claire mentioned Frank, she wondered immediately

why she did. She never wanted to talk about her dead husband, not with anyone, and yet she often did bring him up with George.

She said, "I don't know if I'll finish the thesis, I really don't. I'm good at getting the facts, I'm even pedantic about getting all the facts, but when it comes to writing the text I become lazy or something, suddenly."

The next reference to life in London would have to be about Claire's daughter Rachel, but as they walked along the gravel drive to the hotel, the windows of the dining room lit up so she could see young men in white shirts and black bow ties setting the tables for Sunday lunch, she thought: Not now, not now.

She was, however, always aware of Rachel in London in their house, which, away from it, Claire thought of as a big, dark house. And though she was sure George was right to have convinced her to come with him on this, their first weekend together, he hadn't dispelled her anxiety about leaving Rachel alone. And though George had been right to insist she tell Rachel she was coming on a weekend with him, he hadn't dispelled her anxieties about this either. And George sensed her anxiety growing as the time to return to London came nearer.

George said, as if at a business lunch when he would come around to the point with coffee, which was just poured, "Tell me about Rachel."

"Sometimes I think she's being difficult because of us, then sometimes I think she's trying to be understanding and really is just behaving the way a sixteen-year-old girl would. I don't know. She's been called in more and more lately to be spoken to by the headmistress of her school. I never know what mood she'll be in when she gets home. She might be angry because Miss Hemmings called her in to reprimand her for wearing earrings that hang below her lobes. Only earrings that don't hang are allowed at her school. Another time she might come home so incensed by the injustices of the headmistress against her, her in particular, she'll refuse to discuss them with me, and when I try to get her to talk she'll just press her lips together so her cheeks swell and shake her head and refuse to say anything. But the next time she comes home she might say that the headmistress asked her to read out a psalm at the three hundredth anniversary of the school, to be celebrated in Westminster Abbey."

"And this makes you anxious?" George asked.

Claire said, "It's like what I was saying about —" She stopped and said, "As I was saying about organizing my research material but not being able, for some reason, to get down to my thesis, I feel that as much as I do for Rachel, there's something that I can't get myself to do for her but that she really needs. And now she needs so much more from me than before she knew about you and me."

"You're frightened that now you won't be able to give her what she needs?"

"Frightened? Yes, maybe, even more than anxious. I wonder what we mean to her."

George laughed a little. "I think you imagine we mean more to her than we do. What Rachel needs is a boyfriend."

"Rachel, have a boyfriend?"

"You can't conceive of that?"

Claire frowned. "Not really."

"She's old enough. She's old enough for one to wonder why she doesn't have a boyfriend."

"You know, I can't think of Rachel as being any older than when her father died."

"Three years in the life of a girl are enough to make her a very different person from what she was. Aren't you stunting her with her father's death?"

Claire frowned.

"It's about time you got over his death," George said.

"Me?" Claire asked. "I? You think I'm not over it?"

"I know you're not."

"And both Rachel and I need to get over it?"

Swirling the last of his coffee so the sugar would rise up from the bottom and swirl into it, George said, "I would like to help you both get over it," and he drank the little black whirlpool.

Claire went still. "Is this a proposal?"

"What do you think my intention might have been, inviting you to come spend a weekend in the country?"

"Oh," Claire said.

"I know how anxious you are about Rachel," George said. "I know you wouldn't agree to marry me if she didn't agree also to your marrying. If she did agree, I know I could help her, perhaps in ways you can't quite, at least until she has a boyfriend. Will you discuss it with Rachel and ask if she agrees?"

"I'll have to find the right moment," Claire said, which she thought sounded evasive, and she had meant it to sound not evasive but decisive.

They had second cups of coffee and sat at the table, which, with its rucked cloth and large, stained napkins thrown on it, looked a little like an unmade bed, and they both evidently didn't want to leave, though they didn't say much to each other.

Claire emitted a faint groan when George, raising his torso with the effort to rise entirely and stand, said, "I guess we'd better pack and get on our way back to London." But he sank again and didn't stand. He put his wide, big-knuckled hand flat on the table, and Claire reached across and put hers on his, and he turned his over and gripped hers in his.

Claire said, "You're so kind to me," and she tightened her grip on George's hand.

George laughed. He had a way of commiserating with her and being slightly ironical at the same time, which was one of the reasons why Claire loved him. He said, "You always sound surprised that I am."

"I suppose I am."

"Someday," George said, "I may surprise you in an altogether other way."

Their room was as they had left it, and rain was still falling against the window. It took George just minutes to pack, after which he sat in the armchair. Claire took longer, especially now, when she felt that all her movements were made slow by the heaviness of her body. She stretched out her nightgown on the rumpled bed and began to fold it, but her arms were so heavy she wondered if she'd be able to move them. She looked toward George, who had been looking at her, and a feeling, perhaps similar to the laziness or whatever that made it difficult for her ever to make herself do what she knew she must do, came over her, came over her like an impulse, and she said, "Couldn't we stay till tomorrow morning?"

"We could," George said quietly.

"I'd have to ring Rachel."

"That could be done too."

Then Claire seemed not sure about giving in to her impulse. "She's never gone off to school when I haven't been in the house to say goodbye to her."

"It'll be a first for her," George said simply.

Claire went to the window, not to look out but to think of a way out of what, without thinking, she'd proposed, resenting herself for not just giving in to the impulse. She said, "We'll leave it to Rachel. I did say I'd be back Sunday afternoon, and if she wants me back, we'll go back."

"That's fair enough," George said.

If only, Claire thought, Rachel would say to her in a bright voice when she rang, I'm so glad you're having a good time. But that wasn't the kind of thing Rachel said.

Claire took off her shoes. All she wanted to do was lie on the bed and close her eyes, and this she did, for a moment; then she sat up and reached for the telephone by the bed and dialed Rachel in London. When the telephone was answered, Claire inserted her feet back in her shoes.

Rachel's voice sounded far. Though she said she was all right alone in London, and she'd be all right getting off to school in the morning, Claire felt, the moment she hung up the receiver, that she had made a mistake, and she wished George had told her that it'd be better if they didn't stay but got back to London because she would feel bad about leaving Rachel another night and the time added to the weekend would be spoiled. Claire saw herself, a middle-aged mother, sitting on the edge of the bed, and instead of lying back she got up and put on her shoes and, swinging her arms, walked about the room and said, with a false voice, "What about another walk?" The time added to the weekend was spoiled.

George understood her confusion and kept up his light, easy talk, as only an Englishman could keep up light and easy talk. Claire loved the way his wavy blond hair was combed flat and parted with such a straight parting.

Claire couldn't stop thinking of Rachel in the big, dark house.

In the morning, she wondered if she should ring Rachel before the time she knew Rachel would leave for school and tell her, as she would have if she'd been home, to have a good day, but she didn't because she didn't want to do it in front of George, and even when he left her to pay the bill she didn't.

The rain had stopped but the morning was so moist that tiny drops condensed on Claire's thick black hair as she waited on the gravel drive for George.

In the car, George said to Claire, "What, really, I'd like to do is invite you and Rachel to my flat for dinner. Would she come?"

"You'll find out if you ask her."

George, maybe to reassure her that everything was going to be all right, wanted to make plans that would involve Rachel, but Claire didn't want to talk about Rachel.

She asked George to let her off with her weekend bag in front of the Courtauld Institute, where she said she would, as it was early, do a little research in the library. But she spent the day there, mostly thinking of Rachel at school, of Rachel and herself, of Rachel and George, of Rachel and Rachel. And was she using Rachel as an excuse for not being able to do the work she had come to the institute to do, and too for not marrying George? The lights hanging from the library ceiling were reflected in the windows, behind which the afternoon got so dark the streetlamps were lit. She tried to read an eighteenth-century text in Italian, but her eyes kept focusing on the tiny brown marks of the foxing instead of the words. She forced herself to read.

Claire's thesis was meant to be on the Lucchese painter Pietro Testa, who, a melancholic young man, killed himself around the age of forty. There were references to Pietro in books, a catalogue of a major show of his prints and drawings, but not a full study on him. But Claire wondered if she was up to a full study.

She put the book back in the stacks and left the institute, near Marble Arch, to be at home, in distant Clapham, before Rachel got home from school.

It hadn't been right, she thought, to stay that extra night away from Rachel, and maybe it hadn't been right to spend any night away from her.

To Claire, London seemed dark, and as she walked along the fenced-in and locked garden in the square outside the institute, she looked in. The darkness of London always seemed filled with leaves, close about her, and she wasn't sure what the white and red lights behind the leaves were, though at the same time she knew they were car lights and shop lights.

She might be late getting home, and Rachel would find the house empty, and this made Claire panic. Then she thought, she had stayed at the institute all day, and even left late, because she didn't want to be at home when Rachel got in. This made Claire panic more, and she rushed with her bag to the bus stop.

As Claire was waiting for her bus from Marble Arch to Clapham, standing silently among people also waiting, she heard a voice call her, and she looked, not around but up. She had thought that her husband Frank was calling her.

She did get home before Rachel, who should, however, have arrived before she had. Claire thought: She's been called in to Miss Hemmings's office again.

Claire didn't want to stay in the house, a gray-brick house with a slate roof where she and Rachel had lived the three years they had been in London. She knew she mustn't, however, go far, and she went out into the back garden and picked up a rusty trowel from the lawn and began to dig in a bare bed. The air was chill enough for her breath to steam as she dug.

Her trowel struck something, and Claire dug around it — an earth-filled drinking glass. Flatirons, broken cups and plates and medicine and milk bottles and even cracked spectacles, she had dug up in the past when she'd worked in the garden. Claire threw the glass back into the hole and buried it.

Surely, Claire thought, Rachel had been kept in school by the headmistress.

The garden was entirely dark, and though the garden walls, of the same gray brick as the house, were high, Claire had a sense that someone was behind the holly bush at the bottom — a bottom that, as in all English gardens, didn't seem to be a boundary but seemed, with the rotting potting shed and the compost heap and old, mildewed fruit trees and broken machines under tarpaulins and holly bushes, to open farther out beyond the wall.

When she was anxious, as she was now, about Rachel, about doing or not doing what was right for Rachel, she thought about Frank, and what she had done or not done to help him. And she always told herself, whatever she had done or not done, she couldn't have helped him. He had needed too much help for her to have been able to give it.

That she was writing about Pietro Testa, the large, dark man who had committed suicide, because Frank, also large and dark, had committed suicide, was too obvious a connection for her to think it was anything but accidental. But she did know that in talking with Rachel about Pietro Testa, Claire would no more have said he'd killed himself than she would tell Rachel her father had.

But, then, on mad impulses, Claire wanted to tell Rachel.

III

CLAIRE, IN THE KITCHEN, heard the front door of the house open and shut, and she waited for Rachel to come in. Rachel didn't come in, and Claire, wondering, went out into the passage, saying, "Rachel?" Rachel was standing against a wall, staring, her uniform jacket unbuttoned, her blouse out of her skirt, her socks around her shoes. There was blood on the inside of her leg, as if a vein had been torn out and hung dangling to her knee.

Claire put a hand over her mouth and thought: I knew, I knew. When, with her other hand out to touch Rachel, she went toward her, Rachel ran into the sitting room, where she sat, her legs up and her arms around them, sideways in an armchair, and, staring, she pressed the side of her head into the back of the chair. Her hair was filled with what looked like the down of birds.

Again Claire, stunned, went to her, but Rachel jumped up from the chair, screaming, screaming as if her vocal cords had been scraped and were now raw, and emitted a sound that Claire had never heard from her daughter — "Don't touch me" — and flung herself on the sofa, her legs raised and her arms tight around her knees.

With her arms held out and leaning forward, Claire said, "Please, please, darling, please."

Rachel shrieked, "Don't touch me, don't touch me, don't touch me!"

Claire dropped her arms. "My God," she said.

Rachel threw herself on the floor, curled up on her side, her eyes always staring out, and was rigid. Her school jacket and skirt were twisted about her, the sleeves of the jacket almost up to her elbows and the cuffs of her white blouse, held around her wrists by the buttons, turned round. She lay for a long while, her mother, her arms by her sides but still leaning forward, as rigid as she was. When she began to kick, Claire, startled, stepped back, then stepped forward again, her arms extended. Rachel kicked the furniture, and she pulled at herself as if to pull her clothes off, her hair, the flesh of her face. Then, in an instant, she went still again, more still than before, more rigid than before, and, her head sideways on the floor, she stared out so her eyes bulged.

Claire held her arms out wider to her and said, "We have got to ring the police."

Moving only her mouth and jaw, Rachel shrieked, "No!"

She frightened Claire, who again stepped back and sat on the edge of a chair.

Claire said, "We have got to get the doctor at least."

Rachel shrieked, "No! No! No!" She became terrifyingly rigid.

Weeping, rocking back and forth a little, Claire said, "Please let me help you. Please. Please." She keened more and more, repeating, the word guttural with tears, "Darling, darling —"

With a frightening command, Rachel shouted, "Shut up!"

Claire, more than ever frightened of her daughter, shut up.

She watched Rachel, breathing heavily, her jaw set, stand, and she panicked at what she might do and raised an arm across her face. But Rachel, as if she had, lying on the floor, decided that nothing, nothing, nothing had happened to her to make her lose control of herself, and that she should be punished for losing control, stood almost at military attention, waiting for a command. She was still breathing heavily and her eyes were bulging and staring, and she blinked a lot and rapidly. She was as if waiting to be told what she must do.

Her mother said, "We have got to —"

But it wasn't her mother she was waiting for to tell her what to do. Rachel shouted, "Shut up."

Claire began to tremble. She waited with Rachel for what the command would be. Rachel stopped breathing heavily, and her eyes closed halfway, as if she were listening, and she winced.

She said to her mother, "I want to wash."

Trembling, Claire said, "You've got to let a doctor take specimens for evidence —"

"I told you to shut up," Rachel shouted in a voice that was less hers than before, as if the wounded vocal cords had hardened and gave off very little vibration but were only capable of the tone of the command Rachel had learned when the command had been given her.

Weeping, pulling at her own clothes, Claire rushed upstairs ahead of Rachel to fill the bathtub. She was frightened into doing anything Rachel said. Weeping, and trembling too, she watched Rachel, in the midst of the rising steam, take off her jacket and throw it on the floor, then her shoes and socks and skirt and blouse and slip, and when she saw that Rachel was not wearing panties she was so shocked she began to sob, and she trembled so she couldn't shut off the taps on the bathtub. Rachel did, and asked her mother if she would please find a disinfectant and pour it into the water. She seemed unaware that Claire was sobbing and trembling, and Claire, trying to do what Rachel asked, looked for TCP in the medicine chest. There was none there, and she said in the breaths she took between sobs that she'd look in the downstairs bathroom. She went out, but she couldn't descend the stairs, and stood holding the round wooden globe on the newel post and shook.

When she did come back with the bottle of disinfectant, she found Rachel sitting on the toilet, her naked body tilted and her knees up. She shouted, not at her mother but simply shouted, "I can't pee."

Claire said, "You're tensed, your body is so tensed from the shock —"

Rachel, commanding herself, shouted down at her body, "Pee, pee," and she did.

Claire knew that now the evidence may have gone, and she felt a great sense of defeat. The man who did it would not, even if he were caught, be convicted and punished.

She poured the TCP into the bathwater and Rachel got into it and sat and, holding her nose, leaned far back and submerged herself totally, her hair billowing out under water and the bird's down floating up to the surface. When she rose, she asked her mother for a mouthwash to be made with the disinfectant, which her mother did in a tooth glass, and Rachel, sitting in the bath, gargled and spit the mouthwash into the water around her. Her mother helped her wash her hair.

Trying not to say anything that would rouse Rachel, Claire suggested that this bath be drained away and Rachel have another scented with oils, and Rachel let her mother do this for her. She sat as the water became lower and lower about her and left her exposed. The bird's down was on the bottom of the bath, and there was a ring as if of earth about the sides. Rachel stood out of the bath as her mother scoured it, then got back in and crouched, her arms crossed over her breasts, and clean water gushed from the taps. Her mother poured in oil from a blue bottle. She let her mother rub her with a clean towel and, while she sat wrapped in the towel on the cork-covered stool, comb out her hair as she dried it with an electric drier. Rachel was will-less. Her mother brought her her robe and told her to stand and helped her to put the robe on.

Quietly, Claire asked, "What would you like now?"

"I'd like to go to bed," Rachel said.

Trying again, quietly, Claire said, "Darling, you know how important it is for a doctor to see —"

But Rachel shook her head and began to breathe deeply, and her eyes began to bulge.

"All right," her mother said quickly. "I'll do anything you want."

Standing before the closed bathroom door, Rachel fell backward against it. She said, "What I want —"

Claire didn't touch her, though she looked as though she might fall to the floor. Rachel seemed about to sob, and Claire said, "Cry —"

But Rachel sniffed back the mucus and, her chin puckered, looked away. She asked flatly, "Can I sleep with you?"

Claire, amazing herself because she thought she was empty, began to sob wildly. She sobbed so wildly, losing her breath and then getting it and with it releasing, in staggering rises, greater sobs, Rachel had to put her arms around her. She did so lifelessly, her arms hanging limp, and after her mother became calm, she didn't look at her.

Claire led her into her bedroom and helped her into a nightgown and pulled down the covers for Rachel to get into one side, and when Rachel did she turned over and pressed her face into the pillow.

Downstairs to shut off the lights, Claire got the switches wrong and kept turning on lights, which she couldn't then turn off. She knocked an elbow against a doorjamb and stubbed her toe on the overhang of a stair tread.

As early as it was, she prepared herself for bed.

When she got into bed, Rachel raised her head without looking at her and said starkly, "He said it was my fault and he was going to cut me up inside and cut off my breasts as a punishment." She hurled herself over onto her stomach.

Claire would go out and find that man and kill him, kill him with a knife. She kept the light lit on the bedside table near her. She and her daughter lay side by side, she, in her rage, making her plans, knowing nothing about the man and knowing that Rachel wouldn't tell her if she asked and that Rachel didn't want to remember where it happened, what he looked like, what he wore, what he said. She couldn't put her daughter through that, and she couldn't let the police put her through it. And yet, by instinct alone, by the force of an instinct so concentrated she could see in the dark and pick out the man hiding in the dark, she knew that if she went out she would find him and kill him.

Her body shuddered a little and she yawned, and her body shuddered again.

She knew Rachel wasn't able to sleep, but she also knew that if she turned to her daughter to touch her, her daughter would draw back, shouting that she did not want to be touched. Claire sweated and from time to time moved an arm or a leg.

She shut off the light. She saw transparent black-and-white blobs, like diseased cells, appear to rise up into the air each time she blinked, then fall slowly.

She said, "Rachel?"

Rachel didn't answer, and for a moment Claire, with a strange fright, thought she might have gone, and she turned her head to see her daughter lying straight, her hands folded on her breasts, her eyes open.

"Please talk to me," Claire said. "Please tell me —"

"I can't," Rachel said quietly.

"Of course you can't. Of course you can't. But please try."

"There's nothing to say."

Claire rose up on an elbow. "Oh, but there is."

"I don't think there is."

"If you let me ask you —"

"Please."

"I won't ask you any questions, I promise. But there's so much we have to talk about."

"I don't know what."

Tears welled into Claire's eyes. It seemed to her that the enormity of what she had to talk about with her daughter itself brought tears to her eyes.

Claire said, "There is so much, so much."

"No," Rachel said, "not really," and she said it in a dead way.

Lying back, the tears running down her cheeks and jaw and neck, Claire thought: What will save her?

"At least cry," Claire said, "please, please, cry."

Rachel lay silent.

IV

AFTER THE FIRST NIGHT, Rachel slept in her own room, but with the doors between the rooms open.

Claire didn't sleep, and she wondered if Rachel did.

For three days, the only time they were separated was when they went into their rooms to bed. Claire didn't even leave Rachel alone in the house to go out to a shop. On the third afternoon, while they were having tea in the sitting room, Rachel put her empty cup down and checked her watch, a gold one given to her by her father for her thirteenth birthday, and asked, in hardly more than a whisper, if her mother would telephone her headmistress to tell her that Rachel had been away from school because she had been ill. Miss Hemmings would be in her office now, the time when she always asked Rachel to come see her.

Claire said she'd ring from the telephone in her bedroom, and Rachel followed her up and sat on one side of the wide bed and Claire on the other. With the receiver in her hand emitting a faint buzz, Claire asked Rachel what she wanted her to say, apart from her being ill.

"Tell her I'll need a week," Rachel said.

"And then?"

"And then I'll go back."

Claire said, "Darling, how can you go back without knowing — ?"

Rachel raised her voice. "You told me to use my will."

"Yes," Claire said softly, "yes, I did."

After Claire spoke to Miss Hemmings, the headmistress said to her, "I'd like to speak to you about Rachel."

"Yes, yes, of course," Claire replied, trying to make her words sound very matter-of-fact.

After she hung up, Rachel asked, "What did you say 'yes, yes, of course' to?"

"Darling, you can't become suspicious of me, you can't do that to me," Claire answered.

"You're right," Rachel said. "I won't."

And yet Claire felt that Rachel had every reason to be suspicious of her, not only for her agreeing with Hemmings to talk about Rachel without Rachel's knowing, but for all her feelings about Rachel, as if all of them were not above suspicion. Claire felt so terribly false, fake, and she wasn't sure why.

She was sure Rachel knew when she made an excuse to go out that she was going to see Hemmings — going without ringing to make an appointment with her, at the hour Rachel indicated she was in her office for meetings.

As Claire went down the long corridor, the brownish linoleum floor shining in the fluorescent strip lighting along the ceiling, she imagined Rachel going to the headmistress's office, and she wondered if the slight apprehension she felt was what Rachel had felt. There were tennis rackets leaning against the bottom edge of the greenish walls, these walls also shiny in the light.

Hemmings was a thin woman with wrinkles all around her lips radiating into a blond face, her blond hair parted in the middle and cut short so her ears showed.

On the desk between Hemmings and Claire, who sat on a wooden chair Rachel must have sat on, was a fossil, a large stone, rough and uneven all around and cut flat across the top and polished and revealing, in its slight amberlike transparence, white spirals.

Claire kept clasping and unclasping her hands while Hemmings told her, briefly, that she was worried about Rachel's becoming more and more withdrawn, so much so that she had made a point of asking her to read a psalm at the Abbey when the anniversary of the school was celebrated. And as withdrawn as she was becoming, she was also becoming stubborn, performing, though warned, small acts of insubordination, like wearing earrings she knew were too long to be allowed. Was there any reason Mrs. O'Connel knew of for this?

Claire unclasped and clasped her hands. She said, "Rachel doesn't know I'm here."

"There's no reason why she should know. At this hour, none of the girls would have seen you come in."

"If it did get back to Rachel that I'd come and was talking about her —"

"I can assure you," Hemmings said, and her face appeared to contract a little along the radiating wrinkles.

Claire clasped her hands as if praying.

"What is it?" Hemmings asked.

"On her way home from school, she was attacked —"

Hemming's voice was flat. "Was she raped?"

"Yes."

Hemmings looked down, and after a moment put a finger to her lips. When she raised her eyes, she said, her finger still to her lips as though to keep the secret, "How horrible."

"Horrible for any girl," Claire said, "and for Rachel especially."

"I know how it would be especially horrible for Rachel. I know her well enough to be pretty sure she'd refuse to go to the police."

"Yes."

"But she's seen a doctor."

Overcome, all Claire could do was shake her head a little.

"No?" Hemmings asked.

"She refuses, and I can't make her."

"You must get her to a doctor."

"She won't have anyone know."

"She must absolutely see a doctor, and if this is traumatic at first, in the end it will be best for her. I'll tell her I insist on a report from a doctor before I let her back into the school, on the grounds that she may spread her flu to the other girls if she isn't totally cured of it. I will never let her suspect I know. She's aware how tough I can be."

Claire tightened the fingers of her clasped hands. She said, "She would kill herself if she knew I told you."

"She won't. She's tough too."

Claire unclasped her hands and held them up, and as though she were sobbing and couldn't help herself, she said, "I know she'll kill herself. I know what a failure she feels she is and what a horror she has of anyone else knowing."

Frowning, Hemmings asked, "You think Rachel feels a failure?"

"Oh, I know she does."

Frowning more, Hemmings asked, "But what has she failed at? She is one of our best students."

Claire closed her eyes. When she opened them, she said to Hemmings, "Please don't ask her to do what she can't do. Please. She'll come back to school. She'll do everything she can will herself to do. Please don't ask for more."

Hemmings's face appeared to contract to her pursed lips.

Claire saw each morning that Rachel willed herself to get into her school uniform — a green skirt with a green jacket and green knee socks and the school badge sewn to the breast pocket — and willed herself to collect her books together and willed herself to go out. Claire waited, almost by the door, each afternoon for Rachel to return, and she saw the exhaustion in her young, smooth, pale face from having had to will herself through the day. She didn't telephone friends, and when friends telephoned, she didn't answer but asked her mother to say she was in the bath or something. And Claire kept watching out for the special look of fatigue and the dark circles about the eyes.

After dinner Rachel did her homework, and then, however early, she went to bed.

Claire waited until Rachel was in bed and went into her bedroom and sat on the foot. She watched Rachel braid her hair at her nape, which she had begun to do before she went to sleep. Her breasts rose and fell under the yoke of her nightgown. Claire asked quietly, "Have you had your period?" and Rachel answered starkly, still braiding her hair, "No."

Claire could only guess at Rachel's horror. Though her face remained stark, Rachel dropped her arms and seemed to be waiting for what her mother said next.

"You know you've got to go to the doctor about this."

"Yes," Rachel said almost inaudibly.

Claire telephoned Hemmings, who said this was what she'd thought would get Rachel to the doctor. Then Claire made the appointment with their G.P.

While her mother talked with the doctor in his surgery, Rachel remained in the waiting room. In the middle of the room was a large round table covered with old magazines, and on the wall was a wide picture of a snow-covered landscape with birch woods and the sun setting behind the birch woods. Rachel went to look at it.

Claire came into the waiting room and saw Rachel studying a picture, and she joined her to look too at it, and she asked, "Where do you think the scene is set?"

"Russia," Rachel said.

Claire leaned closer. "There's no one in it."

"No," Rachel said.

"And it looks very cold."

"I wish I were there," Rachel said. "I wish more than anything in my whole life I were there."

"I know," Claire said.

"Do you?"

"Yes, I do know."

The thin shadows of the birch trees cast by the setting sun were long on the snow.

"The doctor is waiting for you in his surgery," Claire said.

Rachel said nothing as she went out.

That word, *surgery,* was a word an American found difficult to get used to in England. In England it meant the doctor's office, but in America it meant operations. And Claire felt that Rachel was going in to the doctor for some kind of terrible operation.

Rachel had never had a boyfriend, and Claire's feeling was that Rachel had always been withdrawn from sex and had never thought that her life, and certainly not her happiness in life, would depend on it. Claire hadn't known what Rachel imagined her life, and the happiness of her life, depended on, and she'd thought Rachel hadn't known either. But Rachel had to have had at least a sense of something that would happen to make her life different, as Claire at Rachel's age had had. But that sense would have been frail in Rachel, and now, Claire thought, it no longer existed. Her daughter seemed to her to exist without any sense of the possibility of anything happening to her that had not already happened.

Claire sat and, as she often did, closed her eyes. It seemed to her that she and her daughter lived within the awareness of unspeakable imagery occurring, appearing and disappearing like faces, in all the darkness around them. Claire knew that there was no more to be done to change this awareness than to make what had happened not to have happened. She worried about what face among all the faces appearing and disappearing, what image among all the images, Rachel would finally center on. It was up to Claire to try to focus Rachel's shifting attention on a face that was different from the faces that kept showing themselves to her; it was up to Claire to focus Rachel on an image that was different enough from the images that showed themselves to her to make her believe it was possible to be, herself, different. But she feared that Rachel's will was such that, seeing face after horrible face appear to her, she would decide that the face that was most powerfully the image of her feelings was one that offered no other possibility but self-hatred and destruction, and this would destroy her life, and her mother's too.

Shame came from self-hatred. Claire had prayed that Rachel would know nothing of self-hatred.

Rachel came into the waiting room, and before she and her mother left she looked again at the landscape.

On the way from the doctor's Harley Street surgery to Clapham by taxi, Claire and Rachel sat silent in the black back seat. When the taxi made an abrupt stop, they lurched forward a little, then fell back together. Claire put her arm around Rachel, and Rachel let her mother hold her.

The sun was setting when they arrived home. Rachel didn't go up to her room but went to the sitting room and sat in the dimness. Claire followed her and sat with her, and when it got dark didn't put the lights on. As if the soft darkness itself caused Rachel's face to soften, her cheeks appeared less sharp and her eyes less staring, and her body, her hands held, palms up, loosely at her sides, softened too and sank back into the sofa.

Claire asked, "What are you thinking, darling?"

She felt a little thrill when Rachel, instead of sitting upright, seemed to soften more, and she waited and felt another thrill when Rachel said:

"I was thinking —"

Claire waited more.

Rachel laughed, a small, dry laugh, but didn't speak.

"You're wondering if the center of your life has been taken away from you —"

Rachel looked down, not sure, perhaps, if this was what she had been thinking about. Then, with a slight frown, she asked, "Did you first make love with Daddy?"

Claire hadn't expected this. She said, "Yes," because that was the truth.

"And how did you feel after?"

"How did I feel about no longer being a virgin?"

Rachel frowned more.

Tears rose into Claire's eyes. After a while, tyring to keep her voice quiet, she said, "When I was growing up, I was told by my mother, by the nuns who taught me, by the parish priest, by everyone in the world, how much being a virgin *had* to mean to me."

Rachel's frown was like a metal band that kept her face from expressing anything, even too much interest in what her mother said. "It only meant what they told you it meant?"

Claire pressed her tears away with her knuckles. "It's difficult to remember. What did I feel at my first communion, wearing my white dress and crown and carrying white satin blossoms? I think I felt great joy. I felt great joy because everyone admired me, my mother and father and aunts and uncles, who all took photographs of me standing on the church lawn holding up my clasped hands and, in the midst of the satin blossoms, my white prayer book and my rosary of pearls. But I think I felt, in myself, joy too —" All their intimate talks had always been unreservedly intimate and without embarrassment, but they had always been about Rachel — Rachel's failing a quiz, Rachel's fight with a school friend, Rachel's eczema, Rachel's puberty. It was with a quiet amazement that Claire now found herself talking about herself while Rachel listened. With a jump of excitement in her voice, which she tried to keep calm, she said, "What I most remember is crowning the Holy Virgin Mother as the culmination of the May Day procession from the parish school to the church. Because the school was right next to the church, the procession went round a block of the neighborhood so that it would last and so that people standing on the sidewalks could see it. And I, in a long blue satin gown with long sleeves and lace cuffs and a lace collar and wearing a golden crown of gilded paper, walked behind a boy in a white satin suit and cap with a white plume and carrying a red pillow with a crown of May flowers on it, followed by someone carrying a white satin banner with gold fringe and with an oval picture of the Sacred Heart in a sunburst of embroidered golden rays."

Claire had never told Rachel any of this, because after she met Rachel's father it had all ceased to mean anything to her, and if she had ever thought about it she had with amusement. She was even now amused, a little. She had brought Rachel up without any religion at all.

She said, "I must have been about thirteen when I was chosen as May Queen, my last year in my parochial grade school, so of course I remember it all. I remember climbing, in a daze, the ladder, an old, paint-spattered ladder the janitor had put before the side altar in which the statue of the Virgin stood, and I remember the silence of the congregation, and I remember placing the crown on the painted blue chalk veil over the head of the statue, and I remember that it slipped sideways and a dangling flower covered one of the Virgin Mother's eyes. And I remember getting down from the ladder, which the janitor took away, and looking up into the one eye that wasn't covered, filled, I felt, with a slightly sad love, singing, singing with the whole congregation and with my whole heart, Ave, Ave Maria, in Latin, and thinking as I looked up at her —" Claire raised her hands, then let them drop. "I'll never forget it."

Rachel said, "That's a strange idea, isn't it, the idea of a virgin mother?"

Claire was moved, but Rachel had taken in no more than the idea of what she had said. And no doubt Rachel was right. "Yes, a strange idea," Claire answered. She sensed an odd defeat, as if she had wanted to tell Rachel what it was she had felt at that moment when, singing, she'd looked up at the statue, had needed to tell Rachel what she had felt, and she couldn't. She couldn't because she was embarrassed even by the memory, which she could re-member only with amusement. Then, all at once, she felt that she had been raised high by this embarrassing, this silly memory, which Rachel was right to reduce to nothing more than a strange idea about a virgin mother, and now she felt let down. She thought she must continue to sound amused by the silliness of the story for Rachel's sake. Laughing lightly, she said, "When you think about it, you wonder how the idea ever occurred to anyone, because it is a total impossibility."

"Yes," Rachel said, in a way that indicated she wouldn't say more, or listen more.

Suddenly Claire thought: What have I done? She had spoken to her daughter about the joy of virginity.

Why had she done this? There was nothing about virginity to give a woman joy. Rachel had lost nothing by having been brought up without any religion and any religious experiences, especially those that had to do with being a virgin, and she must be made to see clearly that she had lost nothing in losing her virginity that might even make her wonder what virginity could mean. Leaning forward, Claire said with a jump in her voice, "The fact is, I was a fool. The fact is, I was a will-less fool for feeling I was in any way glorified in my virginal purity, for believing that the Virgin Mother loved me and took joy in me and listened to my prayers more than to others' prayers because I was, like her, a virgin. I was told all this by my mother, the nuns, the priest, and I believed it all." Leaning farther forward, her elbows on her knees, Claire insisted, "All virginity can mean to a woman is having her will taken from her by another will she's made to believe is bigger and better, exactly in the way I was told the Virgin Mother accepted the will of God imposed on her. But a woman has her own will, of course she does, of course."

Rachel was listening. Claire's voice rose higher, but, panicked, she thought that what she was saying must be more confusing than clarifying, because she herself was confused. And she felt embarrassed.

"Of course a woman has the right, the absolute right, to make love for the first time with the person she chooses, whenever and wherever she chooses. What you should feel is rage at what was done to you against your will. That is what should be upsetting you most — that your will was taken away, brutally, in the worst way a woman's will can be taken away from her. That man, in his hatred of woman, tried to destroy your will. That was what he wanted to do, and you mustn't let him succeed, you mustn't let him destroy your will."

Though she wasn't clear about what she was saying, Claire saw Rachel's eyes become clear, and she thought, excited: She's listening.

"You have a strong will. You know you do. I know you do. If you didn't have such a strong will, you wouldn't be so upset. Don't give in. The more you do nothing, the more you sit silently in a dark room, the more he'll have succeeded in doing what he wanted to do to you." Claire was almost shouting, and she saw that the more she shouted, the more attentive Rachel was to her. "Ring up your friends, ring up your headmistress, tell them, 'I was raped, but the fucker didn't really touch me, that fucking coward left me feeling sorry for him.' Your will is what makes you you, and yours, your own will, is everything that is great, grand, beautiful about you. Act on it. That's all that's required of you now, to act on it slowly, very slowly, but with the absolute conviction that it has only been shaken and not destroyed —"

All the while Claire spoke, she thought: No, none of this is true, not about anyone's will. It's all false. I don't believe any of it. Nothing she'd said was clear, and all she knew clearly about what she'd said was that she had condemned her daughter to willing her life, which was everything she had always hoped to save her daughter from, because she was aware of the horror of having to will one's life. She had said to her daughter, Use your will, use your will, when what she had wanted to do for her was offer her something bigger and better than her will, in which she would find — Claire bit her lower lip. She didn't know, she didn't know.

Rachel, her eyes large, was looking away from her mother.

V

FROM A FIELD in Regent's Park none of the buildings of London were visible beyond the green, rounded, spring trees. The trunks of the trees were spaced so distances among them were open to views of trees beyond trees in the bright morning light.

On the other side of the field was a bridle path of yellow-brown sand, and a white horse, without a rider but with a saddle, walked quietly along the path, its reins dangling. It passed by Claire O'Connel and George Sedgely, whose blond hair was combed flat on his head and always appeared to be wet and just combed.

George said, looking at the horse, "Someone should go and rein it in."

"And take it where?" Claire asked.

She watched George stride toward the horse, which was still walking quietly, its head up. When he approached the horse, it stopped and shook its head and neighed. George took hold of the reins that hung from the bit and the horse turned toward him, and George led the horse toward Claire, who was standing on the grass.

Claire patted the horse's neck. The horse remained still, blinking its large eyes.

"You understand, I know you understand," Claire said.

"Of course I understand."

She could, she had always been able to, count on his understanding. He seemed almost to be disinterested, and it was at moments when she felt she most needed him that she could count, with relief, on his disinterest, and his concern, help, generosity, and even affection in his disinterest. He understood that they couldn't get married, not now.

She reached out and put her hand on his arm holding the reins of the horse and said, "You're so good to me," and he, as if this demonstration weren't really necessary, blushed a little, though she knew he liked her to be demonstrative.

"I understand what a terrible state Rachel must be in," George said, holding the reins of the horse, which lowered its head and stood as if waiting. "But I don't understand what you plan to do about it."

"Practically?"

George nodded, wondering what other way there was to do anything but practically.

"I don't know," Claire said. "I keep praying something will happen that will make all the difference to her."

"It won't happen."

"I know. What can I do?"

"Well, frankly, I think our getting married and our all having a settled family life would be the best for her."

"You don't know what the risk is. Supposing it didn't work out?"

"I can take care of myself. And what would the risk be, anyway?"

"I'd be so worried about our pulling you down."

George said, "Pulling me down? What does that mean?"

"We're trying so hard, Rachel and I, to make everything go right, straining to make everything go right, day after day, but I know, I know how horrible it can be when everything goes wrong. You don't know how horrible it can be. I know."

George snorted a little, and the horse, shaking its head, stepped back and pulled a little at the reins, and George stepped with it. He asked, "How horrible, tell me? As horrible as demons in flames, that kind of thing? You know I don't believe in demons in flames, and neither do you."

"Sometimes I think I do."

"No, you don't."

"You make everything simple."

"It is simple."

"Not for us," Claire said. "If something goes wrong between Rachel and me and she pulls me down, I would grab at you and pull you down too."

George wrinkled his brow and smiled. "Pull me down into hell?"

"You don't know what it is to have someone grab at you and pull you down."

He laughed a little. "No, I don't."

A girl in a riding cap and jodhpurs came along the bridle path, and as she approached George and the horse and Claire she took off her cap and her long hair fell to her shoulders. She was too embarrassed to say much more than "Thank you" when she took the reins from George. He and Claire watched her lead the horse away. She didn't mount the horse but walked it back along the bridle path.

George said to Claire, "Let me see both you and Rachel together, without her knowing I know anything about what happened, and you'll see, I'll make everything seem quite normal."

Claire bit her lower lip.

"I've got to go now," George said. "I've got a meeting at the office."

George worked for an investment bank. Claire wasn't sure what that meant exactly, but she was not so naive as to imagine it wasn't important for the world.

Claire kissed him and thanked him for lunch, and stood leaning toward him, hoping he'd put his arms around her and hold her for a moment. He did.

She left him to walk among the trees toward Marble Arch and the doctor's surgery, and he in a different direction toward the Bayswater Road to hail a taxi to go to the City.

In the taxi, George thought about Claire's naiveté. She was too emphatically sincere when she made such intense statements as "You're so good to me," which were embarrassing. And she herself must have known she was embarrassing, but she counted on her emphatic sincerity, her intensity, to make what she said believable to him. And she succeeded. He believed her.

The taxi went down Oxford Street, and George saw Claire among the pedestrians, and he thought how he'd been so distracted by their conversation in Regent's Park it hadn't occurred to him to offer her a lift in the taxi to Harley Street, but just as he lowered the window to call out to her the taxi sped through a yellow light, and he looked back at her, tall, her dark hair pulled back from her head and plaited at her nape, wearing a loose black dress, walking slowly among the other, hurrying people, the display windows of the department store behind her gleaming. She never hurried, always walked slowly. His impulse was to jump out of the taxi and go to her, because it seemed to him that she was lost.

The taxi got jammed in traffic in the City just outside a finance building with a grand entrance of fluted columns and a portico, its high, bronze, double doors open, and the view inside of a hall lined on either side with green mottled pillars leading to a grand flight of red carpeted stairs. George saw a man in red trousers and a blue shirt go in and climb the stairs.

He thought of Claire and Rachel, who were so different. He didn't think that Rachel enjoyed her life, but he knew that Claire did, or wanted to. Because Claire enjoyed her life, he felt tender, protective toward her, and he would help her. He wasn't sure he liked Rachel very much.

On her way to the doctor for the results of Rachel's tests, Claire, walking down Oxford Street among hundreds of people who passed her coming and going, wondered if the man who had changed not only Rachel's but her life was there among the crowd. An elderly man in a stained shirt with rolled-up sleeves and sweat patches and bagging, dirty trousers passed her, and she turned her head away from the smell of his body. To the extent that she could imagine at all the body of the man who had raped her daughter, she imagined it rank with body odor. She would have liked to find him, however the idea disgusted her, by smelling him out. She didn't know what Rachel felt about him — Rachel had never, ever talked about him — but Claire felt that he must be destroyed as he had destroyed the lives of a daughter and her mother, and she wasn't sure George, kind and gentle George, could help.

She had to wait for a while in the doctor's waiting room. She studied the picture of the sunset over a snowy countryside, the birches' shadows against the red and purple, and she thought the scene reminded her not of Russia but of New England, of Maine, where she was from. She was thinking of the landscape when the doctor told her that Rachel was pregnant. Claire discussed an abortion with him.

On the bus home, she looked out at the crowds of people on the sidewalks, and a revulsion came over her for that child of rape, which itself would destroy not only Rachel's life but Claire's own life.

She found Rachel lying on her bed, waiting for her to return.

Rachel knew she had gone into London to see the doctor for the results of the tests, which Rachel had left to her, as she left so much to her mother. Claire stood over the bed.

Rachel said, "I know I'm pregnant."

Claire nodded.

Rachel kept looking at her mother, as though waiting for her to tell her what, now, to do.

I will lose her, Claire thought, I will lose her unless I act quickly, and she said in a flat voice, as though this was what Rachel would have expected her to say, "I have already spoken to the doctor about an abortion." She began to shiver a little.

Looking away, frowning, Rachel said, "I'm going to have the baby."

This was what Claire had been most frightened of.

Shivering, she said, trying to keep her voice flat, thinking that Rachel might still listen to her if she kept her voice without expression, kept it as though the voice of someone slightly distanced and disinterested, "Think of the baby." But she couldn't keep her voice flat; it jumped in her throat, and she said, "You have a chance of getting over what happened, of forgetting that man, by not having his baby. You will forget, I promise you will. I know about forgetting. But not if you have to take care of his baby —"

Rachel raised a hand over her head and lay it, bent at the elbow, on the pillow. She said, "I'm going to have the baby."

Claire kneeled by the bed. She said, "Please look at me. Please do."

Rachel loosely turned her head toward her mother and, without focusing on her, seemed to look round her face.

"If you have this baby, you won't have a life. There'll be someone you'll fall in love with, really fall in love with, and you'll have a life with him that you've chosen."

"I'm going to have the baby," Rachel said.

As weak as if all her will had been taken out of her, Claire sat sideways on the floor by the bed, turned away from Rachel. She heard her daughter breathing. Dust, she noticed, had collected in rolls under a table with framed photographs of herself and Frank and Rachel as a baby, and she told herself she must give Pauline, the cleaning lady who came once a week, a lecture about the dust mop. Rachel's breathing was loud. Claire turned to her and said, as if she were giving way to something she didn't in any case have the strength to resist, "All right, all right."

Rachel closed her eyes. She had the heavy lids of her father.

The next morning Claire told Rachel to stay home from school, but Rachel, smiling a strained smile, said she'd go, there was an exam she couldn't miss, and Claire stood at the open doorway to watch her, in that uniform that must have reminded her of what had happened the whole time she wore it, go down the street, past the blossoming white and purple lilac and yellow laburnum bushes leaning over the black iron railings of front gardens.

Alone, Claire telephoned Hemmings, who was almost curt with her when she said that Rachel was after all pregnant, healthily so, but she didn't say that Rachel had made up her mind to have the baby. She told this to George when she telephoned him at his office.

He asked, "And she can't be made to change her mind?"

"I wouldn't want to try," Claire said.

"Can I see you both?" he asked.

"You'll try to change her mind?"

"I wouldn't dare to try," he said, and he laughed a little, and Claire was grateful for that laugh.

He came to Sunday lunch, and when he asked them if they'd like, on the next Sunday, when clocks were put forward and summer time began, to take a day trip to Ely in his car to see the cathedral, he looked at Rachel, leaving it to her to say yes or no. Rachel said she'd go if her mother wanted, and as soon as lunch was over she excused herself and left the table to go to her room.

George said, "Anyway, she is polite."

"Of course she is," Claire said. "Why does that surprise you?"

"Willful people aren't usually polite."

Claire was offended. She said, "She is doing her best."

"Of course she is," George said. "I'm sorry."

On the way to Ely in George's car, Rachel lay on the back seat, apparently asleep. At Ely, she remained, asleep or not, lying on the back seat of the car when George and Claire got out.

Claire followed George about the high, thin-pillared, arched nave of the cathedral, details of which he pointed out to her. The light edged in fine and brilliant tracings the pillars and arches. George said he knew nothing about art, but he did, and he put himself down by saying he didn't. Claire was embarrassed about Rachel, but George, as he would, seemed to accept that she had remained in the car and wasn't interested in the art of the cathedral. He seemed to accept so much.

In the lady chapel, he pointed out the arcade all around, delicate pillars holding up arches so intricately carved they appeared to be not stone but fine-leafed vegetation, and in the midst of the vegetation were half-hidden holy figures.

George said something about the nodding ogee arches, and Claire in fact nodded. He did know a lot, but if she took him too seriously in what he knew, he would say really he knew nothing, was just an amateur. He couldn't bear to be taken too seriously, and even now blushed a little for having used architectural terms he no doubt thought he wasn't entitled to use. His fear of pretension always touched Claire, and made her want to reassure him that she for one appreciated his knowing about nodding ogee arches.

Among the holy figures, she looked for an Annunciation, and found it in a corner. The angel's wings were broken off.

Yet Claire wasn't able to be as attentive as she wanted to be, and she knew this was because she was thinking of Rachel out in the car.

George too was thinking about Rachel. Being with her and her mother was more trying than he'd imagined it would be, though really Rachel had done nothing to try him. She could, he thought, have at least made the effort to come into the cathedral and sit in the nave.

Claire told herself: I will have to make a choice between him and Rachel.

This made a pang of love for George occur in her. She couldn't choose not to see him.

George suggested quietly that they walk again around the cathedral, and they did, slowly, side by side, among the high, high arches.

He all at once said, "If Rachel were English, I'm afraid I'd say she were spoilt."

"And you're trying to make allowances for her because she's American," Claire said.

Thrusting out his chin a little, George said, "She can be very stubborn."

Claire winced. "Yes, stubborn," she said. "Her father was like that."

"Is the fact that she is like her father a reason for indulging her in her stubbornness?"

"I so long for her not to be like her father."

"Then —"

Claire said, "She is too much like her father to be different. I know. I know how I tried to help him to be different."

"Did he need help so much?"

"Oh, so much more than I could give him."

"People have to get over their suffering," George said. "Even what has happened to her she'll have to get over. She can't live it the rest of her life."

George's face was, in the slanting light, gentle and beautiful, with clear and shining eyes. She wanted to kiss his face. She wished he would put his arms around her and hold her, and she would press the side of her face against his and kiss his temple. She knew that he didn't understand at all.

She said, "Do you believe it's possible to suffer something one isn't fully aware of?"

"I don't think I understand, but as much as I do, I have to say that no, I don't really believe in unconscious suffering. I think suffering has to be conscious to be real suffering. I believe people in Russia wondering what will happen to them with the fall of communism are suffering."

Claire bit her lip, then said, "I've told her, as I thought I had to, that her will is all she has. I didn't know what else to tell her. But Rachel, as strong as she is, suffers her will. I know how much she suffers it."

"I see."

"Do you?"

"Perhaps."

"Rachel is so much like her father. He had her kind of will."

"How can a strong-willed man be in need of help?"

"You think that's a contradiction?"

"Well, I know people can be contradictory."

"Frank certainly was contradictory," Claire said.

"Do you think I am?"

Claire smiled at George for saying this. "No," she said.

He took her hand. As they were approaching the car, no longer holding hands in case Rachel saw them, he said, "But the fact is, Rachel has a life to live, and she's got to live it with other people, especially with a baby, if she's going to live it at all happily. She's got to learn she's in the world, for better or worse, as we all are."

A stark stillness came over Claire, though she moved, and in the stillness she thought: He really doesn't understand. His mind was too positive for him to be aware of anything invisible and beyond the world. And Claire needed this mind to rely upon, so the very recognition of it in him made her realize how much she needed it to help her. But she felt it was just because of the positiveness of his mind that she wouldn't be able to rely on him to help her with Rachel, and what she needed more than anything was help with Rachel.

She impulsively said, "As strong-willed as Frank was, he killed himself."

"Oh," George said.

"I thought I wouldn't tell you that. I haven't told Rachel. But perhaps my telling you gives you an idea of what Rachel has in her to do. It frightens me."

"Why should anyone want to do that?" George asked.

"I've asked myself that question often. I don't know, and I'm glad you don't know."

He put his arms around her, but though she wanted to give in, she pulled away.

She said, "I'd better go see how Rachel is."

She was sitting up in the back seat. Claire got into the front seat and turned to her. She wanted to ask her please to show some appreciation to George for what he was doing, because George liked them both, very much, but seeing the pain in Rachel's eyes, Claire simply asked, "Did you nap, darling?" Rachel shook her head a little.

George insisted he was not going to leave Ely until he had tea, and if Claire and Rachel wanted to remain in the car, they were perfectly entitled to, but he was going to look for a tea shop. Claire gave Rachel a pleading look, and Rachel got out of the car. George found the tea shop, and at a small wooden table they ordered cream teas, the pot and cups served on crocheted doilies. George kept up the talk, and Claire helped, and Rachel too, when her mother looked pleadingly at her, talked. However, the little party, as the English might have said, was not a success.

They were silent for the drive back to London, and Claire saw in George's eyes that as reasonable as he was, he would allow himself to be a little unreasonable, which his legitimate demands on Claire allowed him to be. It was Rachel who must be reasonable.

Driving through the City, deserted on Sunday afternoon, George, to test Rachel, said to her, leaning his head back, "I wonder if you'd mind my leaving you off at a convenient stop and your taking a bus to Clapham. You see, I was hoping to spend the evening with your mum."

After a silence, Rachel said, with quiet reasonableness, "No, I don't mind."

But Claire became annoyed with George. She wouldn't let George presume on Rachel's being reasonable at a time when Rachel had every reason in the world not to be. Claire said to him, "I really am rather tired," and she thought she sounded like an English woman.

"No doubt we're all tired," George said lightly. He drove on a little more, and asked, more lightly, "Would either of you mind if I left you both at a convenient stop so you might both get a bus?"

Claire said, trying to make her voice lighter than his, "Not at all," but her voice cracked.

A sense of desolation circled her as she stood with Rachel at the bus stop. Neither mother nor daughter could look at the other. The sun began to set, and when the bus finally came its headlights were on.

Sitting next to Rachel in the empty bus, Claire thought: I'll see George again, of course I'll see George again, but —

In bed that night, she thought: Rachel *is* destroying my life — And she suddenly felt all throughout her that Rachel had *wanted, willed* the rape, and she found herself imagining herself shouting at Rachel, You wanted it to happen, it was just what you have always wanted. As suddenly as the resentment occurred to her, the horror of the resentment occurred to her.

And what, she told herself, was Rachel, in her bed, thinking? That her mother had a lover, and she and her lover were more seriously committed to each other than she had known, and that she, Rachel, kept them from committing themselves entirely?

And then, this thinking following inevitably from what she had been thinking, Frank came to her, and for the first time she was aware of she told herself: But my life was already destroyed by Frank, by my love for Frank. She imagined he had willed his suicide to destroy her and her love, she who had done so much, everything, to — But again the horror of her resentment stopped the thinking.

In the morning, the day when Rachel was to read in Westminster Abbey, they had breakfast together. They seldom had breakfast together, but Rachel wanted to, and set the table by the garden window. The cherry tree in the garden was beginning to blossom, and under the tree was an old enamel tub filled with water in which the tree was reflected.

Rachel said in a calm voice, "You would have married George if what happened to me hadn't happened."

There was nothing Claire could answer to this. She asked, "Have you decided what you will wear today?"

"My school uniform," Rachel answered.

In Westminster Abbey, Claire was ushered to a side seat from which she saw the ceremony, which was within the choir, only in glimpses through the openings in the carved stone screen. She noted that all the women around her wore hats, and she didn't; the English would know that this was an occasion for hats, and she hadn't known. She heard Miss Hemmings speak, then the school's girl choir sing a hymn, and then, as if she hadn't expected it and was startled to hear it in such a strange place, Rachel's voice sounded throughout the Abbey. She heard the voice say:

"I will praise the Lord with my whole heart —"

A prickling sensation spread through Claire's sinuses and head, and she formed the words, under her breath, "Oh please."

Hearing her innocent daughter read out the psalm, Claire felt that she herself was guilty of what had happened to Rachel, felt that it was her fault. Her very expectation that it would happen had in some way made it happen.

During the choral singing, she thought: Our wills destroy us —

She would devote herself to her daughter for as long as her daughter needed her.

But Rachel, isolated in the dark circle with her baby, did frighten her.

If Rachel did kill herself, Claire thought, she would also kill herself, she would, she would —

She had never left America, was back where she had been with her husband, and that place really did frighten her.

After the ceremony, Claire saw the headmistress, Hemmings, before she saw Rachel, and she went to her quickly, though she was speaking with two other women. Hemmings glanced at Claire, then resumed what she was saying to the two women as though she hadn't really seen Claire: "The usher didn't know who I was, barging in to get a good seat, and he asked me, and I wondered, well, shall I tell him and embarrass the poor man or say nothing and sit in a lesser seat he showed me to?" The women laughed, and when Hemmings turned to Claire, her hands out to take both of Claire's, the two women left.

Hemmings said, "I've been thinking. Rachel must take a year off from school. I'll make the arrangements."

"And then?" Claire asked, as if what happened next could all be arranged by the headmistress.

"And then I should think you will have your hands full with the baby while Rachel is at school."

This made Claire smile.

Part

T W O

I

THE HARD BRIGHT WIND blew the rain and made the blank plate glass windows of the New York side street appear to have turned into splashing water. An open umbrella, twisting and turning as if held by an invisible tightrope walker rushing crazily along an invisible wire over an invisible, bottomless crevasse, blew down the trafficless street, struck a lamppost, fell into the gutter, but, tumbling, rose again and was blown up and farther along the street. Sometimes the wind, shifting, seemed to rise up in gusts from below.

The weather gave Claude a sense of event, and though his socks and his trousers up to his knees were wet and the shoulders of his trench coat soaked, and his umbrella, held tensely close over his head so it wouldn't turn inside out, was streaming with water, he felt, in all the surging world around him, that something great was happening, and that something greater would happen. The wet wind pulled him in one direction, in another, and yet in another, and he felt he could go, if he just let go of the umbrella, in all directions at once. The cold fresh rain hit the side of his face and dripped down his cheek. He stayed in the middle of the street and moved to the side only when a car, its headlights blurred in the rain, came slowly toward him and passed him, and jumping over a swirling puddle, he went back to the middle of the street, from which some of the tarmac had gone so the old cobbles below showed. The light was bright and dark at the same time.

He was on his way to an opening of a show of paintings in SoHo, and this was enough to give him a sense of event. He knew about openings, had been to them, partly because of his job, often, but he was perhaps still young enough and, after eight years, still new enough to New York to feel the excited promise of being on his way to a place where lots of people were gathered in a celebration of sorts, an excited sense of promise which, even though it would most likely not last beyond entering the gallery and seeing the familiar faces, made him feel lively before he got there.

He went to openings for the art. Of course he went for the art. But if he'd gone only for that, he would have gone after the openings, when, with practically no one in the gallery, he'd have been able to look at the art in the concentrated way art demanded to be looked at. He went for people as well, and he went, in the same way he anticipated seeing artwork entirely new to him, for the people in New York he didn't know. There were many, many people in New York he didn't know, and there were always some of these who appeared at an opening.

Claude Ricard was from Brookline, outside Boston. On his father's side he was French American, and on his mother's side he was Russian American. He had come to New York as a freshman to do his undergraduate years at Columbia, and he had stayed on at the university for his master's degree, but not his doctorate. He felt he didn't really need a doctorate, because by the time he finished his master's degree, he already had an interesting job that made it possible for him to be more original in his work than any job his doctorate would have given him. He was a junior editor in a publishing house that specialized in art books.

He turned into a wider street, where cars splashed puddles, and he kept to the sidewalk, turning his face from side to side against the gusts of rain, and noting as he passed red and black graffiti sprayed on a dented metal door, a pile of bulging, shining black plastic garbage bags, a rolled oriental carpet nailed to the side of a wooden loading platform as a bumper, an old metal filing cabinet with two drawers missing, the crisscross pattern on a metal trapdoor set in the cracked cement pavement. And over all was the light that was both dark and bright.

The gallery was on the ground floor of an old cast-iron building that had thin pillars with fancy capitals between the windows of all the upper storeys and a fire escape, and the wide plate glass window of the gallery, on which the name was painted in black letters, was lit up. For a moment, Claude stood outside and looked in at people gathered in small groups or alone with little white pastic cups, not many of them looking at the paintings, red, white, and black, that hung on the white walls.

Near the inside of the window, a painter friend, Duncan, was standing and talking with someone Claude didn't know, a young woman in a short, long-sleeved black dress that fit her like a stocking, the material stretched a little across her breasts and thighs. As they talked, she and Duncan slowly revolved, glancing over each other's shoulders at others, and Claude saw that her brunette hair was drawn up from her nape and tucked with combs behind her head, and that her neck was slim and curved, and that the dress at the back was cut, as at the front, in a low swoop that revealed just the tops of the angles of her shoulder blades. She revolved, and he saw again the tops of her breasts revealed by the swoop of the dress. Claude saw her lips move as she spoke, but he couldn't hear her.

Inside, he went, without looking around, to the back of the gallery, where the office was. He unbuckled and unbuttoned his coat and hung it on a freestanding rack with other wet coats. In the toilet off the office, he dried his face with paper towels, pulled at his trousers along the creases to try to restore them, and settled his shirt and jacket more neatly on his body by lifting his arms, raising and lowering his shoulders, stretching his neck. He also wiped his shoes, untied them, and tied them more tightly about his wet socks, which he drew up taut. His socks were red.

Glancing in the mirror, he held his chin in his hand and turned it from side to side. The skin of Claude's face appeared, like that of a prepubescent boy, to be so clear in its whiteness that no matter how recently he had shaved, the black whiskers, those of a fully mature man, showed through. There was also a clarity to the structure of his face, as if the skull beneath it defined strongly his forehead, the stark planes of his cheeks, his jaw. His lips were full and soft, however, and he often bit them. His eyes were pale blue but sharp. He always kept his thick black hair clear cut, his sideburns high and squared, the hairline at the nape of his neck keen.

His clothes too always had an edge to them. He wore a white sailcloth shirt with a button-down collar he left open at his neck, a V-neck woolen pullover and a tweed jacket, trousers with cuffs, all in tawny to khaki-green tones, and wingtips. His extravagance was his socks: he wore bright red, yellow, green, even purple socks.

He went back into the gallery, where the wide floorboards had black spaces between them and the ceiling was covered with decoratively embossed squares of tin painted white, and the pipes and valves of the sprinkler system were also painted white. In a corner was an old cast-iron radiator, a decoration in relief on it, painted white, tilted as one leg had gone through the floor.

First of all he looked at the pictures. They were all the same size, narrow and high, in oil, painted in wide strokes and roughly, one with the top half red and the lower half black, another with a thick white band between the red and the black, another all red with a fine black margin on one side. So far, the most interesting, maybe, was the all-red one with what appeared to be a black hole in it — at least, the paint was applied in concentric strokes as if to imply a hole. From time to time, people got out of Claude's way so he could stand in front of a picture and, his arms crossed, study it.

He never made up his mind whether or not he liked a picture. It was enough to find it interesting or not, and usually he found a picture interesting. That word, when pronounced "inneresting," had its ironical subtleties in New York, so that the statement, said with an angled pitch to the voice, "Yeah, I find that real inneresting" could be much worse than flat-out dislike, could be (another expression that had its New York meaning) totally devastating. Claude didn't think the pictures at this show were all that interesting, but he very seldom dismissed painting with the ironical "inneresting," partly because he never felt comfortable (another New York expression) with using ironical New York terms, and partly because he did honestly feel that any work of art was in some way really interesting.

All the while he was concentrating on the painting with the black hole, he was aware, somewhere at the back of the concentration that had become itself a black hole, of the woman Duncan was speaking with, if he was still speaking with her. She seemed to stand at the reverse end of the long black hole down which he looked, and to see her he would have to turn completely around. If she were no longer talking with Duncan, how could Claude get to meet her? He couldn't ask Duncan to introduce him, as he wasn't that kind of person. That is, he felt he should never press himself on anyone. Maybe he'd better hurry through the remaining pictures in the exhibition and try to catch Duncan and her still talking, if they were still talking. But then, it was impossible, he knew it was impossible, so why should he hope for what he knew was impossible? Why was it impossible? Be bold, he told himself; find out.

But he picked up a white plastic cup of wine from a tray a young man who worked in the gallery was passing around and stopped to speak to a small group of people he knew, postponing what he still felt was going to be a disappointment. They looked around to make sure the artist wasn't near. Someone, a bald man, said the paint was sure applied with vigor. Someone else, a short woman with gray hair, said she didn't feel comfortable with the paint, which was so vigorously applied it was pretentious. And then someone else, a tall thin man wearing a black shirt and a black vest with a green bow tie and with his black hair slicked flat, said, with a sharp laugh, "Very inneresting." Claude said, "Well, he's got a vision, you've got to give him that." The others looked at him, and he said, "All right, I know a vision isn't enough to make for very interesting art." Leaving them, he hoped that when he got to the front of the gallery, near the window, he'd find that Duncan wasn't after all speaking to the woman.

No, he didn't hope for that at all. Stop this silliness, he told himself. But he was silly, just a little.

Beyond the people at the front of the gallery was the window, against which the dark rain fell.

Duncan was still speaking to the woman. She was listening and he was speaking. Claude stopped about ten feet away from them, not looking at them directly but all around them. He sipped again and again from his cup of wine until there was none left, and he continued to sip the air at the rim. He'd be pressing himself on them both by going over to say hello to Duncan, he knew. He was just about to turn away to go for another cup of wine when Duncan saw him and raised his hand toward him and called him over and, as easy as pie, introduced him to Penelope, Penelope Madge, who, smiling, held out a hand to him, which Claude took in his.

It was all so easy, and Claude felt swelling in him gratitude, not only to Duncan, his friend, but to whatever circled high and around that made such things possible.

He held her hand and leaned toward her, close to her face, and asked, "I'm sorry, what is your name?"

"Penelope," she said, smiling.

He smiled back. He had gotten her name. She spoke with an English accent. He let go of her hand.

And instead of speaking with her, he spoke, as if she weren't there, with Duncan. Duncan was a large man with a beard who wore black-and-red lumberjack shirts and jeans. From time to time, Claude glanced at Penelope, who, he noted, looked at him calmly. He didn't want to talk with Duncan, he wanted to talk with her, but he didn't want Duncan and her to know this, because they'd been talking for a long time together and he shouldn't break in except to get this little business with Duncan settled. But Duncan stopped him. Duncan said, "Let's talk about this another time," and added, looking at his watch, that he had to get back home, and he left Claude alone with Penelope. Nothing could have been made easier, and Claude was as aware of the circle of possibility around them as if he could see it, or almost, just outside the periphery of his shy glances to the side. He told himself not to keep glancing shyly to the side like a boy, and he fixed his eyes on Penelope's as he thought a man would. He saw that she was searching in his eyes, and he tried to keep them steady for her to look into as deeply as she wanted.

"You're from England?" he asked.

"I am, yes." She waited.

"I've never been to England," he said.

"Then you must come."

"With you?" He laughed, and the laugh caught in his throat.

"With me."

"What would you show me?"

"I'd show you everything you've ever wanted to see."

"There's a lot I want to see."

"Then I'd make sure you saw it all."

What they talked about wasn't in itself interesting, but something else they weren't talking about was, and what the connection was between the two, between what they said and what they didn't say, he didn't know. In the midst of the gallery filled with people, to whom they were just another couple talking in a jokey way, they were to themselves two couples, the audible, visible couple joking with each other and making funny faces at each other, and around this couple was a bigger couple, inaudible and invisible to everyone else in the gallery. But the smaller couple knew that something was happening between the bigger couple, some event that occurred so rarely it amazed the smaller couple, whose talk was jokey and lively because of the great event occurring between the bigger couple. And Claude said to himself, I knew this was going to happen, I knew it.

Penelope Madge had a smooth, wide face with large, dark eyes that appeared far apart, so that looking at him, she seemed too to look all around him.

Then their joking came to an end, and it was as though they had nothing more to say to each other. Claude kept squeezing his plastic cup. Penelope now looked around the gallery.

She said, "I suppose I should look at the pictures."

"You haven't yet?"

She frowned. "Not yet."

"We could go around together," Claude said, "and I'd give you expert commentary."

"I think I'd better do it on my own," she said, and, smiling, she nodded at him and went off into the crowd.

All right, he thought.

He went off in a different direction, looking for more wine. His plastic cup was cracked, and he had to ask for a new one when one of the waiters passed. Sipping, he wandered toward the back of the gallery, avoiding the artist, whom he hardly knew and who was surrounded by people. Claude avoided someone he knew who was standing alone. At the back of the gallery, he saw Penelope wandering toward him, and as they approached each other they laughed.

He asked, "Well, what do you think?"

"You tell me," she answered.

"Tell you what?"

"What I think."

He asked her about herself. She was from London, and she had been living in New York for six months as a journalist for a glossy magazine.

She said, "Not that I know the first thing about journalism," and he found the way she put herself down sort of endearing, though he wondered what she was doing writing journalism if she didn't know anything about it.

Then again they seemed to have nothing more to say to each other, though that bigger couple about them, in their inaudible and invisible way, continued to communicate, animated perhaps by the great event that had occurred and brought them together.

"I really ought to see the rest of the pictures," Penelope said.

"They're very interesting," Claude said.

"Are they?"

He smiled. "If anyone asks what you think, you say you find the show very interesting."

"That's the word, is it?" She paused, then said, "Well, off I go," and she went past him.

He continued in the opposite direction, not looking, now, at anything but a point in the air just ahead of him, and people moved to let him go by. At the front of the gallery, he put his cup down on a long trestle table and stood facing the window. Rain was still falling.

When he turned to the side, she was standing beside him.

A sadness came over him, maybe even a sense that was deeper than sadness.

He looked away. Gathered in groups or standing alone in the white space of the gallery with white plastic cups of wine, everyone inside, reflected in the wide window, appeared to be outside in the dark street, and among those people standing out in the rain he saw himself and Penelope side by side. As if all his senses opened and made more present than ever everything that was inaudible and invisible, he knew that the something that was happening to them was, at its greatest, great in its sadness, and more than sadness. That they had been chosen to be attracted to each other, to fall in love at least for the moment with each other, filled him with a quiet grief, for her, for her and himself, for any two people chosen to be attracted and to fall in love with each other. He saw in the reflection that her eyes were on him, and he turned again to her. They smiled at each other.

He asked, almost whispering, "Shall we go?"

She nodded, but then, her eyes narrowed, she glanced into the gallery with what seemed to Claude a slight fear that someone would come to her right now and take her away, and she'd have to go.

He bit his lower lip, then asked, "Is there any reason why we shouldn't be seen leaving together?"

"There may be," she said, and she too bit her lower lip.

Again he bit his lip and frowned, then laughed. "We'll have to think of a way out," he said, and he felt suddenly at ease, intriguing. He said, "I'll get my coat and umbrella and leave, and I'll be waiting just around the corner of the next block. You come as fast as you can."

"I'll have to make an excuse before leaving."

"That's up to you. Do you have an umbrella?"

"He has the umbrella, and I came with him."

Claude wanted to know who he was, but at the same time he didn't want to know. He said, "I'll leave my umbrella on top of the radiator in the corner."

"But you'll get wet."

"How wet I get depends on how long you take coming with the umbrella."

Her eyes bright, she said, "I'll be as quick as quick can be," and she turned away. But she turned back and asked, "Do you want to know who he is?" and laughed. Her laughter cracked a little.

He felt a tenseness in his stomach, and with it a sudden sexual impulse, and he almost said, Yes, show me, but he shook his head and said, "No."

"You're worried he may be sexier than you?"

"If he were, then why wouldn't you be going off with him?"

She laughed, again with the cracking sound in her laugh, and said, "You'd better be waiting for me."

Was that a warning? he asked himself as he went for his coat.

Hurrying out, he left his umbrella on the radiator. When he got to the door, someone called at him to tell him he'd left his umbrella behind, and he, in a stilted voice that was too loud, had to call back that he'd left it there to dry and he'd be back in a little while. Raising the collar of his trench coat and buckling the short strap at the throat, he rushed in the rain down to the next block and turned the corner. His shoulders hunched, he waited. There were chicken feathers floating in a puddle of water in the gutter. She didn't come. He looked around the corner. As if followed by a dimly illuminated circle of splashing drops that hit the cement sidewalk and exploded like sparks, she, in a raincoat, was hurrying in the opposite direction, and she didn't have the umbrella. His head was running with water. He shouted, "Penelope," and she turned and hurried toward him, wincing, that circle of exploding water drops around her. She said when she got to him, "Someone accused me of trying to steal your umbrella." "Oh," he said starkly. She put her hand over her mouth and started to laugh, and he hit his forehead and laughed too. Laughing, she bent over and put her hands to her stomach, and he leaned backward against a brick wall. Her hair was coming undone, so wet strands hung from her forehead, and when she stood up she smoothed them back and tried to arrange all her soaking hair, but she was still laughing. "I'll go get the umbrella," he said. "No, no," she said, "don't go back." He wanted it for her, and he placed her in a doorway and went quickly. He came back laughing, hardly able to say, "They told me some woman tried to steal my umbrella." Laughing, she pressed her forehead against the bricks at the side of the door and bit her fingers. They laughed as they went down the street looking for a taxi, and in the taxi continued, in bursts, to laugh. And when the taxi stopped, she laughed even more and asked, "What's happening? Where are you taking me?" He, laughing, said, "I don't know what's happening." And they laughed when the taxi driver, black and bald, turned around after Claude paid him and asked, his bulging eyes bloodshot, "You two all right?"

Claude took Penelope up to his apartment, a third-floor walkup in a brownstone on the West Side.

They threw their wet coats across a table in the narrow hall, and in the apartment Claude went quickly to a closet for a towel, a large, soft, clean towel, which he pulled out so it unfolded as he held it out to her. She took it and went into the bathroom. He went into the bedroom. The bed was unmade, and he left it as it was. He undressed.

His body was more bony than muscular, as if his muscles, strong and taut, were a little too small for his bones, which were large and long and apparently simple, so the structure of his body appeared simple. The skin of his body was as clear as the skin of his face, and through the black hair on his chest, swirling around his pink nipples, his skin showed white. He had large, big-boned hands and feet.

She came into the bedroom, the towel wrapped about her, her hair, slightly damp but full, down to her bare shoulders.

Not they but that larger, inaudible and invisible couple made love, slowly, slowly resolving all the problems of the world. He said, kissing her ear, kissing under her lobe, kissing her neck, kissing her temple, "I love you. I love you." And the greatest happened.

He felt impelled, with an added impulse of passion, to say, "I love everyone." He loved the whole world.

And then, just after this high moment of love for the world, he felt come to him again that sense like sadness, or more than sadness, a sense like grief, which made him suddenly expel his breath on a plaintive "Ah" from deep in his lungs.

She comforted him by running her hands gently over his shoulders, along the back of his neck, over his head.

She didn't spend the night. She didn't even stay to have something to eat with him, not even a drink. But she took his telephone number, and, dressed while he was still naked, she kissed him and said she'd telephone him.

He asked, "Can't I have your number?"

With a laugh, she said, "You know, I can't recall it. I simply can't recall it. I'll give it to you when I ring you."

She left, and he realized that as much as he had always hoped for what had happened to Penelope and him in just the easy and bright way it had happened, it had never happened before with anyone else. I'm happy, he thought; I'm really happy.

II

SHE DIDN'T telephone him. Every time he went back to his apartment, he expected a message from her on his answering machine, but the little red light blinking in the darkness filled him with the apprehension that the message wouldn't be hers. It never was.

His apprehension went deeper. He wondered if she didn't get in touch with him because he hadn't made what happened mean much to her.

Then he thought, she couldn't telephone him. She may have

wanted to, but the circumstances of her life, whatever they were, didn't allow her to.

Except that she couldn't have been locked up, as if in a cement cell, and could have gotten away just long enough to telephone from a pay telephone in the street.

But whoever it was who fixed the circumstances of her life might have made her admit what she'd done after she'd left the gallery. It could have been that, accused of stealing the umbrella and drawing attention to herself in that way, she'd made the person she'd lied to in order to get away from him suspicious of her, and when she got back home, he'd forced her to explain what had really happened, and his condition for not making things more difficult than they already were was that she wouldn't see Claude again — wouldn't even contact him by telephoning to explain.

This made Claude feel terrible, and he wondered what he could do to make things easy for her, if they were difficult. Well, the best way would be not to contact her. But he needed to contact her. The need had to do with more than finding out how she was and trying to help if she asked for help, it had to do with making love with her.

But he couldn't get in touch with her. He didn't have as much as her telephone number.

After days of heavy rain, New York started to get unseasonably hot, and Claude thought there would be no spring, but the city would go right into summer. The heat deepened with each day, and when he woke in the morning he saw it shimmering in the early light on the street.

Claude wanted to let Penelope know that he didn't give a fuck if she didn't get in touch with him, and he thought a way of doing that would be to telephone Duncan and say he was going away, and Duncan would no doubt relay this to her. But he couldn't go away — he had his work, and also, when he thought of going away he thought of going back home, but his parents were dead, and he never went back to Brookline, though he had some relatives on his father's side there.

He had one relative — a distant cousin, if she was in fact a cousin, of his mother's — who lived in New York, an old woman called Lidia Rivers. She was born in Russia, had married a professor at Columbia University, a Yankee, now dead. She lived on the Upper West Side of Manhattan. Whenever he felt that he wanted to get out of his life in New York, as he did now, he visited her and had a cup of tea with her. She had nothing to do with his New York.

The heat was bad, and going to visit Lidia Rivers, he wished he were living in some other city.

She lived in a small apartment, the living room with many shelves with sliding glass panes behind which were not only books and piles of brownish writing paper but big pine cones and crystals and multicolored Hopi Indian dolls and beaded belts and, propped against the spines of the books, old black-and-white photographs.

On the wallpaper above the sofa was a framed picture of Christ as the Man of Sorrows.

Lidia, a small woman whose bones showed through her sagging flesh, sat on the vinyl-covered sofa among small throw pillows, and Claude sat beside her.

She said, "Marie is coming."

"Who's Marie?" Claude asked.

"You don't know her? Marie Clark? She's a niece of mine."

Among Russian Americans, "niece" could mean just friendship between an older person and a younger, in the same way "cousin" could mean just friendship between people of the same age.

"The one who's studying singing?"

"Yes."

"Of course I know her."

"She's going to Russia."

Just then, Marie opened the door with her key and came in. She was wearing a sleeveless white cotton dress and, with her long ashen hair, looked cool. Claude wondered why he hadn't remembered her right away.

He said to her, "Maybe I should come to Russia with you."

Marie smiled a little sadly at his wish to go to Russia with her. She said she had come to bathe her aunt, and Claude left.

He had no particular feelings about Russia. All that connected him to that country were some old czarist bonds that had belonged to his mother's father and that, when he'd come across them in the attic of the house in Brookline, his mother had given to him to hang in his bedroom. They were worthless, so his interest in them couldn't have been financial. Also his interest in them couldn't have been one of nostalgia, because he could not conceive of Russia enough to have any feelings for the country that were strong enough to have any true meaning to him — his mother had been born in the United States, so she too didn't have any truly meaningful feelings for the country. His attraction to the bonds, framed and hanging over his desk while he was living at home as a student, was simply in the delight of images that had survived their real significance in the world and existed entirely for themselves. That he had, even as a high school student, thought of an exhibition of such images — valueless bonds, valueless printed money, valueless stamps — was an early indication of his interest in the world of art from the point of view of an organizer of exhibitions, of a curator, of a critic. He'd kept the bonds after his parents' death, which didn't leave him with much else, in a closet in his apartment in New York, and when Russia ceased to be Communist and no one knew what the country was going to be, he remembered them and, for a joke, took them out and hung them in his bathroom. He did wonder, in the same way some surviving old White Russians might be wondering about restitution of property taken from them during the Communist Revolution, if the value of the bonds might be restored. That was very unlikely, but he still took delight in the images.

Everyone in the publishing house made jokes about the heat. Claude wished he could.

Hot mornings, Claude would wake up restless, thinking, the thought a continuation of his restless night, of Penelope. It seemed to him that a very long time passed, though he knew it was only a week; but the length of the time was extended, hot day after hot day, by his waiting for Penelope to telephone him and by his deepening resentment that she didn't. She was willfully not calling him, forcing him by her willfullness to miss her more and more — or miss her body, of which he remembered details that centered all his concentration, even at work, on a mole.

In his restlessness, he went to visit Lidia. She told him Marie had suddenly returned from Russia. They were all, Claude included, invited by a cousin, James, for dinner the next evening, so that Marie could tell them about Russia. Lidia said, "I want to hear everything, everything, everything." Then she added, "But why did she come back so soon?"

Claude's restlessness about Penelope was like that of someone locked in a cell, but a cell he imagined contained an inner cell, and that cell an inner cell, each smaller than the last and each one the cell in which he would find her. Claude didn't want to see Marie, but he said he would. He was to meet her in a children's playground near where she lived, on the Lower West Side. She used this place to meet people, as she never invited anyone up to her apartment. In the hot darkness of the New York night, the playground was illuminated with bright white lights. Through the battered chainlink fence, Claude saw her standing among huge, smooth cement animals, seals and bears and a snake, the paint worn down to the cement. Beyond her, someone wrapped in a blanket was lying on a bench. There were no children in the playground. Marie was looking away, and as Claude entered he was struck for the first time by her beauty: her thin face turned to the side and her thin hands raised, palms out, her long hair shining gray in the light. The playground was asphalted, with holes and trenches.

Uncertainly, Claude said to her, "I wasn't sure I'd recognize you."

"Why?" she asked quietly.

He laughed. "After your visit to Russia."

She didn't laugh. "You think that should have changed me?"

He shrugged.

They walked out of the playground and along the sidewalk in the heat. Below a grating, far below, were black pipes illuminated by a bare bulb, and fetid hot air blew up through the grating.

"Surely it's different there," Claude said.

"The big difference," Marie said, "is that three days ago, in Moscow, I was in the depths of cold and snow, and here in New York it's hot."

"It was snowing?"

"Snowing and snowing and snowing —"

Claude, sweating, was carrying his jacket. "And cold."

"Very cold."

"I'd like to be in a cold place. Tell me about the snow."

Marie said, "You walk along a street in Moscow, and a white comet falls from a bright winter sky and explodes on the ground in front of you."

"Oh?"

"It's snow flung down from roofs by men with shovels."

In the street was a plywood enclosure, and out of it rose, tilted, a wide plastic tube from which steam raged in a big cloud. The cloud was illuminated pink, red, and green by the streetlights. Marie and Claude waited by the plywood for a traffic signal to change before they could cross.

Claude ran out into the street before the light changed. A car raced past him.

"You could have been killed," Marie said, laughing lightly. "Why did you run out like that?"

"Tell me more about Moscow under snow," Claude said.

They walked to the apartment, in the Village, of Lidia's nephew, if he was a nephew, named James Long.

Lidia was sitting in a deep armchair. Her short white hair was wild, and she studied Marie approaching her as if for a difference in her. Marie kissed her and drew back and Lidia continued to study her.

Marie smiled. When she smiled, only her lips moved, and the rest of her delicate face remained still.

"Tell me, tell me," Lidia said.

James, standing by the armchair as though attending to the old woman, said, "There's probably nothing to say."

"It was very cold," Marie said simply.

"But there has to be more to say than that it was very cold," Lidia insisted.

Again Marie smiled and again kissed her old aunt, if she was an aunt.

James's air-conditioned living room had brightly varnished wainscoting in dark wood with raised and beveled panels at regular intervals, each panel incised with fine arabesques. The walls above were white. The door was varnished oak, heavy, with big hinges. The living room was also the dining room, where the table, as highly varnished as the wainscoting and door, might once have been used in a waiting room for magazines, ashtrays, and fedoras. The chairs around the table were straight-backed with leather seats. The wooden floor was bare except for one small Turkish rug. On a tall, square table in a corner, placed on an embroidered cloth the size of a napkin, was a silver samovar surrounded by glasses in silver holders, and above the table hung a brownish photograph in a heavy wooden frame and wide passe-partout of a woman in the costume of a muzhik, taken in a studio before a painted backdrop of birch trees. The woman may or may not have been James's grandmother.

Marie helped her aunt to the table.

There were many small dishes and bowls spread out: herrings and onions, tiny pickled eggplants, sliced tomatoes and capers, cold meat with gelatin and horseradish, salted watermelon rind, a boiled, skinned salmon, black and green olives. James opened a bottle of wine.

Lidia said to Claude, "Do get Marie to tell us about her visit. It's cruel, her not telling us anything, really."

"I've always suspected it'd be a big, big disappointment," James said, "and that's why I've never wanted to go."

He may not have wanted to go to Russia, but it was James who, for all his cynicism, tried to keep Russia alive in America: even at the risk of being picturesque, he prepared Russian food, bought big picture books on Russian churches and wooden architecture and icons, organized a crowded party in his apartment after Easter service. He could not speak Russian except for a few words, like *dvayoradnibrat*, which meant cousin.

He was a tall, bald man, wearing an open-neck white shirt and a brown cardigan.

Lidia, now touching her face lightly all over, asked, "Was it so God-awful? It was my country. Weren't you interested to know where we came from? I am shocked, Marie, that you should feel so disconnected. Even a tourist would have been more interested. And you —"

"Please —"

"Very well, very well," Lidia said, but her shoulders and elbows moved as if in little spasms of agitation.

James, who, always stylish, liked his supper parties to be sustained by a slight formality, started to speak about opera, and the others, who appreciated this formality, listened to him.

Marie was studying music, and James asked her if she was learning an aria, and she said yes, she was. He asked her if she would sing it, and with simplicity she pushed her chair back and clasped her hands and held them away from her waist and she sang an aria in French, her voice quivering at the high notes.

The sadness Claude felt was perhaps for Marie; perhaps it wasn't. He sat back and his mind expanded in that sadness he felt, and when he looked at Marie singing he saw suffering in her face, or grief. Lowering her eyes when she finished her song, she looked at him.

James served coffee, the white pot on a little straw mat, the white cups on the larger straw mats at each setting, and at the end of the varnished table, bottles of brandy lined up behind four empty snifters that reflected the lights of the room.

Lidia kept licking her lips and pursing them and licking them again as if she wanted to say something to get Marie's attention but stopped herself. Marie held her head turned just a little away from her old aunt.

When James offered brandy, Marie said that she had to go. She offered to take her aunt home, all the way back uptown by taxi, and her aunt, who appeared to want to say something else, said after a pause, and as if a little defeated, yes, she'd appreciate that.

James went ahead with Lidia, and Marie and Claude stood together for a moment at the living room doorway, facing each other. Startling him, Marie put her hand on Claude's head. Down a narrow corridor with shiny wainscoting, James was holding the door to the apartment open, and Lidia was by him. In a voice that sounded like a quiet plea, Lidia said to Claude, "Kiss her, kiss your cousin." But Marie dropped her hand and stepped back. Lidia said, "Marie." Her niece went past her and out of the apartment. Lidia regarded Claude with a continuing expression of pleading in her eyes, and then, step by step with her cane, she went out.

James came back from having hailed a taxi for Marie and her aunt and Claude asked him if he had any early appointments with patients the next morning, and James said yes, but it didn't matter — coughing, sweating, and shivering with high fevers, holding the places where they hurt, they'd sit and wait for him. He suggested they go out for beers in a Village bar.

"No," Claude said. "I think I'll go home too."

At home he found a message from Duncan on his answering machine. He hadn't been in touch with Duncan in a long while, maybe because he both wanted and didn't want to find out if Duncan knew what had happened to Penelope. He telephoned, but Duncan wasn't in, or wasn't answering, and Claude left a message after the beep, as instructed.

There were friends in New York who communicated only by leaving, after the beep, messages on one another's answering machines.

As Claude was going to bed, his telephone rang, and the apprehension took him over like a threat, and he hesitated in answering because he told himself it wouldn't be Penelope. He even thought of not answering. Duncan was on the other end of the line.

Claude's only interest in talking with Duncan was, after they'd finished their business, to say, "There's something I need to talk about —"

"Talk," Duncan said.

"You remember Penelope —"

"Yes."

"Well, she and I —"

Duncan laughed. "I know all about it," he said. "Including the part played by the umbrella."

"Who told you?"

"Penelope did."

"She did?"

"Shouldn't she?"

"I guess she doesn't have any reason from my side not to tell anyone. I thought that maybe from her side —"

"What was it you wanted to tell me about you and Penelope?"

Claude's voice sank. "She hasn't been in touch with me since."

"Why didn't you get in touch with her? Why are you making things difficult for yourself?"

"I don't have her number."

"Wait a second and I'll give it to you."

Claude dialed her number slowly, though it was late, and listening to the ring, he told himself she wouldn't be in, or she'd be in bed, and he'd get her machine. She answered.

"Oh Claude," she said, in a high, bright voice. "How thoughtful of you to ring me."

But, he thought, she knew he didn't have her number, had even made an excuse for not giving it to him, so why did she now take it for granted that he did have it and could have called her up at any time? As he thought this, however, the thought became vague, and he wasn't sure she hadn't given him her number — and in any case, whether or not she had didn't, after all, matter. They were in touch, and she sounded very pleased.

She said, as with an urgency of her own, "Now when can I see you?"

"Whenever —"

"As soon as soon," she said.

He was about to say, What about right now? but said, "What about tomorrow?"

"What about the next day?"

"All right," he said.

"Come here," she said. "Come here to supper."

"There?" he asked.

So she lived alone.

Space seemed to open around him that he could go out to, and he thought: This must be a little like freedom, just a little, but enough to recognize the wonder of it.

The freedom should have promised a sense of the whole world, a sense at least of something so large it could only be expressed by including in it the whole world. It should have made him want to open up his arms wider to it. But it didn't. He felt that in his freedom to see Penelope he chose to be drawn to some small particular, like a mole on her body, which at the same time his excitement made him anticipate seeing the mole and pressing the tip of his tongue to it, disgusted him for his being excited by it. He should have been excited by the thought of her whole naked body, should have anticipated in her full body an immensity that drew him all outside himself, and not particulars that thrilled him in a particular, inner way he didn't like.

He didn't want to be on his own the two evenings before he was to see Penelope. He saw James the first, and on the second he went, with a little cake powdered with confectioners' sugar and a bottle of sweet wine, to Lidia's apartment, and was surprised to find how pleased he was to see that Marie was there.

His sense of relief made him attentive in a way he hadn't been before, and when she came from the kitchen carrying a tray with the bottle of wine and wineglasses and the cake on a crystal cake stand, it occurred to him again how beautiful, in her fine way, she was. She carefully placed the tray on the coffee table and served glasses of wine and slices of cake on plates to Lidia and to him, sitting together on the sofa. She sat on the edge of an armchair across from them, and she looked calm and cool.

Lidia said, "I suppose I can understand Russia being a disappointment. Well, what vision is there to replace the vision of communism?" She closed her eyes for a moment and seemed to fall asleep, but with a little jerk of her head she opened her eyes and said, "It was, it was a wonderful vision, but perhaps after all impossible, because no one is capable of suffering for the world the way communism demanded." Again she closed her eyes for a moment, and again opened them with a jerk of her head.

Marie turned to look, Claude thought, into the distance.

He asked her, "What do you think?"

As if considering this, or perhaps not, Marie raised a hand to her cheek. She said quietly, "I think we suffer the world."

Claude's sense of relief at being with her loosened his body, his arms and legs. He hadn't realized how tense he'd been.

Lidia asked Marie to sing, and, unembarrassed, she did, standing in the middle of the living room, her hands clasped at her waist, her breasts rising and falling, her face glowing with perspiration. As he listened, a feeling rose in Claude that he could only think of as deep, strange nostalgia, a nostalgia he was sure Marie too felt, more deeply, more strongly than he. Though he did not feel any sexual pull toward her, the pull he did feel toward her was deep and strange.

Perhaps in what he felt for Penelope there was nothing deep or strange.

He anticipated her exposing her breasts and his touching that mole on the side of one of them.

She lived lower down the West Side, and he walked down Ninth Avenue. Her apartment was in a new building, the lobby carpeted and with floor-to-ceiling mirrors and yucca plants in wooden troughs along the bottoms of the mirrors. The doorman, in a uniform and cap, called up to announce him.

She was standing at the door to her apartment, holding her arms out and smiling. She was wearing a white silk blouse and black velvet slacks and black pumps, and her hair was down. When he hugged her, he felt with his fingers that she was wearing nothing beneath the blouse. She hugged him more closely than he did her.

As if no one in the world existed but for him, she was entirely attentive to him. She put him in the most comfortable armchair — a great gray plush armchair that looked inflated and straining against its upholstery buttons and seams — and placed his drink, in a tall, thin glass, before him on the low glass table whose gleaming chromium legs sank into the white shag rug that showed through the glass top, and sat at the corner of the sofa nearest him — the sofa, too, gray and inflated — and tucked her feet up under her and asked him to tell her what he'd been up to. There were pairs of shoes on the rug and books and newspapers and a bath towel in a heap, and on the glass-topped table, among more books and newspapers and magazines and their drinks, were potholders and a wooden spoon and a little hourglass egg timer and a coffee cup with coffee in the saucer. And in the midst of all this was a glass bell jar containing a bouquet of flowers made of wires and colored beads.

He felt at ease talking to her. Her attention put him at ease, though he remarked moments of inattention, which made him aware she was thinking about something other than what he was telling her. But he saw that she quickly reattached her attention just by lowering her head and staring right at him from under her brow. Though he in fact felt at ease in her attention, he thought that she was attentive in a broad and vague way, with an attempt to belie the broadness and vagueness by staring at him from under her brow.

He wanted to say something that would make her react in a sharp way.

His voice raised, he said, "You know, I've really suffered."

And all she said in reaction was "My oh my oh my."

She doesn't understand, he thought; she doesn't understand what I've said, what I've revealed.

He asked her, "What are you thinking?"

"Well," she said, frowning, "I'm thinking of what I can do to cheer you up, and wondering if a bottle of champagne would help."

He was surprised by how unoriginal she was. But Claude always imagined that people were more original than he, and he thought that Penelope, in her greater originality, was like an artist who will take a banal object — a shoe, a loaf of French bread, a glass of water — out of its context and display it in the context of a gallery and in that way give it a bright, new meaning, and she simply assumed that her received idea would be seen by him to be, just because she stated it, bright and new with all the ironical meanings she would of course give it. Claude was not always very comfortable with irony. Maybe, he thought, what she'd said was brilliant.

He said, "That's brilliant."

She smiled.

He felt uncertain.

She hadn't got around to cooking anything — hadn't, if the truth be told, got around to buying anything for supper — but if he went into the kitchen with her she'd no doubt find something for them. She threw a pile of newspapers from the seat of a chair onto the floor and told him to sit at the table while she, as she said, scavenged about in the refrigerator and cupboards for something to eat. She seemed never to throw out newspapers. The kitchen table had on it a lamp with a cracked ceramic base and a torn shade and the wire coiled around the bottom, a hairbrush, and some old turn-of-the-century postcards of Atlantic City. The meal too was sort of a strange mix — sliced beets from a can, half a slice of pâté, rice with mushrooms, leftover chop suey, and a few eggrolls — but to Claude the ease of it all was more than pleasant, it was reassuring. She cleared the table, set it with starched linen placemats and napkins, fine bone china, and silver and crystal glasses, and lit candles, and she asked him to open another bottle of champagne.

And they got into a very interesting conversation about England and America.

But he was still uncertain, and just when he wasn't sure what was going to happen next, as if it weren't up to him, and as if it weren't up to her either, they went silent and still, and he knew what was promised in that silence and stillness.

She was very loving. And this time, at the risk of trying to raise the passion to a high level rather than letting the passion itself raise them to a high level, the risk being that they might suddenly become aware that they were trying to force into happening what they knew they couldn't force but had to happen of itself, he did make her feel there was meaning in their lovemaking for her, as much as there was for him. Really, it all did seem to happen of itself.

And after, or almost with it, he felt that pang of grief.

He lay by her in her bed in the room lit only from the light of nighttime New York through the window. Again they were silent and still.

He turned around and took all her naked body into his arms and held her close, as if out of pity for her, or pity for everyone.

When he let her go, he said, "Why is it that in making love I feel —"

"What?" she said.

He had never told anyone this, and maybe he wanted to tell Penelope because she made him feel it more than any other woman. Was this because he loved her more than any other woman?

Biting his lower lip, he raised his head and tried to see into her eyes. He said, "— very sad."

"For what?"

"For everyone making love, for all the lovers in the world making love."

"Oh my oh my," she said.

His head dropped back. He thought: I shouldn't have said it.

Maybe one of the reasons why he was so drawn to her was that she didn't indulge him in what she saw as his pretensions. He was filled with them.

He was, in his seriousness, so negative, and she was, in her lightness, so positive.

He spent the night with her, Friday night, and Saturday morning they went around the galleries in SoHo. Among the crowds, both in the streets and in the galleries, they kept running across people, so often that after the third time they'd smile at each other, and after the fourth they'd say a few lively words to each other. They also met friends, and meeting friends here was like meeting them at a party you needed a special invitation to and where you didn't expect they'd be, and this made them all feel special. Penelope didn't seem to mind that she and Claude were being seen together.

She wanted to look at what was being shown in every gallery they passed. She'd say, "Let's go in here," and if he said, "It won't be interesting," she pulled at his arm and insisted, in the bright voice, "Oh, but I must see it. There may be something wonderful in it." Inside, with the floorboards painted white and patched with tacked-down pieces of tin, the rough walls white, the ceilings water-stained, she always saw a painting she said was wonderful, absolutely wonderful.

Before a painting of the Madonna and Child, the figures taken from a Renaissance painting and surrounded by a toaster, a food mixer, an electric coffee grinder, an electric griddle pan, and chickens and rabbits and a porcupine, all in flat, garish colors, Penelope clasped her hands to her breasts and said, excitement gurgling in her throat, "This is too wonderful." It was a terrible painting. "Isn't it wonderful?" she asked. He said, also clapping his hands as she did, "It is beyond being wonderful." They laughed.

She made everything that was difficult, such as not getting a taxi or finding that no tables were available at a restaurant he wanted to take her to uptown, seem not to matter, made everything light and easy, and she responded with such appreciation to the not-good restaurant he found.

Back downtown, he took her to Duncan's studio, where she hadn't been. The studio was in TriBeCa, in a building where some floors were still occupied by light industry, and they went up in a freight elevator set into motion by pulling cables, and passing the floors with the industry saw the machines through the crisscrosses of the elevator gates. The elevator opened right into Duncan's studio. The floors were black with old oil and had holes from where the machines had been bolted to it.

Duncan showed them some of his paintings, having to turn them around from the walls they faced by grasping the middle bars of the stretchers and backing up and in the middle of the studio turning around so he disappeared behind them; it was as if the large, square paintings moved of themselves back against the walls. He emerged from behind them, and stood with Penelope and Claude to look at each one in turn.

Only Penelope commented, and her comments were banal enough for Claude to be embarrassed by them. He tried to make them sound more original by saying, "That's an interesting observation when you think about it —" Duncan, inclining his head from side to side as he studied the paintings, didn't seem to hear.

They stood before a painting that was bigger than the others.

On an impulse, Claude asked Duncan what he knew was the most banal question anyone could ask an artist, but a question that Penelope would be right, he thought, to ask, because it was essential: "Tell us what that painting is about."

Duncan said, "Come on, Claude."

"Come on, you," Claude said. "Why won't you say? Is it about love? Death? God?"

"You know that's something you can't talk about," Duncan said.

"Why?" Claude asked.

He looked at Penelope, who was looking away, toward a window covered with grime through which was seen, in a blurred way, a large cube wrapped in khaki quilts being hoisted to the floor above. She didn't seem to be interested in this conversation, which Claude had risked for her.

Duncan was annoyed. He knitted his brows and stuck out his chin so his beard jutted out.

Claude said, "The only reason I can think of for not being able to talk about it is that there is nothing there to talk about. Is that it?"

Duncan pulled at his beard so it jutted out more. "You're being silly," he said.

"I am silly," Claude said. "You know how silly I can be."

"I do."

"Or is it all too great to talk about?" Claude asked.

Penelope watched the bottom of the cube disappear, then she turned toward Claude and smiled vaguely.

"Get out," Duncan said to Claude. "Just get out."

Claude laughed. He had spoken to Duncan as he had for Penelope, to show her that he too could be light-spirited, could be easy. But she hadn't listened.

He spent Saturday night with her.

The fact was that whatever it was that he felt was most important to the world — which was impossible to talk about, either because there was nothing in it or because it was too great to be talked about — was expressed for him by grief, had its depth and height in grief, the grief that made him want to cry out at intense moments. And to him the world had its highest meaning in that grief. But maybe this was wrong. Maybe Penelope was right, and not grief but light and easy everyday social intercourse was what most made one a part of the world and most gave meaning to the world. Maybe there was no great reason for feeling grief for the world, and he was simply seeing the world from a point of view that was entirely personal, and he was projecting onto the world the indulgences of his self-pity — indulgences because really the world wasn't in such a bad state and didn't need pity. Penelope found the world "so delightfully lovely," and she was right, because even if *she* were projecting herself onto the world, it was better to project one's sense of delight than one's sense of sadness. If the world were a projection of oneself, then hers was, simply because of what she was, the better world. And his was the worse.

But he did take delight in the world, took the greatest delight in most delightful images of the world.

Holding her in his arms long after they had made love, he still awake and she, sleepy, keeping herself awake only because he was, he said to her, "Wouldn't it be wonderful to always see the world in terms of the most beautiful images of the world?"

"Oh yes," she answered, "wonderful."

She didn't understand, didn't understand what a deep wish this was. But then, whenever he said something to her he felt deeply, he felt a little foolish having said it. However, she might have been right again. She might have said to him, as if speaking to a little boy, All your desires are unrealizable. All the deepest of them were, especially the desire to see the world in terms of beautiful images of the world. She never thought in terms of the world; she knew that all images about the world had nothing to do with the world, the world being too big to be contained in even the greatest thoughts, but were about oneself. Really to think about the world would be to think about every single detail in the world; thinking about the world was like thinking of *everything*, which could only ever be a self-enclosed idea and never a fact, because it was impossible to think of *everything*. Penelope thought about this thing and that thing, but not everything. She had no possessive desire for everything. He did.

And long after the fact, when she, turned away from him, was asleep and he was still awake, he thought she was right in her attitude toward lovemaking. Her passion was total, and it was a passion that made all her hot, damp body entirely body. Never, in making love, had he been so possessed by a body in itself, as if her body were surrounded by darkness and not even the bed, the sheets, the pillows, existed. It was as if her soul evaporated from her in the heat and sweat of lovemaking, and nothing but body remained. What was strange was that his passion was roused more by her than by anyone else he'd ever made love with, as though possessing that body, that naked body, were more impossible than possessing everything, and he wanted this impossibility. He had chafed her thigh with his rough beard until a bruise appeared, had sucked at her neck until a black-and-blue mark formed, had bitten her. She'd liked this, and had held his head down. She was right: there was nothing to lovemaking but making love to the body in all its particulars, and the rightness of this was justified by the intensity of their lovemaking.

He wanted to leave her. He wouldn't be able to sleep if he stayed with her, and he felt suddenly exposed vulnerably, all his spent, naked body, to something he shouldn't be exposed to, and he wanted to cover himself. He got up and in the darkness found his clothes, dressed, and, feeling sticky all over, left.

Back in his apartment, he wasn't able to sleep either, trying now to settle something in his mind about Penelope. He wasn't sure what needed to be settled, but not doing so left him feeling that nothing in his life was settled, that his job wasn't really the job for him, that nothing in his apartment gave him a sense of being anywhere, except maybe the old czarist bonds in the bathroom, which were becoming warped with steam.

He told himself that he would go the next evening to Lidia's, where he would see Marie. But he was embarrassed toward Marie — the last time he'd seen her he'd felt something he imagined she'd also felt, something that embarrassed them both toward each other.

Without explaining, but very politely, Penelope told him when he telephoned her the next day that she couldn't see him for four days, and he had to accept the lack of explanation because she was so polite.

He saw James instead of going to Lidia's. He said nothing to James about Penelope, though James asked him what he'd been up to, and by his look implied that whatever he had been up to wasn't doing him much good. The second evening he spent on his own but trying to telephone friends, including Duncan and his family, who were not in. The third evening he went to Lidia's without returning to his apartment after work. He didn't have to telephone, as the old woman was always in. With her short white hair wild and the round opening at the neck of her dress off to the side and revealing her bony clavicle and the overlapping pink and yellowish underclothes, Lidia, at the doorway to her apartment, offered a cheek for Claude to kiss, then turned the other cheek to him to be kissed, and again turned her cheek so he would kiss her a third time. Marie was not there.

Falling onto the sofa, Lidia said, "We won't have tea until Marie comes and makes it for us."

When he knew she would come, he felt relieved.

"Sit, sit," Lidia said, "take off your jacket and sit," and he removed his jacket and sat across from her. "You know she always comes now in the late afternoon, early evening, to help me with a light supper and to get into bed."

"I guess I did."

Lidia said, "It is so very hot in here, isn't it? If I could afford air conditioning, I would have it. Will you open the window more?"

At the window, Claude said, "It's as wide open as it can be."

"Sit, sit," Lidia said, and Claude sat again.

Children outside were screaming.

As if she couldn't breathe, Lidia put her bony hands over her face. Outside, the children were screaming and seemed to be throwing bottles and smashing them against a cement wall. Lidia held her hands over her face, and when she took them away her cheeks were wet with tears.

Claude leaned toward her.

Lidia raised her hands again to place them over her face, but she lowered them and said, "I had so hoped going to Russia would make a difference to her." Then she half shouted, "What are those children doing out there?"

Claude sank back into his chair. A man shouted at the children from a window, so they ran away. In the silence, Lidia closed her eyes.

When Claude heard a key in the door to the apartment, out in the little hallway, he stood. Marie, coming in, didn't expect to see him, and drew back when she did. Claude silently indicated Lidia, asleep on the sofa. Marie came to her and Lidia opened her eyes.

"Marie," the old woman said, questioning Marie's presence before her in the dim room. She put out a hand and Marie held it. "Marie," Lidia said, asking if she were in fact there.

"I'll make some tea for us all," Marie said.

"Lidia told me you come every day to help her," Claude said.

"I come because it's a pleasure to help her."

Tea was at the table in the kitchen, where the yellow light, covered by a yellow shade with a burn mark on one side, hung from a long cord from the ceiling. The linoleum tiles on the floor were cracked and curling at the edges. With the tea, they had soup and crackers. In a tired voice, Lidia talked about her neighbors when Marie, who seemed to know them, asked about them.

Claude remained in the living room while Marie helped Lidia bathe in the bathroom. He heard water running and splashing, and Marie's voice, quiet, telling her old aunt what to hold on to and where to step.

When Lidia was in bed, Marie came out and told Claude he could go in to her to say goodbye. In the hot room, a cool freshness rose lightly from her.

Lidia said to Marie, as she and Claude were leaving, "If I didn't have you to help me, I could do everything on my own."

"I know," Marie said.

She left a lamp lit.

She and Claude took a subway train downtown. A young man, face up and eyes closed, was lying along the plastic seats, his cheeks and chin and forehead covered with sores. Marie and Claude sat across from him.

Out on the street again, they walked to the children's playground, where Claude knew he must leave her. But instead of saying goodbye to her there, Claude went inside the playground, and Marie, as if she were not quite following him but wandering about where he happened to wander, entered behind him. The glare of the lights revealed the playground empty except for them. A torn blanket was thrown over a cement bench, and on the asphalted ground was a stained pillow.

Claude went to the cement animals and sat on the back of one.

Marie leaned against another and bent her neck back and swung her head so her shining grayish hair seemed to float out, then sink. "It is hot," she said.

"And I think it'll never get cold again."

"Imagine, I was just a while ago in the midst of winter."

"I can't imagine it."

Again Marie shook her head and with the tips of her fingers brushed long, loose hairs from her face.

"Do you think there's anything Russian left in us," he asked, "born and brought up in America?"

"Very little, if anything."

"So for us Russia is a country we imagine."

She asked, "What do you imagine Russia to be?"

"A country of great sunsets over forests deep in snow."

She smiled.

"I'm sorry I didn't go with you," he said.

"You might have been disappointed."

"Or I might have kept you from being disappointed."

"You might have."

"Anyway, I wish I were there now."

She liked their talk, and when she asked, "Why?" she didn't mean the question to be merely polite. She wasn't the kind of person who was merely polite. Penelope was. If Marie wanted to leave him, she would simply have gone.

"To get away from here," he answered.

"Why do you want to get away from here?"

He waited, then he said, "Have you ever been drawn, really drawn, to something you knew was wrong to be drawn to, but you couldn't help it?"

Marie looked beyond him.

Claude said, "I know I should get away."

"And someone has to help you to?" Marie asked lightly. She was still looking beyond him.

He said, "Yes."

Marie looked at him before she came toward him, smiling, and touched his cheek. She said, "I'll leave you now."

"Do you have to?"

"Come to Lidia's tomorrow."

"Tomorrow evening," he said, "I can't."

"Ah," she said, and she turned away.

Later, in bed and trying to fall asleep, he told himself: I'll see her again soon, I'll go to Lidia's the day after tomorrow, after I see Penelope, and see Marie.

On his way to Penelope, to make sure she was in her apartment waiting for him, he telephoned her from a public telephone, and she told him to come on over, honey, right away. She was developing an American accent. He went, but telling himself he didn't really want to go. While he was with her in her overly air-conditioned apartment, the telephone rang, but she didn't answer. A man's voice, English and sounding as if coming from abroad, left a message, and as he left it she and Claude too listened to it. Whenever you heard someone leaving a message on the machine, it was a little as if the message were already recorded and you were listening to the recording. The man's voice said, "Are you there? I do want to speak to you, urgently. Please answer if you're there." Though it sounded like a recording, it wasn't; the man was speaking at that moment. Penelope didn't move, and after a pause a click sounded from the machine and a beep, and the little red light began to flash. Penelope not only didn't explain who the man was, she apparently felt that there was no reason why she should explain. She hardly seemed to be aware that the man had telephoned and said he must speak urgently to her. This was her right, and Claude himself had no right to want to know who the man was. Penelope went on talking as if nothing had occurred, except that her eyes were unfocused.

In bed, making love, she asked, "Do you want to know who that man was?"

A surge of jealousy went through him, and with it a surge of greater sexual desire. And as if he hadn't been aware before of a difference, he now thought, a desire not to make love with her, but to fuck her.

"No," he said.

But the sex was very exciting, with delicate, hypersensitive nerves excited as never before, and he felt chills run about his body and also pricklings of heat. And his mind became clear and sharp with the intention to do to her what he had never done before, and while he pinched her nipples hard he wondered what he would do to her next.

Writhing, she said, "I'll tell you if you ask me."

He drew away, knelt, and, looking at her, bit his lip.

She asked, "You haven't gone cold on me, have you?"

Looking at her splayed before him, her legs stretched out on either side of his knees, her arms stretched out, her hair tangled, her breasts hanging sideways on her rib cage, he felt a sudden pity for her. He lay back on her gently, and ran his hands over her, hardly touching her.

He felt, after, no sadness, no expansive sense of grief, but a feeling that something that should have happened hadn't, and that it had been up to him to make it happen and he hadn't done it.

She didn't seem to feel this about him, however. She said, "Thank you, darling," and she fell asleep.

He got up, dressed, and left. He walked back to his apartment, keeping to the avenues, which, even at three o'clock in the morning, were crowded. As he was opening the door to his apartment, he thought: I shouldn't have left her. He had done something very wrong. To calm himself, to take possession of himself, he masturbated, but he didn't sleep.

Early, when he knew she would be at home but not so early that he would wake her, he telephoned her. She didn't reply, and he didn't leave a message.

Over the next days, he kept trying to telephone her, but he kept getting the machine, and he always hung up before the beep.

He told himself not to call her. However, he couldn't stop calling her. He wanted her to respond to him, that was all. In the same way a person lets a telephone ring and ring and ring, in a rage that no one answers and determined, just by letting the telephone ring on forever, to make someone answer, he kept calling her, but the machine always answered, and he slammed down the receiver. He wasn't going to leave a message knowing that she was there listening to him but not responding to him.

He thought of Marie, but his embarrassment toward Marie, an embarrassment that seemed to him more and more incomprehensible the more it grew, kept him from going to Lidia's.

Walking along Fifth Avenue, Claude saw on the street corner outside the Cathedral of Saint Patrick a group of women, their faces shining with perspiration, standing at a collapsible table on which was propped a big colored picture of a naked woman, blindfolded, gagged, and bound hand and foot with nylon stockings, and piercing the nipple of one of her large blond breasts was an instrument that looked like a clamp with a needle. On the table before the picture was a pile of sheets of paper, with signatures, in black, blue, and even red, in protest against such images of women. Claude stood just to the side of the stairs up to the cathedral, looking at the picture and wondering about signing the protest. Traffic was passing along Fifth Avenue, the sunlight glaring off the tops of the cars, and he looked into the traffic beyond the picture, and beyond the cars to the other side of the avenue, where Marie Clark was standing before a store window, looking, it seemed, beyond the traffic toward him.

She appeared thin, her neck long and her wrists, sticking out of the cuffs of the sleeves of her white blouse, long. She was leaning a little to the side. Perhaps she didn't see him.

When the light changed, Claude crossed the avenue and went to her. She didn't seem surprised that he came up to her, but she blinked and smiled slowly, then she put her hand on his extended arm. Pedestrians passed them. Claude kept his arm raised.

"You look lost," he said.

"I've just been wondering if I should go uptown or downtown," she said.

"I suppose that depends on what you want to do."

"I suppose."

He lowered his arm and she dropped her hand.

"Which way are you headed?" she asked.

"Downtown."

"Then maybe I'll go downtown."

They walked down Fifth Avenue, their shoulders touching from time to time, along the curb edge of the sidewalk. Hot, fetid air blew up through the gratings, and bits of paper and pigeon feathers and dust rose up on it.

Claude thought: I made a mistake in Penelope, a terrible mistake. He asked Marie, "How are things?"

She shrugged one shoulder. "They could be worse," she said, and laughed lightly. "I could be a lead singer at the Metropolitan instead of a secretary taking dictation."

She was being ironical, and he liked that in her.

"I'm told lead singers are given a tough time at the Met," he said, and laughed too, a little.

"They're made to sing on their knees, sometimes lying flat on the stage, which is never all that clean."

"Really tough," he said.

"And as glamorous as their public lives appear, they always have miserable private lives."

"I'd rather have a happy private life than a glamorous public life any day," he said.

"Any day."

He changed his tone. "How's the singing?" he asked.

She shrugged both shoulders and laughed more.

He dropped a quarter into the paper cup held out by a homeless man standing against a building.

When they were standing together at a crossing and waiting for the light to change, Marie asked, "Do you still think of leaving New York?"

"I do, yes," he answered.

The light changed, and among others, they crossed the street, but they walked more slowly than the other pedestrians.

"To go where?" Marie asked.

"I haven't thought of that. I've only thought that if I stayed here I'd give in to something I don't want to give in to."

He remembered that the last time he had seen Marie, she had left him just when he'd started to talk intimately in this way. This time, she appeared to be considering carefully what he said and what she'd answer. They walked steadily and more slowly. She said, "Giving in to something is always frightening."

He too took time to consider their talk. "Yes," he said.

He wanted to go on walking with her, though he had no idea where she was headed, and it seemed to him that he didn't know where he was headed either. But at Thirty-second Street, she said she had to go west, and he knew that if he said he'd go with her he'd be imposing himself on her, and he didn't want to do that. In the windows of a shop some storeys up were many large Chinese vases, white and blue and green and with red dragons on them. Claude looked at them, and after a moment he realized Marie was looking up at them too. She didn't want to leave him.

Marie said, "You told me you need help."

He said, "I do, though I keep telling myself I should be able to help myself. Isn't it strange, very strange, that people can't help themselves?"

"It is what is most strange about the world," Marie said, and she glanced at her watch.

"You're not going to leave me now," Claude said.

She smiled at him. "I was thinking it's getting to be the time I usually go to Lidia's to give her her supper and bath and put her to bed."

"I'll go with you."

"Well, I wasn't going to go for an hour or so yet."

"Shall we go on walking, then?"

Marie kept the slow pace Claude set. They talked about singers and singing and opera. With her, he felt come over him that curious nostalgia, though it couldn't be nostalgia as he didn't know what it was for. Perhaps they did, though born and brought up in America, remember Russia, or some Russia that didn't exist and had never existed, and when they were together they felt nostalgia for that country. And he also felt that she was taking a risk being with him, and he was concerned about her vulnerability in taking such a risk. While he was talking, he wondered how he could reassure her that she was safe in having taken that risk, safe in knowing they were at a deep and strange level so alike. He wondered if she too felt the promise he felt in this.

They walked to Washington Square, where, in the long light, three homeless people, a woman between two men, were, with a supermarket trolley filled with bulging plastic bags parked before them, sitting on a bench.

They stood together in the square, and he said to her, "We're so much alike —"

She narrowed her eyes, but she stared intently at him.

"We —" he started to stay, and seeing her eyes open slowly, he felt a sudden sense of embarrassment come to him, and with the embarrassment the slight resentment that Marie herself presumed they were alike when he knew how different they in fact were.

He looked away from her to the homeless people on the bench.

When, after a moment, Marie said, "I guess it's time for me to go to Lidia's," Claude knew that she was offering him the choice of going with her or not. He didn't want to go with her.

It wasn't, he thought, that he wanted to go to Penelope. He wasn't even sure whether Penelope was in, and he didn't in any case want to go to her, he really didn't. It was that so suddenly he had no idea how it had happened, he was embarrassed by what he and Marie felt. There were no deep and strange levels in Penelope, and she had no sense that there were any in anyone else. She was not sentimental.

Claude said, "Oh."

Promptly, Marie said, "You can't come to Lidia's."

He laughed, or tried to.

"That's all right," she said. "I'll leave you now and go get a West Side train uptown."

"I'll walk you to the subway station."

"No, no," Marie said. "That's all right."

She left quickly, without saying goodbye. She disappeared in the long, dusty light as she walked away from him, then reappeared momentarily in the shadow of a tree, and again disappeared in the light.

He felt he had betrayed her, but then, walking around Washington Square to give her time to get ahead of him before he too went to the West Side for a subway train to his apartment, he thought: I can't, I can't. And Marie's delicacy, her depth and strangeness, appeared to him to characterize a girl he had all his life felt it his duty to reassure, and he didn't want to do this anymore. He wanted to think that Marie and he were not at all alike. Marie may have been, but he was not helpless. He had his will, and that was strong.

In his apartment, he dialed Penelope's number, though he didn't want to. He was a little jolted when she answered. Taken aback, he said with an apologetic tone, "I'm sorry."

She laughed. "What do you have to be sorry for?"

He said, "I've been wanting to talk to you."

"But I've been away," she said.

"Away?"

"Yes."

"Why didn't you tell me?"

She didn't answer, perhaps not knowing how to react to his presumption.

Then she said, "Didn't I tell you?"

"No," he said.

Again she laughed. "I am silly," she said.

He waited.

"Well, please, let's see each other as soon as soon. You come this evening, this very evening."

He always took pleasure in what he saw, but walking to Penelope's apartment, he didn't take any pleasure. His vision was of a city of surfaces, destructive stone and cement and metal surfaces: graffiti-covered metal shields pulled down over shop windows, doorways and windows of a derelict house blocked up with cinder blocks, a cement yard behind a high chainlink fence with razor wire along the top, the gray brick walls of the sides of buildings along alleyways. This vision occurred to him now because, he told himself, he was selecting the details that most corresponded to the feeling he had about Penelope. It was she who made him imagine that the people who lived in New York ate stone, slept in stone beds, and covered themselves with cement blankets.

What he didn't understand was how someone who was so vague could make him feel such hardness toward her and the world.

In her apartment, she couldn't open a saltshaker to refill it, tripped over a book left on the floor, spilled wine pouring it into his glass at dinner. He helped her wash the dishes, and they remained in the small kitchen as if there were something more to do. She, apparently not wanting to look at him, opened and shut cupboard doors, searching for something. Puzzled, he watched her, and when she went still he put his arms around her, but she seemed to go more still. Though she didn't move, he felt her entire body rejecting him.

More puzzled, he stood back, and she smiled a wide smile that floated out from her face.

"What's up?" he asked.

She smiled everywhere but at him. She asked, "Where did I put my passport?"

"Your passport?" He thought: Nothing is happening, really, except that she lost something. Once she finds it, everything will be, as there is no reason for it not to be, as easy as pie between us. Keep things simple, he said to himself, and help her find her passport. He said, "Well, let's find it."

Walking out of the kitchen, she said, "I don't know, really," and he didn't know what she meant.

He walked close behind her to stay close. "What don't you know?" he asked.

She made loose gestures with her long, thin arms. "I simply don't."

His voice rose when he said to her, "Look at me and tell me what's wrong."

She turned toward him but didn't look at him, and she put her fingers to her chin and rolled her eyes, wondering where she had put her passport.

He thought he heard a distant crack, and he thought: I was wrong, something has happened. He asked, "Do you want me to go?"

Now she did look at him. She said, "I think that would be best."

"Now?"

"Yes, now."

He had a curious sense of leaving himself there as he went out, or leaving himself somewhere other than where he was, so that out in the street he didn't know where he was, and all he could think was, What happened?

He told himself, It's all right, it's all right, take it easy and it'll all be all right —

But in the New York street, a halo seemed suddenly to descend on him, and he felt he was nowhere in the world. He had to keep reminding himself, street by street, how to get back to his apartment.

More than ever unable to sleep, he walked around his little apartment and picked up a cup or sunglasses left on a bookshelf or a ceramic bowl filled with loose change and felt his muscles tense to throw it, and he had to restrain himself. Back in bed, still tensed, he tried to twist himself into positions he'd never been in before, as if just that would make a difference to everything he thought and felt, which locked him, inside, in one position, and only some violent contortion, even breaking something, would relieve him of that one position that possessed him.

He thought of getting up and drinking a whiskey, but didn't. His will was too strong for him to allow himself to get drunk. His will was so strong he thought the possession must be broken by willing it to break. He willed himself to get up in the morning and go to work. At sunset, when the workday was over but when his concentration on his work was most in gear and seemed, to his surprise, to be turning over of itself and he was no longer forcing it to turn over, the sight of a scarf in a shop window roused the possession again, and he was as if held into one place and one time by that halo above his head. He couldn't bear the possession.

Possession by what? he asked himself.

This was not what he had talked with Marie about when they had talked about giving oneself up to something. This wasn't giving up to anything, this was being imposed upon.

When he thought about Marie, a flush of shame spread over his body. He couldn't make himself go to Lidia's to see her, and he felt he had betrayed Lidia as much as Marie.

But he saw Duncan and his wife Susan and their teenage children. They lived on the top floor of the building in which Duncan had his studio, the vast space divided by partitions of plywood that had never been painted. In the kitchen–dining area, the doors on the cupboards had never been put on, and the bulb hanging low over the long table didn't have a shade. The window frames had been partly scraped down to the original wood, but most of them had layers of old, cracked paint; and there were only blinds pulled halfway down the dark, dirty windows.

Duncan and his family were close, and at the long, wide table the meal was lively. But Claude told himself that he felt, frankly, an intensity had gone out of these family meals, though the food was from the best shops in SoHo and always included something special, like yellow watermelons, or even extravagant, like Cabrales blue Spanish cheese or Valrhona truffles or Ethiopian Yrgacheffe coffee. He told himself that the intensity lacking was sexual, though he didn't quite know what he meant by that; but it seemed to him that these close friends were sexless. At the same time, he knew that this was untrue, not at all true, and the sexlessness was all in his eyes.

Clarissa told them about a relationship she was having with a cripple. Clarissa was eighteen, and beautiful. She didn't say if her relationship with the cripple, who had a withered leg, was sexual. She said that both she and her friend were allowing the relationship space, and they found the developments in that space interesting. They were experimenting, sort of.

"Experimenting?" Claude asked.

"Well," Clarissa said, "maybe just observing, without interfering."

"How can you do that?"

"By letting things happen but being aware of them all the time."

"Yes, I see," Claude said.

He felt low, and leaned back in his chair and didn't speak. Susan, a small, slow, calm woman, refilled his glass of wine and asked him a question about work, but he said only that he didn't know.

She said, "Claude —"

"What?" he asked.

"I wish you could just let things happen," she said.

Tears rose into his eyes and startled him. There was nothing he wanted more than to be in an open, clear space where things just happened around him. It seemed to him he always had to make things happen, and he didn't want to any longer. He wasn't sure he had the will to, but more, whatever it was he did make happen he knew had no meaning, no meaning at all, because he had made it happen. Only what happened in the open, clear space beyond your intentions mattered, and he was out of touch with that open, clear space beyond him. The very idea of it was what made the tears come to his eyes: open, clear space, and the freedom of it.

He said quietly, "I wish I could."

There was in him, always, the impulse to give in, to be will-less, but where then would he be? Giving in, he would not be in control, and he was, in an essential way, someone who had to be in control. Friends saw this in the way he dressed, in his neatness. But what especially frightened him was that in a still more essential way, he did want to give in, did want to be will-less, did want to give up control to what was beyond him. To do that, however, he had to be sure first that what was beyond him was clear, open space and freedom. He wasn't sure. Perhaps he didn't have enough faith in that surrounding clear and open space, in its power to give him the freedom he so wanted, and in his uncertainty, in his lack of faith, he imagined that out there was nothing, and by giving up control he would be giving in, not to what was beyond him but to what was inside him, dark and as closed in as a cement cell in which things more terrible than he could imagine took place, and he had, by the strength of his will, to keep himself away from that, all destructive. He couldn't let that just happen. He was not crazy.

At home, alone, he asked himself again and again what possessed him. Did it any longer have to do with her?

About Penelope, he thought, it wasn't her fault, what had happened to him, it was his.

Claude finally went to Lidia's, and he went, he realized as he stood outside her door, knowing that Marie would be there, but Lidia didn't answer when he rang the bell. He telephoned James, who said Lidia wasn't well and was staying a few days with Marie's mother. Then Claude thought James was the person to see, James, whose irony Claude was incapable of and wished he was capable of. Claude suggested that they meet in a Village bar.

They stood together with bottles of beer. Claude had wanted to talk with James about Penelope, or about himself, but they talked about Marie, and Claude knew that after all it was about Marie that he wanted to talk.

He asked James, "Do you think she could do something to herself?"

"You mean kill herself?" James asked.

"Yes."

"No, I'm sure not. She's a survivor." James drank from his glass of beer, then asked, "Have I ever talked to you about my idea of the halo?"

Claude slowly shook his head.

"I'll tell you," James said. "It's a halo that hangs over everyone's head, and sometimes it suddenly descends, there's no saying why. It destroys the weak, who believe there is nothing, nothing at all, above and beyond themselves, and all there is in the world to be aware of is themselves. But the tough ones know how to survive."

"How?" Claude asked.

"They are capable of a delicate point of detachment that itself bears the weight of their awareness of themselves. Marie, in her detachment, bears her halo with great poise."

"Marie doesn't think about herself," Claude said.

"Marie thinks only about herself," James said. "But Marie won't give in. Believe me. She has her poise to sustain her."

"I really don't know."

"Well, neither do I."

They went to a restaurant for a simple meal. Leaving James, Claude told himself he could hardly remember what Penelope looked like, and back in his apartment and undressing to go to bed, he thought that all he did remember of her was light, and light was his possession. It kept him awake. On his way to work in the morning, he posited this light around any woman or girl who struck him as beautiful. The brighter the light, the more he felt he couldn't have the woman, that she was in every way unattainable in her inviolability to him.

Then he saw Penelope at an opening of a show of paintings by Duncan. The floor, walls, and ceiling of the gallery tilted in odd angles around her. She was wearing a pale blue dress. She was looking away, talking with a tall, balding man in a dark suit. He heard the man talk with an English accent. Claude stopped about ten steps from her.

It would be so easy, so incredibly easy, for everything, everything that was wrong to be put right.

She looked toward him, then, for a second, at him, right into his eyes, then, with the slightest refocusing of her eyes, right through him, and she turned back to the man she was with as if she had turned away only to think about something he had said to her. Claude heard her say, "What I think is —"

His rage uncoordinated him even more, but it also impelled him, shambling, toward her, and he grabbed her arm.

Raising her chin on her long neck, she turned to him and, as though surprised to see him, said in a high voice, "But how lovely to see you."

Claude held her arm. The man with her was smiling a thin smile with his thin lips.

She said, "Tell me about yourself. What have you been up to? I want to hear it all, all."

Squeezing her arm, he said, "There's too much to say."

She smiled, and it was a truly charming smile, clear and open, and without any tension. He dropped her arm.

Right then and there, he could have, struggling to coordinate his enraged body, killed her.

Still smiling, she looked away from him and around the gallery.

"Goodbye," he said.

She glanced back at him, as if she had forgotten he'd been there and was surprised and pleased to see him, and she said, smiling more broadly, "Oh, goodbye."

Shambling, he went to find Duncan, who was in the office with his dealer. Claude broke in on them and, his voice harsh with anger, asked him why the fuck Penelope had been invited. Duncan said, Wait a minute, wait a minute, but Claude said he wasn't going to wait, he was going. Clomping, he left the gallery, his motions made even more shambling by his trying to put on his coat as he left and not finding the sleeves.

The taxi driver said he couldn't change a twenty, and Claude shouted, what did he expect him to do, give him twenty dollars for a seven-dollar fare? and the driver said that was Claude's problem, not his, and just waited, and Claude threw the twenty-dollar bill across the back of the seat, through the opening where the bullet-proof plastic shield was slid back, and got out and slammed the taxi door hard. He heard the taxi driver call him a mother, and he turned toward the closed window and hit it with his fist and shouted at the driver to come on out and repeat that. He threatened the driver enough that the driver put his taxi in gear and with a lurch sped off to the red light ahead, where the taxi swerved when he stopped short. On his way up to his apartment, Claude hit the banisters, the walls.

If anyone had told him a year before that his greatest hatred in the world would be England, he would have said that was impossible, as he had never been there. But, oh God, he hated England.

Dressed, he lay on his bed, and not only did he feel that he was looking down at his body from above, he felt that there was a self lower than his body which he was aware of below him, and this body lying below him was dark and still.

The room was dark and still, and it seemed to him that something was about to occur in it, and he waited for it to occur.

Get up, the self above said to him, get up and eat and read, or even better, telephone a friend and make a date to go out and eat with him. It's early yet. Don't lie here.

If he had had Marie's telephone number, he would have called her.

He didn't move, and the stiller and darker that body below him became the more motionless he became, feeling himself pulled down and giving in to the pull.

The self that was above said, Don't lie here. It's wrong to lie here. Don't do it.

But he didn't move.

He said to himself, Let yourself go and just watch what happens. As long as you watch, just watch, you'll be all right, and nothing will happen to you, nothing will touch you. Give in to the pull and let yourself fall, and observe what happens as you fall.

He let go, and he felt himself fall inwardly.

In the closed and dark cement cell of his imagination, he watched a man seen from the back who was not himself, not entirely himself, standing before a woman, who was not entirely Penelope, and the man raised his hand and hit the woman across her jaw so she fell, stunned, against a wall.

Go on, he said to himself; see what happens next, see what you're capable of imagining.

A chilling and at the same time hot prickling spread all over him, as when, alone, a person is suddenly aware that someone else is in the big, dark house.

The man hit her again, so she bent over. When she stood, her nose was seen to be bleeding and she was also bleeding from the corner of her mouth.

She was naked, and as the man approached her, she raised her hands to her breasts. He knocked her sideways so she fell on her side, and he kicked her to make her lie flat on her back on the cement floor. Shoving the toe of his shoe under her knees, each in turn, he lifted her legs. When again she covered her breasts with her hands, he kicked her arms away. Her body was matte white, and rough with gooseflesh at her thighs. She was trembling. He spit on her.

Claude's self that was above said, Stop this.

I only want to see, he said.

He saw the man put a shoe on her stomach and press down and the woman groaned, but because everything was taking place in silence the groan was inaudible. The man stood on her, and when he stepped off her, she doubled up in pain, holding herself about her middle, but he kicked her to make her lie flat on her back again. Then the man became fixated on a mole on the side of one of her breasts.

Stop this, the voice above said.

Go on, Claude said to himself; go on and see, see as far as you can see into what you can imagine, because it's interesting to see farther than you've ever seen.

Don't, the voice above said.

Go on, Claude said.

The man had a knife in his hand —

That's enough, the voice above said, that's enough.

Claude felt all his strength leave him, and as it did he trembled.

The man raised the knife to the woman's breast, the tip pointing at that mole —

That's enough, the voice said, that's enough, you don't have to imagine more to know what more you can imagine.

Claude jumped up from bed and unbuckled his belt and unzipped his fly and pulled off his trousers, pulled off his socks, and taking off his shirt rushed into the bathroom and turned on the shower. He pulled off his underpants, and, frightened and not knowing what he was doing or why, he stepped under the shower turned to cold. He felt very weak, and he wondered if he could stand.

He knew that what had occurred to him was only the beginning of what could occur to him.

Pressing his forehead against the side of the shower stall, shivering now with cold, he closed his eyes and tried to think of something that would block even the possibility of more occurring to him. He tried to see a glass of water on a table.

And then he thought: Don't think that what occurred to you hasn't in fact happened, and is at this moment happening, in the world.

He concentrated on that glass of water.

It is happening, it is happening, he thought, right now in the world.

III

CLAUDE ASKED JAMES over the telephone how he could get in touch with Marie.

James said, "She doesn't like people to know where she lives."

"But you know."

"She trusts me. You want to see her?"

Claude said, "I do, yes. I do."

"Then I'll arrange it," James said.

In James's air-conditioned apartment, James told Claude to sit still as they waited for Marie to come to lunch, and then, after, they would all go uptown to the opera.

James had prepared an elegant meal, on a table set with a cloth embroidered along its borders with stylized, squared red flowers, which were also on the napkins. There was a crystal compotier of oranges and thin champagne glasses. Half an hour after Marie was supposed to have arrived and hadn't, James said he and Claude should sit and eat.

"She's never late," James said. "She's too conscientious."

Claude bit his lower lip. "Well, she's late now."

It became time for them to leave for the opera.

"Let's wait another five minutes," James said. After ten minutes, James said, "I'll try telephoning her." There was no reply. "I could try telephoning her mother."

"It's possible," Claude said, "she could be there at the opera house, waiting."

"Let's go, then."

Claude didn't move. With one hand, he pulled at the fingers of his other hand.

James said, "You're the one who's getting into a state."

"I'm not," Claude said, and he made fists of both hands.

James narrowed his eyes at him. "I tell you, Marie will be all right."

"Will she?"

"You don't think so?"

Hitting the edge of the table with his fists, Claude said, "No, I don't."

"I see I'm going to have to help you rather than Marie. Where is your poise?"

Claude put his hands, palms down, on his head, and then made fists and tapped his skull.

His eyes narrowed, James asked, "Do you often get into this state?"

Swinging his arms, Claude got up from the table, and still swinging his arms, he paced about the room.

"I am amazed," James said. "With your colorful socks and all, I thought you were such a stylishly detached and undemonstrative person."

Claude sat again at the table and pressed his hands between his knees.

With a light laugh, James asked, "Do you sometimes get violent?"

Biting his lower lip, Claude turned his head away.

"We're going now," James said.

When the taxi stalled in traffic, which was often, a smell of tar and oil wafted in through the open windows with the heat.

Claude sat hunched forward. "Sit back," James told him. Claude slid back against the seat.

The heat in the plaza in front of the opera house was blown about by a wind, which brought with it torn pages of newspapers, dirty paper napkins, gum wrappers, and fine, warm spray from the fountain gushing at the center.

Through the glass doors of the opera house, Claude saw ticket collectors wearing black suits and black ties standing together and talking, and no one else in the red-carpeted lobby.

"She's not here," he said. "She's not."

James opened a door and went in, talked to the ticket collectors, walked back and forth across the lobby, then came out.

"No," he said to Claude, frowning, "she's not here."

Claude ran across the plaza to get a taxi, and James walked slowly after him. At the taxi door, waiting, Claude was pulling the fingers of one hand and then the other. To stop him, James touched one of his wrists, and Claude clasped his hands tightly together.

As they approached the door to James's apartment, they heard the telephone ringing inside. The telephone stopped ringing just as James was opening the large brown front door with his key.

Angry, Claude said, "Telephone her mother. Please telephone her mother."

James did, but there was no answer.

Claude sat on a chair and James turned on the radio to the broadcast of the opera, and he sat too. The voices, a male and a female, rose one above the other, higher and higher. These voices expanded the apartment into an invisible world in which an invisible man and a woman were singing, on long, long, overreaching rises, about their love for each other. And their song sounded like a lament, sounded anguished, the more it rose with the urgency to rise so high it would rise to a level in that invisible world where everything that was impossible in the visible world became possible. There was a thrill from the violins that impelled from the voices a higher, more anguished thrill.

The telephone rang and James got up quickly to pick up the receiver. His face was stark, and he said, "Yes, yes," then, "Yes." He replaced the receiver and lowered his head; then, after a still moment, he raised his head and said to Claude, "She gave in." Claude rose and as he went toward James to hear better in the midst of the singing, James said, "She's dead."

The voices of the man and woman, rising one above the other, paused, then rose together, and their singing was as if out in space. James went to the radio and shut it off.

Claude bent over and groaned, then he walked around the apartment and began to hit himself, hard.

James shouted, "Stop it."

Hitting his chest, shoulders, the sides of his head, Claude walked faster and faster, and he groaned.

"Stop it," James shouted more.

Claude put his hands over his face and sat on a chair.

At Marie's funeral, he felt such shame he avoided Lidia, as if she knew, even more then he, why he felt the shame, and he left the church right after. But a few days later, when James told him Lidia was back in her apartment, he went to see her. He heard the rubber-tipped cane before she opened the door. Tears filled his eyes as he kissed her cheek. He drew away and saw tears were also in her eyes. He kissed her other cheek, then again the first.

He followed her into her living room, where, as if Marie were there, Lidia seemed to look a little past Claude to ask her, "Shall we have tea?"

Claude waited for a moment, then said, "With lemon, please."

He was alone in her living room while she was in the kitchen, and he examined the books in the shelves. There weren't any in Russian. Maybe Lidia didn't really remember Russia concretely, any more than there was concrete evidence of her early life in Russia in her apartment. The apartment might have been that of an old American woman who had married an academic and lived all the life she could remember, or cared to remember, in her husband's academic world, with holiday trips to the West, where they had bought souvenirs from the Indians.

With one hand held out to keep her balance while the other held her cane, Lidia, her thin body swaying, came into the living room. "You'll have to bring the tray in here," she said. It was the kind of order an old Yankee matron might give. Unable to fold her body up and sit, she fell backward stiffly onto the sofa, her cane between her legs. Claude hurried to get the tea tray.

It was black, painted with red flowers. The cups had red flowers on them too. Tea bags were swelling in the hot water, and on the saucers were slices of lemon. Claude prepared a cup for her.

She drank her tea down, then took the lemon slice out with the tips of her fingers and ate it to the rind. She held the empty cup out and he took it from her.

He sipped at his tea. "Do you remember Russia?" he asked.

With a little jerk of her stiffened body, needed, maybe, to get herself to talk, she answered, "I do, oh yes, I do." Her body seemed to stiffen again. In a soft voice that belied all her stiffness, she said, "I remember looking out the window and seeing soldiers."

"Fighting?"

"No. They had come to take all the furniture out of our house, a big house. I had six sisters, and each one of us had her own room, each painted a different pastel color. I remember the empty rooms of the house."

"And you left then?"

"Not just then. My oldest sister said the attic, where the soldiers hadn't gone, should be searched for old furniture to replace what the soldiers had taken. And enough armchairs and tables and chaises longues were found to refurnish the entire house. We lived like that for some months, I think, until my father heard the soldiers were coming again, this time to take over the house, and we bundled up clothes and left, my father, mother, and their seven daughters, before the soldiers arrived."

Claude asked, "And did you have any notion of what was going on, what the Revolution was about?"

"Some of my sisters spoke about it. One or two of them, I think, were quite in favor of it, and would have joined it if my father hadn't been such a dominatingly bourgeois father and forbidden them to do anything but stay with the family, at least until we got out of Russia, and that was the end of the family. I'm not sure I understand the Revolution now any more than I did when I was a little girl. But I do think it was a wonderful, impossible vision, even though it finally almost destroyed Russia before the Russians recognized just how impossible it was and gave it up."

Claude stared as if into space.

"Claude," Lidia said.

"I think you must be tired," he said, "so I should leave."

"No, don't."

He waited for her to go on with the talk, but she didn't.

"Do you ever think of returning to Russia?" he asked.

"I do, sometimes."

"To see what it's like now, after communism has failed?"

"It's more than just curiosity, you know, that makes me sometimes think I'd like to go back."

"What is it, then?"

"Some kind of longing, I suppose."

"Longing?"

"Yes. I sometimes have what I think is a great nostalgia for Russia."

"Even though the country's almost been destroyed by the will of communism?"

Lidia lowered her chin and her entire hunched body fell forward, about, it seemed to Claude, to fall from the sofa. He was going to jump up to hold her, but she fell backward, her face as if crushed by pain. Her mouth was stretched open and the tip of her tongue trembled on her lower lip, and coursing tears followed the wrinkles of her cheeks. "What did she want?" she cried. "What, gentle soul that she was?" And then, leaning forward again, so the vertebrae of her long white nape and back showed, she rocked back and forth slowly in her grief. From time to time, she said, "What did she want?" When she went quiet and lay back, her face was wet with tears and mucus.

Claude sat by her on the sofa, and with the tissues he gave her Lidia wiped her face and blew her nose. He held her arm.

She asked, "What did she want? Do you understand?"

"Maybe, a little," he said.

"What was it, then?"

"I don't know if it's possible to say."

"Impossible?"

"As impossible to say as it's impossible to say what vision could possibly save us."

"You believe there may be, still unknown to us, a vision that will save us?"

"I have to believe it."

"You have to. But like Marie, you don't really believe it."

"Maybe," Claude said, "it's too embarrassing to talk about."

"Is it?"

"James would say —"

Lidia raised her voice a little. "James? James would say all a person can ever talk about is himself, and would deny that a person can speak disinterestedly about the world. He's wrong. James would say that Marie's killing herself had only to do with her, and not with the world. He's wrong."

"Is he?"

"The best James can be is entertaining. That's a lot, but it's not enough, not for me. Tell me, tell me, without embarrassment, what you want."

"To believe the world can be saved."

The afternoon was waning, and the room was dim.

Lidia said, "You don't believe in God?"

"No," Claude said, "I don't. But it's not true that if there is no God everything is possible. If there is no God, nothing is possible."

In the dimness, it appeared that things in the room — the books and papers, the pine cones and crystals and Indian artifacts, the cups — were in space, and this space was very deep.

"I'll wash the teacups," Claude said, "and then I'll go."

"That's kind," Lidia said quietly.

"Is there anything else you'd like me to do for you?"

"Do what Marie used to?"

"If I were able to, I would."

"Thank you, but I can manage without her now."

They didn't move, and the apartment got dimmer and the spaces deeper.

Then Claude took up the tray with the cups and went into the kitchen. When he came out, the living room was so dim he hardly saw Lidia Rivers on the sofa.

She said, "I'm not going to put on a light."

"Please don't," he said.

But there was a yellowish light outside the front door on the landing, and they stood in it.

"I want to tell you," Lidia said, "that nothing could have been done to save her. I believe that now, and you must believe it."

He said, "I can't believe it."

"You must."

"I can't," he said, and his voice rose in pitch. "I refuse to believe it."

"You'll be hurt badly —"

"Maybe I've already been hurt," he said.

She leaned her cane against a wall and took both his hands in hers and shook them. "I would hate to see you hurt more," she said.

He walked down to SoHo for a Saturday afternoon opening of a show. Duncan and Susan were in the gallery and asked where he'd been, they hadn't seen him in, it seemed, a long time. He said he'd been around. They didn't ask about Penelope.

Claude asked about their daughter Clarissa. "How is she doing with her crippled boyfriend?"

Susan said it was understandable that someone with a withered leg would have so many shifting defenses, there'd be no way for Clarissa to get around them, however far she'd go in trying to be large and just let things happen. He'd said he couldn't stand just letting things happen. He wanted to make something happen.

"They've split," Duncan said.

Susan said to Claude, "I think you should know that Penelope has left New York."

"To go back to London?"

"Yes," Duncan said.

"We thought you should know," Susan said.

When Claude, with roses in cellophane, went to see Lidia Rivers again, James answered the door.

"Are you here as her doctor?" Claude asked.

"Just as something of a nephew, to see how she is."

James thrust out his chin, paused, then turned quickly, his hand held out, all his fingers as if pinching together something too small to be seen. He pinched his lips together, too. Then, after a pause, he swung his hips and went forward, effeminate in his movements.

Claude followed him to the bedroom, where Lidia Rivers was sitting up in bed with many pillows behind her, wearing an Indian man's shirt of different-colored diamonds as a bed coat, her short white hair parted at the side and combed over her ears. Her hair had just been combed and the bed looked newly made, and Claude knew that James must have done these. She laughed, with a sparkle, when Claude kissed her cheek and said how beautiful she looked.

"You never tell me the truth," she said.

He didn't know how to answer.

"We're having a tea party," she said.

On the bed, to her side, was the black tin tray painted with roses, set with the cups decorated with decal roses, the teapot, and a cake and plates.

"James has done it all," she said, her voice still sparkling.

"I'm her last serf," James said, "for whom she graciously accepted to be godmother."

Claude gave Lidia the roses. She held them to her bosom for a moment, then held out the bouquet to show it to James.

"Look," she said, "how beautiful."

"Now you're the one who's not telling the truth," James said to her. "It's a cheap bunch out of a plastic bucket in front of a grocery shop."

Lidia laughed. "You're so insolent —"

"I try to tell the truth."

"Now go find a vase for them. There'll be one on a shelf high up in a cupboard in the kitchen."

James bowed a little when he went out with the bouquet.

"It's still hot," Claude said.

"And will never cool off," Lidia Rivers said quietly.

"Oh," Claude breathed.

Lidia said, "You asked me if I'd like to go back to Russia. I've been thinking about it. I would. But how would I go? How would I apply, even, for a visa, given I can hardly write my name?"

"Are you asking me to help you?"

"More, I'm asking if you'd come with me."

A thrill passed through Claude. "Go to Russia?"

"To try to see what Marie couldn't see —"

James returned, carrying in two hands a big vase that was matte black and had diamonds of red and orange about the base and rim, and one red and one orange handle. The pale pink roses, separated from one another, leaned in a circle over the wide rim.

"It's so beautiful," James said, and he held it up high by the pointed handles.

"Oh yes, oh yes, quite beautiful," the old woman said, playing with the word *beautiful*.

James put the vase on the bedside table. He kept Lidia Rivers amused while he poured out the tea and cut the cake. When Lidia asked for two spoons of sugar, he retorted that if she trusted him with the keys to the storeroom where the sugar was kept, she'd have her sugar, but as she didn't he was going to give her, helpless old thing that she was, only one spoon, and that was how serfs got their revenge.

"Insolent, insolent," Lidia said. "If my father were here, he'd get out the flail —"

"There's nothing you can do," James said. "And you know what I'm going to do when you die? I'm going to find those keys and steal everything from the storeroom, including the jars of pickled mushrooms."

Claude sat on a padded stool with a red skirt by a liver-shaped dressing table with a mirror top on which there were a comb, a brush, and a wooden box inlaid with a harlequin pattern.

James said, "Hey."

Claude turned his head to him slowly.

"Where were you?"

"Where was I?" Claude asked.

"If you're with people, pay attention to them."

"Wasn't I paying attention?"

"No."

"I thought I was."

Lidia was asleep.

"I'll clear up the tea things," James said, and he piled the cups and plates onto the tray, and first thrusting out his chin, then pausing, then giving a little forward jerk of his body, he went out with the tray.

When James came back into the bedroom, Claude whispered to him, "She wants me to go to Russia with her."

"Go with her, then. Go."

At night, when he was falling asleep, a picture came to Claude of a white bowl of red currants on a white cloth and two eggs loosely wrapped in paper and then a comb on a table in a room where someone was expected, and beyond an open window was a willow in sun-filled mist and flies darting among the branches. Claude wondered where this picture came from, how it occurred, and while he was wondering the telephone rang.

James, who was always the first to be informed about anything, told him that Lidia Rivers was dead.

"Go to sleep," James said quietly. "Go to sleep now."

Claude didn't sleep.

In the early morning, when the streetlights were still lit in the reddish, hot dawn, Claude walked down Ninth Avenue.

On a street corner was an asphalted lot behind a chainlink fence, coils of razor wire along the top, and in the lot nothing but a black plastic bag of trash and torn newspapers.

He kept his eyes to the ground, to the broken cement slabs of the sidewalk spotted with black gum, to the rusted metal trapdoors on the sidewalk that gave way with a clank when he walked over them. There were empty whiskey flasks and beer bottles in brown paper bags left in doorways and on the curbstones. He came across a sleeping body lying on the sidewalk wrapped completely in a dirty pink blanket, a stream of pee flowing from beneath the blanket to the gutter, and he couldn't bear this sight.

Farther up the avenue, a skyscraper was being built, and a workman high up was welding. He seemed to be the only person working. Sparks fell from where he was welding, fell from girder to girder, sometimes hitting the edges of girders and exploding into showers of more sparks, like stars exploding into more stars.

After the funeral of Lidia Rivers, James invited the mourners, about twelve of them, to his apartment for champagne. Retaining a Russian custom, instead of putting the empty bottles on the wooden floor under the table, as James would have done ordinarily, he made a point now, after a funeral, of lining the empty bottles up on the table.

Claude, leaning against the wainscoting, stayed away from Marie's mother, whose presence made him feel ashamed of himself. A boy, about nine, wandered as if lost among the older people standing or sitting in the room. Claude stood away from the wall, attentive to the boy, who was now sitting on the Turkish rug and following the pattern with a finger.

James said, "Come on, Claude."

"Sorry," Claude said, and he went to where James was talking with two friends about opera.

"Pay some attention," James said.

"All right, all right," Claude said, but his attention remained on the boy on the floor, sitting sideways, supporting himself with one arm, his head tilted sideways, lightly tracing a design in red and black. He was as beautiful as a girl.

James continued to talk and Claude went to the boy on the rug. When he sat, the boy rearranged his position and sat upright.

"What are you thinking?" Claude asked.

Bashful, the boy, whose name was Michael, said, "Nothing."

"You have to be thinking of something."

"Your name is Claude, isn't it?" Michael asked.

"That's right."

"You tell me what you're thinking."

"I'm wondering if I should go to Russia," Claude said.

"Why not?"

"I guess because I'm scared."

"Why are you scared?"

"I'm not sure. Does anything make you scared?"

Michael nodded.

"What?"

"The dark does."

"Me too."

"But," Michael said, sitting up rigidly, "my dad says there's nothing in the dark, nothing."

Claude put his hand for a moment on the boy's head.

Marie's mother, Louisa, was above them, and Claude stood. She was a big-breasted woman with moles on her heavy cheeks and chin, and on a nostril. Michael stood beside her and she hugged him to her side.

"Will you go to Russia anyway?" she asked Claude.

"No," Claude said. "I won't."

"I'm glad. I'm glad you won't."

Part

THREE

I

CLAIRE O'CONNEL had heavy black hair she wore pulled back and loosely braided at her nape, and her pale face was long, her nose long and straight, her cheekbones high and her cheeks long and angular, and her eyes were large and bright black. Her neck was a little fleshy, and the slopes of her breasts, too, which presaged the fullness of her body when she would be ten or fifteen years older. She was tall. By blood she was Irish American, but a strain of some other past, Mediterranean or Jewish, seemed to have come out in her, a strain that mysteriously seemed to refer her Irishness to the Mediterraneans or the Jews.

Lonely, she often wondered if she should telephone George. She had not seen him since he had left her and Rachel in the City to take a bus back to Clapham. He wasn't the only person she knew, but his absence made her feel he was. She didn't telephone him, but neither did she telephone friends.

In London, while Rachel was at school, finishing up the few weeks that remained of the final term of the scholastic year, Claire went from time to time to the library of the Courtauld Institute to do research for her thesis. She did this, she told herself, to keep her sanity, not so much to finish the thesis, which she wasn't sure she'd ever finish.

If she were honest with herself, she thought, she'd admit she'd probably never finish the thesis, because she was lazy. What attracted her about Pietro Testa was his vision, and this vision seemed to her to rise above the context of his life and of his age and become a vision in itself, become a vision she reacted to with an interest that was more personal than academic. Maybe her laziness about doing hard and boring research disposed her, she told herself with self-deprecation, to being something more of a visionary than a scholar.

Claire, who did not believe in God, was like someone who wanted, as immediate as a revelation, effulgent enlightenment without the reasoning to it. For some people with a direct approach to art this was possible, but for scholars, even lazy scholars, who had only themselves to blame for the indirect approach they had taken, it was not possible; they had to go by way of study, and only hope the enlightenment would be greater in its effulgence when they made the leap of faith into it than if they had taken the easier way, the naive, unlettered way — the way she would have liked to take.

On her way to the institute, walking along the pavement around the garden in the center of Portman Square, she looked in through the black iron pickets of the fence and among the trees to where, deep in the garden, two young men were struggling with each other on the grass. Shocked, she did not know what they were doing, and their struggle made her think of Rachel's rape. They were silent except for grunts that came from them. Perhaps they were wrestling for the sport, but she saw one, on top, hit the other on the head with a fist. The garden was one of those private gardens in London squares with locked gates for which a key was needed, and only the people who lived on the square were entitled to have keys. By the young men a small fire was burning, and the smoke rose in a column up to the branches of the trees, where it swirled about the new leaves. Claire watched the young men until the one on top fell away from the other and lay flat on his back and didn't move. The second, also lying motionless, was on his side, turned away from the first. Uncertain of what she had seen, Claire went on to the institute.

She had been to Lucca and Rome, to Vienna and Chantilly and to Edinburgh to see the few Testas there were to be seen. She had seen the one in the Metropolitan Museum in New York before she had left America and even begun her research. She hadn't seen the late *Aneas on the Bank of the River Styx* in a private collection, but she had a transparency of this. And she had a reproduction of *The Presentation of the Virgin in the Temple* in the Hermitage, in what had been called Leningrad and was now recalled, after more than half a century, Saint Petersburg. Of course she knew the paintings of his contemporaries and was knowledgeable about the important division in the art world of his day betwen Pietro da Cortona and Andrea Sacchi, whose differing beliefs in the nature of painting set up opposing schools, and she had tried to determine, by his painting and by his writing, what Testa's true allegiance was and to what degree he adhered to the principles of a school and to what degree he ignored these principles and innovated —

But what she thought of as his ultimate vision, the vision that floated above all her notes and paragraphs and yet that could never be directly referred to without making the notes and paragraphs suspect from the point of view of art history, kept descending like a cloud on what she wrote, and she couldn't see through the cloud. In her usual place, at a table by a window, she decided that what she would do was, for just one day, just one hour, allow herself to write out what it was she felt about Testa, write what she felt without any consideration of any of the facts, and she would then have defined this cloud and filed it away. She might even look into it later for the question that would most attach her to Testa, because she knew that for her thesis to have any life in it, there must be somewhere in her a personal interest that animated her scholarly interest in it, a personal interest raised, of course, to a disinterested scholarly interest. And this interest had to be, from the point of view of art history, more about his work than about his life, so that, say, his suicide wasn't itself enough to justify a full study of his works. What her personal interest was, she thought, might be revealed by her writing out, without considering anything at all but her most free-floating feeling, her own ultimate vision of the painter.

She had read Testa's treatise on art, in which he professed the superior vision of the classicist, the clear arrangement in a painting of but a few figures in a simple landscape. He was by his own intention a classicist, but by temperament he was a romantic. What there was that was classical in his work was expressed by a reduction in color, so that he worked in white and subdued ochers and grays and he preferred, above all, to work in the sharp-edged black and white of engravings; and as a classicist he often limited his painting to one figure, which took up the entire picture plane, and in his elimination of anything that was extraneous, such as flowers or carafes of wine or baskets of oranges, in his apparent desire to depict only the essential, he was as classical as a classical playwright who does not even give chairs to his characters, abstracted from the everyday world of chairs by the nobility of their great suffering, to sit on. But with his use of *finto di notte*, he romantically made the background of his large, muscular figures so dark they appeared to stand in darkness, darkness as if itself reduced to and revealing, at its simplest and clearest, the essential, as if the darkness were itself the condition of the most severe classicism. *Testa* meant, literally, head, but the darkness Claire was aware of extending behind the artist's figures, even beyond the artist's paintings, was not the subjective darkness of the romantic locked inside his own head — it was an objective darkness, classical in being clear and simple, a darkness that replaced the objective, clear, and simple light of Poussin, whom he so much admired. The paint, thin and broad, appeared itself to have been brushed on darkness, which showed through the pigment. All of Testa's vision was in that darkness.

Claire, writing quickly, asked herself what was the quality in his work that made her so aware of flesh, of heavy, muscular flesh, but at the same time of the insubstantiality of the flesh, flesh about to disappear into the darkness that surrounded it eternally. Was it that darkness? After looking at a painting, she retained a stronger impression of the eternal darkness around the figure than of the figure, as if the intention of the image was first of all (or, perhaps, last of all) to make the viewer aware of the darkness in which the figure appeared — as if the highest moral implicit in the picture was the awareness of darkness.

And so, she thought, what inspired her in Pietro Testa's pictures, with an immediate appreciation, was his vision of clear and simple ultimate darkness, as great as all of outer space.

Having written this, she felt suddenly that there was no reason for her to write a thesis on Testa. She had said everything she wanted to say.

In the entrance hall of the institute, going out, she met Henrietta Ridge, also a student but younger, coming in, and they stopped to talk while other students went up and down the curved double staircase. Henrietta's hair was pinned up at the top and strands flew lightly around her face, and all the seams of her clothes seemed twisted; she wore a necklace of what were supposed to be pearls, but the pearly skin was mostly gone, and the translucent plastic of the beads underneath showed. Her teeth were twisted, and not in very good condition. She said she was longing to get away from London and planned to go to Lucca. Claire knew that Henrietta was the niece, or perhaps grandniece, of the art historian Roger Leclerc, who lived outside Lucca, so she would be staying with him. Everyone knew whom Henrietta was referring to when she mentioned her uncle. But she wouldn't say, now, that she was staying with him, which would be rather showy. And because Henrietta felt embarrassed about going to stay in Lucca with her uncle, she had to say to Claire, "Why don't you come too?"

"To Lucca?"

"Aren't you doing work on a Lucchese painter?"

"But I've seen all the paintings there are to see by him there — altogether, just one. He might have been born in Lucca, but he left early and spent most of the rest of his life in Rome."

Henrietta was made to feel more embarrassed about her going to Lucca by this, as if she should have given Claire a better reason for going. Her eyes became unfocused as she tried to think of a better reason, but she couldn't, and she said, "Well, ta."

"See you," Claire said. She never consciously used English expressions, but she had lived long enough in London for the American "see you" to sound odd, a little.

She had looked for references to Pietro Testa in the books of Roger Leclerc, but she had found little more than references to his having drawn ancient works of sculpture for the *museo cartaceo*, the museum in a book, of Cassiano dal Pozzo — that kind of thing. When she had been in Italy, in Lucca itself, where Pietro Testa came from and where she knew Sir Roger Leclerc lived, she had wondered if she could meet the art historian. Now, when she knew his niece, she was as shy about asking her to meet her uncle as she would have been to go and meet him herself. In America, she would have asked another American, "I wonder if your uncle could help me?" But she didn't know how, in England, one did this. She told herself her research had advanced enough that really there wasn't much point to meeting Roger Leclerc.

Out in the square, she looked through the fence into the garden to where she had seen the two young men fighting. Where they had been was a little girl standing and looking at the fire, which was still sending up a thin column of smoke.

She got home, as always, before Rachel arrived back from school, and she prepared tea for her arrival. Rachel liked to sit quietly for half an hour with a cup of tea and chocolate-covered digestive biscuits before she went up to her room and took off her school uniform, and Claire made a point of sitting with her. She heard the front door open and shut as she was setting out the cups and saucers. Rachel came in, slightly languid in her movements, and kissed her mother, who smoothed out and fluffed out her hair, a little disheveled and matted after a day at school. Claire wished she would take more care of the way she looked. She often told her she was beautiful, but this only made Rachel wince. They sat at the table.

With all the will in the world, talk between them, even about Rachel's exams, was a strain. The strain wasn't so much in what they had to say but in what they couldn't say, or what Claire couldn't say, because Rachel more or less left the talk up to her mother. The talk was surrounded by a vast subject that must never be referred to, though Claire was sometimes not sure what that subject was. It could introduce words into the talk — words like *venereal* or *abortion* or even *miscarriage* — which made Claire and Rachel go silent, listening to the other talk around them about the as yet invisible pregnancy. Then Claire would talk quickly about something she was sure had nothing to do with that greater talk. But Rachel seemed to go on listening to it.

Rachel this afternoon sat at the table listening to it, and after an attempt to engage her in talk about school, Claire had to give up and they both listened to that other talk. It frightened Claire, and she wondered if it frightened Rachel, too. When this occurred to

Claire, she felt an added thrill of fear, thinking Rachel wasn't frightened by but attentive to the strange, inaudible talk, and knew, as her mother didn't, what it was about.

Preoccupied, as always, with Rachel and what was happening to Rachel, Claire returned to the library of the institute the next day, and looking through the shelves for a book, she saw out of the corner of her eye the spine of an old book that made her go to it and take it down. Her adviser had told her that research should always be done by oneself and never by an assistant — as though she could possibly have had an assistant — because one could make important discoveries by having a title of a book some way along the shelf catch one's eye. The old book was leather-bound and embossed, and on its foxed and slightly warped title page was printed

Il Forestiere
Informato
delle Cose di Lucca
Opera
Del Reverendo Signore
Vincenzo Marchio
Lucchese
Dedicata
All' Illustrissimo Sig.
Ippolito de' Nobili
IN LUCCA MDCCXXI

It was an early eighteenth-century inventory of works of art in Lucca at the time, done by the Reverend Vincenzo Marchio. Claire took it with her to a desk, and in a faint cloud of mold-smelling dust she read page after page, and when she saw the name Pietro Testa she felt a little jump of excitement. She knew, she thought, all the paintings listed under his name, including the Saint John the Baptist in the museum in Lucca, except for an

Annunciation, which was described in the inventory as being in the sacristy of a church in Lucca, but which Claire, going to the shelves again, did not find listed in any more modern catalogue of his works.

When she returned home, she noticed, opening the front door, that the shoes Rachel wore to school were on the floor of the entry hall, and a thrill of apprehension made her skin tighten. She found Rachel out in the garden, where the cherry tree was now dropping pink petals onto the water in the oval enamel basin. Rachel was standing still and staring out, and Claire didn't want to startle her by approaching her too quickly. She tapped her knuckles on the glass of the door and Rachel turned her head toward her, but she still seemed to be staring out.

"You came home early," Claire said to her when she went to her.

"Yes," Rachel said vaguely.

Smoothing, as she always did when Rachel came home from school, her daughter's hair, she asked quietly, "Why is that?"

As quietly, Rachel said, "I couldn't bear it any longer." Then she looked into her mother's eyes, all at once pleading with her to do something to help her bear it. "I can't bear it any longer, Mommy."

Claire continued to smooth Rachel's hair, gently rounding it out at her shoulders. "Tell me what went wrong," she said. "I'll ring Miss Hemmings —"

"Oh no," Rachel said, "no, there's nothing wrong at school, and Miss Hemmings has been kinder toward me than she's ever been, all that's all right. What I can't take any longer—" She stopped for a moment. "It's just making myself do everything I know I must do. I get so tired. Why?"

"It's very, very tiring to have to will yourself to go on."

"Have you ever had to do that?"

"I have. I know how tiring it is. I know how tiring it can be just to get up out of bed in the morning."

At tea, Claire told Rachel about her discovery of the Annunciation, and Rachel, knowing how important the discovery must have been for her mother, made herself attentive, Claire saw. She knew the pain of that attention.

Claire leaned back and said, "I've just had an idea."

"Oh?" Rachel asked.

"We'll go to Lucca this summer. We'll look for the painting."

"Oh," Rachel said again, but this time in a tone that suggested disappointment that her mother's idea hadn't been what she'd hoped it would be, though she wouldn't have known what idea to hope for.

"We'll go," Claire said.

Rachel drank her tea.

Claire thought it would be a good idea, not only for her but for Rachel, to go to Lucca, and she made up her mind to ask Henrietta Ridge if she could talk to Henrietta's uncle while they were in Lucca. But she found out the next day that Henrietta had already gone, and Claire wasn't able to ask her if her uncle would help her in finding out more about the Testa Annunciation.

Sometimes, attentive with Rachel to the inaudible and strange talk that went on around them while they were silent, Claire would feel the impulse to tell Rachel about her father, and she would, very frightened, begin to talk about anything at all in a loud way that made her daughter look at her.

II

CLAIRE HAD a tourist map of Lucca, and she and Rachel, in
the lobby of their hotel, located on it the church of Santa Maria
Misericordia, in the sacristy of which the Pietro Testa Annunciation had been noted by the Reverend Vincenzo Marchio.
Following the narrow streets as indicated on the map, which they
from time to time stopped to look at, they found the church, with
its flat façade with three circular windows, the one in the center
higher than the ones on either side, and three wooden doors, the
central door grander than the side doors. All the doors were shut

and didn't give when Claire, holding the handles, pressed her body against them. The wood was painted a faded green and cracked. Rachel too tried opening the doors. An old woman crossing the little piazza before the church looked at them. The air was bright and warm.

"Surely it'll open for Mass," Claire said.

"When's Mass?" Rachel asked.

Claire couldn't recall when she herself had last been to Mass, and could only recall that the celebration usually took place early in the morning. She did recall those early mornings in Lent when she had gone out into the cold to go to church, day after day. She wasn't now able to imagine herself that pious girl, not any more than she was able to imagine Rachel pious.

They walked around the wide, tree-lined top of the great brick walls that surrounded the medieval city. As they walked, the angles of the houses, palaces, church façades, and church towers, lit in one direction by the declining but clear sunlight and shadowed in other directions, seemed to shift, and streets appeared among them, then, moving sideways as if on the radius of a circle, disappeared. Only a high medieval tower with trees growing on it, apparently at the center of the circle, remained visible. Shifting walls revealed palm trees, gardens, terraces, open windows, with a view through one of a room with a huge wardrobe with a mirrored front, and reflected in the mirror a woman brushing her hair. The near walls appeared to shift more quickly than the ones deeper into the center of the city, and over them the beams of sunlight appeared too to shift. The view away from the city, out over poplar trees, was of distant mountains, dark blue against a pale blue sky, some covered on their high crags with snow.

Rachel was looking, her eyes shifting to take in the apparently shifting multidimensions of the city, and too the people they passed on the battlements — running children, two strolling old women arm in arm, a priest on a bicycle. Here in Lucca, Claire could imagine making Rachel happy simply by showing her something that would, in its simplicity, be a revelation to her. There was so much to see here.

On their way back to their hotel, at the center of the walled city, Rachel said they should pass by the church again to check if it just might be open. It wasn't, but Rachel's interest in finding the painting, though she hadn't said as much, gave Claire, for the first time in months, some faint faith in the possibility that things could be different.

But she should have come more prepared to find the painting. She was an art historian, after all. She should have written to the Italian Belle Arti for special permission to get into the church. That, however, might have taken months, years. If only she could talk with Sir Roger Leclerc. If only she would run across Henrietta in a street, in a shop, on the walls.

As they were separating that night to go to their different rooms, Rachel said, as if slightly embarrassed, "Maybe we can get up early and go to the church."

Claire's amazement made her hesitate. She said, "Well," and paused and said, "yes."

She had no idea why, but all the sleepless night she anticipated, with fear more than any sense of relief, going to the church the next morning with Rachel.

She woke her when it was still dark out, as Claire thought that if there were to be a Mass in the church, it would be at six o'clock. She could tell it took Rachel all the will she had to get up and get dressed in the chilly air, the dim lamp on the bedside table hardly lighting the dark room. Rachel didn't speak as she dressed.

Claire whispered, as if they were already in a church, "Wouldn't you prefer to stay in bed?"

Rachel shook her head angrily, and her hair flew out.

The early morning light in the city seemed to rise from the stone walls. The church was shut, as were all the shutters of the windows on the piazza. One shutter opened, and a young man wearing an undershirt, his hairy chest showing above the loop of the white, looked out, then he shut the shutter. Claire and Rachel stood uselessly in the piazza.

Then Claire said quietly to Rachel, "Go back to your room and sleep."

Rachel didn't move.

"Go on," Claire said.

Rachel kissed her mother before, reluctantly, she left, as if she were going far.

Claire walked about the narrow pedestrian streets, deserted except for a young black man arranging on a blanket spread on the cobbles tooled leather wallets, until she came to an open café, where she had a coffee. Claire prayed that she could at least save her daughter from the small disappointments of, say, not finding the church open when she had made such efforts to go to it. How, she wondered, could she get in touch with Roger Leclerc?

In the café, under a wall telephone, was a shelf with a telephone book on it, and she looked up his name. She couldn't find it because he didn't live in Lucca, she was sure, but outside, perhaps in what was called *una frazione,* and his name would be listed under the name of that *frazione.*

As she walked up the main street of Lucca, the Fillungo, back to the hotel, she met Henrietta Ridge coming down.

Henrietta said she was thrilled, thrilled to see Claire. She was really finding it very trying, staying with her uncle. She invited Claire to have a coffee with her. Why Claire hesitated to accept this invitation she had no idea. All her reactions were off. She said, "I really should get back to Rachel." Henrietta said, "Oh please," and Claire consented. Meeting Henrietta had thrown her off when meeting Henrietta was just what she had wanted.

They went to a café where they sat in a corner at a round marble-topped table. In the middle of the café was a white grand piano with a vase of flowers on it. With their coffees, they talked about the Courtauld Institute for a while, then Henrietta asked:

"Who is Rachel?"

"My daughter," Claire answered.

"I didn't know you had a daughter."

"I do, yes."

Claire lowered her head and put her hand to her forehead, and remained still. When she sat up, Henrietta was looking at her.

"Are you all right?" Henrietta asked.

"I don't know what to do," she heard herself say. "I came to Lucca with Rachel, thinking she needed to have a change —"

Henrietta hunched her shoulders a little and seemed to look up at Claire.

Hearing her voice and telling herself to stop, telling herself that Henrietta Ridge was the last person in the world she would confide in and who would be interested enough in Claire to want to be confided in, Claire said, "She had something horrible happen to her, and I had hoped coming to Lucca would make a difference."

Hunching lower and looking more up at Claire and frowning, Henrietta asked, "What happened?"

Claire stared at her in a hard way, and said in a hard voice, to do nothing but state the hard fact, "She was raped."

Henrietta sat back. "Oh," she said.

And Claire wanted to get away immediately. She had said the one thing she shouldn't have said, the one thing that would make Rachel, if she found out about it, kill herself, and she'd said it to someone who had nothing to do with Rachel and her own life with Rachel. It was as if she had destroyed any possibility of Lucca's making a difference to Rachel or her. Still staring at Henrietta, she narrowed her eyes, and as she did tears rose into them.

"I am sorry," Henrietta said.

Her voice strangled in her throat so she was unable to say anything more than "Thank you so much for the coffee," Claire got up and walked out of the café quickly, pressing the tears from her eyes with her knuckles. She rushed out into the Fillungo, where a man in whiteface, wearing a long white shirt and long white trousers and a black skullcap, was walking on stilts over the small cobbles among a small crowd of people. She rushed past them but, at a corner, stopped when she heard Henrietta call her. Henrietta was hurrying to her, holding out a piece of paper, and she said, handing the paper to Claire, "Here's my telephone number," and as if she had been the one to rush away, turned and hurried back down the street, ahead of the man on stilts and the group around him.

Rachel was still asleep. Claire had to explain to the maid that she needn't go in and make Rachel's bed, as her daughter wasn't well and needed to sleep. Claire waited in her room. She dreaded seeing Rachel again, as though Rachel would have found out what she had said. Claire stood against a wall and pressed her forehead to it. She jumped away when Rachel entered the room without knocking, and her face twitched a little when she smiled at Rachel.

Rachel did sense something was wrong. She asked, "Are you all right?"

"Just disappointed that that church was shut," Claire said.

Rachel shrugged. She said, "Isn't there anyone we can talk to who'll get us in?"

"I've been thinking of that," Claire said.

At lunch, Rachel asked her mother about Pietro Testa. Claire said, "He was a big man, with a very big physique, and noble looking."

"What else do you know about him?" Rachel asked.

"Some people said he was rather pleased with himself and was made so despondent by slights, especially to his painting, that he'd have something like breakdowns."

This made Rachel laugh a little. She asked, "Did he ever get married and have children?"

"No," Claire said, and she found herself about to tell Rachel about his suicide. She stopped herself, wondering why she was about to say something against her will.

In the afternoon, alone in her hotel room, white and all clear, sharp-edged planes with a gray tile floor, Claire telephoned

Henrietta Ridge. Henrietta's voice resonated over the receiver as Claire's voice resonated in her stark room.

There was the sound of dogs barking behind Henrietta's voice. The sound got louder and louder, and Claire heard Henrietta shout, in Italian, *"Zitti!"* and the dogs seemed to obey her and go silent. "We must meet," Henrietta said.

While trying to think how to suggest a meeting that would include her uncle, Claire heard the dogs bark again.

Henrietta shouted down the telephone, "I can't hear a thing."

Claire shouted back, "Perhaps we should talk later, when there aren't any dogs."

"Just a moment," Henrietta shouted. "Just a moment. My uncle has come."

Over the barking of the dogs, Claire heard a command shouted that made her go silent and still. So, evidently, did it the dogs.

Henrietta said, "I hate it when he kicks them."

"What?" asked Claire.

Now addressing herself to Claire, Henrietta said, "He's silenced the dogs. Now where were we?"

Claire said, "There seems to be such chaos there, perhaps it'd be better if I rang another time." She sounded English to herself, and she told herself to stop this. "What about my calling some other time?"

"Oh no," Henrietta said. "Of course we must make a plan now."

And Claire, thinking Roger Leclerc must be standing near Henrietta, said, "I'd like to invite you to lunch."

"That would be lovely," Henrietta said.

Claire thought it only polite to add, "And of course your uncle, if he'd like."

"I'll ask him," Henrietta said, and as Claire didn't hear even the echo of a voice, she thought Henrietta must have put her hand over the receiver. She came back a moment later. "He said he'd be delighted."

"My daughter Rachel will be there —"

"Just a moment," Henrietta said, and again must have put her hand over the receiver to talk with her uncle.

Claire wanted to say, I didn't tell you that in order for you to ask your uncle if he deigns to meet my daughter.

Back on the receiver, Henrietta said, "He'd be delighted to have lunch with your daughter as well."

Claire said, with a pronounced American accent, "That's just great."

"Tomorrow or the day after tomorrow would do for us," Henrietta said. "Where do you want us to come?"

The restaurant in the Piazza Grande, Claire suggested, feeling that she was being taken advantage of and that she should say she was busy those days and give them other days, days that would do for her, to choose from. She felt humiliated — humiliated for talking to Henrietta after what she had told her in the café, and doubly humiliated for trying to overcome that humiliation with an invitation to lunch which Henrietta must have sensed was a ploy to get to meet her uncle. "What about tomorrow?" she said.

"That will do nicely," Henrietta said and hung up, as Claire knew some English did, without saying goodbye.

She went to Rachel's room thinking she would telephone back the next morning and say, without explaining, that she couldn't invite them to lunch, and not make another date and not telephone again. But then she thought, It's just a manner, and that seemed to make Henrietta's arrogance all right. She knocked on Rachel's door.

There was no answer, and, apprehensive, Claire opened the door onto a white room like hers. Rachel wasn't in, and Claire felt her scalp stir. On the floor before the unmade bed were her panties. Then Claire saw her, naked, in the open doorway to the bathroom. She was drying her hair with a towel and she was looking out the bathroom window. The door frame cut most of the window off, and all Claire could see of what Rachel was looking at was sunlit yellow stucco wall. Concentrating on what she was looking at, Rachel stopped drying her hair and her arms slowly dropped, one hand holding the towel, which fell in folds on the tile floor. She was in three quarters view to Claire, and the light from the window defined her young body in a fine bright line. Her breasts were fuller, and her nipples stood out more, than when Claire had last seen her naked. Her thighs too were fuller, and Claire saw just enough of her stomach to note that it had filled out. Rachel's dark hair, still damp, stood out wildly from her head. She was so beautiful, so beautiful, Claire thought.

As always, she wondered what Rachel was thinking, because it seemed to Claire she wasn't looking out so much as looking in, and was concentrating on what was invisible to her mother but sharply visible to herself.

When Rachel became aware of someone in her room, she turned just her head, and as Claire was about to apologize for coming into the room without her knowing, Rachel, her head tilted, smiled at her. Claire knew that smile, knew the tenderness in her daughter, but seeing it now surprised her, and uncertain how to react, she reached out a hand. Rachel raised a corner of the white towel up between her breasts. Her hand still held out, Claire looked at her, and tears, as she found tears did more and more the more she felt out of control, filled her eyes.

She thought she shouldn't let Rachel know she was weeping, and rubbed her eyes with her knuckles as if they suddenly irritated her and then sniffed as if something in her nose irritated her.

"I thought we might go out for another walk around the walls," Claire said.

The smile, now slight, still on her face, Rachel came into the room and finished drying her hair with the towel, sometimes swinging her head to let her hair swing back.

Not knowing quite why, Claire went behind her and to the bathroom door to look out the window Rachel had been looking out, or seemed to have been looking out, and Claire saw, on the building across from the yellow stucco wall, a scaffolding against another wall, and standing on the planks of the scaffolding, a young man naked to the waist was plastering the old stones over with fresh stucco. His belt was low on his hips, so the vertebrae of his backbone were seen almost all the way down. The muscles of his back and shoulders moved as he moved, smoothing the stucco with his trowel in wide sweeps, and the black hair in his white armpit showed whenever his arm swung out on the arc of a sweeping motion, and also one of his nipples. The thick black hair on his head was covered with white powder, as was his brown body.

Claire stood still for a moment, then, as if the young man might see her, she drew back into the room. She drew back really because she didn't want Rachel to know she had seen him, didn't want Rachel to know she had found out what Rachel had been looking at outside the window, which was not at all inside her but perhaps as far outside as Rachel imagined the outside was. Claire didn't want to embarrass her. But once again, and so much so that she couldn't smear them away with her knuckles as they came, tears rose into Claire's eyes, and embarrassed by herself, she glanced out the window at the young workman on the scaffolding.

Rachel said, "Mommy."

Keeping her head lowered, Claire turned a little toward her. She asked, "Yes?"

"Will you brush my hair?"

Claire couldn't hide the tears but must honestly present them to Rachel, and she raised her head and tried to smile and said, "Of course." She blinked and asked, her voice gurgling a little with the tears in her throat, "Where is the brush?"

Rachel, the towel wrapped around her, stared at her mother, wondering why she was crying, and then she seemed to understand. Her body went limp and she sat on the simple chair before the simple desk, her shoulders slumped.

"Where is the brush?" Claire asked again.

Rachel didn't tell her.

Claire stood in front of her and said, "Please look up at me."

Rachel raised her head and, her lids half closed, looked not at her mother, but all around her.

Claire said, "You will have a happy life, I promise you."

Her chin raised from her long, thin neck, Rachel said quietly, "Will I?"

Her slightly unfocused eyes magnified the gentleness, the sad gentleness, Claire knew was in her, and the vulnerability of the gentleness. She gave no more certain answer to Rachel's question than "I promise." Rachel smiled with the corners of her mouth. Aware of what she wouldn't be able to do for her daughter, Claire went weak.

All Rachel said, quietly, was "The brush is there on the bedside table."

Rachel leaned forward, and Claire brushed her hair up from her bare nape and said, "We're having lunch tomorrow with some interesting people who might help us find the painting."

Rachel didn't ask who they were. When her mother finished brushing her hair, in deeper silence than before, she stood and ran her hands through her hair and thanked her mother, then said, "I don't know if I'll come to lunch tomorrow."

Claire knew she mustn't argue. She said, "I wish you would. It means a lot to me to meet the art historian who may be able to help us with locating the painting."

Rachel let her head loll, so her hair fell.

"You were keen to know about the painting," Claire said. "Aren't you still?"

"Yes," Rachel said, and she raised her head and with both hands drew her hair away from her face and smoothed it back.

In a dry, quiet voice, from the back of her throat, Claire said, "Please believe me. Please believe when I promise you you will have a happy life."

"I'll come to lunch," Rachel said.

Rachel was using her will, and if Claire could have willed it for her, she would have made Rachel's life happy right now, right now and forever. And if Rachel was like a nonbeliever who held by her will alone to her beliefs, because she knew that if she didn't she would be destroyed, Claire was like this too. Claire would have, if she could have, willed her daughter, in her pity for her, into believing that in letting go they wouldn't fall, condemned, but would rise and be saved.

By what? By what?

Claire didn't know. She was a nonbeliever.

While Rachel dressed, Claire sat on her unmade bed and waited. Rachel then presented herself to her mother and said, "Shall we walk around the walls now?" Claire wanted to lie on the bed but, straining her muscles, got up and said, "Sure thing, sure thing."

When they came out of the hotel into the street, Rachel went around her mother to the other side of her so she wouldn't be on the side of the street where the young workman was still on the scaffolding. This evasive action roused in Claire a recklessness — a recklessness that often came after something heavily serious had happened, as if in defiance of the seriousness — and she moved closer to the side of the pedestrian street where the workman was. Rachel didn't stay with her but walked, now, separated from her mother by the width of the narrow, cobbled street. Passing close by the workman, who was just a little higher than her on his plank, Claire loked up, and at that moment the young man turned his head and looked down, and giving way to her recklessness, Claire smiled and said, *"Ciao."* He too smiled and said, *"Ciao."* Claire stopped.

She felt her pulse beating, not because she had stopped to speak with the young man, but because Rachel would be watching her speak to him.

Rachel could make her defiantly reckless, as Rachel's father had made her defiantly reckless.

Claire said to the young man, *"Che lavoro."*

"Ah si," he said, and then went on in Italian about all the work being done in Lucca to restore the façades of the old palaces, or so

Claire understood. The young man, holding his trowel up, asked, *"Da dove venite, Voi?"*

Claire didn't know where to say they were from — England, America? She said, *"D'America."*

The young man asked if they liked Italy.

Yes, yes, Claire said. And he, she asked, was he Lucchese?

He shook his head. He was from Naples. He laughed and said, *"Non sono toscano. Per i toscani i napolitani non sono ne anche italiani."* He was not only not Tuscan, he was not, according to the Tuscans, Italian. Claire laughed.

She could have had such fun just joking with him.

At her feet was a wide wicker basket filled with chipped-off fragments of stucco. On some of the flat surfaces were the remains of painted decorations, such as red berries and blue tendrils.

Claire turned to look back at Rachel, who was standing almost at the end of the short street. Her arms were down by her sides and her hands were clenched into fists.

Pointing to Rachel, Claire, with greater recklessness, said to the young man on the scaffolding, *"Mia figlia."*

She thought: And if Rachel were different, if Rachel were only a little like me, what fun she could have. But she was like her father.

The young man smiled a large smile across to Rachel. There was a sparse stubble on his chin and even less along the smooth edge of his jaw, and a few dark hairs grew in the middle of his young chest.

Claire gestured to Rachel in the Italian way — downwards — for her to come over. She knew she was taking a risk with Rachel, but she was, however much resentment there was in it for her, having fun, a little.

Frowning, Rachel came over to her mother without even glancing at the young man.

Claire asked the young man, using the familiar, *"Come ti chiami?"*

"Carlo," he said.

"Carlo," Claire said, feeling her blood pump throughout her, *"questa è Rachel,"* and she placed her hand on her daughter's shoulder.

Carlo squatted, his knees wide apart and his legs open, and reached down to Rachel a rough, large-knuckled hand that appeared too big for his slim body. Rachel studied it, but didn't raise her hand to take it. The big masculine hand hung in space. It was callused and the nails were thick and cracked and the fingers seemed to be a little out of joint. Rachel lowered her eyes to the ground.

Laughing, Claire took Carlo's hand and said, *"Mia figlia è timida,"* trying to make up for the timidity she excused Rachel with. She felt the strong, rough palm of the young man's hand in her palm, and she squeezed it a little, then let it go.

Rachel had gone. She stopped down the street, at a corner with another street, and on the corner was a medieval palace, brick, with delicate columns and arches along the storeys, and a tower. Rachel faced her mother squarely as she approached her, and when her mother got to her she said, her fists held out in her rage, "Why did you do that? Why did you do that? Why did you do that?"

Still a little inspired by her recklessness — because, Claire told herself, she had of course expected Rachel to react in this way, so why not do what she had wanted to do? — she smiled and said, "But darling, I did it for you."

Rachel turned and walked away, fast. Claire, skipping a little, kept up with her. Pedestrians in the *zona pedonale* of the city center got out of their way. "Please, please," Claire said.

She told herself: She's right, Rachel is right to be angry, because I didn't do it for her —

"Please," Claire repeated.

She followed Rachel across a piazza and down a narrow street to the city walls, and up stone steps onto the walls, as if Rachel knew just where she was going and once she got there would do something, she alone knew what. But on the walls, she seemed not to know why she was there, and went and sat on a bench. She was breathing hard. Claire, also breathing hard, sat on the bench with her. They were under a large plane tree.

Rachel said, "I want to go home."

"Home?" Claire asked. "You mean London?"

Rachel began to weep silently, the tears running down her cheeks and even down her neck. Claire didn't speak, but simply sat by her on the bench. Sunlight flickered in the leaves of the tree over them, and sometimes Claire looked up into the tree. She would let her daughter weep and weep, and though Claire knew she was in part the cause of her daughter's weeping, though she knew she had taunted Rachel in a way she shouldn't have and Rachel had every reason for being angry at her, she felt curiously unmoved by the tears. She felt curiously unmoved by her daughter's aloneness. All she really felt was great patience. She would wait forever if Rachel were to weep forever, and she would follow Rachel after wherever Rachel went — if Rachel didn't ask her not to follow her.

People passed them on their walks along the walls, and among them were young couples with their arms about each other's shoulders or waists. Sometimes a couple would bump their thighs against each other, and push each other to the side, each in turn, so that they walked in a rambling, zigzag way, until one or the other, usually the girl, would break away and, raising a hand, shout in Italian at the other; then they'd both laugh and put their arms around each other again and go on. Beyond them was a brick wall, and beyond the wall poplar trees and red tile roofs, and beyond the poplar trees and roofs, far, were mountains clear in the clear, cloudless sunlight.

Claire closed her eyes.

A long time passed, and Claire heard Rachel say, quietly, "Shall we walk?"

Opening her eyes, Claire saw her daughter's red eyes appear before her as if in momentary darkness.

She said, "Yes, of course," and stood.

They walked around the walls in silence. They had lunch in silence. After lunch, they went to their separate rooms, and when they met later, at dusk, all Claire asked Rachel was if she had rested, and Rachel said, Thanks, a little. They had dinner in a *trattoria* in silence.

It was not a closed silence, but open, and Claire knew she would be able to talk if she wanted. But it seemed to her there was nothing to talk about. She was very tired, she realized, and so too must Rachel have been. Perhaps it was because they were tired that they remained silent.

When they were about to leave each other in the stark white corridor of the hotel, Claire said, "I want to apologize for what I did earlier today."

Rachel shook her head.

"I shouldn't have," Claire said.

For a moment Rachel stood silent, then she went to her mother and kissed her on her cheek and said goodnight. Her eyes were still red.

Claire placed her hand on her daughter's head and said goodnight.

III

IN THE MORNING, Rachel answered "Come in" to Claire's knocking on her door, but when Claire opened she found her still in bed, the shutters on the window shut and the dim room striped with the light through the slats in the shutters. Rachel was not so much covered as wrapped in her loose sheet, and she raised herself on her elbows, wincing.

"Did you sleep?" Claire asked.

"No," Rachel said in her hard voice.

Maybe Claire should leave her alone. But she wouldn't leave her alone.

Rachel fell back onto the bed and drew the sheet up to her mouth.

"Remember," Claire said, "we're having lunch today —"

Now Rachel drew the sheet up over her face.

"Are you coming?" Claire asked.

The body in the sheet didn't move.

Claire said, "Rachel, for God's sake, I'd rather you didn't come if you're determined to ruin the lunch for me."

She was again saying something she didn't want to say, but the moment she said it she realized that before she had told Henrietta that Rachel would be at the lunch, she had hesitated a second, doubtful if Rachel should come, and against her own doubt had said Rachel would come; she had been anxious about Rachel's being at the lunch, and had even wished that Rachel would insist on not coming.

Rachel lowered the sheet from her face and said, with a slight frown, "You don't want me to come, then?"

"Of course I want you to come," Claire said. "But I want you to be lively, otherwise there's no point to your being there."

"Who for?" Rachel asked. She was going to be argumentative.

Her voice raised, Claire said, "For the people we've invited. For them. You don't invite people and then behave as though you don't want to be with them. You've got to know that."

"All right," Rachel said. "All right, Mommy." She sat up but didn't get up, and a faint smile appeared to float about her mouth.

Her voice raised to a higher level of pleading, Claire said, "I'm sorry. I hate being made to feel I'm forcing you to do what you don't want to do. But I don't know of any other way but forcing oneself to do what one doesn't want to do but has to do."

"Why has to?"

Claire hit her thigh. "Please don't ask such ultimate questions."

"All right —"

"Because," Claire said, again hitting her thigh, "because —" She hit her thigh again. She was becoming exasperated; she shouldn't become exasperated, or all the calm silence, the calm silence that had encircled them the night before, would be this morning lost, and instead there'd be the strained contention. She remembered evenings of calm silence, calm dark, and mornings, always mornings, of strained contention. There was a deep boredom in the midst of her dread. "Because one has got to live," she said in an even higher voice.

Rachel's voice, too, went high. "All right —"

"You believe that, don't you," Claire said. "Don't you?"

Rachel put her hands to her stomach and in a high, hard voice said, "You know I believe it."

This made Claire step back. It was as if she only now knew that her daughter, her innocent daughter, was pregnant, was going to have a baby, and she couldn't understand what this meant. She couldn't even understand how it had happened that her innocent daughter had become pregnant, and was amazed. Because she hadn't before fully accepted what her daughter had done, it amazed her that Rachel had decided, herself, to have this baby, and Claire almost felt that her decision to have it was what made her pregnant.

She thought: I don't understand her, I don't understand my daughter at all.

She said, "Oh Rachel."

"What?" Rachel asked, her voice still hard.

Claire sat on the edge of the bed and put her hands flat on the undersheet and studied them, then she turned them over and continued to study them, not sure whose they were. When she looked up at Rachel, she saw that the hardness had gone from her face, and after a moment she said, her voice, it seemed to her, swollen larger than the opening of her throat so that she wasn't sure it would be audible, "Of course you were right to keep the baby. Of course you were right." And then she said in an even less audible voice, "I would have kept it too."

Rachel pressed her hands to her breasts, covered by the sheet.

Claire said, "If you're wondering whether or not you'll ever be able to live without having to make yourself live, day by day, the answer is yes. It will happen. It does happen. You'll see, you'll wake up one morning thinking, How lovely, I have the whole day, and you'll wonder why you ever dreaded having the whole day before you."

"When will that happen?"

Claire put her hands on Rachel's shoulders. "I don't know," she said. "I wish I could make it happen, but I don't know how, really. I try."

"I know you do."

"Maybe it has to happen mysteriously of itself." She smiled.

Rachel smiled faintly.

"But it will happen," Claire said. "I know it will happen. I've told you before, and you must believe it, that you will one day know you're happy, maybe even without quite knowing what's happened to make you happy. It will happen. It'll be like a revelation to you. You must believe that."

The smile that her daughter gave her made Claire press her hands to the sides of her face.

It took Claire a moment to say, "If you want to sleep longer, I'll go out to the museum. And if you don't want to come to lunch but stay in your room, I'll say at the desk that you're not well and ask for some food to be sent up to you."

Rachel said, "If you'll wait for me for five minutes —"

In her room, Claire, while compulsively putting order to her toiletries and makeup on the shelf below the bathroom mirror, asked herself why she still wished, a little, that Rachel wouldn't come to lunch with her. Her mind was going in so many different directions, she thought she had a fever.

Why should she be so anxious about meeting the kind of man Roger Leclerc must be, a man who shouted commands as he did, and kicked? She shouldn't want to meet him. And perhaps she should count on Rachel to express her dislike of him, which Claire herself would never do, but she was also anxious that this was exactly what Rachel would do. She wet the corner of a towel in cold water and pressed it to her forehead, but her mind really did seem out of control with fever.

Before lunch they went to the museum. Rachel looked out an open window into a courtyard, in which a large dark cypress stood.

Claire studied a Baroque engraving of an allegorical scene, not unlike the allegories Pietro Testa engraved — for which, more than for his paintings, he was really admired — and, like one of his, called "An Allegory of Reason." Concentrating on a figure of an old, naked, grimacing woman carrying a sackcloth over her head, she thought that what was odd about Baroque allegories was that the artist tried hard to make the figures as realistic as possible, as the artist had tried to make this figure of an old hag, as if to dissemble rather than intensify the allegory — as if to make it more difficult, rather than simpler, to understand. Why? To bring the allegory closer to life? Or to conceal, more and more, the banality of the allegory's meaning, as if the artist thought that an allegory in which the meaning was obviously illustrated wasn't really art, whose meaning, for art to be art, had to be unstateable, and never, ever obviously illustrated? Maybe the artist was beginning to think that stateable and obviously illustrated ideas in art made his art pretentious. He had to hide, dissemble, his meaning, because of course he had a meaning, of course. But it would have to be a meaning that could not be abstracted from the work of art but would be absolutely one with it, so that in the end he would say his work of art had no meaning, no meaning whatsoever. He couldn't be accused of being self-conscious and pretentious about that. What he'd really be saying, however, was that his work of art had no meaning, no meaning whatsoever, that could be stated, or that was in any way illustrated in the work. So the meaning, which was of course there for the work of art to be a work of art, was ultimately as unstateable and as incapable of being illustrated as the highest mystery. But the artist wouldn't even say this, because mystery was the most self-conscious and pretentious meaning for a work of art to proclaim. But there were moments, there were strange moments, when Claire believed that the only really great art had to have been done for the greater glory of God. This momentary belief was all that was left in her of her having once been a Catholic.

All Rachel had was her will, and Claire must support her in that, mustn't let her let that go, must make her believe that she must live. But what, overall, she wanted Rachel to believe in was that something *would* occur, something *would* be revealed to her, to make her happy she was alive. This *wouldn't* occur, *wouldn't* be revealed, but Claire wanted her to believe it, and she prayed for the inspiration for her.

As they were walking from the museum to the restaurant in the Piazza Grande, Claire didn't want to have lunch with Henrietta and Sir Roger Leclerc.

The restaurant had an awning outside, and under this, on a low wooden platform, were round tables set with starched white cloths and white napkins standing up in points on the white plates, the wineglasses and the silver gleaming as if not in shade but sunlight.

Claire realized she had not made a reservation, and she hurried ahead of Rachel to make sure of a table. Not having made a reservation was, she thought, just like her. If anyone would destroy this lunch, she would. And what would she do if there weren't any tables?

Inside the restaurant, standing by a long table covered with straw punnets of wild strawberries, cakes on cake stands and pies with lattice crusts, and slim clear bottles of liqueurs, were Henrietta and her uncle, listening to a man talking Italian. This man wore a dark suit and was holding leather-bound folders for the menus, and must have been the maitre d'hôtel. Blushing, Claire held back, not knowing what to do. Henrietta saw her and smiled, and Claire went over, and before Henrietta introduced her to her uncle she said:

"I'm afraid we got here a little early. Uncle is so punctilious, he's always a little early."

Sensing the heat of her blushing face, Claire simply smiled at the uncle, who didn't smile back.

He was a thin, straight man wearing a light gray jacket from one suit and the darker gray trousers from another suit and a checkered shirt with a knitted red tie. His shoes were suede Hush Puppies with black-and-red ribbed socks that were so short the white skin of his shins showed between them and the cuffs of his trousers. His face was very wrinkled, as if the sagging flesh above his eyes hung in flaps over his lids and hid them. His skin was matte white, colorless except where he had nicked himself shaving; there was a dry trickle of blood at the side of his neck. His white hair was combed flat at the top but curled over his ears, and his mouth was turned down at the corners, his long nose hung at the tip, and his chin turned up sharply to meet it. His eyes were bright blue and intense, and he looked at Claire intently as Henrietta introduced them. Sir Roger held out a hand to her, and grunted when she took his large, warm, strong hand in hers. Claire supposed this grunt was some form of greeting, and she said, not knowing what she was saying, "And a pleasure for me too." Sir Roger drew his hand back, and the four, including the maitre d'hôtel, stood still.

"But of course," Henrietta said, and introduced Claire and Signor Castrucci, who tipped his head to one side as a sign of recognition.

"Ho dimenticato —" Claire started to say.

Signor Castrucci said, in English, "I have just the table for you, the one Sir Roger always asks for when he comes to our restaurant."

Blushing more, Claire didn't know if she, as the one who had invited the others, should follow behind Signor Castrucci and lead the others out to a table under the awning or go last. Without smiling, Sir Roger took her arm and they went out together.

Rachel was standing in the sunlight beyond the awning, her hands clasped at her waist. For a moment she closed her eyes and threw her head back with an abrupt motion and shook her long hair, and when she opened her eyes she looked away from her mother and the others in the shade of the awning.

Claire called to her, "Rachel."

Rachel came toward the group standing at a table in a corner and waiting for her. Sir Roger held out both his hands to her and said, "And this is Rachel, is it?" She smiled a gentle smile, and Sir Roger took both her hands in his and leaned toward her as if to speak only to her. "I dared hope," he said. Rachel's smile widened. Claire felt a little glow of pleasure.

"I'll have you on one side of me," Sir Roger said to Rachel. "And your mother on the other side. And I shall be very happy."

He discussed the meal with Signor Castrucci, and Claire, looked at from time to time by Sir Roger to check with her if she, the one who had invited them, agreed, said yes to everything. Sir Roger said to her after Signor Castrucci left with the folders under his arm, "I've made sure not to have ordered extravagantly."

"Oh, well," Claire said, and shrugged. The thought passed across her mind that Sir Roger was being patronizing, but she dismissed this thought with another: he was just acting according to his own code of manners. And the English code of manners was peculiar.

To Rachel, Sir Roger said, holding an arm out toward her, "For your first, I have ordered a very simple dish, I'm afraid, but as I think you should know something about the history of the area, I've ordered an historical dish called *farro,* made from a kind of wheat the Romans called *spelta* and we call spelt, made into a soup that the Roman legions lived on." He made a face, pressing his lips together and forcing the corners of his mouth farther down and opening his eyes wide in the folds of flesh about them. "For those of us who already know enough history, I've ordered less simply."

Rachel asked, "Didn't the Roman legions eat spaghetti?"

Bread in a basket lined with a napkin, a tall green bottle of mineral water, and a carafe of red wine were put on the table by a waiter wearing a stiff white jacket.

Shaking his head at Rachel, Sir Roger said, "The ignorance of the young makes me wonder if I was ever so ignorant myself. I dare say I was, but I can't recall. I remember myself as always knowing everything."

Rachel laughed.

As he poured out wine in the glasses, he said to her, "I will leave it to you to do a little research on the history of spaghetti and find out when and how it came to Italy. Tomatoes, also, with which spaghetti sauce is made. You might do a little serious study in the *biblioteca* while you're here."

"In the what?" Rachel asked.

In a voice she knew was too loud, Claire said to her, "Because I haven't had any luck with my own research, I'll help you in yours." She meant this, of course, to let Sir Roger know that she herself was an art historian.

Sir Roger looked right past her, as if she had no existence at all as an art historian, and she thought: Well, compared to him, I don't. It was better for Rachel to be at the center than herself.

Henrietta lifted her arms high and exclaimed, "I'm starving."

The first course came, and everyone, under the command to remain silent as long as Sir Roger was, ate in silence.

In his self-centeredness and arrogance, Sir Roger probably never thought about the world, but only about what was of immediate concern to him, as if responsible only to his own world and not to any other beyond him. His own world would, he'd assume, include all the artworks about which he was such an authority; he would be called upon to authenticate a picture in dispute, to advise on the cleaning of a work, to sign a petition to keep a work from being exported, to help voice an appeal to raise public money to buy a work for the nation, and all of this he would consider in the interests of a world that was his. Sir Roger belonged to a world of people who believed they could change their world at will. Claire had read his books, and she knew how original Sir Roger was; he had the ability to determine new and revealing points about the creation of a work that shifted all the known perspectives about it. Just because he was as original as he was, he would never sign protest letters against imprisonment and torture in Third World countries, or send contributions to organizations meant to stop pollution and the extinction of animals, or even when younger have joined protest marches against wars and dictatorships — all of which Claire did and had done — not because he knew they would do no good — Claire knew they would do no good, but even so she must sign, must contribute, must protest — but because the world that was to him most meaningful was his own, radiating with always newly discovered perspectives.

When Sir Roger spoke, at the end of the course, it was to ask Rachel if she'd enjoyed her *farro*.

"I kept telling myself I was having a historical experience," she said, "and that helped."

Sir Roger seemed to smile, though Sir Roger's smiles were reverse smiles — instead of the corners of his mouth going up, they went down. He asked Rachel, "How old are you?"

"Seventeen," she said.

"I once knew a young woman of seventeen."

"Just turned seventeen," Claire said.

Henrietta said, "I'm still starving."

Sir Roger unexpectedly asked Claire, "You're a student of art history?"

Claire sat up. "Yes," she said demurely.

"You came to Lucca to do research?"

More demure, Claire said, "On a very small hunch."

Sir Roger grunted.

Claire said quickly, "I found a reference to a Pietro Testa Annunciation in Vincenzo Marchio's inventory of artworks in Lucca, and I came to try to locate it, in the sacristy of the church of Santa Maria Misericordia. It's not mentioned in any of the catalogues of Testa's work, and I thought the Marchio reference might be worth a visit to Lucca."

"You'd hardly expect it to be in the Misericordia, would you, even if it did exist?" Sir Roger said through his teeth.

"No." Claire sat back, and she felt like a fool.

"But one has got to begin somewhere to locate pictures. I've never heard of the picture myself, I must confess. I wasn't even aware of its having once existed. Most likely it no longer exists, or I would know about it, and I know of no Annunciation by Testa, certainly not one in Lucca or Italy or, I might add without undue modesty, most of the Western world."

The second courses came, and everyone ate in silence. Sir Roger chewed his food carefully, his mouth a little open, and sometimes he drooled and wiped the saliva away, not with his napkin but with his fingers, which he then wiped on the napkin.

Claire and Rachel exchanged looks past Sir Roger, and Claire smiled when she saw Rachel smile.

After the plates were removed, Sir Roger said to Claire, "You know that Napoleon's sister Elisa, to whom he gave Lucca as her very own duchy, suppressed the churches and made a collection of the paintings she took from them —"

Of course she knew, but Claire composed herself to show him she was attentive.

"— and after she died, her collection was sold by the grand duke, son of the Bourbon Maria Louisa, because he needed the money. The king of Holland bought the Lucca Madonna by Van Eyck, which is now in the Städelsches Kunstinstitut in Frankfurt. The Testa might have been sold then. But who would have bought it?"

"You have no idea?" Claire asked.

"I have no idea."

Telling herself it was not so important — not for her life as an art historian, because finding a painting by a minor late Baroque artist was not going to be a revelation to change the known history of the period, and not really for any other life she led — Claire tried to sit still against her disappointment. She noted that along the hanging edge of the awning was a fringe, and sunlight was flickering through the fringe.

Moving not just his head but his entire body toward Rachel, Sir Roger said to her, "That young woman I once knew, she had a most horrible secret."

A shock made Claire feel that she rose from her chair, but she saw Sir Roger smile a little, and Rachel too smiled a little.

Sir Roger said to Rachel, "Young women always have horrible secrets."

Smiling more, Rachel asked, "What was the secret of the girl you knew?"

Sir Roger grunted. "I can't say. She made me swear I would never tell anyone. But I can say it was horrible."

Rachel wrinkled her nose.

"Don't wrinkle your nose," he said. "You're beautiful, and that makes you hideous."

Rachel laughed, and the laugh amazed Claire. The conversation Rachel and Sir Roger were having amazed Claire.

"I think young women should all have horrible secrets they only reveal to old, kindly men who will never tell anyone," Sir Roger said.

"All?" Rachel asked.

"All."

Pressing a finger against her forehead, Rachel thought. Then she shook her head so all her long hair shook in loose waves, and she said to Sir Roger in a little girl's voice, "I have a secret."

Sir Roger grunted, as he often did, but more loudly.

Feeling she was still high with shock, Claire said to Rachel, "You don't."

"I do," Rachel said.

"Of course she does," Sir Roger said to Claire. "And if I'm lucky she'll tell me, but no one else."

Rachel thought again, and seemed to dare herself to go on with the joke. Her voice came out a little twisted when she said to Sir Roger, "You really promise not to tell anyone else?" She bit her lower lip.

Sir Roger put his large white hand over his heart.

He said, "But I hope it's a really horrible secret, you know. If it weren't, I'd forget it, and there's no point to a secret if you forget it."

"Oh, it's horrible," Rachel said.

"I hope, a story filled with blood and gore. Those are the secrets I like best to keep, stories filled with blood and gore."

Rachel laughed like a little girl.

Claire frowned. She wasn't sure that Sir Roger and Rachel weren't indulging in something that was English, that Rachel got from her deeper contact with the English world than Claire's contact, and this something else, English or not, wasn't anything Claire, with her own sense of what was funny, found funny. There was something sinister, something crude, in the English, and the higher they were in the class system, the more deeply sinister and crude. If all Claire was frightened about in Rachel's darkness turned out to be the English sense of what was funny, she must get Rachel out of England right away. She wanted to get her away from Sir Roger.

But before she could think of something to say to end the lunch, Sir Roger threw his napkin onto the table and said, "I won't have pudding or coffee." He stood.

Everyone else stood.

Bowing a little, Sir Roger said to Claire, "Come to lunch tomorrow at my house," and turning and bowing a little to Rachel said, "With your delightful daughter." Leaving the table, he said, "My niece Henrietta will tell you when and where." Without saying thank you or goodbye, he went into the piazza, where the sunlight was brilliant white. He stopped, looked back, and held up an arm.

"He wants something," Henrietta said, and went to him.

Claire sat, but Rachel stood. They didn't look at each other.

Henrietta came back. She said, "He'd like Rachel to walk to the car with him."

Without asking her mother if she could, Rachel went out into the sunlight.

"I can only sit for a moment because I must drive him back to his house," Henrietta said and, seated, told Claire that the next day at twelve-thirty she should take a taxi to the Villa Fabiano. The taxi driver would understand where that was. Henrietta picked up the green mineral water bottle and poured some into her glass and drank, then said, "I must tell you that I've told my uncle about Rachel."

Claire narrowed her eyes.

"I was sure he would want to do everything he could for her, knowing what happened to her. You saw that, didn't you? He was so attentive to her, and she responded to him. He may seem to be a hard man, sometimes terrifyingly hard, but he's really quite gentle. And he saw how gentle Rachel is. She is, isn't she?"

When Rachel came back to her mother, she didn't say anything about Sir Roger, ashamed, maybe, of the way they had joked. And Claire didn't ask her what she and Sir Roger had talked about on the way to the car, as if to ask her would be to make her more ashamed of the joke she and Sir Roger shared.

Feverish, Claire spent the night wondering if she should take Rachel to Sir Roger's villa. Their joking worried her. Their joking would take away from Rachel something that was fundamental to her. Joking couldn't be all that Rachel's horror meant. It had to mean more than a joke that a strange old man perpetrated on a vulnerable girl. It had to. What had happened to Rachel must be meaningful, as any fundamental must. The world itself would become meaningless in the jokes it told about itself to try to distance itself from its horrors — the jokes the world told itself about the rape, the torture, the murder, the war that occurred in the world, that were occurring now, right now, as Claire lay in a hotel room in a peaceful Italian town within its old walls.

She knew that Rachel was counting on seeing Sir Roger again.

IV

On the marble bar of the café was a bright silvery bowl with two round handles hanging from the mouths of lions. The bowl was filled with ice, and thin, long-stemmed glasses were embedded upside down in the ice. Claire saw herself, shortened and widened, reflected in the contour of the bowl as she drank her midmorning espresso standing at the bar. The side of the bowl also reflected the misty sunlight behind her, out in the street.

She put her small, thick white coffee cup and saucer on the marble bar. Tired because she had not slept and because of what she imagined to be the continuing fever, she did not want to see Sir Roger today. Neither did she want to see Rachel, who was probably still asleep, so she would have to wake her. And she kept wondering how she could prevent Rachel and Sir Roger from coming together.

She wouldn't have minded staying in this café. Other customers were reflected in the silver bowl, which was to Claire the center of the café, and these customers, the man behind the bar, the gleaming espresso machine, the bottles of red and green and yellow liqueurs on glass shelves behind him and behind the bottles a mirror, the glass cases in other parts of the café of boxes of chocolates and cellophane-wrapped baskets of marzipan fruit, the shelves of cigarettes and cigars, the highly polished gray and white marble floor, and the light too, the misty light that seemed to surround everything as if everything formed a globe — all this appeared to Claire not so much to be reflected in the bowl but to be projected from it. She shivered, feeling not only feverish but alone.

When a middle-aged man and woman came in and asked for and were served glasses taken from the ice and filled with *pro secco,* they too were projected from the bowl into the air not far from Claire, who, listening to them speak Italian, thought they must be married.

On the way back to the hotel, she lingered at the shop windows to look at the shoes, the purses, the gloves, the crystal perfume atomizers with golden nozzles and crochet- and silk-covered rubber balls, the cases of delicate instruments for manicures, the cloisonné-backed mirrors and hairbrushes.

Rachel was waiting for her in the small lobby.

"I thought you might still be asleep," Claire said.

"I've been up for a while," Rachel said.

"You were sitting here, waiting for me?"

Rachel seemed to be wondering what else she could have done but wait for her mother.

"It's a beautiful morning," Claire said. "We have lots of time before we go to Sir Roger's. We could take a bus out into the country."

"Would we be sure of getting back in time?" Rachel asked.

No, Claire thought, she couldn't prevent Rachel from seeing Sir Roger again.

"Then we'll just walk," she said, "and look around."

As they walked, Claire pointed to bronze memorial plaques, carved architraves, wrought iron window grilles, terra-cotta bas-reliefs of saints along the palaces; the multiple columns and inlaid patterns of green and white marble, and the carved lions and statues supported by stone sconces on the façades of churches; the arches and pillars of old, bricked-in porticoes; the fountain; the palm trees over an old pink wall. She pointed them out, and she hoped Rachel would point out details to her.

They passed the church of the Misericordia. Its two main doors were open. Rachel paused before the doors and looked in. The outside brightness made it impossible to see inside. Rachel went before her mother.

Claire, disoriented, followed Rachel. Taped on the partition of the little wooden vestibule were pink-and-white notices, badly typed and headed with childlike drawings of lilies. Rachel opened a side door of this vestibule and went in, and Claire followed her into the stony gray, narrow, Gothic nave. Under a suspended cross a marriage was being celebrated at the altar in the apse, a long low table with a white cloth covering the middle of it. The priest was standing behind it, facing the bride and groom, who were kneeling before it.

At the priest's back was the old high altar, carved in gray stone, with *putti*-filled clouds floating high above it, and in the midst of the clouds a tarnished golden sunburst surrounding the tarnished golden tabernacle. It was at altars like this, with steps up to them and tabernacles and high candlesticks and candles, that, when Claire was a girl, the Mass all over the world was said, the priest facing away from the congregation. By the time the Mass was changed and said on the substitute table-altar, the priest facing the congregation, Claire no longer went to church.

The edges of the paving stones of the church were rounded, and the stones had dips in them and grooves. A tomb with a bas-relief of a bishop was worn down to a shadow. The chill inside air smelled of dust and mold and incense.

There were not many people attending the wedding. None of the women wore hats. That too was a difference from the time when Claire had gone to church, when it would have been forbidden to women to go into churches with bare heads. Claire had sometimes put her handkerchief over her head if it so happened, passing a church, that she wanted to make a visit and say a prayer and wasn't wearing a hat. One of the young women, with long blond hair, was wearing jeans and a tight halter, and standing, she shifted her weight from one leg to the other often. She was standing between a man and a woman who were probably her father and mother. The elderly attending sat on little rush-bottomed chairs.

Claire and Rachel stood toward the back, Claire a little behind Rachel so that she could often look at her looking at the ceremony.

Along each side of the nave was a row of high, thin, opalescent glass vases, fluted about the rims, with white carnations. The bride, in a white satin dress and a veil that stood out in soft angles about her head, and the groom, in a blue suit, turned away from the altar and walked down the aisle between the rows of carnations.

Rachel, and Claire too, stood farther back. Claire saw that Rachel watched the couple as they passed. The bride and groom smiled at them, and Claire, while Rachel remained silent, said, "*Gloria a Voi*." She didn't know if this was an appropriate salutation, but the couple laughed and said, "*Grazie*."

The bride pressed her veil down at the back of her head with one hand and with the other hand gathered up her long skirt, and the groom opened the wooden door by its brass handle for her to go out. The other members of the party came quickly and, talking, went out too, and there were shouts and bursts of laughter from outside.

Rachel walked farther into the now empty church, along the side aisle. She stopped at each stone altar there, raised on a wooden platform with steps up to it, all with large, dark paintings above them. Above one altar was a glass case and in it a statue of a saint with a smooth black veil over her head and a yellowish robe, carrying roses in her arms. The glass case around her was filled with faded paper flowers. Before the altar was a metal stand for votive candles. One thin white candle held by a clamp was burning.

Claire had once known about all the saints' lives and what to pray to them for. She had forgotten it all. She was thinking of the sacristy, which had to be just a little way farther down the aisle, which she was anxious to get to but also didn't want to go to.

Rachel frowned a little, then went on to examine the other altars, the large paintings above them in worm-eaten and blackened gilt frames, the canvases warped. She examined too the dusty chandeliers hanging crookedly, with prisms missing, from the apex of the stone arches along the side aisle. She was calm in her attention. For a while she stood still and silent, and she didn't look at anything.

Claire said, "Shall we look in the sacristy?"

Rachel nodded. Claire could see her pulse in her neck.

The sacristy, with a floor of cracked black-and-white marble squares and high cupboards of dark, cracked wood, had no pictures in it at all. The air smelled of dampness. Neither Claire nor Rachel said anything, but left the sacristy as if they had not been looking for anything in particular in it, but just looking at it, as they had looked at the church.

Sir Roger had told them the picture wouldn't be there.

Was a revelation possible? Claire thought. No, she answered herself. But she had once, as a Catholic girl, believed in revelation, and she asked herself if it was a loss for Rachel, having been brought up without any religion, not to have believed anything that religion gave, such as belief in revelation. She, Claire, had not made a mistake in giving up her religion, she was sure of that, sure that she had done what was right, because her religion would have killed her by not allowing her a life of her own, which she had insisted on, which she had needed in order to live at all. And in any case, it was too late to go back to her religion, because her religion was no longer there to go back to, no longer what it had been when she grew up in it and found her moments of consolation. Claire could not go back, and she could not take Rachel back with her, but for the first time in her life she realized, without being able to or wanting to do anything to amend this, that the worst that had happened to her in her life was that she had lost her faith. For Claire, faith and religion were one, and to have lost her faith meant losing her religion, because she could not imagine finding her faith in any other religion, not even in her love of paintings and statues or silver bowls filled with crushed ice and champagne glasses. And Rachel knew nothing about this, nothing at all —

On the cobbles of the piazza were hundreds of minute gold-and-silver paper horseshoes.

Crossing the piazza, Rachel asked Claire, "What does marriage in a church mean?"

"I'm not sure I understand," Claire said.

"Well, what's the difference between being married in a registry office and a church?"

"You know what a marriage in a registry office is."

Rachel nodded.

Claire said, "A marriage in a church is —" She had to think. She said again, "It is —" She didn't know, really; she couldn't remember. Then she remembered this: "The ceremony in church is meant to commemorate the marriage of Christ to his bride, the Church."

Rachel laughed. "The marriage of Christ to his bride, the Church? When did that happen?"

"After his resurrection, I think. I'm not sure anymore about any of it."

"You and Daddy weren't married in church?"

"No, no."

"Why?"

"Because we didn't believe."

"Didn't believe that your marriage was the marriage of Christ and his Church?"

"That, and everything else. Didn't believe in Christ or his Church."

"I guess I don't understand. Believe how?"

"Just believe in them. When I was a girl, I was made to believe in all kinds of things that I later realized couldn't possibly be true."

"Like what?"

Claire walked slowly, and she talked slowly. "I was told by the nuns that I must believe in the great mysteries of the Church, such as the Immaculate Conception, the Resurrection, the Ascension —"

"What are they, exactly?"

"It would take such a long time to explain."

"Explain one," Rachel said.

"The Immaculate Conception, then. You don't know what that is?"

"I'm not sure. It has to do with that strange idea of a virgin becoming a mother and still being a virgin."

"You don't know the mystery?"

"Who would have told me?"

"I guess I wouldn't have."

"No."

Claire said, "When God decided to save the world from its terrible suffering, caused by Adam and Eve's disobeying him, he chose a girl, Mary, to bear his son, Jesus, who was to come down into the world and by taking on all the suffering of the world save the world. Mary was made pregnant by God in the form of the Holy Spirit, who is depicted as a dove. But because she remained a virgin, her conception was called immaculate, and that is one of the great mysteries of the Catholic Church."

"How did she remain a virgin?"

"You mean, physically? I remember being told that the conception occurred through one of her ears."

"An ear?"

"You see how unbelievable it all is? Grace entered one of her ears and she became pregnant."

"Grace?"

"Yes."

"What's grace?"

Claire couldn't say, exactly. "Some beam of inspiration that comes directly from God."

"And this inspiration made Mary pregnant?"

"Yes."

"What did people say about that?"

"She got married to Joseph, who didn't quite understand but accepted that his wife had been chosen by God —" As she spoke, Claire thought: This is an even odder story than I remember. She said, "When I learned a little something about life, there was no way I could believe in what I was told, even though I was told it was a mystery and I couldn't understand it but simply had to believe it."

"Believe it because it was a mystery?"

"Because it was dogma, and my duty was to abide by dogma. And of course I questioned the dogma by questioning my duty to it. I questioned everything. All I believed in was in questioning everything that was a principle one had the unquestionable duty to abide by. That was the Church when I was growing up — a system of dogmas it was one's unquestionable duty to abide by."

"Yes," Rachel said quietly.

"Not that questioning leaves you with much," Claire said, laughing a little. "I have to admit that."

"And Daddy was the same?"

"Daddy was a more fanatic believer in questioning than I. There wasn't anything Daddy didn't question. If anyone, it was Daddy who made me question everything, and no doubt he was right to make me. You know, he was so powerful, so big and dark and powerful, and I loved him, oh, a lot."

Claire thought: How strange. It appeared to her that spaces were shifting, and darkness was opening up all around them. Again she thought: How strange.

Rachel frowned, trying to understand.

They were approaching the parking lot in the piazza, the hoods of the rows of parked cars glinting. In their midst and rising above the cars was the statue of Elisa Buonaparte, the woman who had suppressed the churches and formed a collection of her own from church paintings, among them the Testa Annunciation, which had probably been sold after her death — to whom? She was in neo-classical dress and with a naked boy by her, facing the great yellow-brown palace with heavy grilles over its windows that had been her residence.

The sense of strangeness continued as, in the back seat of the taxi, Claire and Rachel were driven through an arched gateway and outside the walls, through suburbs, and out into the country. The continuing sense of everything shifting was explained by the movement of the taxi, but not the sense of strangeness. It was as if Claire were about to discover a point somewhere in the air that would be the focus of a rearrangement of all the perspective lines of the fields, the osier trees along the edges of the fields, the olive groves, the lines of poplars, the modern white villas with stone walls and the small prefabricated factories and the old farmhouses; and the very possibility of that new point made the green and bluish scenery, with white mountains beyond, appear ready to be transformed into scenery that was completely but unpredictably different. The taxi turned off the main highway into a narrow road up into the hills. It was Claire's fever that made her imagine the landscape kept shifting.

The road to the villa was dirt, with a middle strip of weeds and on each side higher, blossoming weeds. Then the taxi, rocking in holes, went along a gray-pink wall. Dogs bounded out of the gateway in the wall and ran around the taxi, barking. Rachel tapped at the window to concentrate their attention on her, but this made them pause only and bite their haunches, then they ran barking in the opposite direction around the taxi, stopped before the gateway with two square stone gateposts with terra-cotta urns on them planted with spiky agaves.

Henrietta appeared between the gateposts but didn't try to stop the dogs, as if she had decided there was nothing she could do anyway. She was wearing her necklace of beads from which most of the pearly skin had been peeled away. In the midst of the raging dogs, Claire paid the taxi driver.

She let Rachel go ahead of her, following Henrietta, along a gravel path between more terra-cotta urns of agaves to the house, with wings on either side and a double staircase up to glass double doors, open.

Rachel, Claire noted, was taking everything in, seeing the details, perhaps, for what they said about Sir Roger. They went up one side of the double staircase and into a high, wide room with a tile floor and a painted wooden lamp hanging from a beam across the ceiling, on the lamp many small, tilting, brownish shades, and under the lamp a wide table covered with magazines and books, and in the middle a marble bust. Also on the table were an old olive oil bottle and a straw hat and a tin of paint dripping blue down its sides and a stick with blue paint at the end and a sponge that looked as if it had been dipped into blue paint. The few chairs in the room, placed too far apart for people to sit on them and talk to one another, were encased in white covers. There was a haze of light in the room, like smoke that drifted up toward the ceiling.

Outside the back of the villa, within the mottled pink-and-gray walls, was a garden with box hedges and a stone basin in the middle filled with thick green water. By the basin were a rusty metal bucket and broken terra-cotta flowerpots and empty wine bottles and an old, broken bidet.

The loggia was at the back of the garden, under an old cedar, in the branches of which a cicada thrilled.

It was only when you looked carefully, Claire noted, that you saw how rundown everything was. But Claire, who always wanted to see everything in the best possible way, thought that that was just as it should be according to Sir Roger, who would have disdained anything too done up, too carefully arranged.

The wicker furniture under the loggia was falling apart, so the chair Claire sat in listed.

Henrietta said, "I'm rather looking forward to getting back to London."

"Why, when you're in such a beautiful place?" Claire said. "Don't you think it's beautiful, Rachel?"

"It's great, it's really brilliant," Rachel said, then said, more quietly, "Yes, I think it's beautiful."

"Oh, it's that, I suppose," Henrietta said. She pointed to the house, and showing her twisted teeth by raising high her upper lip, she said, "It's him."

Rachel laughed. "What about him?"

"Well, I wouldn't mind a little freedom to do what I choose, just a little. I can't sleep in the morning, but have to be at breakfast by eight. Elevenses are exactly at eleven. Sherry under the loggia at twelve-thirty. You'll see, he'll be here in eight and a half minutes precisely with the bottle and glasses. And —"

Sir Roger was coming across the garden with a tray.

Henrietta looked at her watch and said, "He's early."

Hardly greeting anyone with more than a grunt, Sir Roger gave them all small glasses of sherry, then, with a glass himself, sat in a wicker chair.

He looked at Rachel for a moment, but without expression, though her face opened up when he looked at her.

The first words from him were for Claire. He said, "Your Testa

Annunciation might have been done while he was back in Lucca from Rome for a few months, trying to get the patronage of Cardinal Marcantonio Franciotti." He looked away, staring as if into the branches of the tree.

She wondered if he was testing her. "Yes," she said, "in 1637. Or he might have done it on an earlier visit, in 1632."

His eyes still averted, he said, "When he did, or tried to do, the fresco in the Cortile degli Svizzeri in the Palazzo degli Anziani, and make his name in Lucca."

"The fresco of Liberty conquering Time," Claire said. "I've seen the original sketch in the *cabinet des dessins* in the Louvre and the more worked drawing of the subject in the Ashmolean."

"Quite," Sir Roger said, and looked at Claire for a moment with his lower lip stuck out.

She wanted Sir Roger to know she possessed her artist.

Then he diminished Pietro Testa. "He never really learned about color," Sir Roger said.

"He would have preferred to work only in black and white."

"Those last paintings are very dark. I don't think I like them."

These were just the paintings Claire most liked, the ones that drew her to Testa. All she said was, "Yes, very dark —"

"He killed himself, didn't he?" Sir Roger said.

With a pang, Claire said quickly, "It's thought so —"

Sir Roger's voice rose in pitch, interrupting her. "That's something I've never been able to understand, never, the impulse to kill oneself. And if my lack of understanding means I'm deficient in the understanding of the sensibilities of certain artists, I can't honestly say I feel the deficiency is so great that it keeps me from enjoying something I might otherwise find deeply interesting. Suicide is not very interesting, I think."

Claire thought that Sir Roger knew everything, everything, and the fact that Sir Roger pronounced suicide uninteresting was a pronouncement against everything that gave her life meaning, and made her life itself uninteresting. He took away all her darkness. And he seemed to know exactly what he was doing.

Rachel, raising her head, asked, "How did he commit suicide?"

"He killed himself by drowning in the Tiber," Sir Roger said. "He jumped off a bridge."

"He might have just slipped and fallen," Claire said. "Some friends swore that he had only slipped and fallen."

"That," Sir Roger said, "would have been so that he'd be buried in consecrated ground, where suicides weren't allowed to be buried."

"Yes," Claire said quietly, and slouched.

"Why weren't they allowed to be buried in consecrated ground?" Rachel asked.

"Because they were, quite rightly, considered sinners," Sir Roger said.

Claire wondered how she could change the subject.

Sir Roger said to her, "That reference to a Testa Annunciation by Vincenzo Marchio you mentioned to me —"

Claire sat up.

"Marabottini also mentioned it."

Claire went red in her cheeks. She had read Marabottini — she had read Marabottini and Calabi, Harris and Hartmann, and the dispute between the two sets of art historians over a painting of the Nativity in the Musée Fabre, Montpellier — but she couldn't recall any mention in Marabottini or anyone else of an Annunciation. She wanted to say she'd read all the relevant works, she really had, but she knew that because she hadn't read this one relevant passage, all that she had read went for nothing.

"And he mentioned seeing what he thought was that very Testa Annunciation in Moscow, in the collection of Prince Volkansky, before the Bolshevik Revolution." Sir Roger delivered this, again looking into the branches of the tree, as if it could not be of much consequence to anyone. He pressed his lips together as though to keep himself from smiling.

"Where does he mention that?" Claire asked. "Not in *Il Tratto di pittura' e i disegni del Lucchesino.*"

"No, nor in *Novità sul Lucchesino,*" Sir Roger said. He did smile a little, and Claire thought he was not going to tell her. "He told me so himself. I remembered just this morning, looking through various books in an attempt to help you in your quest, that he told me years and years ago that he had been in Moscow before the Revolution and seen what he thought to be a Testa Annunciation in the collection of Prince Volkansky. He never published anything about this, as he hadn't had sufficient time to study the work, and he didn't want another disagreeable battle on his hands, not after both Harris and Hartmann attacked him for attributing the Nativity in Montpellier to Testa — attacked him, he finally had to admit, so brutally he had to retreat and say that he himself was doubtful of the attribution. And he was never able to get back to Moscow."

"How could a Testa have ended up in Moscow?"

"Oh, that's not so difficult to imagine. When the son of the Bourbon Maria Louisa, the grand duke, ran out of money, he began to sell off the collection he'd inherited, and at that time any number of Russian noblemen touring Italy might have bought a painting by Testa, who was no more fashionable then than he is now and whose work would have been cheap. But to find out that you would have, I suppose, to do research in Russia."

Claire sat back. "Russia," she said. As if she were trying to see Russia, she looked into space. She said, "I wonder what happened to it during the Revolution."

Sir Roger raised his hands, palms up, and said, "God knows."

"I should forget about it," Claire said. She could not find a painting in Russia any more than she could be Russian.

"What?" Sir Roger said. "But that the painting may be in Russia only makes your research a little harder."

Claire laughed. "Pretty much impossible, I'd say."

"Not if you really and truly want to find the painting."

"I do."

"Then you must find a way."

It was Rachel who asked, "How?"

Sir Roger said to her, as if she had taken the place of her mother, "When you are back in London, you might contact my old friend Maurice Kuragin, a White Russian who has lived in London since the October Revolution of 1917. We were undergraduates together in Cambridge. A simple, kind man, he forgot more than he learned. At Cambridge, he forgot all his Russian. But he might very easily know if there are members of the Volkansky family in London, or elsewhere in the West, who might know what happened to the family collection. You see, what appears to us to be a hermetic world isn't at all to those people who live in the world. All that's required to get into the world is an introduction, and I'll give you the introduction. You may find your painting quite easily once you get into the right world, and I think you would be amused by the search."

He looked at his watch and stood and collected the glasses on the tray, which was a wooden Florentine tray gilded all around its elaborate edge and with a picture of the Bargello on it, and it was in parts worn down to the wood. He asked Rachel to take the carafe of sherry. "Now it's time for lunch," he said.

The dining room was in the basement, off the kitchen. Sir Roger prepared lunch, and allowed no one in the kitchen, not even to take the dirty dishes out. There was silence kept during the first course, a rather gummy *risotto con funghi*, but when Sir Roger went out with the dirty dishes, Henrietta talked until he came in with the next course.

Raising her eyebrows, she said, "Tomorrow is Sunday, and I'm going to have to drive him into Florence for Mass."

"For Mass?" Claire exclaimed.

"Oh yes, he insists on going to Mass, and given my uncle, it has to be a very special Mass in a very special church in Florence."

"Is Sir Roger a Catholic?"

"Why does it surprise you?"

"I don't know why, it's just —"

"I thought everyone knew. But then, how would everyone know?"

Sir Roger came in with a small roasted chicken.

After this course, as if he thought it formally correct to have a pause and to entertain his guests, or at least Rachel, he asked her, "Have you done any of your research yet on spaghetti?"

"I promise to start on Monday."

"Monday the library is shut."

She said, "Then I'll start on Tuesday."

"I can see you're not a serious scholar, letting the fact that a library is shut stop you from somehow getting into it."

"How do I get into it?"

"You might ask me to find a way for you."

Rachel laughed.

Sir Roger leaned toward her and said, involving her in no good, "I could even help you, in my own modest way, with finding out fascinating facts about pictures. Or don't you have any more interest in pictures than you do in the history of pasta?"

Rachel moved a little in her chair, wondering, maybe, if she could get away with saying she was terrifically interested, but aware that Sir Roger would know if she wasn't telling the truth. "I don't know much about pictures," she said.

"There you are," Sir Roger said. "I'm sure your mother has often offered to teach you something, but, stubbornly ignorant girl that you are, you've refused. Now, why have you refused?"

Rachel looked at her mother across the round table and blushed.

"After our pudding," Sir Roger said, "I'll show you my pictures."

Henrietta said she had things to do and went off into the garden. Sir Roger led Rachel and Claire up a curving stone flight of steps to the wide landing with the big table, on which the tin of paint and stick and sponge, dribbled with or coated with or soaked in blue paint, still were. They went into a drawing room off the landing, with a terra-cotta tile floor and white walls and shutters shut against the afternoon sunlight, and the dogs, asleep on a large sofa. There was a blue-paint-splattered ladder standing in the middle of the room. On the walls were paintings in heavy gilt frames.

They stood near the ladder, and before Sir Roger even pointed to a painting, he said to Rachel, as if Claire weren't there, "What drew me to pictures, many years ago, was that they had stories, or so I thought in my great naiveté, and, I may say, in my continuing naiveté I still think. I'd ask myself, why in heaven's name is that man wearing a brown robe standing so still, his hands clasped in what I recognized as prayer, with a great stone on his head and blood pouring down his pate? Why, would you think?"

"It sounds weird," Rachel said.

"Weird, indeed. And why was that man lying on his back and having his bowels wound out of him by soldiers on a big wheel?"

Rachel winced.

What, what was the strange man doing? Claire thought.

"And," Sir Roger asked, "what could that woman be doing with her breasts on a serving dish?"

Claire's body jerked, and she raised a hand to stop him. He knew what Rachel had suffered, and he was blatantly referring to the most telling image of her suffering. It was as though Claire had been struck by a fist in the face, and she was hit again when Rachel asked:

"Why?"

"Ah, you see. I've got you. You want to know the story."

And Claire thought: I understand, I understand. This, like the stunning effect following on a shock, made her go weak.

Of course Sir Roger knew what Rachel had suffered, and knowing that she was unaware he did, he was offering to her the images of her suffering, not only images that would, he might believe, help her by making her suffering part of the human condition, but images that at the very least were wonderfully interesting. This appreciation of art, which had nothing, nothing at all to do with art history, so amazed Claire that she could hardly hear what Sir

Roger went on to say. All she could think was that he was trying to help Rachel, and Rachel was responding, she was opening up to him. He was right, he had her, and he would, with time, with visits he would want her to make regular, with, perhaps, visits he would invite her to extend into weeks in this villa, help her as Claire hadn't been able to. In what Claire had thought his crude and sinister English way, he had made Rachel feel that horror could be joked about, however stupidly, and that it could be interesting, even entertaining, when seen depicted in pictures of the exotic tortures endured by saints. And then Claire thought: He is a practicing Catholic, and ultimately what he would make Rachel see, in time, was that the images of the suffering of these saints were images of a devotion that could transcend suffering. He was very deeply Catholic. She understood this because it was something she had as a girl been taught. She felt her heart move in her, and she felt sudden love for this macabre man. She understood too how Rachel could come to love him, and it occurred to her that she had wanted Sir Roger to know what had happened to Rachel, that she had told Henrietta wanting Henrietta to tell him, to move him to help to find the picture, for Rachel's sake.

He said in answer to her question, "Well, you see, Saint Agatha was very brutally raped and had her breasts cut off."

Rachel went totally still. Claire made a slight movement toward her, but held back and went still also.

Sir Roger said, "She is a saint many women have prayed to."

Claire saw Rachel breathe in and out, but when Sir Roger said, "Now come and look at this and learn a thing or two about an artist named Carlo Dolci, who particularly liked painting pious martyrs," she, as if drawn, followed closely behind him to a painting hanging above a bookcase.

Claire felt too weak to stay, and also she thought it would be better if Rachel were alone with Sir Roger. She didn't follow them to the picture but went out of the room, and from the landing into the garden. Henrietta was under the loggia. Claire sat down heavily, and once seated, she felt slight shivers and imagined that everything could at any moment shift around.

Henrietta said, "He likes Rachel."

"I'm glad," Claire said.

"He doesn't like me."

"Well, I'm sorry for that."

"I thought I'd do a lot of work while here, but I've done nothing, having to do for him."

Claire said, "I'll drive him into Florence tomorrow for Mass, if you'd like."

Henrietta said lifelessly, "Oh, that would be kind."

"What is so special about this Mass in this church that he must go?" Claire asked.

"It's the old Latin Mass, the Tridentine Mass, which is celebrated in a Franciscan church in Florence by dispensation from the Vatican."

"That," Claire said, "was the Mass of my youth."

She saw Sir Roger and Rachel coming toward her across the garden.

Henrietta said she would take Claire and Rachel back into Lucca by car. As Sir Roger led them along the gravel to the front gate, Claire noted smoke rising over a wall of the garden, in the distance, and she said, "Is that from a fire a farmer set to burn off his fields?" Sir Roger stopped to look, and he frowned. While they looked, the smoke spread over a wider area, and Sir Roger, frowning more, went out through the open gateway and the women followed. Fields, with trees along the edges, extended out from the walls of the villa's garden, and in the clear, bright wind the fire was spreading from field to field, toward the villa.

They stood still for a while and watched it. Henrietta said, "Shouldn't I go get Adriano?" but Sir Roger didn't respond, and Henrietta went to a stone house just outside the gate where the old peasant who took care of the land lived. Sir Roger went to a cypress tree and with difficulty, twisting it round and round, broke off a branch, and he went into the burning, smoking fields. Rachel too broke off a branch and followed him, and Claire, not knowing what else to do, did the same. Sometimes the flames disappeared into the grass, though the cracking sound, as of many little twigs being snapped, was audible; then the flames would reappear farther on in a sudden blaze. The fields were very uneven, with ruts and holes and dry lumps of earth. Claire saw, ahead, Sir Roger, in the smoke, thrashing the grass with a long stick. Rachel went toward him, but Claire, trying to avoid a ditch, went along a bank, then found herself among brambles, the ditch separating her from Sir Roger and Rachel. The flames were coming toward her, and she thought that once they caught in the brambles they'd roar. Pulling her sleeve away from where a thorny bramble had entangled it, she hurried back along the bank of the ditch, crossed it where she could, and hurried on to Sir Roger and Rachel, who, back to back and in the midst of the flames, were beating them out with their branches. Claire joined them, and, she between them, they formed a line and beat out the flames in the grass as they walked together.

It was difficult to breathe in the smoke, and sometimes the beating itself, instead of putting the flames out, fanned them, and the flames raged up and the three had to stand back from the heat. They were surrounded by fire, and formed a circle, each going out in a different direction, and while beating the flames right in front of her, Claire was shocked by a flame shooting up beside her, and she jumped back. Just where she had been standing the ground burst into flames, as if the fire issued forth in bursts from the earth itself, then it roared up around a clump of hawthorn trees and the branches of the trees twisted as if in a violent wind, twisted and went black, and the flames died away.

Sweating now, and frightened, Claire beat and beat the low

flames, which died out as she whacked them. She didn't know where Rachel and Sir Roger were. She kept beating the flames, which seemed to come from everywhere, from the air, but which died when she hit them. She was covered with soot and dust. And then, suddenly, there was a deep silence, as if something live that had been struggling had been killed. Claire looked around to where Rachel and Sir Roger were standing, their cypress branches still in their hands, in the smoking but fireless field. In another field, the old peasant Adriano was putting out the flames that had spread there. Areas like continents on a map were burned black on the field that Claire, Rachel, and Sir Roger were on, and when they walked across those areas of thin black ash, they left footprints of pale yellow unburned grass below.

Henrietta was waiting by the gate into the garden of the villa. She said to her uncle, "You'd better go wash and lie down."

But he didn't even appear to be breathing hard. "Show the ladies up to the guest bath," he said. "And make sure they get clean towels and a clothes brush." He didn't look at the ladies as he left them, still frowning, to go into the villa. Just as he got to the bottom of one side of the double stairway, however, he stopped and turned back to them and called out, as if to reprimand her, "Rachel, come here."

She went, and Claire saw Sir Roger talk to her for a moment before he climbed the stairs. She came back, smiling a little.

"What did he want?" Claire asked.

She smiled more. She said, "He wanted to thank us." But Claire was sure that wasn't all he'd said.

In an old-fashioned bathroom with white tiled floor and walls and a large, claw-footed tub and empty blue scent bottles on the small windowsill, Claire and Rachel brushed each other, shook out their hair, washed their necks and faces and feet. They laughed, as if they had been to a celebration. But it was a celebration that puzzled Claire.

When Henrietta dropped them off in the car outside a gateway to the walled town, she reminded Claire of her offer to drive her uncle into Florence in the morning for Mass.

Walking back through the town with Rachel, Claire noted that her daughter would from time to time smile, but when she did she'd turn her head away to hide the smile from her mother, and then shake her head so her hair would swing.

In her deepening feverishness, her mind expanding and contracting, Claire imagined that that fire had meant something, and her mind kept delving to understand the meaning, though she knew that it meant nothing at all.

V

THE PRIEST, in a green chasuble and carrying a stiff green veil covering the chalice, one hand flat on the square burse on top and the other holding the chalice beneath the veil, came down the main aisle of the small white and gold church. Two servers in surplices were with him, one carrying a smoking censer by its chains and the other the little silver boat of incense. The choir in the loft at the back of the church sang. The priest went up the steps to the altar and placed the veiled chalice on it before the tabernacle and descended the steps, made the sign of the cross, and turned to the congregation and held out his arms and said, *"Introibo ad altare Dei,"* and the servers, on either side of him, said, *"Ad Deum qui laetificat juventutem meam,"* and Claire felt a strange movement in her. She was sitting on one side of Rachel, and Sir Roger sat on the other. The aged man had a missal, bound in black and with red page-top stain and silk page indicators, in which he followed the Mass. The Confiteor was being said by the priest, and when he, bowing, struck his chest three times, Sir Roger struck his chest. Again Claire felt a movement in her, when the priest went up to the altar and kissed it. And she felt a movement yet again when the priest blessed the incense in the little silver boat, spooned it out onto the burning coal in the censer, held open by a server so a cloud of smoke rose up, then took the censer to swing it by its delicately clinking chains about the altar, releasing more of the resin-smelling smoke. The chorus sang.

She remembered it all. She remembered the Latin, she remembered the parts of the Mass, and she remembered the way the wide chasuble of the celebrant of the Mass, facing away from the congregation, moved. She remembered the Bible on its stand being changed by the server from one side of the altar to the other.

Rachel sat still, staring at the ceremony.

Claire remembered, too, the boredom of the sermon, given now in Italian and only vaguely understood by her. Even after all these years during which she had not been to Mass and the Church had changed so she no longer had any idea what the Vatican stood for, she felt the resentment of being preached to. She remembered the boredom and the resentment she had felt at those Sunday sermons in her Irish parochial church in her town in Maine, remembered how she felt that some will, beyond her choosing it or not, was pressed down on her, and she must behave strictly according to that will. She had said to herself during those sermons, No, I won't, I won't. And after she met Frank when she was in college in Boston, she never entered a church again unless it was to see a painting or a statue, and she never genuflected before the main altar.

Rachel listened to the Italian sermon as if she understood it, which Claire knew she couldn't.

She was right to have broken the will of the Church, and she knew she was right not to have brought Rachel up under it.

She watched the priest lift the purse from the veil and remove from it the corporal, the white linen, handkerchief-like cloth, which he spread on the altar, then remove the veil from the chalice and place the chalice, covered by the pall and the purificator, on the corporal. She remembered all of this, she remembered the names. She remembered going to Mass early on cold winter weekday mornings, when there would be no sermons, her missal in her mittened hand, and the sense of calm in the dim church with the altar candles lit and the quiet voice of the pastor intoning the Latin and the altar boys responding.

And she remembered the moment of the elevation and consecration of the host, marked by the delicate chiming of bells rung by a server, and the bowing of the congregation in adoration of the high white circle. And this moment of devotion had had nothing to do with the sermon, with what had been preached to her, with the dictatorial will of the Church imposed on her.

She looked at Rachel during the elevation, which Rachel stared at.

Oh God, Claire thought, her feelings swaying in her as if keening.

She didn't know what to think, she simply didn't know what to think.

All, all she cared about was the happiness of Rachel, of her beloved daughter, and she prayed:

Give her back her virginity.

Blue-gray clouds of incense filled the nave, and Claire felt ill with the feverish vividness of the smell. She felt ill with the feverish vividness of everything she saw and heard, too.

Following Rachel, who followed Sir Roger, Claire wasn't sure she wasn't swaying from side to side as they left the church to go into the piazza, where the congregation gathered. In the midst, Sir Roger stood still, Claire and Rachel on either side of him, as if the ceremony weren't quite over and he were waiting for something to happen before they could go. People came to him and spoke to him and sometimes shook his hand as well, and he, grunting a little, inclined his head in recognition of their greetings. He didn't introduce any of these people to Claire and Rachel. It was only when an elderly woman with a black veil over her white hair came toward him that he raised his arms to embrace her, and then the young woman, her long hair uncovered, with her, and he introduced them to Claire and Rachel: the Contessa Bonpianti and her niece Francesca.

Taking off her veil, the contessa said to Claire, "Now I do insist you come to me for coffee and doughnuts. Whenever I'm in America, I'm always invited after Mass for coffee and doughnuts, and I adore, simply adore, this habit. I'll never make it catch on in Florence, but whenever here I meet an American, as Roger has told me you are, I insist, I absolutely insist, on coffee and doughnuts at my home." She spoke in a loud voice, forming each word with her entire mouth, emitting from time to time a fine spittle. She smiled at Claire.

"Of course we'd love to," Claire said, "but Sir Roger —"

The contessa raised her hands. "Roger has no choice."

Sir Roger laughed.

"You will come, won't you?" the contessa asked Rachel. "Francesca would love it if you would."

Francesca swung her hair and said to Rachel, "It'd be great if you came."

Rachel smiled. The two were about the same age.

On the way, by foot, the contessa said enthusiastically to Sir Roger, "Did you remark the singing of the Gradual? The music was pre-Gregorian, wasn't it?"

"You know, I think it was," Sir Roger said. "I do think it was."

"Anyway," the contessa said, "terribly, terribly old. It might even have been Roman."

"It might well have been," Sir Roger said.

The drawing room of the contessa's apartment was oval, with a wide window on one side, a wide double door on the opposite side, and single doors at either end, and on the curving walls among the window and doors were four symmetrical frescoes, within elaborate trompe l'oeil frames, of the four seasons in country landscapes. The concave ceiling was painted blue, with pink-tinged clouds. There were no rugs on the highly polished parquet floor.

A woman wearing a blue smock over a flower-patterned dress and heel-less mules came in carrying a tray of coffee and a plate of doughnuts, and the contessa cleared a space on a table for her to put it down. The maid went out with the tray.

"Imagine," the contessa said, "it is now possible to get honey-glazed and chocolate-coated doughnuts in Florence. The old city is finally becoming civilized."

Claire laughed and said she wasn't sure they were available in London. Of course they were, Rachel said.

"Ah," the contessa said, "you live in London. That's why you have English accents. I was worried for a moment that Roger had misinformed me and you were in fact English, and I should have had crumpets, if the English still have crumpets."

"Never," Sir Roger said, "in the summer."

"There, you see how one's always getting things wrong in cultures one presumes to know?" the contessa said.

"I know about that," Claire said.

"Rachel, my dear," the contessa asked, passing around cups of coffee, "do you have a boyfriend? In America, young women are always asked if they have boyfriends."

Rachel frowned for a moment, and Claire, with a slight twinge, wondered if she would remain silent, but she said, "I live in London."

"I keep forgetting," the contessa said.

Rachel said, smiling, "And in London one has doggies and kitties and girlfriends desperate to have boyfriends."

Everyone laughed, especially Claire, who was surprised by the little flash of irony, which she'd never remarked in Rachel before. She thought: Rachel *is* capable of being different.

"You see," the contessa said to Francesca. To the others she said, "She's so influenced by America, where she thinks everyone has a boyfriend, she feels something is wrong with her for not having one." Again the contessa said to Francesca, "Perhaps you should go and live in London for a while."

Francesca said longingly, "I'd love to live in London."

"A dark and menacing city," Sir Roger said. "I don't like it at all."

The contessa said, "You will all help yourselves to the doughnuts, please."

They did, and they all sat, and there was a momentary lull, and the contessa said, as if she had just remembered something she had been wanting to say, "Roger, you haven't asked me about my trip to Moscow."

"Haven't I?" he asked. "I'm pretty sure I did, you know."

"Did you really?"

Claire wondered if this was her way of introducing a subject, and she said, "Well, I'd like to ask you about your trip."

"Aren't you kind to be interested," the contessa said to her. "What would you most like to ask me about?"

"What most struck you."

"What most struck us? I went with Francesca, so you must include her. Francesca, what most struck us?"

"How very dented, rusted, cracked, broken down everything appeared."

"That's it," the contessa said. "We were shocked at how bad a state communism has left the country in. My old friends who believed all their lives in communism are in despair, you know, despair, and don't want to know about what is happening in Russia. Well, you can't blame them." She said to Sir Roger, "Like Claudio. I can't tell you what Claudio feels about the fall of communism in Russia after having devoted his life to communism. He tells me he thinks the only way for him now is suicide."

"Claudio will not commit suicide," Sir Roger said.

"My personal opinion is that the Russian Church will give back to the country the vision it was not allowed under communism," the contessa said.

"You say that," Francesca said, swinging her hair, "only because you wish the whole world were under the Church."

"I didn't say Russia should be under the Catholic Church," the contessa said. "Not at all. Though that is what the Russian Orthodox Church thinks the Vatican has in mind. Well, I could tell them, not at all. However, it is true there are a great, a very great number of Catholics in Russia who feel the Vatican should have more power to represent them in their country."

"I don't know what's worse," Francesca said, "a country under the dominating power of the Church or the state."

To Claire's surprise, Rachel said, "I honestly think the only way is anarchism."

Claire thought: Anarchism? What does Rachel know about anarchism?

Francesca said to Rachel, in a soft, almost lazy voice, leaning so far toward Rachel that her hair fell to the side, "You are right."

The contessa said, "You two girls go discuss your anarchism somewhere else, please. Francesca, take Rachel up to the *altana* for the view of the city. Go on."

The two girls left the room, and Claire thought Rachel's friendship with Sir Roger might be the most important relationship in her life so far, more important even than her relationship with her mother, because not only was Sir Roger helping her himself, he was introducing her to a world that would help her. And Claire was pleased to see how well Rachel acted in this world, a world that, Claire knew, made you feel you were at its center while you were in it but that closed around itself, in its embassy receptions and weddings and memorial services and special openings of museum exhibitions, once you were shown out of it. But Rachel, she felt, would be kept at the center by Sir Roger. She began to wonder if Rachel, once she had the baby, should move to Florence, if both daughter and mother should move to Florence, and in Florence Rachel, if not her mother, would begin a new life, one Sir Roger would keep round and full about her.

The contessa said about Rachel, "She is divine."

Claire said quietly, "Thank you," and then, as if gently to secure Rachel's place in the contessa's world, she said, "She and Francesca seem to have the same radical views. I hadn't known Rachel was so radical."

The contessa made a gesture. "All young people are anarchists now. They don't know what anarchism means. All they think is that it does without visions, which they are convinced are bad. Well, we know different, don't we?"

Do we? Claire wondered. She thought she should change the subject, and asked, "Do you know anyone in Moscow?" Immediately, she asked herself if Sir Roger would suspect her of trying to find out if the contessa knew anyone there who might know the whereabouts of the Pietro Testa Annunciation, and she covered herself by adding, "I'm told the people are wonderful." In fact, she had been thinking of the painting somewhere in dented, rusted, cracked, broken-down Moscow.

The contessa said, "I only really know an Italian Jesuit or two who now live there and whom I went to speak to. But yes, the Russians I met were wonderful. It is true that they have souls." She seemed to think Sir Roger was being left out of the conversation, and she more or less shouted out to him, "Do the English have souls, Roger?"

"None at all," Sir Roger answered.

"Do the Americans?" the contessa asked Claire.

"You know," she answered, "I feel they do."

Then Sir Roger asked the contessa questions that had to do, Claire surmised, with activities of the Catholic Church in Russia, about which the Contessa Bonpianti knew a lot. She sat on the edge of her chair, sideways, her knees bent and her narrow legs together, one hand, palm turned outward, on her narrow bosom, the other on her lap.

She apparently thought Claire was being left out of the conversation and, turning to her from Sir Roger, asked her, "Tell me, my dear, what church do you go to in London?"

A blush rose up Claire's neck. The contessa assumed she was a practicing Catholic. Sir Roger probably assumed she was a practicing Catholic. Turning her head a little from side to side, as if something were constricting it, Claire felt the blush rise up into her cheeks. And then she said, "I don't go to church."

The contessa lowered her eyes. "I see," she said.

Claire's blush seemed to expand out from her face into the air, so she felt the heat of it around her. She said, "I was born a Catholic, but I'm not one any longer."

She heard the voices of the girls in another room.

Laughing, she said, "I haven't been a Catholic since I was a college student, and thought better of it."

His elbows on the arms of his chair, Sir Roger asked her, "You're lapsed?" There was a slight tone of pleading in his voice that she might say she was, because to be lapsed wasn't to be lost.

"I'm an atheist," Claire said. "I didn't have Rachel baptized."

Claire looked, with overvividness, at a fly flying, with an overvivid drone, around the room, and it seemed to her the fly meant something, but she couldn't think what. She felt her fever break in perspiration on her forehead.

The girls came into the drawing room, and Sir Roger stood.

He said, "Well, I think I should be on my way back to Lucca," as if he had come to Florence on his own and was returning to Lucca on his own.

Claire had suddenly destroyed everything — had destroyed it not for herself, because she didn't care about it, but for Rachel, who was standing before the fresco of a landscape in summertime, the foreground a stream with reeds growing along it and in the distance a hill with cypresses and the sun bright in a pale blue sky. Standing too, Claire drew her shoulders back and clasped her hands at her waist and raised her head and said to Rachel, "Come, darling, we're taking Sir Roger back to Lucca now."

Francesca said, "I was hoping Rachel might stay."

"I'm afraid she can't," Claire said. "Sir Roger would like to get back to the Villa Fabiano."

Sir Roger didn't say that Rachel needn't go back, and the contessa didn't invite her to stay.

The silence in the car was all the evidence Rachel needed that something had gone wrong. Claire had to drive with great concentration, because it seemed to her for a moment that when she accelerated, the car went backward.

Sir Roger was polite when they got to the villa, and insisted they come in for what he said would be a simple lunch of ham and salad, which he prepared. Claire would have preferred to go back to the hotel and to bed. Henrietta joined them, and as no one was allowed to talk while they ate, there was no need to try. Sir Roger also insisted that Claire and Rachel go out to the loggia in the garden for coffee, and here he told them a story about a woman who ate — he said "et" — her husband. Rachel laughed, but Claire could tell she laughed uncertainly, not sure why Sir Roger seemed to be telling his story to no one. He also insisted on having a taxi come to collect Claire and Rachel and return them to Lucca, and he stood at the gateway as the taxi left, raising his hand as if giving a vague benediction.

Claire really had no more idea what had happened than Rachel.

She didn't tell Rachel she wasn't feeling well, and she didn't mention Sir Roger as they walked around the walls in the afternoon. For a while they walked behind a young woman pushing a baby asleep in a stroller, then, when Claire noticed that Rachel was staring at them, she hurried, and, Rachel following her, they passed and went on ahead. But there were other babies being wheeled in strollers, and there were many older children running around or clinging to the ambulant legs of adults.

During the night, Claire's fever broke out in a sweat all over her naked body, then went, and she woke up feeling light, though still disoriented. Though she felt better, she thought there was no longer a reason to stay in Lucca. But she told herself Italy was the place to see things, the place that offered up itself in images, and she took Rachel to see the big villas in the hills. Rachel was attentive to what Claire pointed out to her, but behind her outward attention was the inward sense that something had gone wrong and that whatever had gone wrong had occurred in that brief time in Florence while she was out of the drawing room with Francesca. Claire kept telling herself she must let Rachel know that whatever had gone wrong hadn't had to do with her, in case this idea came to her as a possibility — and especially hadn't had to do with anything her mother might have said about her. But Claire was reluctant to say that what had gone wrong had had to do with herself, with Claire, maybe because she couldn't understand how her saying she was a nonbeliever could have changed Sir Roger's view of her.

She kept hoping that Sir Roger, or Henrietta for him, would telephone the hotel. There really wasn't any reason why he wouldn't get in touch with them again. Only three days had passed since Florence. He wouldn't, in any case, be in touch before that, even before a week. She saw, however, that the more days that passed, the more Rachel suspected that Sir Roger wouldn't get in touch because of some occurrence unknown to her. But Rachel didn't give in to her suspicions, not entirely — she waited, and in the meantime she went along with her mother on excursions to Bagni di Lucca, to Barga, to Carrara. She slept later and later in the mornings.

A few days before they were to leave, Claire, descending the steps to the lobby of the hotel on her way for a morning walk about Lucca while Rachel slept, found Henrietta at the reception desk writing a note.

Henrietta appeared a little embarrassed. She laughed, her crooked teeth showing, and held up a sheet of notepaper, and said, "I was just leaving you a message."

"Are you in such a hurry?" Claire asked. "Can't we go for a coffee?"

More embarrassed, Henrietta said, "What a lovely idea."

In the café with the white piano, on which was no longer a bouquet of flowers but a stuffed toy bear in white and blue, the two women sat at the same table as before.

Henrietta asked about Rachel.

"I had hoped —" Claire began, and raised her hands but, dropping her hands, stopped.

"I am sorry things didn't work out with my uncle," Henrietta said.

Bluntly, Claire asked, "What happened?"

"Oh, he's so peculiar —"

"What did happen?"

"You mustn't take offense. If I took offense at everything peculiar he says to me, I'd be like one of his dogs cowering before him. And there's no knowing what offends him."

"Was it my telling him I'm a nonbeliever?"

"He wouldn't have minded that. He's perfectly aware that if he refused to see nonbelievers, he wouldn't see most other art historians, though I'm not sure he'd mind that, as he's not particularly interested in other art historians. He thinks their attitudes to art are all wrong."

"I don't understand, then. What did I do that was wrong?"

"What he took offense at was your going to Mass as a nonbeliever."

"Oh," Claire said.

She understood this, she felt. She understood the offense.

"But if he doesn't want to see me, why not Rachel? I thought he liked her."

"He's such a peculiar person."

"You don't think he'd even consent to talking to her over the telephone, saying he's been terribly busy, that kind of thing, but he wishes her —" She didn't know what she wanted him to wish Rachel.

Henrietta took a torn-off bit of paper from her purse and handed it to Claire. "He wanted you to have the name and address of Maurice Kuragin in London, and told me to tell you that you can use his name when you write. He didn't give the telephone number, as he thinks one shouldn't ring up someone one doesn't know with requests. But you can write."

Claire took the piece of paper. She asked, "Did he say why, particularly, he disapproved of my going to Mass as a nonbeliever?"

"He said he couldn't understand any reason for going except as a believer. He really disapproves of people going for what they call aesthetic reasons. He hates anyone doing anything, even looking at pictures, for aesthetic reasons. Just between us, I think my uncle hates beauty and can't see it as a reason for appreciating anything, from religious rituals to ladies' hats."

"He suspected I went for purely aesthetic reasons?"

Henrietta stuck out her chin.

"He might have thought for a moment," Claire said, "that I went simply as his chauffeur."

"He told me to tell you he sends all wishes in your quest for the painting."

Claire put the bit of paper, crumpled, into her purse. "And he had nothing to tell Rachel?"

"Of course he did. He wishes Rachel great happiness."

"I'll tell her."

Lowered, Claire went to her hotel room to lie on her bed.

In her soul, she understood Roger Leclerc's disapproval of her. He's right about me, she thought; he's right.

But about Rachel — did he believe that Rachel, unbaptized, could not be saved?

When Rachel, coming into her room, woke her, Claire felt more lowered than when she'd lain down, and she wondered if she had the strength to move. She thought: I'm still not well. Rachel didn't seem to be surprised to have found her mother asleep, though it was almost noon. She sat on the bed. She too looked as if she didn't have much strength. Her heavy lids were half shut.

With a hoarse voice, Claire said, "I saw Henrietta this morning."

Rachel's eyes opened.

Claire stretched and yawned, and she hoped this conveyed to Rachel that whatever she had suspected had happened with Roger Leclerc, it was revealed by Henrietta to be of no real importance. She said, "Sir Roger has been terribly busy."

Rachel blinked.

"Too busy, he's sorry to say, to see us before we leave. But he wanted to make sure we had the name of the man in London who might be able to help us find the picture in Moscow. He's keen that we should go on looking for it."

Rachel, blinking a lot, waited.

"Also," Claire said, "he sends many wishes to you."

"Yes?"

"And prays for your happiness."

Looking down, Rachel seemed to think. She wasn't convinced, Claire knew, but she would not have been convinced by anything her mother said. She was never, ever really convinced by anything her mother said to her.

With an effort, Claire sat up and shook her head. "Shall we go out?" she asked.

"Where?" Rachel asked dully.

"There are many things we haven't seen."

"Are there?"

"I thought you were interested in looking."

"Oh," Rachel said loosely.

Claire herself couldn't think of anything to see. "We could walk around the walls."

"If you'd like."

"No, if you'd —" Claire started, and realized they were back to where they had been once, it seemed to her a long time before, when they'd contended with each other to get the other to say what she wanted. Claire said, as if finally she were thinking first of what she wanted and she intended Rachel to know this, "As a matter of fact, I want to walk around the walls." She didn't really, but they had to do something. Claire would panic if they did nothing.

The day was misty, and from the walls the mist was seen to swirl about the city. The trees, and people walking along the walls, appeared and disappeared in it, sometimes in aureoles of pale sunlight that penetrated the mist.

She asked Rachel if she'd like a sandwich in a café. Neither was hungry. They didn't talk as they ate their sandwiches.

Everyone at the other tables, the young, sleek, groomed Italians, were talking and laughing. A girl shouted something in Italian at a boy and hit him over the head with a rolled-up magazine, and he grasped the magazine, opened it, and pointed to a photograph of an old fat woman and evidently said the girl looked just like her, and they laughed. They were no doubt in love. The other young people at their table all talked at the same time.

On the way back to the hotel, about five o'clock, Claire saw that the doors of a church they hadn't been into were open, and she asked Rachel if she'd like to go in, and this time Rachel, instead of saying, "If you want," said, "No, I don't want to." They went back to their rooms to lie on their beds.

After the room got dark, Claire thought she must not go on lying on the bed. She must go to Rachel. She knocked on Rachel's door and opened, and saw her daughter, in the darkness, standing by the bed and holding her stomach with both hands, and it seemed to Claire that she was standing and holding her pregnant stomach in universal darkness.

Part

FOUR

I

CLAUDE RICARD went to Long Island to talk to an author whose book had been assigned to him to edit, but the author was too drunk to make sense and Claude left him early. The train he took to return to Manhattan was not a through train, and he had to change at Jamaica. From the platform, while he waited for his connection, he saw, over a fence made of corrugated sheets of iron, piles of wrecked cars, their windshields smashed with holes that glinted about the edges.

Every single thing Claude saw, as if it glared painfully, made him look beyond it.

The train passed a cement wall covered with aerosol graffiti, and above the wall appeared the buildings of Manhattan in heat mist.

On Eighth Avenue, a white man was lying face up on the sidewalk, his nose bleeding so the blood flowed down his cheek. Pedestrians walked past him. Staring beyond him, Claude walked past him too.

When he got back to the office, the editor in chief called him in to offer him the possibility of spending six months in London. The job there was an exchange with a young editor from a similar, English publishing house who would come to New York. London, Claude thought, was the last place he wanted to go to.

In his apartment, he absent-mindedly flipped through old copies of art magazines he kept piled under the coffee table in his living room, wondering whether he should accept the job in London or not, and he stopped at a photograph of a naked man lying on a bare wooden floor, his head and hands thickly wrapped in white bandages, and placed here and there on his flesh — at the base of his throat, near a nipple, below his navel, on the groin, on a thigh just where the glans of his penis rested — were razor blades. Claude threw the magazine down. He didn't want to go to England. It would have been, it just would have been, London he was asked to go to.

He told his boss he'd go.

Duncan and his wife Susan, who knew London and had friends there and were pleased by Claude's decision to go, not only gave him names and telephone numbers but arranged for him to have a friend's flat that would be empty while he was there.

The strangest thing, which he wouldn't admit to anyone, was that the real reason he had for going was the possibility of meeting Penelope.

He arrived in London at dawn, and from the window of the taxi saw the windows of three- and four-storey terrace houses blazing with light, and sometimes saw right through houses out the back windows into gardens with trees. London appeared to him to be without shadows, transparent, and as there were no skyscrapers, the sky above the low, flat roofs rose high, high, cloudless and transparent itself.

The flat he was to stay in overlooked Primrose Hill, and while standing with the driver on the sidewalk to pay his fare, he glanced past the driver making change and down the green hill with blossoming cherry trees lining a pathway, then up at the pale blue sky. A woman was pushing a baby in a stroller along the pathway. The driver had to say, "Here's your change, mate," to get Claude's attention, and held out bills and coins to him. Claude gave him a five-pound note as a tip. It seemed to him he was able to see to far distances but couldn't see what was up close. It took him a while to find the number of the house, with white pillars supporting a porch and a wide black door with a brass number and brass knob. He rang the bell he'd been instructed by Duncan and Susan to ring, and an English woman's voice told him over the intercom to come up and the door clicked open. He had a curious sense of being lifted as he climbed the stairs with his suitcase and briefcase. The stairs were wide, and carpeted in blue. The light through the wide, dusty windows filled the landings, and Claude paused by the windows to look out at the garden at the back and, at the front, a higher and higher view over Primrose Hill. On the third landing, a door was open, and standing by it, made a little dim by the light beaming behind her, was a woman who said in a soft voice, "I was expecting you."

When inside, she showed Claude the flat, told him she'd stocked the fridge with a few staples, and handed him the key. He didn't know who she was, and she left, saying she suspected he'd want to sleep after his trip, without giving her name.

He did go to sleep in the double bed with ironed sheets, and he woke up in a greater blaze of sunlight than when he'd fallen asleep.

Outside, on Primrose Hill, people were lying on the bright green grass.

Naked as he was, he started to telephone people whose names and numbers Duncan and Susan had given him, and was invited for that evening to the opening of a show of paintings in a gallery by a couple called Robin and Hilary.

The possibility of meeting Penelope at the opening excited him enough to make him shower and shave carefully, and to dress, in the careful way that was his style, to quietly impress — wearing, as the one loud accent that belied the quiet style, a tie patterned with red lips. His socks were black.

Robin had said over the telephone that Claude would recognize him because he had red hair and wore spectacles with blue frames.

The sun was still high when, at six o'clock, Claude went out and hailed a taxi to take him into Mayfair to a Cork Street gallery, and on the way he tried to register, as if against a background of light, the details, for details were, for a reason he didn't understand except as an impulse to see everything, important to him: cream-white gateposts with cream-white balls on them, pediments of neoclassical buildings showing over walls, black iron picket fences running along the bushes of a park, a glimpse of a pond beyond trees and ducks and swans, then coming out of the park and turning into a wide street with black taxis and cars and red buses coming in the wrong direction because, to Claude, on the wrong side of the street. He had no idea where he was, and he liked not knowing, because that in itself gave him a sense of possibility.

Cork Street was where most of the big art galleries were, as, just one street up, Savile Row was where most of the famous tailors were. At half past six, all the galleries except the one with a private opening were shut, and so were the shops among the galleries, and the only people in the straight, narrow street, were, at sharp angles to their long shadows, going to the opening. Claude felt he was going to a party in a private house, and at the glass door, through which he saw, inside, people standing about with glasses of wine, he wondered if when he went in someone might come to him and ask who he was. He wasn't sure of his tie.

He went on past the gallery and stopped before the window of an antique shop in which were a marble head with a chipped nose, a pile of large, flat, polished stone rings, and mottled conch shells on which cameo profiles were carved.

Then he thought, why should he, with whatever tie he might be wearing, hesitate to go into a gallery where he knew no one? Knowing no one, which meant getting to know someone, was what always excited him enough to get over any shyness.

Inside the severely spacious white gallery, with large, square, unframed paintings on the walls that were all in black and white — shiny black poured in long drips on matte black, white and gray poured on black, black poured on gray — Claude looked around for a man with red hair and glasses with blue frames, and he saw him standing with two women before a painting. The painting they were standing before was not square but a long rectangle, and white with long, undulating lines of black paint as if flicked across it, some of the flicks almost as long as the painting. One of the women was blond and wearing a yellow T-shirt and yellow skirt, and the other, who was dark-haired, was wearing green tights and a long, orange, loosely knitted pullover that reached down to her thighs and had long sleeves that reached to her fingertips, and what looked like a workman's heavy black shoes. As Claude approached them, they were looking off in different directions but, it seemed, not at anything, as if they'd paused in their conversation to think about what they'd been saying to one another.

He said to the man with the red hair and blue-framed glasses, who must have been Robin, "Hi, I'm Claude."

"Oh, hullo," Robin said. He didn't introduce him to the women but said, "Let me get you a drink," and, as though he was thinking of something that filled his mind, took Claude to a table covered with a white cloth and on which were rows of stemmed glasses of red and white wine and tumblers of orange juice and chromium salvers of cocktail sausages, *crudités* and dip, little vol-au-vents filled with pâté. With glass of wine in hand, Claude was taken by Robin, who, still thinking, hadn't said anything to him, back to the two women. Again Claude wasn't introduced.

Robin said, looking at his watch, "I wonder if I should go to the hospital."

"I don't think they'd let you in to see him," the woman in yellow said. "It's way past visiting hours."

The woman in the orange pullover and green tights and man's black shoes, who was in her twenties and maybe too young to be called a woman, bit the side of her thumb, then said, "I'd like to know how he is, though."

"How can we find out except by going to the hospital?" Robin said.

The woman in yellow sighed and said, "Isn't it just like Gavin?"

"Come along, Hilary," the young woman in orange and green said, "you can't blame Gavin."

So the woman in yellow — who, in her early forties, could be called a woman, and had to have been the wife of Robin, who also appeared to be in his forties — was named Hilary. She said to the young woman in orange and green, "I am not, Judy, blaming Gavin, but saying it's just the kind of thing that happens to him. It's not as if he intended it."

So the young woman in orange and green was Judy.

Claude asked, "Who's Gavin?"

The three glanced at him, then away, as though he didn't mean his question to be answered. If he really didn't know who Gavin was, what was he doing with them in the gallery? Robin and Hilary left him with Judy.

She gathered the ends of her sleeves into her hands so they became like large soft orange paws and brought them to her mouth. The pullover, stretched so the knit was so open in places her pale skin showed through, hung so loosely on her it kept shifting around with her movements, the wide neck sometimes on one side and revealing a clavicle, sometimes on the other side and revealing the top of a breast. She looked at Claude over her two covered hands. Her face was pale, but her eyes were outlined heavily in black. He smiled at her, but she simply wrinkled, a little, her nose.

Judy asked, "Can I get you another glass of wine?"

He gave her his empty glass and she left him, and he, turning to face the picture, thought she wouldn't return, thought he'd been left on his own by everyone, and a small sense of defeat came to him, as if he'd tried his best but had been found wanting. He wondered in what way Judy was like Penelope. If she was like Penelope, she wouldn't come back, and he would find himself, though there were any number of other people to meet, looking for her. She did come back, gave him a glass of wine, wrinkled her nose at him, said, "I like your tie," and went off. He put his hand over his tie.

He left and, back in his flat, though the sky was still bright with the afterglow of the sunset, went to bed.

How could he have been even a little excited about coming to London and meeting Penelope?

In the morning, Claude, in a jacket and red-and-navy-striped tie, went to the publishing house in Bloomsbury where he was to work for six months. The junior editor, a short, plump young man with a mustache and spectacles who was to leave the next day to take Claude's place as junior editor in New York to find out about American publishing, showed him around the offices and introduced him to people.

The sales director, a bald man who wore a suit and tie, said he was inviting these two junior editors and the managing editor, a man with lots of hair who wore corduroys and an open-neck shirt, to lunch at his club. The managing editor grumbled about having to wear a tie.

In the club bar, a high, wood-paneled room where they sat on leatherette banquettes in a corner with a view into a courtyard of a vine growing on a trellis against a wall, Claude listened to his new colleagues talk about people he had never heard of and who weren't explained to him, but he laughed when his colleagues laughed.

Listening from time to time to the conversations of other men in the bar, Claude was surprised and amused to hear expressions he'd thought only parody Englishmen used, such as "I say" or "bloody" or even "crumbs."

The sales director said they should go upstairs to eat. Their table was among others on a wide landing to a double staircase, and the rococo walls were painted pale blue, the decorations silvered, and there was a large chandelier hanging high over their heads. The different planes that made up the table surface were highly polished and uneven, so the plates, served on placemats printed with scenes of old London, tilted a little. All the diners were men, and Claude wondered when he had last been in a place where there had been only men. Maybe a toilet.

The talk was about other people Claude knew nothing about. For coffee, they went down the stairs, where, while the sales director poured out cups from a glass pot kept on a hot plate, Claude looked through the window of a door into a room where he saw a billiard table. No one was in the room. With coffee, the talk was about still more people Claude didn't know.

They were standing together, and Claude saw pass them an old man he thought he recognized from photographs, though older than he appeared in the photographs. He was a writer Claude had imagined didn't quite live in the real world but only in the photographs of him in journals. He was very old. Passing Claude and his colleagues, he paused and looked at his watch and asked, "What time is it?" and the sales director, who as the member of the club took on the duty, said, "Two-thirty," and without any exchange of "thanks" or "you're welcome" — which last Claude learned was not an English expression — the old writer remained where he was, looking at his watch, frowning and blinking. Claude checked his watch, which he knew, as he had set it to the right time the day before, was accurate, and which indicated two-twenty, and he supposed that among the English not the accurate but the approximate was what mattered. No one paid any attention to the old writer, and perhaps the old writer didn't expect any attention in his club. The only reference to him might have been the managing director and the sales director's telling the two junior editors funny anecdotes about authors, and the old writer shambled on.

On the way back to the publishing house in a taxi, Claude realized that nothing about his work had been explained to him at lunch, and at his desk — which was in someone else's office and which he was told was "temporary" until an office was found for him, as the office of the junior editor whom he was replacing was being taken over, in some complicated way, by someone else — Claude realized that nothing would be explained to him, but he must discover for himself even where the toilet was.

No one came to say goodnight to him, and by the time he left the publishing house all the other offices were empty, the late sunlight shining on piles of typescripts and books, and there was no one to say goodnight to.

Alone, Claude wandered about the narrow streets of Soho. He went into a square with a small, lopsided lodge of beams and plaster at its center, and sat on a bench. On the bench next to him were three people, a woman between two men, and they, motionless, were staring out. The long light in the square was filled with dust particles, and shadows were cast through it.

He would not meet Penelope, Claude thought. But he had the feeling that he would meet Marie, as if they were together in the same city, and he knew she would appear across a street as he was walking along it.

The next day Claude went out to a sandwich bar for lunch with three secretaries, one of whom was meant to be his. They were girls, Cambridge and Oxford graduates, and they were pretty. They told him the in-house gossip.

In the afternoon, the managing editor put his head through the door of the office where Claude still had his temporary desk and told him there was to be a book-launching party that evening, if he cared to go, and gave him the name and address of the person who was to give it. The managing editor said, "I won't be going, but I dare say you'll meet someone you can talk to."

II

THE PARTY was given by an expatriate American who had lived in London for almost fifty years, and who, rich, sometimes hosted publication parties for authors he knew. His name was Peter Matthews, and he lived in a large Edwardian mansion block in South Kensington, which was, Claude had already learned, a nice place in London to live. And Claude took what he thought of as the lift. It was lined with mirrors and carpeted in red, and the door to it closed behind Claude as soon as he stepped out of it.

The door to the flat was open and a tall, thin man inside was holding the leash of a dog that was outside on the landing and straining against the leash, its tongue lolling. On the bottom panel of the door was a large sheet of metal screwed to the wood. The tall, thin man, whom Claude assumed to be Peter Matthews, said with a thrill, even before Claude could introduce himself, that just that morning, while he was out for ten minutes, some burglars had cut a hole in the door big enough for one of them to squeeze through and had stolen all his silver. Peter Matthews spoke with an English accent and also, as the English seemed to do, addressed Claude as though he had always known him and was excited to tell him this news, which he was sure Claude would react to with amazement. But when Claude said, "How terrible," Peter said, "It doesn't matter, it honestly doesn't matter."

Claude introduced himself.

The door to the lift opened and Peter said to Claude, "Go on through, go on through," and turning away from him, said with a thrill to a man and woman who had just got out of the lift, "I was burgled," and the man and the woman said, together, "How dreadful." Peter said, "It isn't so bad really, not so bad." The dog pulled at him.

Claude went along a long, narrow passage, on the white walls of which were many small dark paintings in thick scrolled and gilded frames, and wall lights like candles in brackets, with yellowish shades and crystal prisms, the flamelike bulbs lit though the passage was bright with sunlight coming from ahead. Ahead was a wide, high-ceilinged drawing room with three French windows and fine white curtains over the windows through which the evening sunlight shone, and in the light, on oriental rugs spread about the parquet floor, stood small groups of people with drinks, and among them circulated a man in a starched white jacket and carrying a wooden tray.

Knowing no one, Claude went to stand by a group, but he thought he must be invisible to them. Other people came in, none of them from the publishing house, and none of them looked at Claude.

The dog pulled Peter into the room, and as he passed the man serving drinks he said, as if in apology for the institutional-like tray, "The silver tray was stolen."

"How beastly," someone he was passing said.

"Not really. It doesn't matter."

"But it is beastly," someone else he was passing said.

"It doesn't matter, it doesn't matter." Peter never stood with anyone for longer than enough time to mention the burglary, hear a word or two of commiseration, and say it didn't matter. Then, his chin raised and his chest out, he was pulled by his dog to another part of the room, where there was no one, and he had to drag the dog back to where guests stood, only to be pulled away again.

Claude, with his drink, looked at pictures, then wandered into another, small room where an aged man with a lot of white hair was examining a large dark carved chest on corkscrew legs and with many small drawers. The man's face was pink, and he had blue eyes that appeared bright with the attention he was giving to the chest. He glanced at Claude and smiled, and he asked, "What do you think is in these drawers?"

Claude stood beside him and they both examined the chest. "I couldn't guess," Claude said.

With the laugh of a boy, the aged man said, "Shall I open one, just one, to see?"

Laughing too, but not quite in the boyish way the man did, Claude said, "Why not?"

"Which one?" the man asked.

Pointing to one, Claude said, "That."

Tiptoeing, his fine, frail fingers pressed together at the tips, except for the baby finger, which stuck out, the man approached the drawer and, grasping the handle, opened it very slowly, as if it might make a noise and reveal to everyone in the flat what he was doing. Though he was looking down on the drawer, he rose up higher on his toes to look into it and said, "Oh, look." Claude went to look. Inside the drawer was nothing but a tarnished silver napkin ring.

Excited, the man said to Claude in a high voice, "Peter will be pleased. He will, he will. We'll go show him what we've found." He took out the napkin ring.

"He won't be offended that we've been snooping in his furniture?" Claude asked.

This seemed not to have occurred to the man. "There is that," he said, and he thought.

Claude bit his lower lip, also thinking, or pretending to think. He liked this boyish aged man.

"We could always say to Peter the drawer was open and we just happened to glance in," the man said.

"After the burglary, he'd have checked everywhere, don't you think?" Claude wondered if he was already taking on an English accent.

"You think of everything, which is very clever of you."

Claude wasn't quite sure what that word *clever* meant. He said, "A person has to."

"No doubt you're right," the man said. "No doubt you're perfectly right. So how shall we let Peter know we've found a piece of silver the burglars overlooked?"

Again Claude bit his lower lip, pretending to think. He said, "We could say it must have been dropped by the burglar and we found it under a chair."

"You see how clever you are? That's just what we'll do." The man said, "Now, come along, we'll find him and tell him." Holding the napkin ring in the extended palm of his hand, excited, the man went out, with Claude right behind him. Claude followed him to where Peter was being pulled away from someone he was talking to by the dog, and before he was pulled away the aged man got to him with the ring and told him he'd found it under a chair, dropped — but he didn't have time to say more before Peter picked it up from his palm and said, "I can't recall ever having had this," and deposited it on a small, round, pie-crust table. Peter was pulled away, and Claude was left standing with the aged man.

"My name's Claude Ricard," he said.

The aged man said, "And my name's Maurice Kuragin."

"That doesn't sound English," Claude said.

Smiling, the man said, "Oh no, no, it's Russian."

"You're Russian?" Claude asked.

Maurice Kuragin asked, as if Claude's surprise meant he had something to do with Russia himself, "Why do you ask?"

"No reason really, except, I suppose, I'm always surprised to meet Russians."

"There are quite a lot of us."

"My mother was Russian," Claude said.

"Ah. What was her name?"

"Vetrov, Florence Vetrov."

"Vetrova," Maurice Kuragin said.

"She always said Vetrov."

"To make it simpler for Americans, no doubt. What was her patronymic?"

"She never used a patronymic."

"What was her father's name?"

"Peter."

"Then her patronymic would have been Petrovna."

"Yes," Claude said.

Making a face, Maurice tried to remember. "It seems to me I remember the name Vetrov. Was it a Moscow family?"

"I'm not quite sure."

"Your mother didn't tell you."

"She was born in America."

"I see."

"Were you born in Russia?"

"Before the Revolution, if you can believe it. I was born before the Revolution. And sometimes I think I can remember it, something of it."

"How old were you when you left?"

"I was born in 1915 and we left in 1917, but there are moments when I think I remember something. I'm sure I remember a crowded train station, and many people forced to leave the country trying to get on an already crowded train."

"And you've never been back?"

"Some are going back now, you know, after everything the Revolution tried to do has failed. I heard a story of a man who went back to the village where his family had had an estate. The estate had been turned into an orphange. In the village he asked if any of his relatives were alive there, and when the villagers found out who he was they came out with their icons, icons they had kept hidden for some seventy-five years, and presented them to him. Of course he didn't take them, he would have been a rogue if he had, but they said the icons belonged to him. And the estate." Maurice shrugged. "Well, that was a story I was told."

"Did your family have an estate?" Claude asked.

"Oh yes, yes," Maurice Kuragin said, and made a gesture as if indicating something long, long past. "And I had relatives in Moscow. And maybe I should find out if I still do. You know, since *perestroika* many Russians have been looking for their relatives in Russia, and many have found them."

"I can't imagine having relatives anywhere in Russia," Claude said.

Some people from the publishing house arrived and came to Claude. They all knew Maurice Kuragin. Claude didn't want to leave the aged man, and stayed with him even when his colleagues drifted away. Maurice was enthusiastic about everything, as if he knew nothing and everything he heard, about traffic, the weather, the cost of a bottle of whiskey, struck him as amazing. He was interested in everything Claude had to say about New York and America, and he asked questions earnestly, like "Have you ever met any red Indians?" or "Is it true that George Washington had wooden false teeth?" or "What is the feeling going up so high in a skyscraper in a lift?" as if there were no skyscrapers in Europe. Everyone at the party came up to him and said hello, and Claude saw that he was very much loved by everyone, and thought how honored he, Claude, was that the aged man should want to spend all his time at the party with him.

But thinking he should, Claude went to speak with a group of colleagues from the publishing house when he saw them gather in a corner. They were talking about the huge advance another publisher had paid for a book, which the book couldn't possibly earn back.

Claude said, "The fact is, we hope it doesn't make the advance back just to show them up," and laughed. He would never become a brilliant publisher because he wasn't interested in such issues as advances, sales figures, or any kind of figures, but he would always be kept on as an editor because he was basically interested in good books.

He was pleased when he saw Maurice Kuragin just outside the little group, as if shy about breaking into it but making a sign with a raised finger to get Claude's attention. Claude went to him and asked, as he knew an American would, "What can I do for you?"

Maurice Kuragin laughed. "What can you do for me? I don't know. I wanted to ask you if you'd like to come to supper at my home. I'd be very pleased if you would."

Claude's first impulse was to say he couldn't, he was sorry. He didn't know why Maurice was inviting him, and he suspected the old man might be drawn to him in such a way that it would be better if Claude weren't alone with him. But then he saw that the old man would be disappointed, because in whatever way he was attracted to Claude, he did take delight in him, an attractive young man, and Claude thought he just couldn't disappoint him. He was from New York, and would be able to deal with anything that happened. He smiled and said, "Sure, I'd like to come."

"Now that's lovely, lovely," Maurice Kuragin said.

The fact was, the old man made him feel attractive and, more, made him feel he was amusing.

Excited, the elderly man seemed to have forgotten how to get back to his home. He asked Claude, "How shall we go?" Then, worried that he was pressing Claude too much, he said, "But I'm sorry, perhaps you don't want to go yet," and he stepped back. He had the blue eyes of a boy, and his white hair ended in points at his sideburns as if he didn't shave and in a point in the smooth groove at his nape like a boy's.

"I'd like to go now," Claude said. "And how we go depends on where you live."

"Yes, yes, of course. Where do I live? I live in Holland Park."

"Where's that?"

"Too far to walk, I'd say."

"Then I think we should take a taxi."

"What a good idea. I see you're filled with good ideas. We'll take a taxi. Buses can be damnable, you know, damnable."

It occurred to Claude that Maurice Kuragin mostly took a bus, and rarely a taxi, because he couldn't afford taxis often. And it also occurred to him, out in the street, that Maurice was leaving getting a taxi to him, as if he didn't quite know how to do that. When Claude raised his hand to hail one and it stopped, square and black and shining, before them, Maurice said to him, "You really are clever." Claude asked Maurice the address, which he then relayed to the driver, and he thought he would, in any relationship with the old man, have to do all the organizing.

In the taxi, the old man, his face faintly pink, said, "You'll have a very simple meal, I'm afraid. I dare say you are used to feasts, so I can only hope you'll accept my modest fare with *noblesse oblige*." He put a large pink hand flat against his chest, and said, as if confessing, "Really, I should be fasting, but that is not the reason why we will have a simple meal. Sinner that I am, I never keep the fast."

"What fast?"

"Don't you realize this is Holy Week? Today is Holy Thursday. You can't say you don't know the holy days of the Orthodox Church? You should be fasting too, when it comes to it."

"I didn't know."

"You weren't brought up Orthodox?"

"I wasn't brought up anything, really."

"Not even Christian?"

"We celebrated Christmas and went to my father's church, a Catholic church, on Easter, but we went to church only while my paternal grandmother was alive, and after she died no one went."

"And your mother never went to an Orthodox church?"

"Never, that I know of."

"Well, obviously you wouldn't know about Holy Week."

"I do now," Claude said. "Tell me what I should and shouldn't be eating."

"Meat, of course, you shouldn't eat. You shouldn't eat any meat or fats, or any dairy products, like milk and butter. But caviar is allowed. You can eat as much caviar as you like." He laughed, a bright laugh.

Maurice Kuragin insisted on paying for the taxi, and pushed Claude aside when Claude tried, with his money out, to get in front of the old man, but Maurice Kuragin carefully counted his change from a bill when the driver gave it to him and, squinting, took a long time choosing the coin he would give as a tip.

The flat, where he lived alone, was small, the overstuffed armchairs slightly soiled at the arms and where heads rested, the wallpaper yellowish and with what looked like burn marks of flames over the radiators. There was nothing Russian in it. This disappointed Claude, who realized only there that one of the reasons why he had wanted to come was to see in just what way Maurice Kuragin led a Russian life in London. Claude did not even see any Russian books on the bookshelves that covered one wall. In front of the books, on the dusty shelves, were many dusty rock specimens, an old collection. It did not look as though a book had been taken from a shelf in a very long time.

First thing, the old man poured out sherry, and handing the little stemmed glass to Claude, he looked him in the eyes and smiled with the delight of Claude's being with him. Maurice raised his glass to Claude, and Claude to the old man, but Claude didn't sip, and in the silence, for a moment, he felt that Maurice was about to put his other hand on his head. The old man simply smiled and sipped at his sherry, then Claude did too.

"Now I am going to leave you alone, I'm afraid, to disappear into the kitchen to prepare our simple but, alas, not fasting meal. No caviar. I hope you'll find something to amuse you. Please feel free to look at anything. Are you interested in rocks? I used to collect rocks. There are some interesting rocks in the collection along the shelves. Quite rare specimens, I might say. Quite rare."

"I'll look at your books," Claude said.

"Oh yes, the books," Maurice Kuragin exclaimed, but said nothing about them, and left Claude to go into the kitchen, from where Claude heard a pot clank against a burner. Claude took down a novel set in New York and read:

Clarence looked from his penthouse terrace out onto the city at night —

Claude put the book back and continued to look for books that were about Russia, and while he was doing this the doorbell rang. Maurice Kuragin came quickly to the entrance phone on the wall by the main door to the flat, in a little hall just outside the sitting room, and in a high voice said, "Lovely, lovely," and pressed the button to release the catch on the street door. So there would be another guest, perhaps more than one. Claude wondered if he weren't disappointed.

Maurice opened the door, went out to the landing, and waited for the guests, who came slowly up the stairs. The first of them was an old woman with a cane with a rubber ferrule at the tip and black shoes with tie-up laces and, though it was warm, a black overcoat, her white hair parted in the middle and wound in two braids over her ears, and as she entered the sitting room she stared at Claude as if with fury in her eyes. There were two other, not old but elderly women behind her, in cotton print dresses, who were talking to each other in Russian.

Maurice came around them and introduced Claude and the old

woman, Maria Polosova. He was happy, was always made happy by introducing anyone to another, simply because he believed all people loved one another, and he couldn't understand why they didn't, if they didn't. His eyes shone. Maria Polosova's eyes became darker in their apparent fury. Maurice Kuragin introduced the two women by only their first names, Ludmilla and Larissa; they were identical twins, and couldn't speak English. Maurice did not speak to them in Russian, but Maria Polosova did, in a commanding tone, and one of the elderly twins took from her shoulder bag a white handkerchief tied at the corners in a small bundle and, on Maria Polosova's command, gave it to Maurice. Maurice simply held the bundle, and said to Maria Polosova, indicating Claude with his free hand, "He is Russian."

The old woman, older than Maurice Kuragin, had an English accent that was too sharp-edged to have been learned in England. She asked, "Are you?"

Maurice Kuragin answered for him, half laughing, "His mother was a Vetrov."

Maria Polosova looked at Claude more closely and asked, "From Moscow?"

"Her father was from Moscow," Claude said, "or maybe her mother. I'm not sure."

Maria Polosova nodded. "She's dead?"

"Yes."

"And there are no more?"

"In New York I used to have a distant relative — cousin or aunt, I was never quite sure."

"What was her name?"

"Lidia Rivers."

Maurice Kuragin said, "That's not Russian."

"Maybe her maiden name was the same as my mother's," Claude said. "Vetrova."

"You don't by any chance know the Vetrov family?" Maurice Kuragin asked Maria Polosova.

She said to him, "You speak as if I'd spent a lifetime in Moscow before the Bolshevik Revolution, my dear." She looked at Claude just by turning her eyes to him. "All I can recall of Russia is leaving." She looked at Maurice, again just by turning her bulging eyes, and said, as if furious, "And I can't imagine you recall much more."

The old man laughed.

Maria Polosova asked Claude, "How many of the Vetrovs survived?" Many hairs hung loose from the coiled braids over her ears.

"Survived?" Claude asked.

Again Maria Polosova nodded, then, her head tilted, not only waited for a response but, blinking often, examined him. Her eyes appeared to bulge with fury.

He said, "My mother never talked to me about —" He stopped.

"About their suffering," Maria Polosova said starkly.

A blush of embarrassment rose up in Claude.

He said, "My mother was born in the United States."

Maria Polosova closed her eyes for a moment, as if to make a pain go still, then, opening her eyes, she said, "Of course, you're too young to have had a mother born in Russia."

He and Maria Polosova looked at each other, and he felt the startling impulse to say, "Ah."

"Did your mother speak Russian?" Maria Polosova asked him quietly.

"A little," he answered.

"And you?"

"None."

Maria Polosova hunched her shoulders a little, then let them drop. She said, "That is probably, for you, just as well." She did not wish Russia on anyone.

The twins went into the sitting room, talking between themselves, and sat.

Maria Polosova said to Maurice Kuragin, raising her cane to point to the bundle, "Open it."

He took the bulging handkerchief to a table below a tarnished, framed mirror and placed it beside a porcelain figure of a shepherd and shepherdess, dusty and chipped here and there, and untied the knot and drew back the handkerchief on three small cakes, round and tall, the rounded tops covered with powdered sugar. They looked as if they were for children. Maurice went back to Maria Polosova and kissed her, three times, and thanked her.

Though she evidently thought the whole business a bother, she was pleased, and she said, "I had the twins bake them today. The least they can do, in the West where they expect everything to be done for them, is do things I now find difficult. Sometimes I do wonder why I searched out any of my relatives in Russia. They were all Communists, and are spoilt and expect everything to be done for them as soon as they're in the West. They have no idea at all about life in the West. They had it easy as Communists. Now they have got to learn to work."

Maurice Kuragin always agreed with everything Maria Polosova said. There was nothing to be said but to agree. She went to sit with the twins, with whom she spoke, always as if commanding, in Russian, and Maurice went back into the kitchen.

Claude studied the cakes. He remembered his mother made them, and he remembered the name.

"Kulitch," he said to himself.

Kulitch was, perhaps, all he could recall of his mother's Russianness, and this Russianness had to do with her Church, which he knew so little about.

In the way Claude became aware of what he hadn't been aware of before, which was the way any moment might suddenly seem to detach itself and become, it seemed, the center of all his life, he became aware, in the miniature cakes, that he was probably more Russian than he had ever imagined. He was outside America, outside, specifically, New York, and being in London was like being in a bright nowhere. In this flat, with these people, he felt that he was somewhere, and over the evening, though nothing was said to remind him of anything his mother used to say, he felt he was among people who were familiar to him. He didn't believe this could really have anything to do with his being Russian, as if he were Russian and nothing else, not French, and not even American, because his being half Russian through his mother had never meant that much to Claude, not any more than being half French had meant to him. He had always been simply American. But away from the particulars of America, away, especially, from the particulars of New York, and nowhere in London, which to Claude seemed to have no particulars in itself, he was attentive, here in the flat, to the particulars of the Russian sounds when Maria Polosova and the twins spoke to one another, of the way Maurice put an empty wine bottle on the floor by the table, of the cakes on a crystal cake stand at the center of the table, and he wondered in what invisible ways he was, through his mother, Russian. The meal was not particularly Russian and not at all Lenten—thin slices of liver pâté, cutlets with overcooked spinach and potatoes, eaten at a drop-leaf table Claude had helped Maurice pull out from the wall and open up in the sitting room—but to Claude there was something familiar in the way they all seemed to lounge about the table long after the meal was eaten. He had the strong and curious sense of having been in the flat, among these people, at this table, before. He wondered: What can Russia mean to me? Maria Polosova did all the talking, mostly in English but, as in asides, to the twins, and everyone listened, even the twins, who didn't understand her when she spoke in English.

From time to time Maria Polosova stared at Claude across the table, as if she too thought he was familiar, and was trying to remember where she had seen him.

She asked him, "Will you come to church for the Resurrection service?"

He sat up. "Oh?"

There was a note of sadness in her voice, or perhaps of pleading, as if she saw something in Claude that made her sad, and she was pleading with him to let her commiserate. She said, "Come to church with us."

Maurice Kuragin said, "You must come, of course you must come."

Claude didn't know why this invitation should suddenly so move him. He said to Maria Polosova quietly, "Thank you, I'd like to."

Maria Polosova continued to look at him, and he lowered his eyes.

She pushed her chair away from the table with a groan and said something in Russian to the twins, who both got up, one to get her cane, the other to pull the chair farther back for her. Standing, she said to Maurice Kuragin, "Give your young friend one of the cakes," and then to Claude, "Mind you don't eat it until Sunday." Claude wondered if she remembered his name, but felt that she knew him without knowing his name.

When Maurice Kuragin came back from seeing her and the twins out, he came back saying, with a laugh, "She does take up an evening."

Claude didn't want to comment on her.

"Will you stay a little longer?" Maurice asked.

Claude wasn't sure, but perhaps it was because of Maria Polosova that, unaccountably, tears rose into his eyes, and he blinked. "Maybe I should go," he said.

"You won't have a glass of port with me?"

He couldn't disappoint the old man. "One glass."

Claude stood before Maurice in the little hall to say goodbye to him after the port, but even after they had said goodbye, Claude didn't move.

Maurice said, "I thought of asking you to the Resurrection service, but then thought better of it after you told me you were brought up without religion. I thought you'd be bored. I'm very glad you're coming."

Claude exclaimed, "My cake."

"Dear, dear, yes, your cake. You almost forgot to take your cake."

Maurice rushed to put one of the small cakes in the white hand-kerchief, which he tied together and gave to Claude, and as he did Claude leaned toward the old man, about to kiss him goodnight, but he drew back and didn't, and left quickly.

On his way back to his flat, Claude remembered how when he was a boy growing up in New England, he would, on a winter day at sunset, find himself walking across a snow-covered field, in the distance a few birch trees, and beyond the birch trees an arctic sun-set, and he'd stop and think: This must be like Russia.

He remembered how a white hand towel embroidered at the edge in red, stylized flowers would make him think of Russia, or even a wooden box of potatoes at the back of the grocery store.

At those moments, it seemed to him that Russia, as if that country were floating high over America, would descend, and he would think: I know Russia. Russia didn't seem to him a geo-graphical place on the earth, but a country that floated above his and that descended in details at those strange moments at sunset in winter, or when looking through his mother's cedar chest for a towel for a guest, or in the grocery store.

And he used to dream about the country. He dreamed that he was in Russia and couldn't get out to return to America. However much he struggled to get out, Russia held him against his will and made him give in to the terrible darkness that Russia was.

He carried his *kulitch* by the knotted corners of the handker-chief.

III

As MAURICE AND CLAUDE were approaching the church, set back from the street in a little square, they met other people going to the service too, and among them was a tall, beautiful woman in a white sari and with a red dot between her arched eyebrows. Claude held the door open for her to go in, then for Maurice, and he followed. The church was dark and so crowded they had to press their way through to a counter where Maurice bought two thin and brownish beeswax candles and disks of cardboard cut from cereal and soap-flake boxes to insert the candles in, which he did before he handed one to Claude. They pressed more deeply into the crowd, Claude looking for the beautiful and strange woman in the sari. People in the congregation were moving about, talking to one another.

There were fewer people toward the front of the church, where a few rows of chairs were lined up and women were sitting on them facing the iconostasis, white and gold and with icons inserted in it, its gates shut, and above the iconostasis was the shell of the coffered, dimly gleaming, gilded apse. Here and there in the church were votive candles burning in small red glasses before icons in what looked like small, chapel-like, onion-domed frames attached to pillars. A woman was reading aloud from a holy book to one side of the closed gates of the iconostasis. The congregation continued to move around in the dark and talk to one another. One of the women on the chairs held a baby, which began to cry, and she quietened it by putting it on her shoulder and rocking back and forth.

In the dark, there seemed to be no walls to the church but only surrounding night, and people were gathered in a crowd in that night. Claude and Maurice were standing near a pillar, and behind the pillar was Maria Polosova with her cane, wearing her black overcoat, a boy and girl, both blond, on either side of her. Before Maurice saw her, Claude went to her, and as if he were meeting somone he had known for years and was seeing now at a moment of crisis, he grasped her hands in his and held them tightly and kissed her three times, and she responded, holding his hands as tightly as he held hers. When he drew back, she retained her grasp on his hands and shook his arms a little, and she said, looking into his eyes, "There will be an end to your despair. You will have your revelation," and he felt the startling impulse to cry out. They were both very still, and again he felt the impulse, which shocked him. He was unable to look at Maria Polosova any longer, and she let go of his hands.

Maurice came to her and kissed her, then put his hands on the heads of the boy and girl. They had clear blond faces, and were shy. Maurice introduced Claude to them — Sasha and Vera, the great-grandchildren of Maria Polosova — and they smiled at him.

Claude might not be any more Russian than that dusky Indian woman in a white sari who had disappeared into the congregation, but here, some self he had been only distantly aware of, some self he wouldn't have allowed himself to be in America, and certainly not in New York, had emerged from him and become him, and he looked toward the iconostasis and held his fist up to his chin, then held his breath.

Maria Polosova said she must sit, and followed by her great-grandchildren, she went toward the folding chairs, where, as if reserved for her in the front row, three were free. Their movements slow, her grandchildren sat down on either side of her after she was seated.

The gates of the iconostasis opened; the metropolitan appeared, in a gold and silver cope and a rounded, sparkling silver crowd, and addressed the congregation in English, asking everyone to be silent.

Claude saw two men, also wearing copes, carrying over their heads a bier covered in a black and silver cloth into the sanctuary, which was lit up. The gates remained open, and Claude could see lit candles and incense rising in clouds from swinging silver censers. The shadows of the men officiating, about which billowed the clouds of incense, were cast out into the church on the light through the open gateway.

If all the atrocities from all time perpetrated on humanity were contracted into three hours, they would make the world, like an eviscerated heart nailed to a post, drip blood.

In no way had he ever allowed himself to consider that what he felt in that secret self was despair, but it was despair.

It seemed to Claude that the choir was singing out not the glory of man's redemption from darkness, but the grief of the impossibility of redemption. Their singing was a lament. The ceremony filled him with unbearable despair, and he held his jaw to keep it from convulsing.

A young woman by him was weeping into a tissue, and Maurice, on the other side of him, kept looking past him at the young woman, concerned about her.

The metropolitan and the servers, carrying candleholders with three tall, thin, lit candles leaning toward one another and crisscrossed at their tops, and swinging censers, then the choir and members of the congregation, carrying unlit candles in the cardboard disks, went out the back door of the church in a procession, and Maria Polosova and her grandchildren got up to join it. Intent on her devotions, she didn't look at Maurice when she passed him, measuring each step with her cane, but as she passed Claude she turned her eyes to him, and they exchanged a look that made him feel she knew what was happening to him. Sasha and Vera also turned to him as they passed him, following close behind their great-grandmother, and they didn't smile. In the procession, Maria Polosova held her jaw up, and it seemed to Claude that her face was defined, under her loose and sagging flesh, by her furious skull.

Maurice stepped back from the procession and so did Claude, and so did the young woman weeping between them.

Those members of the congregation who remained in the dark inside were very still and silent. But it was as though those inside were in fact in a vast outside, and the chanting that sounded from outside as the procession went around to the front of the church came from a circular horizon, too distant to be seen. Everyone waited. Claude waited. The young woman continued to weep, and Maurice, Claude saw, was turned to her and, frowning with his concern, staring at her.

Everyone faced the front entrance of the church and separated to form an aisle down the middle. Through the translucent glass on the front doors the lighted candles shone blurred, then the doors opened and the metropolitan, entering the church, called out, in Russian and Greek and English, "Christ is risen!" and the congregation responded with "He has risen indeed!" and the choir sang out, loud. Lit candles appeared in the dark, and the members of the congregation lit their candles, a few first from the flames of the votive candles, then more and more from those with lit candles, so the flickering flames spread through the church, and in their light shone hands and faces. The metropolitan and those behind him proceeded into the church down the aisle. The metropolitan shouted out again and again "Christ is risen!" and the congregation responded with "He is risen indeed!" and once again this evening tears started into the eyes of Claude.

Just as Claude was lighting his candle from a man standing near him, he heard weeping and, with his candle lit, turned to see Maurice holding in his arms the weeping young woman. His unlit candle in one hand, Maurice was slowly patting her back with the other.

Maria Polosova appeared in the procession, carrying her lighted candle, and behind her, side by side, were her great-grandchildren, also carrying burning candles and detaching and showing to each other the shapes formed by the wax melting down onto the cardboard disks. This time Maria Polosova didn't look at Claude as she passed him, and he, wanting for a moment to join her and her great-grandchildren, almost went to her, but held back.

The young woman in Maurice's arms stopped weeping, and Maurice held her away from him and, looking at her closely, asked her quietly if she was all right, and she nodded yes.

Maurice lit his candle from Claude's, then presented his candle to the young woman for her to light hers. Her face was still wet with tears. She said goodbye to Maurice and walked into the congregation nearer the iconostasis.

Maurice whispered to Claude, "I only come for the Resurrection, so we can go now."

Other people were going out, too, carrying their lighted candles. Before he left, Claude looked about for the Indian woman in the white sari but didn't see her. Outside, people tried to keep their candles lit as they walked along the sidewalks by holding one hand cupped about the flame. For a while, all along the streets were burning candles, the flames blown from side to side, including Maurice's and Claude's own; but one by one the air blew them out, Maurice's and Claude's too. Maurice laughed when his went out.

IV

CLAUDE SAW MAURICE often and, because he knew the old man had very little money, took him to simple restaurants. Every time they met, Claude asked about Maria Polosova. He needed to be told by Maurice that she existed, as there were times when Claude thought he hadn't in fact met her, and that what she'd told him in the church, which had so shocked him, he'd only imagined he'd heard. Maurice laughed and said he needed to feel strong to have Maria Polosova to dinner, but if Claude wanted to see her, he would do it, he would.

One Sunday they went together by train to Cambridge, and after Maurice showed Claude the colleges and the windows of his rooms at Trinity, the old man said they must, they must go punting on the Cam along the Backs. Claude, standing barefoot at the rear of the long, narrow, flat boat, punted while Maurice took delight in pointing out to him views of cows in fields, the colleges beyond, and beyond the colleges the high blue sky with round white clouds. Claude thought he would like one day to travel with Maurice.

They had supper back in London in Maurice's flat. Maurice told Claude he had received a letter from an American woman—he couldn't recall her name, and he looked for the letter in a little drop-leaf desk, where there was a stethoscope and the armband and gauge and little black rubber bulb for taking blood pressure, and he studied the signature a long while before he said, "Claire O'Connel" — asking him if he might help her in any way with locating a painting of the Annunciation by the artist Pietro Testa, which his old Cambridge friend Sir Roger Leclerc, who had suggested she write, believed had once been in Moscow in the possession of the Volkansky family. Sir Roger thought Mr. Kuragin might have some information: were there any members still alive, and if so, how might Claire O'Connel get in touch with them, if this were at all possible?

"Roger wouldn't have given her my name if she wasn't serious," Maurice said. "Though I know Roger has his doubts about my being serious. He always did. He certainly never took me seriously when we were undergraduates, and often told me I got into Cambridge only because I was a Russian émigré, as there was considerable sympathy for Russian émigrés at the time. And yet he wanted to be my friend, and he did tell me a great deal about iconography in art, which interested him particularly. I think it still does. He had me read Saxl, Wind, Panofsky, such people. I've forgotten most of what he told me, though perhaps, given the chance, I'd find I haven't. He never, of course, introduced me to his family. Only once, when I went round to his rooms with Count Peter

Volkansky, who, oddly, hadn't got into Cambridge but was visiting me, did Roger suggest that we all might have tea with his sister, who was about to visit." Maurice laughed. "But when Peter told him his mother had started a catering business in London, Roger remembered his sister wasn't coming until after Peter had left Cambridge. I was in Cambridge, but he forgot to invite me to tea with his sister. But Roger did give me a wonderful, rare book on Renaissance emblems."

"I'm glad you find the English amusing," Claude said.

Maurice laughed again and said, "I do, I do."

Claude laughed with him.

"Well," Maurice asked, "what do you think of the American woman who has written?"

He often asked Claude what he thought about matters that concerned him, however small.

"About whether or not you should help her?"

"About inviting her to tea to meet her. She must be interesting, don't you think? That is, she is an art historian, and they are interesting, aren't they? After all, as you are an art book publisher, I thought you'd be especially interested."

"Most art historians are very uninteresting to art book publishers."

"You don't want to meet her?"

"I was joking," Claude said.

"She included her telephone number. If I were to ring her and invite her over, would you come? You know about her world, don't you, and could help?"

"I've never heard of Pietro Testa."

"Well, then, meeting her would give you a chance to find out."

Maurice was becoming dependent on him, but this worried Claude only because he would be leaving London in, now, less than three months, and he felt the old man had become older. He didn't like the way Maurice would sometimes stop for a moment during a conversation, or out on a walk, and press his hand to his chest and wince a little. Claude had told him he must go to a doctor, but Maurice said he knew what was wrong with him and it was nothing, and Claude stopped insisting on the doctor, as he thought Maurice must know. He said that he would come to tea with the American art historian, with a cake.

"We'll wait a while," Maurice said. "I like to look forward to meeting people."

Claude said, "The person I'd really like to see is Maria Polosova."

"Oh, I must ring her up and have her over," Maurice said. "I must. But she can be difficult."

"How?"

"She can reprimand me, you know, for being childish. Anyway, she thinks I'm childish. It makes her angry when I am."

"What do you do that she thinks is childish?"

"Well, I wanted to buy her a rhinestone pin, just a rhinestone pin, you know, for her drab coat, a pin in the shape of a bow and arrow, but she got angry at the very idea. I was glad I asked her first, as she wouldn't have accepted it if I had bought it. I'd seen it in a shop. It was rhinestone, but it wasn't cheap. I'd childishly thought it would have cheered her up."

"She doesn't look like the kind of woman who could be cheered up by a rhinestone pin."

"There, you see how childish it was of me."

"I'd like it if you invited her."

"I'll do that. I'll invite the American woman, and I'll invite Maria."

"Not together," Claude said.

"No, not together. But then," Maurice asked, "why not?"

The summer light in temperate London lasted until late. Claude stood with colleagues from the publishing house on sidewalks outside pubs and drank pints, the sky above pale and a little strange and the green and red flashing lights of planes seeming to drift across the sky like small, strange planets. He began to think that London was a city in which nothing happened if he remained among the English, and Claude, an American, was always eager for something to happen. He didn't mind going home on his own after the last round when it was certain that nothing was going to happen.

Alone, it seemed to him that that feeling which Maria Polosova had called despair might simply be restlessness, and he would think he should be out with someone to keep him from being restless. The only person he could think of whom he wanted to see was Maurice, who, though he was sometimes boring, mostly gave him as much delight as Claude always seemed to give the old man. But at some times not even seeing Maurice would help him out of the feeling, which was more than restlessness. Claude didn't know what brought it on, but he would at moments find himself walking around his flat, the sun still high and showing through the wide windows, striking his chest with his fist. He would want to see, as if out of a need, Maria Polosova, in whom he was reassured that what he felt was not a feeling he should be embarrassed by, or blame on self-indulgence, the way James would have done. Then, stopped and swinging his arm by his side, in the next minute he would tell himself that James had been right, and any feeling that went unchecked by irony was embarrassing, and almost always self-indulgent. James would have said, with a high voice, Oh, the despair in your Russian soul, and he would have underlined, ironically, exactly what made Claude believe in the despair — it was not American, not New York, it was Russian — but James would have told him it could be in Claude only parody Russian. No, that was not true, Claude thought, what he felt wasn't a parody of any feeling.

He again walked around his flat. He felt it, that despair. Maria Polosova had brought this person out of him, this person who did not have to feel embarrassed by his torment at a despairing world. He wanted to take himself as seriously as Maria Polosova took him, but he couldn't; he needed her to take him seriously. His greatest embarrassment, however, would have been to telephone her and ask to see her. At his worst moments, it wasn't Maurice who could help Claude, it was that woman with the look of fury. Claude didn't understand how Maurice could find her, at best, an amusing dictator. She gave Claude authenticity. She made him Russian. She made it possible for him to walk around his flat and hit his chest with his fist.

What he didn't understand about his feeling was that there was no one to cause it.

He would tell himself he didn't want anyone, and then, in the next moment, he would tell himself that that was all he wanted, he wanted someone.

He became frightened of what he was capable of when once he knelt and bent far over and struck his forehead on the floor. His fear made him jump up, and he told himself, Don't you ever, ever do that again.

When he saw Maurice after this, he asked please to see Maria Polosova again.

They were in Maurice's flat. The old man said, "Well, I'll ring her now, right now," and did. By the way Maurice kept saying, "Oh dear, dear," Claude understood that Maria Polosova wasn't well, and he became anxious. He felt a contraction in his chest when he heard Maurice say his name, and he waited as though a judgment were being decided until Maurice said over the telephone, simply, "I will tell him," and hung up and said to him, "She is not well, but she wants to see you."

"Ah," Claude said.

"Don't worry about Maria Polosova. She will survive us all."

Claude wanted to tell her something. He wanted to confess something to her, though he wasn't sure how he could articulate the confession.

Maurice had supper prepared. When, at the table, Maurice said, "We are all dying now, all of the last of us who were born in Russia and had to leave because of the Revolution," Claude put a hand over his eyes and sat still for a moment, and he felt sadness rise in him and unbalance him. He lowered his hand and looked around the small sitting room, the yellowing wallpaper, the threadbare rug, the soiled armchairs, and it all appeared so familiar to him and itself filled him with hopelessness. There was no reason for him to feel this, none at all, and he was sure that Maurice, who did have a reason, didn't feel it.

He said to Maurice, "I really do want to see Maria Polosova again."

"I know, I know."

Claude again looked around the room.

Maurice said, "But what about the American art historian, whom I've finally invited to tea, next Sunday?"

Claude felt sad, and he even wondered if Maurice, who did not appear to be sad at all, was a childish, soulless man. "I don't think I'll be able to make it," Claude said.

"Perhaps I can ring her and change it to another time when you would be able to make it," Maurice said.

Claude made a gesture with his hand that meant never mind. "Leave it," he said. "It'd be too complicated to change it."

"I could ring her now —"

"No," Claude said, "leave it." He was, for the first time, getting annoyed with Maurice.

"But —"

"I said, leave it," Claude said, and stood; then, seeing the expression on Maurice's face of distress at what he might have done to cause Claude to be annoyed, Claude smiled and said, "It's just that I'm feeling I may be coming down with something, and can't think, really, about Sunday."

"Shall I take your temperature?" Maurice asked.

"No," Claude said. "But I think I should go back to my place and go to bed."

"You won't stay and have a glass of port before you go?"

"I really think I should get to bed."

"Pity, as I know how much you like port, but of course I understand." Maurice's tone was a little formal.

Claude wasn't feeling that he was coming down with anything, but he did go back to his flat and lie on his bed. He felt bad about having left Maurice, and also having made Maurice think he'd done something to offend him enough that he had left. But maybe he was becoming too close to Maurice. He closed his eyes and saw the light on the ceiling as a bright red vagueness, and he thought he wouldn't go to tea with the American art historian. He didn't, he thought, want to meet an American.

On Saturday he went to the National Gallery in Trafalgar Square to look at paintings. He always went to look at great paintings when he was restless.

On Sunday, just before four o'clock, he took the Underground to Notting Hill, bought a chocolate cake from a pastry shop, and walked to Maurice's flat in Holland Park.

Evidently Maurice wasn't expecting him, because when Claude rang the bell to Maurice's flat beside the street door, Maurice asked over the intercom who it was in a surprised voice. Claude gave his name, and he heard "Oh" over the intercom, and the door clicked open.

Claude climbed the stairs with their threadbare runner to the landing where Maurice was standing with the door to his flat open, and the old man said, his voice high, "I'm so pleased, I'm so pleased." Claude, for the first time since they had met, embraced the old man on an impulse, the box with the cake dangling by its string from one hand, and kissed him on a cheek. This seemed to fill Maurice with joy.

Claude said, "Am I late?"

"Only just a little," Maurice said, the joy still bright in his blue eyes. "Come in, come in."

As Claude entered the sitting room, he saw a young woman who turned to him at that moment.

She was very young and very beautiful, with her long black hair about her shoulders, and she wore a sleeveless black cotton dress that was loose and had many big pleats, and her bare arms and legs were smooth and white. After a moment, as if she had caught herself staring at him, she turned her eyes away from Claude, but not her head, and the look in her eyes, one of a woman much older than she was, made him continue to stare at her until Maurice, coming into the room behind him, said, "This is Rachel O'Connel, the daughter of Mrs. O'Connel, who asked if she could bring her along, and I of course said yes, and how pleased I am now that I did." Further in the room, a middle-aged woman, whose black hair was braided at the back of her neck and who wore a dark linen suit, was standing with her hand already out. Claude went to her first, and as he shook her hand, she said, "Please call me Claire." He felt jammed a little, in a position with his back to Rachel, as if he couldn't make himself turn back to her, but he did turn and she was looking at him, her hands at her sides, and waiting for him to come to her, and she was smiling slightly. What pulled him to her was that look in her eyes, and when he held her hand he stared as if into that look. She didn't blink. He smiled slightly and held her hand for a long while, the other hand still dangling the box with the cake, and it seemed to him that as he drew his hand away she pressed it with her fingers.

Laughing, Claude gave the box to Maurice.

A charm came over the tea party. Claire took the box from Maurice and insisted on going into the kitchen and finding her way around and making the tea, while Maurice and Claude and Rachel, in the sitting room, talked. And a great sense of spirit came over the party too, when Claire returned wheeling a tea trolley with tea things and thin, crustless sandwiches of butter and cress Maurice had already prepared and the chocolate cake Claude had brought and the éclairs she had brought, and everyone exclaimed excitedly. Maurice told Rachel and Claude to sit together on the sofa, and Claude felt certainty, such certainty, in their sitting near each other on the sofa. Claire, who seemed particularly excited, poured out the tea.

Maurice asked Claire, "And how is Roger?"

She laughed, as if at a joke she couldn't stop herself from telling, though she knew she shouldn't tell it. "The saints in Sir Roger's pictures look after him." She bit her lower lip to restrain her smile, ashamed, perhaps, to have told the joke, but pleased too.

"I sometimes wonder," Maurice said, "what he sees in me. Not that we see one another often, mind you. He doesn't invite me to his villa. But he does ring me when he's in London, and I invite him round, and he asks me —" Maurice seemed to try to remember. "Oh, about friends who survive from when we were undergraduates together, friends I remain in touch with. He keeps in touch through me. I am in touch with quite a number of people, quite a number —"

Glancing often at Claude and Rachel, Claire asked Maurice, "Are you in touch with any members of the Volkansky family?"

"Oh, let me think," he said. "Let me think." He lifted his head and closed his eyes, then, lowering his head and opening his eyes, he said, "It seems to me I should be."

"You used to see them?"

"I saw some of them in London. They came with nothing. I saw especially Peter, who was my age. Some of the family remained in Russia to try to save what they could, and up to 1924 or so the London Volkanskys were able to keep in touch with the Moscow Volkanskys, meeting from time to time in Berlin, but after that —" Maurice raised his hands.

"I don't suppose you remember the painting from your visits to them in Moscow?"

"Who did you say it was by?"

It was Rachel, leaning forward, who said, "His name is Pietro Testa."

"Tell me more about him," Maurice asked Rachel.

"He was an Italian late Baroque painter, from Lucca."

"And this painting you think the Volkansky family have, you say it's of the Annunciation?"

"Yes," Rachel said.

Claire said, "We have some reason to think it is."

"You don't remember it, do you?" Rachel asked Maurice.

Now he lowered his head so his chin was crushed against his chest and he closed his eyes tightly. Opening his eyes, he said, "There were so many paintings, but yes, I think I do remember an Annunciation."

Claude thought Maurice, in his kindness, must be making all this up so as not to disappoint Rachel and Claire.

Rachel said to her mother, her voice rising as she spoke, "He says he remembers it."

The surprise Claire expressed wasn't so much that Maurice remembered the painting, but that her daughter should be so excited by what he had said.

Claude thought: She's very young.

"Of course I can't be absolutely sure," Maurice said. "You say it's an Annunciation?"

"Yes," Claire said, and, excited herself, she explained how she had discovered the reference, and Maurice made an effort to be as interested, and even as excited, as Claire was.

Claude was aware of the hands of Rachel moving as she raised and lowered her teacup, as she brushed her hair away from her cheeks with the tips of her fingers, as she folded and unfolded her fingers on her lap. He had the curious sensation that as aware as he was of her, she was of him, and he became conscious of his own hands and the movements they made, and he didn't quite know what to do with them.

It was as though everyone became aware of themselves sitting in a circle, of their gestures and talk, and they all went still and silent.

In the circle of stillness and silence, Rachel said, in a quiet voice, "It's such a strange idea, the Annunciation."

"Why do you say that?" Claude asked.

She said, "You wonder how anyone can have ever thought it up, because it's impossible."

Claude felt that he had never heard anything from anyone that had ever meant so much to him.

Claire was studying Rachel.

Maurice said, "Impossible? Why is it impossible?"

Again stillness and silence encircled the party.

"Of course miracles are possible," Maurice said. "Of course they are."

Rachel asked him, "Will you help us find the picture?"

Maurice laughed. He said, "Now, Maria Polosova may be able to help. She is in touch with the London Volkanskys, mainly through the devotion she and they have to the Orthodox Church. But if the London Volkanskys have found that they still have relatives in Russia, as Maria, much to her regret, has found she does, then Maria will know. I myself lost touch with the Volkanskys when Peter died. But I will ask Maria Polosova."

As Rachel looked toward her mother, her eyes stopped on Claude, just long enough for him to sense something in him go out to her, and then Rachel said to her mother, "He'll find the picture."

V

CLAUDE'S SIX MONTHS at the publishing house had only a few weeks left. Though he didn't think he had learned anything he couldn't have learned in New York, except the way the English used vagueness to dissemble inefficiency, he didn't want to return to New York. He wasn't sure now what he had expected, coming to London, but he had expected more than what he had learned at the publishing house.

Sunday morning, Claude took a bus along misty Bayswater Road. He noted that in the mist the leaves in Kensington

Gardens were turning yellow, and that the grass was brown in patches.

The gas fire was on in Maurice's sitting room, and on the table before the sofa was a bottle of sherry and glasses.

Without looking at Claude, Maurice said quietly, "I thought we would sit for a moment before going off to lunch at Claire O'Connel's. We have time." Handing Claude a glass of sherry, he still didn't look at him. Maurice said, "It was so nice of her to invite us. I do look forward to seeing her again, and Rachel."

Claude said, "But when can I see Maria Polosova?"

Over the rim of his own glass of sherry, Maurice said, "Maria Polosova will not, after all, be able to see you."

Claude frowned. "Has she died?"

"Yes."

Claude turned away. He said, "I expected so much from her."

Maurice said, "Please do not be sad. I was able to ask her about the Volkanskys in Russia, and she did help. She was able to get the name of a Moscow Volkansky from a London Volkansky. You'll see, Maria Polosova will continue to help."

A taxi took them over the Thames into South London. There was little traffic. The autumn mist went from sunlit pink to shadow-blue and back again as the taxi passed through it.

Mist floated in waves against the bay windows of Claire's sitting room.

Claire, her back straight and her head raised so she appeared tall even when seated, answered Maurice's questions about Pietro Testa. Claude hardly listened. It seemed to him that the absence of Rachel had to do with the death of Maria Polosova.

"I'm not sure why I got interested in Testa," Claire said. She was wearing a loose, waistless dress, dark, that reached to her ankles, and this undecorated dress too made her appear tall and stately. She placed a hand on her bosom and laughed and said, "I think maybe because he was a desperate person."

"Dear, dear," Maurice said.

Claire sat for a moment longer, in tall and stately silence, then rose slowly, but just as she was standing Rachel came into the room.

Claude turned to her. Like her mother, she was wearing a long, loose dress, also dark but with oriental embroidery along the hem, the edges of the long sleeves, and across the bodice, and as she moved toward Claude, smiling, he saw the cloth move in a swaying way against her bulging stomach, and he thought: She's pregnant. He stood and said "Hi," but he didn't say more. Smiling a little, she too said "Hi," and she went to Maurice, who only half rose and kissed her on her cheek and said, "How beautiful you are," and, sitting back, added, "You and your mother, I must say, are both of a beauty. I must say."

She sat on the end of the sofa her mother had been on, her back, like her mother's, straight, her head raised, and she looked around the room with its overstuffed furniture covered with flowered chintz slipcovers, its small coal fireplace with a black mantel and silver candlesticks on the mantel and over it an etching framed in a gilded frame with a mat, as if not to look at Claude. He remained standing. He bit his lower lip.

Rachel's mother also remained standing, but after a moment she said, laughing, "That's right, I was going to get some reproductions of Testa's work," and she went out.

Maurice said to Rachel, "I hope you're not given a beastly lot of work at school, so you can't ever have a good time."

Rachel raised her head a little higher and said, "I've taken off some time from school."

"Now, that is a good idea. I think it is always a good idea to take some time off from school and enjoy oneself."

She said to Claude, all at once like a matronly hostess who must put him, a guest who was abiding by the formalities, at his ease, "Do sit down."

He sat, but he felt that everything was strange. The way they all talked about the weather was strange, the way Claire came in with large, glossy photographs of Baroque paintings and showed them around was strange, and the way Claire, acting too like a hostess from another century who must put her guests at ease and entertain them, took the etching down from where it hung over the mantel and, holding it, facing outward, against her bosom, asked if anyone could tell her what it represented. It was by her desperate artist, Pietro Testa.

Without rising, Maurice leaned forward and pursed his lips as he peered. Claude rose to stand on one side of the picture, and Rachel stood on the other side, and each leaned toward the other to examine the etching. Claude was more aware of her than of the picture — of the curves of her cheek and jaw, which he saw vaguely from the corner of his eye, of the aura of her long black hair — and he felt she was the strangest person he had ever met.

Maurice said to Rachel, "But surely you know what the picture is about, as you live with it."

Rachel said, with a light laugh, "I never really looked at it."

The picture moved a little with Claire's breathing. The drypoint etching was foxed, and there was a hole torn in a corner, and it looked as if it had been cropped. The scene was a rocky mountain, and a muscular young man with a cape and a crown of laurel was climbing the mountain, led by another, naked young man in an aureole of shining light. Behind and below were monsters, and ahead were women in clinging and diaphanous robes, whom the shining naked male figure was pointing out to the young man with the cape and the laurel crown; the women were gathered about a stream, one with a trumpet, another with books, another garlanded with roses and reaching out for a basket of flowers held above her by a *putto* flying among other *putti*, who were hanging, it seemed, swags in the sky. At the top of the mountain was a winged horse. The young man was wearing a crown of laurel and was looking lovingly into the eyes of the woman garlanded in roses and reaching out for the basket of flowers held by the flying *putto*.

Another *putto* above her carried a flaming torch. Maurice sat farther forward and craned to see better.

Claude glanced at Rachel. Whatever he felt for her, he felt it as helplessly as he felt the helplessness of Maria Polosova's death.

Maurice said, "The Pegasus of course means we are on Mount Helicon."

"Yes," Claire said.

"So, if we are on Mount Helicon," Maurice continued, "we are among the Muses."

"You're very good," Claire said.

"But everyone knows that," Maurice said.

Claude saw Rachel reflected in the glass over the picture, and just as he focused on her reflection she focused on his, and they both quickly refocused more deeply on the picture.

Rachel asked, "Who is the Muse with the trumpet?"

"The Muse with the trumpet?" Claude said, as if he knew but had to think a little.

"That's Clio," Maurice said, "the Muse of history. You didn't know that, Claude?"

"I forgot," he said.

Again he caught Rachel glancing at him in their reflection.

"And the Muse with the books is Calliope," Maurice said, "the Muse of poetry, which means our young man in the laurel crown is a poet. Given that Clio is also welcoming him to heights of Helicon, he must be an historical, maybe a national, poet."

"That's right," Claire said.

Rachel said, "But he's looking at the Muse garlanded in roses. Who's she?"

Claude said, "It looks like she and the poet are in love."

Rachel touched her forehead.

"Who is the garlanded Muse?" Maurice asked Claire. "She isn't carrying a lyre, she isn't carrying a celestial globe and staff."

"She's Venus," Claire said.

"I should have known from the torch."

"Shall I tell you?" Claire asked.

"No, no," Maurice said. "It wouldn't be fair to be told what the meaning of an allegory is, would it?"

"Is there only one meaning to an allegory?" Claude asked Claire.

"They're intended to illustrate a meaning," she said.

Maurice pursed his lips again as he studied the picture, then said, "The poet is being led to the Muses, his source of inspiration. But more than to the Muses, he is drawn to Venus, who is about to give him a basket of flowers she is reaching to take from the little *putto*. That's all very simple, isn't it? What does it mean? Well, the most important personage in the drama is, I think, the naked man in the shining aureole, who has to be Wisdom leading the poet. He is central to the composition, and he is leading the young poet to Venus. The meaning is in him, and it is a meaning that is not, I should imagine, very relevant to the way poets think today — that Venus is meant to inspire not voluptuousness, but the delights of wisdom. Not a very interesting meaning to any of us today, is it? I shouldn't think that anyone today would look at such a picture for its meaning."

"You really are very good at interpreting," Claire said to the old man.

"A useless talent," Maurice said. "An entirely useless talent."

Claire turned the picture to her and studied it for a moment, and as she did, her eyes seemed to go out of focus, and as if she were no longer thinking about the picture but about something that had made her eyes go out of focus, she hung it back over the mantel.

And how was Claude supposed to interpret the luncheon party, each of them at a side of the square table in the small dining room with a mirror that was tilted and reflected them at the table? He couldn't have made a mistake about Rachel's being pregnant, and he had no idea, no idea at all, what that could mean to them at the table, but he was sure it was central to the meaning of their passing to one another the serving dish of slices of roast lamb, the bread in a basket, of Claire keeping the wineglasses filled, of their all talking about films, plays, operas they had seen in London. Claude sat across from Rachel.

After the meal, Maurice and Claude were told by Claire to go into the sitting room. The clearing and washing up would be done the next morning by Pauline, the cleaning woman, she assured Maurice, who wanted to help. The men went into the sitting room and Claire shut the double doors on them, so they were alone. The men stood in silence in the middle of an oriental rug.

Claire came in by a doorway to the side with a tray of coffee things, and she asked Claude please would he strike a match and light the smokeless fuel already prepared with a fire lighter in the grate of the fireplace. He did, and as the flames rose up among the black fuel, everyone settled for coffee. Rachel didn't appear.

Did Rachel and her mother think that her pregnancy wasn't noticeable, that the loose dress she wore, similar to her mother's, hid it?

Claire, among the cushions of the sofa, was a little self-conscious as the hostess, being attentive, two fingers on her cheek, while Maurice spoke, and asking him questions to keep him talking. She seemed to realize that Claude didn't want to talk, and wouldn't press him. But she refilled his cup.

A helpless longing came over Claude, and with the longing he felt a familiar sadness, or grief, and all the while he felt how very strange everything was.

The longing wasn't, nor the sadness, nor the grief, nor especially the strangeness, dispelled by Rachel's coming quietly into the room and surprising him by her appearance. She stood on the rug with her arms folded over her stomach, and everyone in the room went silent. But her pregnancy wasn't evident, and Claude wondered if he'd been mistaken. When she dropped her arms and moved to a chair, he realized he wasn't mistaken.

Maurice said to her, "We missed you."

Rachel didn't excuse her absence.

Claire said to her and Claude, "Why don't you two go out for a little stroll on the common?"

It seemed to be left to Claude to agree to this or not, and he said to Rachel, "I'd like a stroll, myself. Would you?"

She nodded.

And why, he wondered, was her mother making it so easy for him to be close to her?

They wore raincoats because of the mist, but didn't take an umbrella. A fun fair was set up on the common, and the lights of the tents and the amusement rides expanded into the mist and appeared to float and waver. Claude and Rachel walked among the tents and turning rides. Though the music over the loudspeakers was loud, there were few people, and the flaps of the tents were raised on games without attendants, and the rides turned without anyone on them. Claude didn't try to keep up any talk with Rachel, and neither did she with him. They walked away from the fun fair into the mist of the common, in which, here and there, large trees showed darkly.

The longing remained with Claude, and too the odd grief that always accompanied the longing.

In the distance were the red and white lights of moving cars, too far away for the sound of the traffic to reach them. Even the music of the fun fair, floating in its soft illuminations, sounded as if it came from very far.

They walked along a muddy path among bushes, and Rachel stayed close by him. He felt the impulse to put his arm around her, so close to him. She was all he could see vividly in the mist, her presence immediate in its vividness. He wondered if she could possibly know how immediate she appeared to him, and how he wanted to put his arm around her. And as aware of her as he was, he was aware of himself, and it seemed to him they were both immense beings walking side by side along a path through misty bushes.

Her voice, though low, startled him. "I know you know about me."

He stopped, and she did. "What do I know?" he asked.

"That I'm pregnant."

Her face was so close to his that he could have, by inclining his head only a little, kissed her.

He said, "Yes."

And then, as if she had made up her mind to reveal to him what would make all the difference to her life, either to create it or destroy it, she put her hands to the sides of her neck and, after hesitating a moment, said, "What happened was I was raped."

He heard himself say, "Oh."

She lowered her hands and spread them out on either side of her. "I was raped here, in this place."

All of Claude's longing was to put his arms around her and hold her, but he couldn't raise his arms. The longing itself seemed to make him weak. All he'd be able to do by giving in would be to press against her and let her put her arms around him, but he didn't give in. He drew away from her, and as he did she lowered her eyes and stepped away.

Very quietly, she said, "Now you know."

All he could say was "Yes."

On the way back, Rachel said, "You won't tell anyone?" He knew that she was in a state of desperation and was trying to contain her desperation.

She was able to look at him when, in the entry hall, they took off their raincoats. He tried to smile, and his effort was enough to make her smile too, a faint, tense smile. She had risked everything, and she had no idea what the result of the risk would be.

Claire and Maurice were talking animatedly in the sitting room, Maurice's voice rising excitedly over Claire's, then hers rising more excitedly over his. The lamps were lit and the fire was glowing red, fine blue flames shooting up among the red. When Rachel and Claude entered, Claire said to them, "We've decided we'll all go to Russia together. What do you think? It's a marvelous idea, isn't it? We'll all go to Russia together to look for the picture."

Maurice said, "A marvelous idea."

Rachel sat on the edge of a chair and, brushing her hair back from her cheeks with her fingertips, tried to smile.

Maurice said to Claude, "Wouldn't you love to go?"

What he hadn't been able to give in to before, he gave in to now, and he said, "I would love to go."

But Rachel's face remained tense, her smile tense.

Claire's voice jumped when she said, "I'm excited, I really am excited."

Alone in his flat, Claude tried to read the typescript of a book for a meeting at the publishing house the next day, but he couldn't concentrate.

He got up from the table and went to the window to look out over Primrose Hill. A wind was blowing, and with the mist cleared away, stars were visible above the lights of houses.

Out for a walk in the wind, he walked down Primrose Hill to the zoo, and along the sidewalk outside the zoo, from where he could see the cages. Dark animals he couldn't recognize moved silently about the cages. He walked all the great circle around the outside of Regent's Park.

Why was he so attracted to what he didn't know, and why did what he didn't know so fill him with grief?

VI

CLAIRE AND GEORGE were walking along a side street in Paddington, and as they passed under a plane tree a yellow leaf fell so close to them, and so slowly, George reached out and caught it. He showed it to Claire, the yellow mottled with brown, the veins showing still green. She said quietly, "Beautiful," and George smiled and released it as if he were releasing a bird.

They were going to visit a friend, Anne Will, in Saint Mary's Hospital.

Another leaf fell, but Claire, reaching for it, didn't catch it.

251

She said, "I think that Rachel hopes for something to happen in Russia."

"You'll be going into the depths of madness, all of you, and perhaps that will be the best place for all of you," George said.

"Are you being ironical?"

"No."

As they entered the hospital, Claire felt that tightening in her stomach she always felt going into hospitals. George seemed not to find the stairways, the double doors, the corridors much different from those of any other building, and carrying the bouquet of flowers he'd bought in the flower shop attached to the hospital, he went a little ahead of Claire. There was a sharp smell of spirit of alcohol.

He stopped, however, at the door to Anne's room and peered through the little window in the wooden door, then, turning to Claire, bit his lower lip as if to stop himself from smiling nervously. She peered through, and in the square space defined by the small window saw, as though removed to a space that was inaccessible to anyone, Anne lying propped on a bed, her face gaunt and gray, her hair matted, her closed eyes sunk deep into the dark sockets of her skull.

George held the bouquet of lilies and fern out to Claire. "You give them to her," he said.

Claire took them, but she didn't want to go into that room. She did what she was told, however, and went in when George pushed the door for her to go in first.

Anne didn't open her eyes, and Claire and George stood together, side by side, waiting. When Anne did open her eyes, she stared at her friends for a long while before she smiled a little. She had a drip in her arm, the tube attached to a bottle of clear liquid hung upside down from a metal support.

However modern medicine became, Claire thought, it still appeared to be brutal in the way it was made to function. Anne looked as if she were the victim of some unnamable brutality from which she wouldn't recover. Her smile seemed to have nothing to do with her, but to stand out from her face with large teeth.

Clutching the bouquet, Claire realized that for months, for years perhaps, she had been trying to control something, and that she no longer wanted to control anything, but be mad.

She had had to control her resentment toward Rachel for not being able to marry George, and, more, had had to try to control her impulse to give in to her desire for what wasn't possible because of Rachel: flowers, food, music, sunlight, sex. Because of Rachel, Claire had had to deny herself all these.

Stop this, she thought.

Claire said to Anne, holding the flowers out more, "Look, a marriage bouquet for you."

Anne said weakly, "Who'm I marrying?"

"A big sexy blond man," Claire said.

Giving in at least a little to an impulse, Claire sat on the plastic upholstered armchair at the side of Anne's bed and, changing the bouquet from hand to hand, took off her shoes, then stood and searched the room for a vase. There was one on a shelf, and she filled it with water from the washbasin in a corner of the small room, arranged the lilies and fern in it, and placed the vase back on the shelf among other vases and pots of flowers. Anne and George watched her. She sat again in the armchair and stretched, then slouched a little.

In a loud voice, she said to Anne, "I'll bet you can't wait to get out of here."

Anne managed to laugh, a small, dry laugh. The laugh made her cough, so she shook, and afterward she shut her eyes.

Claire thought: She's dying. She sat upright and slipped on her shoes and she reprimanded herself. It always happened when she let go that she went too far.

George went to Anne and kissed her cheek. "What's the news?" he asked.

"They don't tell me," Anne said with her death's head smile. "They don't tell me anymore."

Claire jumped up. She exclaimed, "Oh Anne," and she walked quickly to the window and looked out on a yellowing plane tree.

She thought: Supposing nothing happens to make a difference to Rachel?

Oh, a difference — Claire wanted everything to be different, so that she, barefoot, loose-limbed, her tall, dark body swaying from side to side, could give up, give up, and — she didn't know what, except that giving up would be giving in to the fullness of what her life should have promised, the fullness of her body. She hadn't been able to in so very long. Impossibility forced her to use her will to accept impossibility, as if she had no choice, no more choice than dear, dear Anne.

Claire took a deep breath and she turned around to Anne, and as soon as she did she began to weep. George pulled a tissue from the box by the bed and took it to her, and she continued to weep, blowing her nose into the tissue. Then she suddenly laughed, and Anne too laughed a little, as did George. Claire thought again: Supposing nothing, nothing happens to make a difference to Rachel?

She went to Anne and leaned over her, put her arms around her, and kissed her cheek. She said, "I'm sorry, I don't know what came over me." When she drew back, she said, "As soon as you're out of here, we'll go out, like two hookers off the job, on the town for a good time."

Anne shut her eyes.

A nurse came in and asked Claire and George if they'd step out of the room for a moment while she did something to Anne, and Claire and George went out into the corridor and sat on a bench under a picture of a snowy landscape.

George said, "She doesn't look well."

"No," Claire said.

George got up and walked along the corridor, then returned and sat. He said, "I want us to get married."

"Oh," Claire exclaimed.

"Come on. There's a big difference between us, I know, but there's also a big similarity. I know and you know the pleasure of breakfast brought up on a tray in a hotel when you don't have to get up and rain is falling on the window. You know that I amuse you, and you, believe it or not, amuse me, at least at moments when you're as aware as I am of that pleasure of staying in bed and drinking tea among the pillows and sheets and blankets. I long for those moments with you. You can't deny we enjoy being together."

"Deny it?" Claire said. "No."

"Maybe it's even in Rachel to enjoy being with her friend. What did you say his name is?"

"Claude."

"Maybe Rachel and Claude will also one day have the pleasure of spending a weekend in a country hotel."

Claire pulled at the thick braid at her nape.

The nurse came out of Anne's room and smiled a faintly sad smile as she passed Claire and George, and they returned to the room.

Anne looked even thinner, more gaunt and gray than when they had seen her fifteen minutes before. She said, "Everyone is so kind."

"How are you feeling right now?" George asked.

"I don't know if I can say," Anne answered. "But everyone is being very kind."

Claire quickly reached for a tissue from the box by the bed and pressed it against her nostrils to try to stop herself from again weeping.

George said to Anne, "You know, it occurred to me the other day, while shopping for sheets, that almost all sheets are colored now, colored red, blue, deep purple, but when I was growing up no one would have ever thought of having anything but white sheets. I wondered, what made the change?"

"Washing machines did," Anne whispered. "When it became

easy to wash sheets, there was no longer any reason to prove they were clean by keeping them white."

Anne was a fabric designer. She wasn't married, and had never, as far as any of her friends knew, had a lover. She had had to take care of her mother until her mother's death, when she became ill.

"Of course," George said.

Claire sniffed a little and said, "I saw some sheets the other day with lovely patterns that reminded me of some of your patterns, Anne. Did you ever design fabric for sheets?"

"I think a sheet needs a rather bold design," Anne whispered. "My designs were always a bit too delicate for sheets, I think."

Keeping her tissue pressed to her nostrils, Claire thought that no doubt it was right to be talking about fabric design now, was no doubt right to reduce all the horror of death, the horror of and the longing for death, to talk about sheets.

But when Claire embraced Anne and kissed her goodbye, her friend groaned a little, and Claire turned away and left without looking back. She waited outside the room for George.

In Praed Street, near Paddington Station, they went to a workingman's *caf* with green Formica-topped tables and chairs with orange plastic seats and backrests to have tea, which came in thick red mugs.

There was nothing to say about Anne.

But as if this had everything to do with Anne, Claire said, "We can't get married, George, we can't. You must see that."

"Can I ask you again, when you get back from Russia?"

Claire turned her hand over and looked at the lines in her palm. She said, "I just recalled that when I was a little girl in my parochial school, the nuns made us pray every morning for the conversion of Russia. We prayed to the Holy Virgin Mother for the conversion of Russia. Why do I remember that just now?"

"I think that's beyond me to say."

Claire smiled at him.

George drove her back to Clapham, and in the car kissed her, but didn't go into the house.

When Claire couldn't find Rachel in the sitting room or kitchen, she went upstairs and, leaning silently into her room, found her asleep on her bed.

Claire went into her own room to lie down. If she thought of going to Russia, it wasn't to find the picture, it wasn't even for Rachel and Claude to find each other there, but to return to George, who was not mad, and whose sense of life was the only sense to have. Her very body yearned for a weekend with him in a country hotel.

Left to herself, the last thing she would have wanted to do was go to Russia. Left to herself, she would have forgotten about the picture in the depths of Russia, a country that had only ever inspired fear in her of the enemy country; a country of vast hydroelectric dams built by slave labor, of deep basements in great dark buildings in which executions took place and the blood ran gray on the cement, of mass graves in forests; a country of labor camps with frozen puddles and wooden barracks and barbed wire fences; a country where poets were imprisoned and shot against walls; a country where neighbors denounced neighbors and the secret police searched for letters and people were taken away in their pajamas and never seen again; a country the Holy Virgin Mother, with all the prayers of all the children in the world, couldn't save. George was right — it was mad to go to Russia.

Part

FIVE

I

THOUGH THE TAXI to the train station stalled often in the morning traffic of the City, Maurice sat still and quiet, as though there were all the time in the world. Claude, by him, thought they'd be late for their morning train, and his anxiety made him look out the taxi window with pointed attention. Anxiety always made him more attentive than he usually was. This was perhaps because when he was anxious about, say, being late for a train, he felt that there was much more to be anxious about than just that. There was so much more to be anxious about than he could say, his only way of dealing with so much, all beyond him, was to fix on the details.

Among the high, glassy commercial buildings was an old brick church with a tree in the churchyard and a black iron fence around it, the tree moving in the wind.

It was one thing to be late for a train from London to, say, Oxford, and another to be late for a train from London to Moscow.

Maurice, smiling a little, seemed to be aware of nothing around him.

"We'll be late," Claude said.

"I don't think we will," Maurice said.

Maurice had insisted on going to Moscow by train, as it had been, he said, by train that he had left.

In the 9:35 train to Harwich, Claude looked out the window with the special attention of someone who was going far. Maurice read the morning paper.

Claude noted the wild buddleia with mauve blossoms growing along the sides of tracks, sometimes on abandoned tracks, and the brick walls with aerosol graffiti — He noted the old-fashioned gas lamp in a narrow cobbled street below a bridge and a black woman wheeling a black baby in a stroller along the empty street, a brick wall on one side, and beyond the brick wall an empty lot in which there were old truck tires and more buddleia bushes were growing — He noted playing fields, and the low horizon behind them of blue sky and puffs of white clouds —

An hour outside London and going through farmland, he saw the fields covered with tawny stubble, some plowed, and masses of bramble, heavy with blackberries, on the banks when the train went through a cutting —

He saw everything as if already surrounded by the country he was going to.

Maurice looked out once and said the trees with red-orange berries, rowan trees, grew in the Russian countryside.

Why, Claude wondered, was he so anxious, so frightened even, of giving in to Russia?

On the ferry they sat out in the sunlight. Other passengers were sitting about, some lying, on the wide, wide, blue-painted metal deck of this enormous boat. When a cloud passed, the air became cold. Maurice closed his eyes. A sense of deep, deep — what? — not contentment or even peace so much as letting go, as giving in and feeling he could sleep and sleep in the sunlight, came to Claude. From time to time he nodded and half fell asleep, and images occurred to him —

The image came to him of a glass of water surrounded by darkness. And how, he wondered, had that occurred?

He knew why he was frightened of Russia. He was frightened because he was going there for Rachel, as though there he could do something for her he couldn't do anywhere else, but he did not know what he could do except to help find the picture.

The sky was cloudy, with sunrays beaming through and down into the green-gray surge, and oil tankers on the horizon.

In the train station of the Hoek Van Holland, they got into a Russian car. The back of the seat was covered by a dirty white embroidered cloth. The compartment was paneled in Formica made to look like wood. There was a Turkish carpet on the floor, and over the window two little drawn curtains, white with red-and-blue pictures of Saint George and the dragon printed on them. The smell was as of sour cream.

A Russian steward came into the compartment to give them glasses of tea in metal holders and big cubes of sugar.

Maurice didn't talk, and Claude wondered what he was thinking. Once he sniffed the air and said, as if about the smell of sour cream, "I remember that. That's the smell of Russia."

At night, Claude, in his berth above, heard Maurice in his berth below breathe in sleep.

They woke up in Berlin. Out the window was a construction

site, a concrete basic structure with many rusted iron rods piled around it and a crane high above it, the whole looking abandoned.

In Poland the train went through woods with a floor of purple heather, then passed a neat, well-kept, fenced-in village that looked completely depopulated, or as if invisible people lived there. At a corner where two dirt roads through the woods met was a large wooden cross with a wreath of red and white flowers on it.

After Warsaw night fell, and Claude saw, outside, the lights of cars driving along roads through rainy, bare woods.

What Maria Polosova had promised him, he thought, had ended in death. He thought of what he had wanted to tell her. It seemed to him now that he had wanted to tell her about Rachel.

Maurice went out for a glass of tea. The rain-covered window reflected the compartment and projected it out among the dark trees, with a pale green streetlight or yellow house light here and there, so Claude saw, outside, the jackets hung on wooden hangers above a stack of valises, magazines and a packet of candy and a map of Moscow on top of the valises, and the gray curtain meant to hide the jackets and valises pulled to the side, and, in the narrow open doorway, Maurice standing and drinking a glass of tea. The dark trees and green and yellow lights passed right through him.

There was a long, silent wait at the Polish border before the train crossed to the Belorussian border at Brest. Passengers were standing in the train corridor, under the dimmed lights, still and silent. The platform under floodlights was entirely deserted.

While at Brest the wheels of the Russian cars were changed for the different, Russian gauge, Claude and Maurice wandered about the train station. Big, granite, it was like a fancy train station at a spa, but a very rundown spa. As Claude and Maurice examined the decorations on the building — the carved Soviet stars and wreaths, a plaque with the emblematic head of Lenin — they said nothing. Some three quarters of a century past, Maurice had passed through Brest, on his émigré way out of Russia, but nothing, Claude saw, was as it would have been.

Two hours later they got back into the train car with its different-gauge wheels and into their berths.

During the night Claude was woken by Maurice in the berth below, seeming to gasp, and, worried, Claude listened until he heard Maurice breathe regularly.

In the early morning, Claude got up to go to the toilet and saw in the dawn light, in a blue-gray haze, bare birch woods. He stood in the empty corridor and looked out: woods, woods, vast woods. The train passed a village of small wooden houses, almost all log cabins of square-cut logs interlocked at the corners, but one green house, all listing, sagging a little. They were surrounded by fields, some with scarecrows made of old clothes, then bare woods.

Russia, Claude said to himself, Russia.

The trees went out of focus when the thought occurred to him that Marie had killed herself because of her visit to Russia.

When Claude went back into the compartment, he found that Maurice was still asleep.

The train stopped at a station. Red boxcars were on the sidings, beyond tracks with weeds growing between the ties. A woman railway worker was wearing an orange vest. There were cement posts and many crisscrossing wires overhead. On one side of the yard was a long open structure with a corrugated roof, and beyond that trees and small buildings, wooden or stucco, a bicycle leaning on the corner of one, and on the other side an open expanse with a huge factory in the distance and, on a rise, rectangular cement apartment buildings. As the train left, Claude saw, over the tops of parked cars, the stationhouse: blue stucco with white neoclassical pillars and, in a neoclassical pediment, a relief of double red bunting. A large woman in a green dress and blue apron and red cap with a black visor held up, grimly, a sign as the train passed: a white disk with a black circle.

When I imagine a glass of water, Claude thought, I imagine it in darkness. My wonder at the occurrence of the glass of water becomes, when I shift my vision from it, wonder at the darkness around it. Perhaps the glass of water can occur only because of the darkness, which is, I think, universal awareness. He imagined he stared, beyond everything he now saw as the train passed it, into that vast and frightening darkness.

A blond boy with a red tie among bare trees, carrying a satchel on his back, looked at the train passing.

II

SNOW BEGAN TO FALL when Claude looked out of their high hotel room, out over Moscow. He watched the snow fall on the low, long gray roofs of pink and pale green buildings while Maurice, in the small bathroom off their room, bathed. As the snow fell, the air darkened, and Claude felt, as if the falling snow had something to do with it, less and less well. Perhaps he was tired from the long train trip. In the distance were smokestacks and heavy white smoke rising up toward the snow-filled clouds. He thought he might have a fever.

Maurice came out of the bathroom in his dressing gown, his clear face bright pink, his flat chest also bright pink and hairless. His thick white hair was combed. He looked very fresh and clean, like a boy.

"Is it snowing?" he asked, his voice rising.

"Yes."

"What a blessing on us. What a blessing to have snow in Russia. Isn't it a blessing?"

"Yes," Claude said again.

In the hot water of the small bathtub, his knees up, Claude almost fell asleep, but his whole body jerked back as if in fear of letting go, and his will clung tightly to the edge and wouldn't let go, though he wanted to let go, and knew he wouldn't be able to unless his will let go. The edge it clung to was very narrow.

Dressed but still damp, he came out into the room where Maurice, sitting on the only chair, was squinting as he looked through an address book. The old man shut the book when Claude sat on his bed.

"I'm trying to find the telephone number of the Volkansky cousin. I know I put it in my address book. But it is not under V. What could it be under? The cousin, if cousin at all, is not called Volkansky."

"I hope you find it."

"It wouldn't do not to. What would Claire say if I couldn't? And Rachel?"

Claude got up and again went to the window to look at the falling snow. Turning to Maurice, who was looking through his address book, he said, "Rachel is pregnant."

"Pregnant?"

"You didn't notice, then."

"I don't know if it's proper for an old bachelor to notice such things. In fact, no, I didn't notice."

Claude said, smiling a little, "I wasn't the one to make her pregnant, if you're wondering."

"Was it forced on her?"

"Yes."

"Ah, Rachel." Maurice sighed deeply and asked, "Why should anyone have wanted to do anything so terrible to such a girl?"

"It's no doubt happening right now," Claude said, "right now, not far from us, here."

"No doubt," Maurice said softly.

Claude said, hearing his voice come from a distance and shocking him, "Somehow, I do feel I was the one."

"You do because you're a young man who, morally, would feel responsible toward a young woman who had been so wronged."

"You don't know me."

"I think I do."

"You don't."

Maurice asked quietly, "Do you love her?"

Claude breathed in deeply, then out, and said, "I —" He said, "I really do want to find the painting for her."

Again Maurice looked through his address book. "I must remember the name. It is not Volkansky. That is the maiden name of the woman we want to see. There are so many names in my book. I can't concentrate. Can it be because I'm so excited about being back in Russia? Can't I go out now? I want to find where I was born. Then I'll be able to concentrate. I'll remember everything."

Claude said, "Let's go out, then, and find where you were born."

In the hotel lobby, Maurice said, "We'll need a taxi. We'll need a taxi."

Women stood about the entrance to the hotel in the snow, wearing fur hats and bright scarves and heavy makeup, and the thought occurred to Claude that they were prostitutes. He wouldn't mention this to Maurice, who, Claude sometimes imagined, wouldn't have quite known what a prostitute did.

Claude promised to pay the taxi driver in dollars. He held the taxi door open for Maurice, who walked carefully on the snow.

The old man spoke in Russian to the driver, but when the driver spoke, Maurice, wincing, asked Claude, "What did he say?"

Claude laughed. "I have no idea."

"Tell him," Maurice said, "we want to go to the Arbat. Say it clearly, and he'll understand. *Arbat.*"

"Arbat," Claude said to the driver.

"Da, da," the driver said. "Arbat."

"You see," Maurice said, "he understood." He sat back and said, "I suppose my Russian is pre-Revolution, and he couldn't understand. I dare say I won't be understood by anyone and I won't understand anyone. Perhaps it'd be better simply to speak English."

"A good idea, I think."

Maurice turned to look out the window as the taxi, swerving in the snow whenever it stopped for a red light, sped along.

"I don't recognize anything," Maurice said. "Not a thing."

Claude did not want to say to Maurice that if he was only two when he left, he could not remember much. Maurice was trying to remember a Russia he couldn't remember.

"Well," Claude said, "if the language has been so radically changed since the Revolution, think how changed the city must be."

"Of course it would be, wouldn't it?"

The taxi sped up a wide prospect without traffic lights and stopped at a building with a red neon sign on top that spelled, in Cyrillic, PRAGA. Claude paid the driver, then turned to Maurice, standing in the falling snow, looking up at the sign.

"This has to be the old Restaurant Prague," he said as if to himself. "I must have been taken here as a boy by my parents for a meal. I'm sure I recall my parents saying they ate at the Restaurant Prague, and surely they took me. Perhaps we should dine here this evening." He wasn't wearing a hat, and snowflakes were melting in his white hair. He went to the entrance of the restaurant, and a doorman came out just as Maurice, still looking up at the façade, put out a hand to push the door open. *"Zakrit, zakrit,"* the scowling doorman said. "Tell him I want to make a reservation," Maurice said to Claude. "Tell him in English, he'll understand." "I think he's saying the restaurant is shut," Claude said. *"Zakrit,"* the doorman said, then crossed and uncrossed his arms like blades.

"*Zakrit?*" Maurice asked the doorman. "*Da,*" the doorman said. Maurice said to Claude, "I understood that. That word was used in pre-Revolution Russia too. He says the restaurant is closed." Then Maurice said to the doorman, bowing his head a little, "*Spaseba,*" which made the doorman stare at him. Walking away, Maurice said to Claude, "I thanked him anyway. It's not his fault, is it, that the restaurant is closed?" "I'm sure he was just doing his job," Claude said. Maurice said, "Also, I wanted to let him know that the Revolution wasn't entirely in vain, and that people like me would now be polite to people like him."

Maurice stopped a woman carrying a string bag of oranges by holding out his hand and saying something like "*Gda Arbat?*" Without saying anything, she turned and pointed behind her, then, her bag of oranges swinging, turned away and left. Maurice called after her, "*Spaseba bolshoi,*" and she looked back. As she did, she slipped and fell on her big bum. She was wearing zippered felt boots and a dark gray overcoat and a knitted cap. The oranges rolled out of her string bag.

"Oh my," Maurice said.

Claude rushed to the woman to help her up. He also helped her collect her oranges. She frowned, but she said as she left, "*Spaseba.*"

At the beginning of the Arbat a man was selling oranges from a crate. Some of the oranges, visible through the spaces between the slats, were wrapped in green tissue paper. A long line of people stood before the man. Snow fell more heavily.

Maurice looked carefully at the façades of the buildings along the Arbat, which was for pedestrians only. On the ledges of the shop windows were propped small paintings of snowbound Russian landscapes with birch trees and the arctic purple and red sun setting behind the trees. The snow on the ground was slushy. Maurice said, stopping before a neoclassical house with a medallion of the Three Graces on the pediment, again as if to himself, "Perhaps this was our house."

"You can't remember the number?" Claude asked.

The damp cold was penetrating, and he felt a fine shiver pass through him.

"No," Maurice said. "I should, but I can't." He looked at Claude, disappointed by himself in his enthusiasm. "I've come so unprepared."

As they were walking back along the Arbat, an old man going in the opposite direction slipped and fell, his arms flung up, and he lay still in the snow. Claude started toward him, but others gathered quickly around him.

"What has happened to him?" Maurice asked.

"I don't know."

"Shouldn't we find out if we can do anything?" Maurice said, and stepped toward the man surrounded by other men.

Claude put his hand on Maurice's arm. "He's being taken care of."

Maurice was feeling low, and Claude wondered how he could raise his spirits.

"We'll go back to our room," Claude said, "and we'll look through your address book for the name and telephone number you were looking for."

"Oh yes," Maurice said, but he didn't move except to press his hand to his chest and, it seemed, try to regulate his heartbeats by his breathing. When he took his hand away and, breathing normally, looked at Claude, he said, "But I'm not sure I should bother them, you know."

"They're expecting you to telephone, aren't they?"

"I was told they would be, yes."

"It'd be as terrible a disappointment to them as it would be to Rachel if you didn't."

"Would it?"

"Of course it would."

"I should think they'd be disappointed meeting me."

"Come on," Claude said, "let's go telephone them."

In their room, Maurice handed Claude his address book to read out the names. He said, "You needn't read the ones crossed out. They're all dead." While Claude read the names, the old man kept a hand over his eyes. There were hundreds of names, but most were crossed off. Of those that were left, few were Russian, and there were no Kuragins. Halfway through, a small panic came to Claude with the thought that Maurice would not remember the name even when Claude called it out. But when Claude said "Poliakoff," Maurice dropped his hand and said, "That's it. I couldn't remember because it is so common a Russian name. Names have to be odd for me to remember them."

Claude read out the telephone number and Maurice picked up the black, heavy, old-fashioned receiver, held it up to his ear and mouth as if listening, then, after a moment, asked Claude, "Please, will you do it?"

Claude took the receiver. "Do they speak English?"

"I was told they do. They are Sasha and Vera Poliakoff. He is not a Volkansky relation, she is. Try to speak with her."

She answered. She spoke English with a precise English accent, and said that she had been expecting this telephone call, and that it would be a great honor if he, Mr. Ricard, and Mr. Kuragin would dine with her and her husband the evening of the following day. She slipped, tripped by excitement she could no longer suppress, only when she gave instructions as to time and Metro station where her husband would meet them, which she had to repeat again and again. And she didn't seem to know how to say goodbye over the telephone. She said, "Well then, well then, well —" and she hung up.

When Maurice, in pajamas, got into bed for the night, he said, "Poor Rachel," and turned away from Claude.

The hotel room was small and narrow, the simple, built-in beds on opposite sides. For a long while, Claude couldn't sleep. When finally he did, he was woken by the gasps of Maurice trying to catch his breath, and he wondered if he should get up and go to him, but was worried that this might embarrass Maurice. Maybe Maurice was asleep now, and his seeming to try to catch his breath was part of a dream. Then Maurice went silent. But Claude couldn't fall back to sleep.

Snow was still falling in the morning, and when Claude looked out he saw, below, hunched men and women in dark overcoats and fur hats treading the sidewalks, their footsteps dark in the white.

Maurice appeared to be fine. He wanted to go out as soon as possible after breakfast. He had brought a cap just in case of snow, and had warned Claude to bring one also. Somewhere in this city, Claude thought, there might be the painting. They walked to Red Square and along the narrow parks under the brick walls of the Kremlin, and all the while Maurice kept looking about as if for something familiar, and nothing was. They walked to the Moscow River, and over a bridge, and for a while stopped on the bridge to watch the river below. Over the bridge, they walked around a quarter of old buildings which, without the tramlines and electricity poles and wires, was as it would have been long, long before Maurice left Russia, but standing in a curving street of yellowish stucco buildings, snow collecting on the sills and bulging over the edges of roofs, Maurice simply raised his arms and let them fall to his sides as though he gave up, then and there, trying to recognize anything of the Russia he had been, in any case, too young when he'd lived here to remember now.

Then, standing with Maurice in this street, Claude felt a strange sense that he had been here before. He looked for a detail that would confirm the sense — the grille over a window designed like a sun in one lower corner, emitting long rays — while knowing at the same time that it was impossible he had ever been here. He told himself he was experiencing *déjà vu*, but he didn't quite believe it was *déjà vu*, for the sense of familiarity was so strong. Maybe the sense had something to do with his fever, for with it came the unreasonable belief that the painting would be found, and that could have been the result only of a fever.

"I suppose we should go back to the hotel," Maurice said.

They walked slowly, Claude holding Maurice's arm where the snow was trampled down so he wouldn't slip.

Again Claude stopped on the bridge to look over. Maurice went on ahead and at the end had to call Claude, who, staring down at the swiftly moving black water, didn't at first hear. A plank sank and rose, sank and rose in the current, then was pulled under, and Claude did not see it rise.

Maurice didn't want to go out in the afternoon. Clearly, he felt that whatever he had come to Russia to find for himself wasn't to be found. He and Claude sat in the café off the lobby, reading. Claude saw Maurice turn his book upside down and lower it to his knee and stare out through high, wide panes of glass into what was perhaps a little garden, now thick with falling snow. Maurice said, "I am a fool."

Claude couldn't let Maurice believe this. "What's wrong?" he asked.

"I was only two years old when I was taken away from Moscow by my parents. And I'm a fool for imagining I can remember."

"Perhaps in some way you do remember," Claude said.

"I don't," Maurice said. "I don't even have any unconscious memory of the place. I don't feel it means anything to me at all."

"That can't be true," Claude said. "You've hardly seen anything."

"But I sense it."

"You'll see, in talking with Sasha and Vera this evening, you'll begin to feel something pull at you."

"I've been wondering if we should cancel this evening."

That, Claude thought, was exactly what he would like to do, and withdraw — withdraw from the hard-edged public places of the hotel, from Moscow, from Maurice too — and sleep, if he were able to sleep, but he couldn't withdraw. He said, "I won't let you. I promise you, Sasha and Vera, inviting you into their home, will mean everything to you."

"You think so?"

"I promise you so."

Maurice blinked.

"And you mustn't forget Rachel. We're doing this for her."

"Of course I won't forget Rachel," Maurice said. "Wasn't it my idea that we should come? And we'll find the painting for her."

"Yes, we'll find the painting," Claude said.

Sasha Poliakoff seemed to recognize them immediately at the entrance of the Metro station, because he went right to them as they came out. He was wearing a large black fur hat and black, thick-rimmed eyeglasses. His English had an American accent. He walked between Maurice and Claude through the snow-covered streets under the dim streetlights among the bare white trees. Except for them, the streets were empty.

Sasha said, "I'm told the West exists — I meet people, as yourselves, who say they're from the West — but I can only believe you come from nowhere. You come from outer space."

"Perhaps we do," Claude said.

"I have no way of knowing you don't," Sasha said.

Maurice didn't speak, but kept looking around.

Vera was in the narrow passageway in the apartment, waiting for them. She shook Maurice's hand, then Claude's, and hung their coats among many coats hanging on pegs above a number of shoes and rubber overshoes. Without saying anything, Maurice handed Vera a bag with four bottles of wine from the hotel hard-currency shop, and she, perhaps not knowing what the formal thanks were, said nothing.

Sasha indicated the way down the passageway into a room with a table covered by a white tablecloth and set for supper, and Maurice and Sasha sat. Claude spoke, but not Maurice, and Claude realized that he spoke as much as he did because Maurice didn't at all. Sasha sat and poured out glasses of vodka. Vera came into the room from the passage carrying a square mushroom pie.

Claude was grateful that Sasha took over the talk. He talked about Russia. He kept saying, "In our country —" Behind the thick lenses of his spectacles his eyes appeared to be very small.

The room was papered with faded wallpaper and had water stains on the ceiling. There was very little furniture: a divan at one end and a bookcase at the other. The floorboards were painted black.

"What a beautiful dining room set," Claude said of a table and four chairs and a large freestanding mirror that reflected the diners about the table. These pieces of furniture were of dark walnut, with bronze sabots on the tips of the elegant legs of the chairs and gilt lion's heads at the corners of the backrests and bronze laurel wreaths at the centers of the backrests. On the top of the posts supporting the mirror were bigger lion's heads, and in the middle of the pediment of the frame was a bigger laurel wreath. All the furniture was rickety, the bronze fixtures loose and the finely striped upholstery on the seats of the chairs worn and stained. Maurice appreciatively but silently studied the furniture.

To eat her mushroom pie, Vera sat away from the table and used a knife and fork. Sasha leaned, hunched, low over his plate and ate the pie with his fingers.

Whenever there was a pause, Sasha spoke about Russia, always starting with "In our country —"

Vera went out and came back with a roast pork on a platter, surrounded by pickled apples and cucumbers.

As the four ate, Sasha sat back and said with a sigh, "Ah, Russia, Russia." He looked at Maurice, perhaps wondering why this old man, for whom they were giving this extravagant meal as a celebration of his return to his country, was so silent.

Because of his spectacles, Sasha appeared to have a smaller, inner head within his outer one, which smaller one could only be seen through his lenses. He was about thirty-five, with black hair that hung over his ears, and he wore a gray turtleneck pullover.

Vera said to Sasha, glancing at Maurice, "Please, they have just come to our country. They won't want to hear you say anything about Russia that will make them wish they hadn't come."

She, tall, broad-shouldered, wore a blue woolen dress that fell in loose panels to just above her knees and long black stockings and narrow black shoes. Her hair was cut so it swung across her cheeks.

Refilling the glasses with vodka, Sasha laughed, a clear, light laugh, and said, "Not tell him the truth about Russia?" He said to Claude, "Ours is a dented, rusted, cracked, broken-down, destroyed country." He looked at Maurice again, but there was no reaction from the old man, and Sasha frowned.

Vera said, "Oh, but there is another Russia." The black circles around her beautiful black eyes were deep.

Just as she spoke, a boy came into the room from the passage. He was slim and white and had blond hair, and he stood inside the doorway, looking at the people gathered about the table. He lowered his head.

Vera said, "Alyosha."

The boy raised his head and smiled.

A look of amazement came over Maurice's face. The boy didn't move but kept his eyes as though focused in the air between him and the table, too shy to focus on the table. His eyes bright, Maurice said, "Alyosha," and the boy focused on him and smiled more widely, his lips separated on even young teeth.

Vera called him over to the table. His eyes lowered, he stood by his mother, who spoke to him in Russian and passed her hand through his blond hair, which stood up. Maurice kept his eyes on him, and when Alyosha looked up at Maurice and said, in delicate English, "How do you do?" Maurice leaned toward the boy, then sat back and expelled his breath softly on the name "Alyosha." He leaned forward again and said, with humor in his polite deference to the boy, "I am well, Alexei Alexandrovich, and happy to meet you." Except for his name and patronymic, Alyosha didn't understand this, and turned his entire body to his mother, who, whispering, explained, then, whispering more quietly, told him what to respond in English, and Alyosha said to Maurice, "I am happy to meet you."

Maurice pushed his chair back from the table and said, "Come here, come here" to Alyosha, and with a gentle push from his mother, the boy went to stand before Maurice, who looked the tall, slim boy up and down, then held out his hand, and the boy took it in his.

Maurice said, "I thought that I could speak Russian, but I can't."

He paused, and Vera translated this for Alyosha. The boy's blond hair covered the tops of his ears and ended in a point at his smooth nape. His blond face was made broad by his cheekbones. His nose was straight, and there were fine, Asiatic folds of flesh at the insides of his blue eyes. The boy listened to Maurice.

The old man asked, "Do you speak English?"

Prompted by his mother, the boy said, "A little."

"You'll teach me Russian," Maurice said.

Again prompted by his mother, Alyosha said, "It will be a pleasure to teach you Russian."

Tears rose into the old man's eyes, and he kissed the boy's hand, then let go of it and looked away from him, looked away from the table. When he looked toward Vera, the tears were running down the sides of his nose. His voice choked, he said to her, "I'm sorry." Vera spoke quickly to Alyosha, who hurried out of the room.

Vera, Sasha, and Claude sat still and silent while Maurice wiped his eyes and cheeks with his napkin. He cleared his throat and said to Sasha and Vera, not quite in control of his voice, "The fact is, I have — we, Claude and I, have — come to Moscow on something of a mission—"

"Oh?" Sasha asked.

Claude thought he should explain what their mission was in case Maurice got it wrong. But Maurice was stopped from talking by a tall, thin woman who came into the room. Her face was red from the outside cold. She seemed to have come expecting foreigners, because she spoke immediately in English: "Please do not let me disturb anyone." Maurice and Claude stood, and Vera introduced Katya Platonova, who said, "Please sit, please." She did not want anything to eat. She sat at an angle to the table, distant from it, and she reached out for a sliver of roast pork, which she ate, then a bit of pickled apple, and eating this, she remained leaning forward. Sasha and Vera seemed embarrassed by her and ignored her. Katya said, "I know I interrupted —"

Maurice addressed her, ignoring the others, as if he'd been waiting for her to explain their mission. "A recent friend, a dear American woman, believes there is a painting in the possession of the Volkansky family, a painting by the seventeenth-century Italian painter Pietro Testa, she would like to have a look at for her scholarly studies. I am looking for someone from the Volkansky family who might know where it could possibly be, if in the possession of someone of the family or someone else, or the state."

Pushing strands of her long blond hair over her red ears, Katya listened intently, but just as she was about to answer, Sasha stopped her by speaking to Maurice himself.

"Vera is Volkansky."

Maurice, turning to her, said, "Of course, I knew that, and should have been addressing you."

Sasha said, "But I am afraid to tell you that Vera does not have the painting."

"And you know no other Volkanskys?" Maurice asked Vera.

She said, "There are very few of us in Russia, and I can tell you, with my hand on my heart, that not one has such a painting."

"Not one would even remember it?"

"I am sure not."

Sasha said, "If anyone might have known, it was Princess Volkansky."

Vera said, "Who lived in one room in the palace that had belonged to her father, the palace where she was born and brought up. But the last I heard, which was some years ago, she was thrown out when she was a very old woman and her room was given to a family."

"She must be dead now," Sasha said.

Claude asked, "So you have no idea how to find out about the painting?"

"No," Vera said quietly.

Katya, frowning, asked, leaving out, as Russians often did, the article in English, "Tell me, what is name of painter?"

"Testa, Pietro Testa," Claude said to her.

"Testa, like word for head in Italian?"

Smiling, Maurice said to Katya, "Have you studied art history, then?"

"I know someone —" Katya began, but Sasha stopped her with a look. She stuck out her lower lip and sat back.

"Ah," Maurice said, and, his chin trembling as if he were about to cry again, he lowered his hands to his knees. He didn't look at Claude.

Claude thought: Of course we will not find the painting. He looked about the room as though wondering what he was doing there in that strange place, and yet the room appeared familiar to him, and strange because it appeared familiar. He knew it, he had spent his life in this room. Again he thought: Of course we will not find the picture, of course not.

Vera put the dishes on a tray and went out, and Sasha poured more vodka, for Katya too. He and Claude tried to resume talk about Russia, but their awareness of Maurice, who was himself silent, kept them mostly silent. Vera came back with a walnut cake and a pot of tea and teacups, and Katya had some tea too. Put into her place, however, she remained silent.

Shortly after the tea, Maurice said to Claude, "I think I should get back to my bed." But as he rose, he said to Vera, "Please may I say goodnight to Alyosha?" She smiled a faintly sad smile and said, "Of course," and went for the boy and came back with him to stand, holding him against her with her arms about his shoulders, in the doorway. He was in faded flannel pajamas too small for him, so his wrists and ankles showed. His mother whispered something into his ear and, releasing him, gave him a little shove toward Maurice. Standing, Maurice waited by the table. Alyosha took a couple of steps toward him, evidently sent by his mother to kiss him, and Maurice, in anticipation, held out his hands to embrace him, one hand still holding his napkin. But the boy stopped, and after a moment turned and ran out of the room.

"Call him back," Sasha said to Vera.

"No, no," Maurice said. "Let him be."

He said goodnight to Katya. As Claude did, she reached out for his hand to grip it in her fingers, and she said, "I can help with painting," but seeing Sasha approach, she pulled her fingers away.

The two doors to other rooms along the passage were shut. Maurice and Claude put on their overcoats, and Sasha also, then his large black fur hat and overshoes. It seemed to Claude there was a strange finality to their leaving the apartment, as if he and Maurice would never come back. While they waited for the elevator, Vera, standing at the open doorway, was backlit by yellowish light from inside.

Maurice said suddenly, "I've forgotten my gloves."

Vera closed the door to a crack and said, "Oh, but it's bad luck to come back in once you've left."

Maurice stopped and clasped his hands together.

"It'll be all right," Sasha said, "if he looks in a mirror."

Vera opened the door and let Maurice enter and take his gloves from the shelf above the hooks where the overcoats were hung in the passage, but before leaving he had to look at himself in the mirror hanging on the wall. Then the old man turned to her and tried to smile.

Sasha accompanied Maurice and Claude to the Metro station. Snow was falling in small swirls about the streetlights. No cars passed along the wide, snow-covered streets, and no one walked along the snow-covered pavements. No, that wasn't true: a lone man was walking his black dog.

At the Metro station, Sasha was reluctant to let Maurice and Claude go, as if he too felt he would most likely never see them again.

He said to Maurice, "Would you like to meet my grandmother? You might even have met before you left Russia."

"I wouldn't remember," Maurice said.

"Maybe she would," Sasha said.

Claude said to Maurice, "You should see her."

"Of course I want to see her," Maurice said quickly. "Of course."

"We can go to her dacha," Sasha said.

"Will Alyosha come?" Maurice asked.

Sasha laughed. "I will ask him."

In the hotel, Maurice said he would like tea, he really must have tea, and Claude took him up to the tea shop at the top of the hotel, sure that it would be shut. But it was open, and Maurice got his tea, which Claude brought to him from a counter to a narrow table where the old man sat.

"Lovely tea," Maurice said. He warmed his hands by holding them close around the glass.

"Don't you think we should let Claire and Rachel know that there's no point in coming?" Claude asked.

"No point?"

"If there's no way of finding out about the painting."

"Oh, there will be a way."

"How do you know?"

"You'll see, we'll find a way."

"Sasha and Vera weren't so sure."

"We'll find someone else who knows. We won't disappoint them, we won't disappoint Rachel."

Claude and Maurice waited outside the hotel in the morning for Sasha and Vera to arrive in their car. Snow had stopped falling, but the clouds were dark and low. Alyosha was not in the car, and Maurice didn't ask where he was. Perhaps the boy had said he didn't want to come. Claude, in the back seat, did the talking with Sasha and Vera in the front, while Maurice, in the back by him, remained silent, holding a bag of gifts against his knees. Glancing at him from time to time, Claude thought: He is silent because he's not well.

Sasha talked about Russia. He said, "The Revolution was a terrible mistake."

"But it was such a wonderful idea," Vera said.

"Yes," Claude said quietly.

To see through the window, he had to keep rubbing it with his glove, because the glass frosted over as soon as he cleared a little space, and looking out, he wondered why he felt he had been here before, why his sense of *déjà vu,* if it was that, was so extended and seemed to last all the time.

The high-rise apartment houses stopped, and there were small wooden houses under snow, behind fences, and wide, empty white plains with electricity pylons behind them. The car went among birch woods and dachas. A woman was cross-country skiing through the woods.

Then Sasha got stuck in an ice rut. He kept stepping on the gas to try to get out, but the one back wheel in the rut just spun, screeching. Claude and Vera got out, and as they were pushing at the car, a man in a big black fur hat and black overcoat pulling a sled along a snow-packed path, a large brown-paper–wrapped parcel on it, stopped and came to help. Behind the sled was a woman in a flowered kerchief, her hands thrust into the sleeves of her long overcoat so the sleeves' edges touched and her hands weren't visible. Her boots were big and as chunky as logs of wood. With the help of the man, the car lurched out of the rut. Back in the car, Claude saw the woman through the hole in the frosted window. Her clear round face was red from the cold, and she was smiling at him, her chin held in, her face tilted downward so she looked up from under a wide white brow. Her smile rose into her cheeks. And a strange, maybe a scary longing came over Claude.

Sasha parked at a gate made of solid planks painted blue, and the large dacha beyond the gate was also blue, the edges of its slanting roof rounded out with snow. A middle-aged woman met them in the entrance with a dog that jumped about and barked, and, all of them cramped in by coats on hooks, boots, and shelves of books, Sasha introduced Maurice and Claude to his mother, Natalia Alexandrovna. She wore a knitted sweater in maroon and yellow stripes, and her short hair was champagne blond around a lively face lightly rouged, her eyelids made up slightly with blue. She hurried up the stairs that led from the entrance hall, and left Maurice and Claude to clean their shoes with a besom kept behind the door and Sasha and Vera to take off their boots and put on felt slippers.

At the top of the flight of bare wooden steps was a large room with a painted wooden floor, one small rug, and very little furniture. Natalia Alexandrovna was standing in the middle of the room, indicating, with a slight bow, a doorway into another room, and everyone waited for Maurice, carrying the bag, to go in first.

This was a smaller room. In one corner was a double bed covered with a fake fur spread, and in another corner, near the one window in the room, was an old woman sitting in an upholstered chair with wooden arms at a low, round wooden table. Her gray face, her squared body, seemed to be made of cement.

By her on a stool, sitting with his back to the window so the snow-light behind him made his blond hair brilliant, was Alyosha.

Claude, just behind Maurice, saw the old man stop for a moment. He put his bag down on the wooden floor.

On the cloth-covered table were laid out glasses and small plates and serving dishes of food: tuna fish and mayonnaise salad, slices of cold beef, chicken, onions, cucumbers, caviar, a little crystal bowl of bilberry preserve, pickled mushrooms, bread and butter, and a bottle of vodka.

The old woman stood as Maurice approached her. Her hard, cement-gray face was long, with a long, thin nose crooked at the bridge. Her eyes were deep in black circles.

When Sasha introduced her, Varvara Petrovna, to Maurice, she didn't smile but frowned, as if she had not wanted to meet him but was meeting him against her will. She held out her hand and Maurice shook it, then she withdrew her hand and folded her heavy arms across her waist, and spoke in Russian.

Maurice, his hands raised, looked around the room for someone to help him.

Sasha said, "She welcomes you back to Russia."

Maurice didn't seem to understand this either but, smiling, looked at Alyosha, who was standing by his great-grandmother, smiling at Maurice.

Varvara Petrovna sat.

"Where is my bag?" Maurice asked, turning to Claude. "I have brought a gift for Alyosha."

Claude handed him the bag, and from it Maurice took a large shiny picture book, which he gave to the boy. Vera went around to her son, who was staring at the laminated cover of the book, a picture of a beautiful countryside, and whispered into his ear. She took him to the bed and sat on the edge with him, the book on the boy's lap, and as he turned the pages his mother translated the English text into Russian.

Varvara Petrovna began to shift from side to side and she looked around the room, looked, it seemed, past those near her as if they were, close around her, keeping her in her chair against her will, and she was searching beyond them for a way out. When Sasha asked her something in Russian, she appeared for a second to be frightened back into attention to the people near her, but when, after that second, she focused on her grandson, she raised her head and answered him with a tone of voice that was almost disdainful for his having asked her something so stupid.

No one touched the glasses of vodka Sasha poured out. Perhaps the Russians were waiting for Maurice to pick up his glass first. Claude reached for a glass of vodka and raised it, and Sasha reached for one also. Maurice was looking at Alyosha, as attentive to the boy as the boy was to the book. "Maurice, pay attention," Claude said quietly to the old man, who, with a slight jerk, turned his attention to the table, picked up a glass of vodka, and held it up. Varvara Petrovna also raised a glass.

Not knowing whether he was being forward or not, Claude said, "Let's drink to Russia."

Sasha raised his glass higher, said, "To Russia," and drank his vodka down in one shot.

Varvara Petrovna didn't drink. She moved slowly. Apparently moving gently under great duress, she put her glass of vodka on the table and leaned back and placed her hands, her long fingers gracefully extended, on her bosom.

She focused on Claude, as if Maurice were not even present and this party had been arranged for her to meet Claude. Perhaps, he thought, she imagined she would address Maurice through him, if she were to address Maurice at all. Perhaps she thought there was no reason to address Maurice, whom she took to be as much a child as Alyosha. Claude felt he couldn't turn away from her, because to turn away would be to indicate that he didn't like her studying him, which she seemed to have the right to do. The old woman pressed her hands against her bosom and stated, "Inside —" She spoke in English slowly, and as she spoke she pressed harder into her bosom. "Inside, I have dark feelings."

Claude laughed a little. He didn't wonder whether his laughter was polite or not. He asked Varvara Petrovna, "About what?"

She raised her hands from her bosom and held them out.

Claude had laughed because he was embarrassed by what she had said, but his embarrassment, which no one around him would have understood, least of all Varvara Petrovna, succumbed as a thin piece of white paper floating on dark water would succumb to black depths if a stone were thrown onto it, succumbed especially to the way Varvara Petrovna dropped her hands onto the flat wooden arms of her chair.

Maurice asked Vera, "Does Alyosha like the book?"

She whispered to her son, who smiled from the bed at Maurice and said, "I love the book."

Unable to hold himself back, Maurice went to sit on the other side of the boy. The book was meant to teach the basic English words for house, hill, tree, sun, and these words the boy's mother read out in English and the boy repeated. Everyone listened to the boy say the simple words.

Out the window, icicles hung from the eaves of the house.

Beyond the icicles were snow-covered birch trees and pines. Claude recalled that sense he used to have on snowy winter days in New England when, looking out the window, he'd think: This must be like Russia.

He looked at Varvara Petrovna, who, head raised, was frowning as she listened to Alyosha say the English words.

When Vera stopped talking, the old woman lowered her head and thought. Everyone watched her think. She raised her eyes to Claude.

"In the West," she said, "tell everyone —"

Claude waited.

"Tell everyone —" she repeated.

Sasha spoke to his grandmother in Russian, but she ignored him and made a violent gesture as of pushing him away, and she shouted at Claude in Russian.

Sasha said to Claude, "Is passionate, my grandmother," making a rare mistake in English.

Varvara Petrovna shouted at Claude, "Tell everyone, tell everyone —" and she went on in Russian, in a high voice. Sasha picked up the bottle of vodka very carefully and tipped the neck very slowly to fill Claude's glass, and Varvara Petrovna snatched it from his hand and poured out the vodka quickly. She sat back, her elbows on the arms of her chair, and she spoke to Claude in Russian in a low voice, and then she put her hands over her face.

Sasha said, "She had such faith in our Revolution."

"And now?" Claude asked.

Sasha said, "She has no faith in anything."

On the edge of the bed, Maurice put his hand on Alyosha's head, and the boy smiled, but got up with his book and went to the other side of the room, where he turned back, still smiling, and looked at the old man.

Sasha said something to Alyosha in Russian and the boy smiled more at Maurice. He stepped from foot to foot and also moved his head a little from side to side. He raised the open book, looked at a picture in it, lowered it, and, when his father spoke to him again, looked without smiling at Maurice.

Maurice put his hand to his chest as if to regulate his heartbeats, and there was a momentary expression of pain on his face. Sasha spoke to Alyosha once again, and the boy rushed toward Maurice and kissed him, just at the corner of his lips, and, laughing, drew away.

Varvara Petrovna was sitting with her head held high and her eyes closed. Sasha spoke to her and she opened her eyes and stood, and she put out her hand to shake Claude's hand. Then she went around the table to Maurice, on the bed, who also stood, and she held out her hand for his. Holding his hand, she spoke to him at length in Russian, her head tilted to one side, and when she was finished she let his hand go and left the room.

Sasha said to Maurice, "She regrets she does not remember you, but hopes you had a happy life in the West."

Vera said to Claude, "Perhaps we should go?"

The old man asked, "Must we?"

Smiling, Sasha said to him, "Alyosha will come with us."

The dog jumped about them as they went to the blue gate.

From the road, Maurice pointed to a church on a low hill, the gold onion domes bright in the great gray sky. "Can we go there?" he asked.

Claude wanted to say, You must get back to the hotel, you're not well.

Maurice and Alyosha went ahead, talking to each other partly in English and partly in Russian.

In the churchyard, a little boy with a great fur hat with long earflaps hanging loose was running and sliding, his arms outstretched, on the ice. In the church, Vera bought candles for all of them, and Claude watched Maurice and Alyosha, their heads leaning toward each other, light theirs and stick them in the stand before an icon. The narrowly arched church, with blue frescoes in which tall, narrow churches similar to the one they were in occurred in strange perspectives, was filled with women, some lighting candles at the icons but most crowded into the nave and holding out glass jars and white enamel cups for holy water. The women all wore the same dark clothes: heavy overcoats rounded by their large shoulders and breasts, knitted, dun-colored, or fur hats, and boots.

Outside the church, Sasha asked Maurice if he'd like to visit the grave of Sasha's grandfather. They all went to the cemetery near the church. The plots in the snow-covered cemetery were surrounded by blue- or green-painted iron fences, and the tall, narrow, thin gravestones had photographs inserted in them. Sunk in the snow on the grave were red carnations without stems, and apples, which Sasha said his grandmother had placed there.

That night, Maurice slept, but again Claude lay awake.

He wondered if there was a hotel doctor, not only for Maurice but for him. He listened to Maurice's breathing.

Varvara Petrovna, he thought, understood that everything ended in darkness. Claude didn't know what her positions had been during the years of communism, but her dacha indicated that she must have had the high approval of the Party. There was no room for longing in her thinking, none, and she was right, because nothing could ever be realized from longing but longing itself. Only thinking could realize anything beyond itself, the careful thinking out of a system and the imposition of the system on the world. Claude thought Varvara Petrovna had believed in that, had believed in a system as a vision, and had believed that the vision must be imposed. She had counted on the vision being strong, stronger even than the horrors of what had had to be done to realize the vision, and she had lost. She understood horror, understood what baseness humans could sink to, understood that all that was left was the horror, the terrible baseness, too great for anything but the starkest despair. There was something reassuring about such despair.

That they wouldn't find the painting, Claude thought, was a fact of that despair, and he and Maurice and Claire and Rachel, especially Rachel, must live out the despair, if possible.

He heard Maurice breathing hard, and he sat up to listen.

In the morning, he asked at reception if there was a hotel doctor. There wasn't. Was there any doctor? The woman behind the high counter said that if it was an emergency, he should contact his embassy.

When he went back to the room, he found Maurice ready to go out.

"To go where?" Claude asked.

For a moment, he imagined Maurice would say he had an idea of where the painting might be found.

"I'd like to try to find something to buy Alyosha," Maurice said. He looked pale, and the angles of his skull showed.

"There is very little in the shops."

"I would like to buy him a bicycle."

"A bicycle? Where would you buy him a bicycle?"

"We'll go look."

Claude himself felt better once he was out with Maurice, going into department stores. But there was very little to buy. In one department store, all the dusty glass cases were empty. Maurice's Russian seemed to have improved, and he talked with the woman behind a counter on which there were three pairs of gloves spaced out far from one another. She frowned, but she understood and gave him instructions. He leaned on the counter, breathing hard. In the shop where she instructed Maurice to go were many new shining bicycles, leaning against one another in rows. Excited, Maurice bought one. Claude wheeled it along the sidewalks where the snow was trodden down to pathways, Maurice from time to time touching the bell on the handlebars. He's right, Claude thought, he's right to be excited, and a little thrill of excitement passed through him. He did feel better.

Snow fell as they climbed the rising avenue to the hotel. Claude looked up at the sky, then looked back to Maurice, but Maurice had fallen. He was lying on the snow-covered sidewalk, his hands crossed over his chest, and as Claude looked at him he rolled over onto his stomach. Claude dropped the bicycle, which slid, sideways, partway down the slope, and he knelt beside Maurice, his arms raised, not knowing what to do. Men and women in dark overcoats gathered around them, one with the bicycle, and spoke, but Claude, looking up, simply raised his arms higher. The steaming breaths of the people formed a cloud over the body of Maurice. On the other side of Maurice from Claude, one man stepped forward and crouched and quickly turned Maurice over. The old man's eyes were open, but they were not seeing anything. His hands were still clutched to his chest, and the man removed them and placed a fist on Maurice's chest, and with his other hand, also made into a fist, he thumped the fist on Maurice's chest. Maurice's body jolted as the man continued to hit his chest, but when Maurice's jaw opened and remained open the man stopped, looked at Claude, and said something in Russian. But Claude stared at the man, who, realizing Claude didn't understand, stared back. The people standing separated, and a policeman in a long gray coat and a gray furry cap with turned-up earflaps appeared.

When, hours later, Claude got back to the hotel, he found the bicycle in the lobby.

Stunned, Claude did only what he was told to do by Sasha and Vera. They even contacted people in London through the telephone numbers Claude gave them. Maurice's closest relative, a very distant cousin, said he should be buried in Russia, and Sasha said he would deal with the arrangements with the help of the British embassy. Vera gave Claude some pills she said would help him get over his fever, and insisted he stay in bed in his hotel room. The pills made him sleep, but he had nightmares, and when the ringing telephone woke him he wasn't sure for a moment where he was. Vera wanted to know how he was.

"Did Alyosha get the bike?" Claude asked.

"He did," Vera said, "he did."

She visited him in his hotel room, and brought him a thermos of hot soup. He hadn't got rid of his fever, and was sweating.

But he insisted on going to the burial, in a cemetery under snow.

He found, outside the closed cemetery chapel, Sasha and Vera, Alyosha and Varvara Petrovna standing at an open casket on a carriage, with pale green and pink swags of cloth hanging round the casket, and inside Maurice, in the clothes he had died in, lying with his hands placed one over the other at his waist, his face smooth and white, his mouth a little open. Snow fell on him.

As if by instinct, Claude put his arms around Alyosha and held him for a moment.

Claude wouldn't be able to do anything to help Rachel. He had made her believe something was possible when he should have known it was not.

III

HE WOKE to a blizzard. At the window of his room, the great white and black, involuting clouds of snow, swirling toward him and pressing, as they rolled, against the pane, seemed to draw him out, out as into a high place where he would be pulled in one direction, then another, then another, until he was as lost as out on a tundra. Below were pedestrians in dun overcoats and dark fur hats, leaning into the blizzard as they walked slowly along the sidewalks, the snow rising and falling about them. But above, the snow seemed to convolute itself, in blasts, into that great tundra where there was no one.

Sasha and Vera told Claude he must come and stay with them, at least until he was well, but he didn't want to stay with them, and said he was in fact all right. However alone Claude felt, he didn't feel well enough to see anyone.

He thought of Rachel even when he imagined he was thinking of something else.

As he lay in bed, he tried to figure out something. He knew how his mind worked: it was always in itself trying to figure out something, even when there was nothing to figure out. All it did was distort space. Perhaps what it was trying to figure out had nothing to do with Rachel but only with space.

His eyes closed, he saw himself, from a long distance, fall from a black bridge into a river.

As unwell as he felt, he thought he must go out. Dressing, he kept telling himself he must go out, must at least take a walk, but it seemed to him that to go out on his own must be forbidden. He would make himself go out for a walk.

He put on his scarf, overcoat, a cap, all of which seemed to require him to remember to put them on. Dressed, he realized he had to use the toilet. Then, dressed again to go out, he saw he'd forgotten to put on his gloves, and he couldn't remember where he'd put them. They were on the bed. Opening the door to leave the room, he paused because he was sure he'd forgotten something, and he went through everything he must have on him to go out: wallet, passport, tissues. He'd forgotten tissues.

His confusion annoyed him, and he told himself he must think out carefully everything he did. The floor, walls, and ceiling of the corridor tilted at odd angles as he walked down it. Outside, it came to him that he had forgotten something important, and he stood outside on the snow-cleared sidewalk to remember what.

Then he heard himself say, You came out for a walk, that's all, and not especially to the bridge.

Why shouldn't I walk to the bridge? he asked himself.

There's no reason for you not to, he said to himself. But that's not why you came out. You came out just for a walk, not to see the bridge.

What bridge? he asked as he walked down to the Moscow River.

When he saw the bridge, he stopped for a moment and said to himself, It wasn't to see the bridge that you came out for a walk, so why did you come here?

He responded, I came here only to take a walk. There was no reason why I shouldn't come here.

Then he heard another voice, maybe his but maybe not, say, You came here to see the bridge.

Go on, that voice said, go on and get a closer look. That's what you want.

As he went toward the bridge, he began to tremble.

There was something else he wanted to do, he thought, but he'd forgotten what, and he tried to remember.

A pedestrian, a man in a dark overcoat and large fur hat, came toward him, and just as he passed him Claude was startled by another pedestrian, walking more swiftly than he in his direction, passing him, another man in a dark overcoat and large, dark fur hat. They left bootprints in the layer of newly fallen snow.

Claude had the curious sense that someone, seeing him walking toward the bridge, would know why he wanted to go there.

For the view, he said to himself.

Trembling, he went to the middle of the bridge. Ice capped the wide parapet, and on top of this solid ice fell the light snow, which, with a sudden wind, rose up in swirls and blew out in lengthening drifts over the edge. Claude stood at the parapet and looked over, down into the current flowing from beneath the arches, the floes bobbing. Channeled by the wind, the snow, gathered up and blown out not only from the parapet before him but, it seemed, from the air about him, streamed along with the current of water.

A young woman was crossing the bridge. She was wearing a pink overcoat. He watched her advance. She glanced at him. She had blue eye makeup. Claude wanted to tell her he'd come for the view. She passed.

Again he looked down to where the water, separated by one of the breakwaters, folded into a whirlpool as it flowed together just beyond it. Blocks of ice spun in the whirlpool.

A car crossed the bridge and Claude drew away from the parapet. On the other side, the young woman was standing, looking at him. As soon as Claude saw her, she turned away. He recognized her. He was sure he recognized her. But she walked into a side street.

Claude crossed the bridge. He tried to remember where, before, he had walked along a street with yellow stucco houses. He stopped under a scaffolding on the façade of a building and looked at the little notice, PEMOHT, nailed to it, at the huge, mud-spattered drainpipes. Hadn't he been here before?

A man was shoveling snow off the roof of a house. The snow fell like white comets through the cold, bright blue air, their sparkling tails drifting off, and exploded with thuds on the icy street. The man on the roof waited for the man below to pass the house before he heaved off another shovel load of snow. The man below heard it hit the ground behind him and turned, slipped, and fell to his knees. Somebody rushed to help him up.

Claude heard a loud thud behind him and, frightened, turned and saw a load of snow fallen to the ground, hurled down from the roof by a man with a shovel. Claude lost balance and fell on his thigh. Yet another shovelful hurled down, and lying, Claude watched its tail drift off.

It drifted off toward a woman in a suede coat, suede boots, and a pale beige fur hat who was walking toward him, smiling. He watched her come up to him and, still smiling, lean over him. He did recognize her. She was Katya Platonova, the young woman he had met at the home of Sasha and Vera. He looked up at her with an expression of bewilderment that made her put her gloved hand — the knitted glove with a design of zigzag bands across it — over her mouth and laugh. She laughed so, she couldn't stop herself, but turned one way, then the other, bending from her waist. He could have stood, but he didn't.

"Are you hurt?" she asked him, her glove held just a little away from her mouth in case she needed it to suppress more laughter.

"I don't think so."

"Well, get up then," she said, and she held out her gloved hand to him. He took it.

He let her take him to a café, and at a table with cups of tea and a plate piled with wedge-shaped slices of plain bread, he leaned toward her. He had the sense that he had sat in this café before with her and leaned toward her.

Katya pushed strands of loose hair up under her furry hat. All her gestures were so calm, as if she never acted in a hurry, as if she had, and she knew she had, all the time in the world, and even if she didn't people would wait for her. She had large dark eyes, and her skin was pale, her forehead, her cheeks, her lips pale, and only around those dark eyes was her skin dark.

She asked, "Are you looking for painting still?"

He asked, "Painting?"

She pursed her lips, then, after what seemed a long while, said, "You wait," and she stood and put on her coat and went out. He did not know where he was. She returned and asked him to come with her, and he did what she said.

She took him back to the Moscow River, rushing black between its snow-covered embankments. He followed her onto the black bridge, and he stopped to glance over the rail into the water, but, aware that she was waiting for him, he drew away.

Ahead of Claude, Katya was pushing open a heavy door, and he went to her. The floor was wet, and along the walls were benches with flat pillows where a few people sat at wooden tables. In a corner, at a table, a man with a black beard stood. His name was Viktor. He wore a heavy sweater without a shirt, the sleeves pushed up to his elbows. It was an old sweater, the knit loose, with black hairs caught in the thick yarn. He said to Claude, holding his hand, "Now we will see."

At their table, Viktor and Katya talked to each other in Russian. Claude felt he might vomit. No one in the place but Viktor and Katya talked.

From time to time the door opened and someone in boots came in or left. There was, in the very air of the place, a deep awareness of the outside cold. Hot when he'd been outside, Claude felt himself go cold inside.

Viktor's black beard looked as though cut anyhow with blunt scissors. Crooked hairs grew from the soft flesh at his neck and high on his cheeks. He had a mole on a nostril. The hair on his head, though thin at his forehead, was long, and as he listened to Katya talk he pulled strands of it behind his ear or grabbed a handful of it at the back of his neck and yanked at it so his chin rose, all the while looking at her with large dark eyes. While he listened to her speak, always pulling at his hair, he appeared to be studying her also, appeared to be listening to her closely and studying her at a distance, and he sometimes, perhaps because of what he heard or perhaps because of what he saw, smiled slightly. His cheeks didn't rise when he smiled, however, and his large dark eyes didn't smile but filled with liquid, which almost overflowed the rims of his lower lids in tears.

Cold now, Claude made fists of his hands and blew into them.

Viktor said to him, "You are cold."

"A little."

"Give me one of your hands."

Claude held out a hand. Viktor took it in his, rubbed it, and brought it to his lips and blew on it with his lips formed into an O. Claude felt his beard and mustache all around his warm breath. "Give me your other," Viktor said, and he rubbed and slapped Claude's hand as he breathed on it. Then Viktor grabbed Claude by his shoulders and, pulling him to him, patted his back, his arms, his thighs. Viktor took up both his hands and held them between his and blew on them. Then Viktor contemplated Claude. "Tell me what you want in Russia," he said, "and I will give it to you."

Katya said, "Viktor will help you find painting."

"Tell me about painting," Viktor said. Claude all at once forgot everything about the painting, even who had painted it. "Is by Pietro Testa," Viktor said. Claude nodded. "And was owned by Prince Volkansky in Moscow," Viktor said, and again Claude nodded.

"Viktor will help you," Katya said. "I tell you, he will help you."

"I will help you," Viktor said.

Katya said to Claude, "How bright your eyes are. You have fever."

"I think I do."

Viktor stood and, putting on his padded coat, said, "Come."

Now Claude followed Katya and Viktor down an empty residential street, the yellow buildings stark, with the ventilators of the double-glazed windows all shut. They went into a courtyard. In a corner, spread out on the snow, was an oriental carpet. Viktor held open a door with a glass window in it, the panes painted yellow and some broken, for Katya and Claude to go into a dark corridor that smelled of grease and dust. Along one wall of the corridor was a long shelf made of a wooden plank, and on it were plaster fragments of architectural decorations — a lion's head, a woman's neoclassical hand, part of an egg-and-dart cornice, and broken oriental tiles. Viktor led Claude, then Katya, into a narrow room and switched on a light, a bare bulb hanging from the ceiling by a frayed cord. The wooden floor was covered with black oil, and hanging on the fissured cement walls were old paintings, large and small, in gilt frames: paintings of landscapes, of flowers in vases, of horses and dogs, of people in stiff poses, of interiors in which paintings in gilt frames hung on papered walls. Most of the paint was cracked, and the gilt and plaster had fallen off the frames in places to reveal the worm-eaten wood.

Farther down the corridor, they went into an apartment. It had plywood partition walls and itself a long corridor that went around sharp corners. All the doors along the corridor were shut. There was a smell of cat pee. Viktor took Claude into a room at the back, but Katya didn't come in. Some floorboards were missing, so the joists showed underneath. In one corner was a pile of suitcases, in another cardboard boxes on top of which was a broken chair. In front of an old sofa was a low table, a large jar filled with onions in brown-red vinegar on it. By the jar of pickled onions lay open a magazine whose thick, stiff pages were black-and-white photographs of Cyrillic text and illustrations. Viktor told Claude to sit on the sofa, and he went out of the room.

Claude passed his hands close over his body and head, without touching them but as if to protect them. He raised his knees and folded his arms in close to his chest and shut his eyes.

When he opened his eyes, he saw, between the jar of pickled onions and that magazine reproduced photographically, not Viktor but Katya in the room.

He wondered what country he was in, if he was in any country.

The room didn't have walls, and the pieces of furniture moved out beyond the room, out among lampposts and snowbanks which came in and moved around the room.

Katya said, "Viktor wants to see you."

Why didn't she leave him alone? He didn't want to go anywhere with her. He didn't want to be in this city with her. He didn't want to know her. Russia was her country, not his, and he didn't want it ever to be his country. He hated her and he hated her country.

His shoes were off. Maybe someone had taken them off as he had slept on the sofa. He sat up and put on a shoe, and in his rage he broke a shoelace, pulling at it. He yanked off his shoe and, unbounded as he felt he was, was about to throw it across the room. He wouldn't go out. But Katya was waiting for him. Sweating, he drew the broken lace out of the eyelets and restrung it to make the ends even. They weren't even and he had to restring the lace again. The ends were so short he couldn't tie a bow, so he tied a knot that he couldn't then undo when he found the lace wasn't tight enough and the shoe was loose. His foot slipped a little out of his shoe with each step he took. He put on his overcoat and cap and gloves.

All the control he had was in his politeness, and he was acutely polite to Katya. Her face was made up lightly: pale blue on her eyelids and a flush of powdery pink high on her cheeks. As if trying to detach herself, delicately, from his politeness, she kept a distance from him as they walked along the sidewalk. All his control was in a point of delicate detachment high above him.

The streetlights illuminated the snow piled in banks along the sidewalks, and above them was the Russian darkness. The sky flashed sulfur yellow. Claude asked Katya, "What's that?" expecting her to tell him that America was bombing Russia. He waited, stopped in the street, for that sudden rush of air he'd been told when a schoolboy would occur when Russia dropped the bomb on America. A trio of two young men and a young woman, their arms locked, were striding down the street ahead, singing. There was a distant *whomp*, more vibration than sound, and the sky flashed dull red.

"It's fireworks," Katya said.

The sky kept changing color as she and Claude walked.

They went into a courtyard with fir trees, black in the black night and among them a children's slide. Katya opened a battered door, a rope tied around and hanging from its handle. Another battered door was on the other side of the threshold, and Claude held this open for Katya. She led him up the stairs, the well lit by low-wattage bare bulbs. There were rusty galvanized buckets on the landings.

The apartment also had two doors. The inner one was opened by a clean-shaven man with short cropped hair who didn't smile. He couldn't speak English. His name was Mikhail.

Claude took off his overcoat among rubber boots in the narrow entryway with its wooden floor and runner of old, worn linoleum and its cracked walls and water-stained ceiling, and he saw, in rooms at every side, people on wooden chairs looking out at him.

Mikhail showed Katya and Claude into one of the rooms, where Viktor was sitting at a round table with another man. There was a sagging double bed in a corner, and tacked to the wall along the head and the side was a narrow hanging of velvet printed with an elk standing on a crag. A single bed was in an alcove made by bookshelves. Viktor didn't move from the table.

The other man at the table didn't get up but held out his hand across the table and said to Claude, "My name is Alexander."

Everyone watched Mikhail open a bottle of vodka and fill five small glasses to their brims. Everyone reached for one, raised it, and Claude was, after a few seconds, the only one still holding a full glass. The others had drunk the vodka down in quick shots. Mikhail filled the glasses again, and again they were drunk down. He kept filling them until the bottle was empty.

Viktor wore his sweater. They all wore sweaters: Mikhail a black turtleneck, like a sailor's, that was tight and showed his powerful chest and shoulders, and Alexander a loose, thick, brownish turtleneck, which fell away at the neck and showed the white, unshaven throat of what seemed to be a thin body. Alexander had shaggy, uncombed hair.

Slowly, Claude leaned toward the edge of the table and for a moment closed his eyes. He knew immediately that if he didn't keep his eyes wide open and fixed on a detail, he would lose control, so he fixed on the reproduction of a golden medallion of a naked boy on the green and white label on the empty bottle. He saw, in the vague circle of vision around the bottle, Viktor's hand resting on the table. There was another medallion on the label, and Claude studied this: a woman in a flowing robe carrying in a raised hand an olive branch and holding the globe of the world against her hip with her other hand.

Claude looked at the men around the table, over which a bulb without a shade hung so low that the shadows cast by the foreheads of the men shaded their faces.

His neck rigidly extended, about to vomit, Claude said, "Please, the toilet."

Alexander showed him where it was, off the entryway. In the other rooms, people looked out. Behind the closed door of the toilet, like a small closet, Claude, leaning over the bowl which had no seat, didn't vomit but wept. Water ran constantly down the rusty interior of the bowl, and by it, on the floor, was a pile of shredded newspapers. Claude sweated and wept. The pipe from the cistern high up on the wall was covered with funguslike corrosion and dripped at the joints. Having waited for a while, Claude wiped his eyes with the backs of his hands, then pulled the long chain attached to the cistern to flush.

He came back to the room where the empty bottle was the center. Katya was standing against a bookcase, her arms folded. The three men sat still at the table.

The Russians, silent, stared out into space. That dark space: it went on forever, so there was no seeing to the end of it. That space, which they were always aware of, made all their words and acts, all their thinking and feeling, all their suffering nothing. But that space, as frightening as it was because anyone who went into it was not only lost but could never return from it, made everything possible. They couldn't live, couldn't have endured what they'd endured, without it. It did not need them, but they needed that space.

Claude wiped his eyes with the palm of his free hand. His face was wet with sweat and tears and mucus from his nose. He knelt and lowered his forehead to the floor.

Viktor got up and went to Claude and put his hands under his arms, raised him, and held him up. He said, "You are a little boy." He kissed him, and when he let him go Claude fell.

IV

HE WALKED through a forest of charred trees stumps, the sky above dark with soot. He passed the mounds of mass graves. He tripped on machine guns and the shrapnel of large shells, and he circled around a place where dogs were gathered so he wouldn't see what the dogs were eating.

A hot gust of wind blew up clouds of ash, and he couldn't see ahead but had to lower his head and hold his hands over his mouth. The wind fell, and another gust at a distance blew up a cloud of ash that rolled among the black trunks toward him, then swerved away from him. All *over the burned landscape these clouds of ash rose, were blown about, then sifted down through the air.*

Before him, a cloud rose up and remained, slowly involuting, and in it Claude saw, dark in the gray, a figure. The cloud dispersed from about a young woman. She was naked, and her smooth body was covered in ash. Her uneven hair was singed. She smiled, and raising her hand, she called out, but in a language Claude couldn't understand. She gestured and called again, and Claude went toward her. As he advanced, she turned and went ahead of him, wood ash swirling about her bare feet, and from time to time she looked back to make sure he was behind her. Each time she looked back she smiled.

She led him out of the forest of charred stumps, over burned fields and around the craters caused by explosions. The craters became less and less, and she led him into fields of grass. On a stone in a square of grass was a sickle and a cucumber. When he looked behind him, he saw that the burned landscape was at a distance, and the low cloud of soot that spread over it was drifting away. Above him the sky was clear. Following the young woman, he walked alongside a fieldstone wall. The lichen-covered boulders were fallen away, and the wall became a trail of stones among trees in what were once plowed fields. Then the stones ended and the trees were bigger and older. He followed the girl through blue flowers into the forest.

In the branches of a tree was a bright red and black bird. Claude had never before seen a red and black bird.

The young woman had disappeared, and he went to look for her. Among the bushes an old woman appeared, emptying a tin of berries into a large basket made of interwoven strips of birch bark. Around her head she wore a rag that was stained with blood, and her dress, torn so her wounded body showed, was also stained with dried blood. Other people emerged from among the bushes. They were all wounded, and some used branches as crutches. Some, men and women, were naked, with burns on their thighs, breasts, backs. They laughed.

The baskets held by the handles, and the full tins suspended from strings about their necks, the people all moved off together. Claude didn't follow, but some of the people in the group turned around and made gestures for him to follow.

It was warm in the forest. There were no paths. The natives showed the trees to Claude. They seemed to talk to the trees as if they were talking to one another. The shadows of the trees merged and deepened, but here and there opened with a flash of light when branches high up, moving in a treetop breeze, revealed the sky.

Claude knew that these people were happy. He knew they were happy and didn't desire anything, and they didn't because they were possessed, all together, by their world, which, all together, they loved.

The light deepened. A stork flew down among the branches, and they watched the stork, lifting its feet and placing them carefully, walk about.

The dusk didn't deepen to dark but became pale, as though another kind of light, not starlight or moonlight, were shining from a concave sky, and in this pale but vivid light people were gathering. Children and animals ran about among them.

They were gathering around an expanse of bare, cracked earth scattered with tree trunks that looked as though they had once been burned, rusted oil drums, and rusted, twisted pieces of metal, perhaps the battered fenders and hoods of army vehicles. But on one side water was gushing out from under a raised sluice, the gush like a massive rush of people with banners that burst into a huge and empty square, then momentarily drew back a little before it spread out along the uneven ground in different currents that joined up as they ran toward the bottom of the drained pond. The voices of the women rose above the men's, and both above the splashing roar of the water.

Part

SIX

I

CLAIRE AND RACHEL arrived in Moscow at night. The streetlights cast a low, even level of gray, grainy light, palely reflected from the snow on the ground, where shadowed people moved slowly or didn't move. Above the level of the streetlights was night, high, high, and walking from the taxi to the hotel, Claire kept looking up. Rachel, beside her, glanced at the women with big fur hats and colored scarves standing about the entrance to the hotel.

At a counter they checked in, then, while Rachel walked into the lobby looking around as if for someone, Claire asked the receptionist for the room of Claude Ricard and Maurice Kuragin. The big-bosomed receptionist, in a heavy cardigan, flipped through papers and said, as if she were impersonally issuing a death sentence, "They are not here," and Claire thought: I knew it, I knew they wouldn't be here. Frowning, she asked, "Are you sure?" and the receptionist, frowning more, rudely answered, "I have told you, they are not here." Claire drew back from the counter, startled by the rudeness, but she felt intimidated by the large Russian woman, felt intimidated by being in this country, which she had grown up in America believing was the enemy country, and she and her daughter were alone in this country.

She turned toward Rachel, who held her overcoat folded over her stomach as if to hide it in the coat's wide folds and continued to search the lobby, then Claire turned back to the woman behind the counter, who was tying together a pile of forms into a bundle with a piece of string, and Claire waited until she had finished and put the bundle of forms into a plastic briefcase bulging with other bundles of forms, then politely said, "I'm sorry, but it is very important — were Claude Ricard and Maurice Kuragin here?" The woman frowned and said, "You will have to wait," and left with the bulging case to go across the lobby to an office, where she was behind a translucent glass partition for a long while talking in loud Russian, and when she came back she seemed to have forgotten Claire, who had to ask again. "That is not my work," the woman said, "but the work of the person there," and she indicated another big-bosomed woman farther along the counter. "Thank you," Claire said meekly, and went to the other woman, who had trouble understanding the request, but who, when she understood, said more than Claire could take in, and all Claire could understand was that Claude and Maurice had gone.

All of Claire's skin tightened, and she closed her eyes for a moment before she went to Rachel.

But what would she tell Rachel, who studied her with her brow lowered and wrapped her overcoat more closely about herself as her mother approached her? Claire saw expectation in Rachel's eyes, but she said, as if she were too occupied with getting them settled in this unsettling country to be attentive to anything else, "They give you a hard time here."

"About what?" Rachel asked.

"About everything."

In the room, Rachel went immediately to the wide window to look out over the city at night, then, after contemplating it, turned slowly to her mother and asked, "Where are Claude and Maurice?"

Claire took a breath and said, "They're not here."

Rachel sat, but for only a moment slumped and quickly straightened her back. "Where are they?" she asked.

"I don't know. They were here, but left, and there isn't a message from them." Claire sat too.

Rachel, sitting up straight and rigid, chewed her lower lip, then bit into it so hard Claire thought her teeth would draw blood, and she put out a hand to stop her, but drew her hand back and pressed it to her breasts.

"Maybe," Claire said, "they went somewhere on a side trip, maybe even to find out something about the picture, and they got stuck and couldn't get back in time for our arrival, couldn't even get a message to the hotel. That could happen here. I expect they'll turn up."

Rachel's dark green woolen dress bulged at her stomach. She placed her hands on her stomach, then let them drop.

"We should find something to eat," Claire said, "and go to bed. In the morning maybe Claude and Maurice will be here."

Rachel raised both shoulders.

The restaurants in the hotel were all closed, and even the little café at the top of the hotel, which was supposed to be open, was closed.

"It doesn't matter," Rachel said.

"This country —" Claire said.

For the first time Rachel raised her voice at her mother. "This country is doing its best," she said, "it's doing its best."

"All right," Claire said, "all right." She was hungry and impatient, but she suppressed both hunger and impatience. She found a package of digestive biscuits in her bag which she'd brought for the flight.

Lying in the narrow bed across from Rachel, it occurred to her that the last time she had slept so close to her daughter was just after what she now thought of simply as the horror. Rachel did not sleep any more than Claire did, and Claire wondered what she could be thinking, and wondered if she dared ask her, then thought no, not now — maybe the next day, or the day after, but not now.

Everything Claire had thought of to help Rachel had failed, and coming to Russia would fail too. It was a mistake for her to have come to find the picture.

In the morning, Claire got herself ready quickly and told Rachel she'd meet her in the hotel restaurant for breakfast, if the restaurant was open, and she went first to the lobby to check whether Claude and Maurice had arrived. They hadn't. At breakfast in the big, low-ceilinged, fluorescent-lit hall, Claire and Rachel didn't speak. Perhaps Rachel suspected her mother had checked whether Claude and Maurice had arrived, and the fact that she didn't mention them meant they hadn't.

Rachel said, with a hardness in her voice, "We'll look for the picture."

"How? We have no idea how to begin."

Rachel's hardness became a cast to her entire body, and she said, "We'll find it."

"Darling —" Claire began, but she knew that her daughter's will was set. She said, "All we have to go on is the name of the family Maurice was supposed to contact."

"Then we'll look them up. I can read the names."

"Look them up where? There are no telephone directories."

"We'll go to the police."

"Darling —" Claire began again, but again stopped.

Rachel said, "All that matters is that we find the painting. I won't leave until we find it."

"Very well," her mother said.

It was Rachel who said, after their soggy blinis and sour cream and weak coffee, that they must go out and look around Moscow and think of ways of finding out how to contact the Volkansky family. Claire didn't dare say otherwise.

Claire felt that something would happen to her if she went out of the hotel, that she would be arrested for no reason, or followed, however she told herself this kind of thing didn't happen anymore. Nevertheless, she felt very uneasy out on the streets, and held back Rachel from crossing streets when the pedestrian sign was still red, even though the Muscovites did. If she did something that wasn't correct, she felt, some terrible judgment would be passed on her, and it surprised her that Muscovites, whom she assumed to have been made for years to obey laws imposed on their lives, even to what they wore, and who risked really terrible judgments if they didn't abide by the laws, broke them without even looking to see if a policeman was around. It surprised her very much to see a young woman wearing a bright pink overcoat among older women in dark, round-shouldered overcoats, as if Claire had assumed that a pink overcoat wouldn't have been allowed. She had taken with her the simplest, darkest overcoat she had. Rachel wouldn't let Claire hold her back, but strode out into the street with the Muscovites, the pedestrian light still showing red. Claire hurried behind her.

She followed Rachel over icy sidewalks, up and down streets of mud-splashed blue-and-white palaces, delicate green palaces, orange-pink palaces with grimy windows. Wind was blowing, and looking at the palaces, they blinked and turned from side to side against the wind. Claire continued to follow Rachel, as if Rachel knew where she was going.

The palaces looked abandoned, but people went into and came out of stark stucco buildings through battered, metal-framed doors that seemed to lead into nothing but stark, bare rooms. Many people kept going in and coming out of the battered doors.

Claire asked, "What are they doing? Are they buying things?"

Rachel didn't answer.

They were walking down the middle of a street of shops, where there was less ice than on the sidewalks, stepping to the side to let cars and trucks pass them. The cold struck their bones. Claire stayed close to Rachel because of her intimidation, too great to ask Rachel if they could go into a café or a shop to get warm. In the middle of the street was what looked like an old army truck, its loading platform down, rusted chains hanging from it, and inside a few shriveled potatoes.

Holding her arms close to herself, Claire said, "It's all so, so —"

Her voice suddenly high and thin, Rachel said, "If I could choose, this is where I'd live. You'll see, you'll see what a country Russia will make herself into."

"Yes," Claire said.

"Look at that," Rachel said.

"Yes," Claire said, "I see," not sure what Rachel was pointing to. She saw the smashed door to a public telephone booth open, the receiver hanging from its cord; the high-heeled boots of a young woman who passed, the soles warped and the heels peeling; the large, rusted drainpipe on a building, disconnected from the gutter and falling away, a great icicle hanging from the hole left in the sagging gutter.

They were standing on a corner, and Claire waited for Rachel to decide which way they would go. Her daughter looked in different directions. The cold wind began to blow with stinging flakes of snow, which seemed to strike through clothes.

Rachel said, "We could try to find out through the office of the minister of culture. They would know who has what painting."

"Go to the office of the Russian minister of culture?" Claire asked, amazed by this proposal. There was no intimidation in Rachel.

"Why not?" Rachel asked, and Claire sensed from the tone of her voice that she was inciting her mother to say that going to the office of the minister of culture would be difficult. Claire knew from the past that Rachel did this: proposed something difficult almost to get her mother to object, and then accused her mother of finding everything she proposed difficult, accused her mother of stopping her from doing what she had made up her mind to do. Claire closed her eyes for a moment, then, opening them, simply looked at Rachel with the bewilderment of someone who was in a place that was too strange, if not too rude and threatening, for her to know how one would get in touch with the office of the minister of culture. But that was just what Rachel was expecting of her.

She said, "That's probably a good idea."

She saw a look of pain in Rachel's eyes, the pain of making her mother agree to try to do what she had imposed on her to do. In a low voice she said, "Never mind."

"No, no," Claire said. "I think it's a very good idea. You're right, we came here to find that painting, and we should do everything we can to find it." She turned up the collar of her coat about her neck and blinked rapidly against the sharp flecks of snow. "But I think we should get back to the hotel to get whatever information we can from there about how to go about contacting the office of the minister of culture." She knew in her soul that this would be impossible.

Rachel's look of pain deepened. Her mother was doing this for her, she knew. She put her gloved hand on her mother's arm. "Maybe we should go back to London," she said, "and forget it all."

"No, no," Claire said. She smiled. "We'll find the painting. I know we will."

"I don't know," Rachel said.

"I know," Claire insisted.

"You're cold," Rachel said. "Let's get back to the hotel for a cup of tea."

"I wouldn't mind that."

Rachel turned away, blinking as she looked in the different directions. The old army truck with the few shriveled potatoes was still parked in the middle of the street, and Claire followed Rachel around it.

Claire let Rachel lead her back to the hotel, though she felt Rachel wanted to go anywhere but there, as if returning to the hotel after not having found something, anything, to convince her mother of a different Russia were a defeat. So Claire wouldn't even have to try to find something to point out to her, she walked behind Rachel. And when Claire saw her daughter pause to look, ahead of her on the sidewalk, at an old man in a ragged black overcoat and a molting fur hat, Claire too paused, then stayed behind Rachel as she continued past the man, who held out, in a bare, big-knuckled hand, a few rusty nails for someone to buy. The image of the old man remained with them and confronted them when, on the top floor of the hotel, where the tea shop was supposed to be open, they found the door shut. Angry, Rachel knocked on the door. No one opened. Angrier, she knocked again, harder. No one opened.

Her anger, and more than anger, making her eyes wide, she said to her mother, "I'm going back out to buy the nails from that old man."

Unsure what state her daughter was in, but sure that it was caused by more than anger, Claire asked, "Will you let me come with you?"

"Come with me," Rachel said, and turned away.

The cold was deeper than before, and the ice on the streets and sidewalks like broken stone over which Rachel hurried, sometimes losing her balance, so Claire, behind her, held her elbow to steady her. When Claire lost her balance there was no one to steady her. The old man was not where he'd been.

Claire said, "Maybe he sold the nails."

"Of course he didn't."

It was midmorning. Not knowing what else to do, they went to their room. Her back to her mother, Rachel sat at the built-in, Formica-topped desk before the wide window and looked out. On the desk was a glass of water and an old-fashioned black telephone. For a while Claire walked up and down the room, then lay on her bed. Maybe, she thought, they should return to London, because it seemed to her that if Claude and Maurice should come back, even with the picture, nothing would be made different. She stood, and walking toward Rachel she noted, beyond her, that snow was falling outside. The telephone on the desk rang.

Rachel's arm rose, but she didn't reach for the receiver. Claire went quickly and held her hand over the telephone as it rang again and again, and then she picked up the receiver.

"Hello," she said.

"Hello," a man's voice with a Russian accent, the double *l*'s liquid, said. "I am sorry to telephone you without your knowing who I am. My name is Sasha, Sasha Poliakoff. I am a friend of Claude Ricard."

Instinctively, to keep Rachel from hearing the man, Claire pressed the receiver to her ear. "Yes."

"When I telephoned earlier this morning, the receptionist said that you had arrived last night and were asking for him, so I am telephoning —"

"Yes," Claire said again.

Sitting up, Rachel was attentive, listening, it seemed, not to what her mother was saying but to a voice from another room.

The Russian said, "I have been trying to telephone Claude for days and days. Do you know where he is?"

Pressing the receiver more tightly to her ear, Claire said, "No."

"I wonder if he has left Russia without saying goodbye."

"We were supposed to meet him here. We were supposed to meet Claude Ricard and Maurice Kuragin here."

Rachel sat up straighter, listening to voices more distant than from the next room, or from the hotel.

"I know," the man said.

"Where are they?" Claire asked.

"I thought you might know."

"I don't. We don't."

"Please don't be anxious. I will come to your hotel and find you, you and your daughter. Claude and Maurice told me you would come with your daughter. I will take you to where my wife and my child and I live. We will find out what has happened. Please, please, do not be anxious," the man said, but he sounded himself anxious.

Their hats in their hands while Claire and Rachel waited in the lobby for Sasha Poliakoff, concentrating on every man who passed the uniformed doorman, some of the men showing a hotel pass and others simply walking quickly by him, Claire saw in Rachel's face her frightened expectation. Rachel, biting her lower lip, rotated her hat in her hand.

A man wearing thick spectacles and a large black fur hat and a Chinese padded jacket came in, looking around, and Rachel, startled, stepped toward him, then stopped, and Claire went to him. Yes, he was Sasha, he said to her. He held the windshield wipers of a car in his left hand. "Please do come with me," he said, and he led them out through the snow and among the girls in bright, flower-patterned scarves standing in the snow to a small car parked by a snowbank in the street. Before they got in Sasha fixed the windshield wipers into place and, smiling, said, "They would be stolen if I did not keep them with me at all times." Claire and Rachel sat in the cramped back seat.

Rachel, silent, was trembling. Claire put her arm around her daughter to hold her close to her and said to Sasha, driving, "You saw them, you saw Claude and Maurice?"

"They came to dinner at our apartment."

"And they told you why we were all meeting here?"

"To find a painting."

"Yes, to find a painting. Maurice was so sure he would be able to, would be able to find it before Rachel and I arrived, so that when we did —" She couldn't go on.

Sasha, to lead the talk away from Maurice and Claude, said to Claire, "You are an art historian."

"I am."

"Maurice told us."

"Do you think Claude and Maurice, trying to locate the painting, might have got into trouble?"

"With our police?"

"With anyone. I have no idea what goes on in this country."

"What kind of trouble do you think?" Sasha asked.

"I don't know, either, what kind of trouble a person can get into in this country now. I've heard about the trouble a person used to be able to get into, trouble that meant being arrested and disappearing, and even being liquidated. Maybe that still happens. Do you know?"

Sasha laughed. "You never know, in our country."

Claire held Rachel, trembling more, closer to her, and she kept her arm around Rachel to protect her as they followed Sasha to the blank front door of a cement apartment building. And Claire kept her arm around Rachel as they ascended slowly in an elevator rising in a cage of crisscrossed wires.

When Sasha opened the door to his apartment, a little blond boy ran down the passage toward them. A tall, beautiful woman was rushing behind him to hold him back, calling, "Alyosha, Alyosha." At the door, the boy stopped and stared at Claire and Rachel, and the woman, whom Sasha introduced as his wife Vera, crossed her hands over the boy's chest and drew him to her. Introduced to Claire and Rachel as their son Alyosha, the boy, smiling, held out a thin, long-fingered hand and said in precise English, "I am pleased to meet you." Down the passageway, beyond hanging coats, was a new bicycle leaning against the wall.

The boy couldn't wait for the guests to take off their coats but, pulling at Rachel's hand, led her, with Claire following, down the passage to see the bicycle. He said, as carefully as he had prepared it, "This bicycle Maurice gave me," and he rang the bell on the handlebars.

Then, as if that were only the beginning of what he wanted them to see, he led them to the end of the passage and into a room where an old woman stood against a wall. Alyosha was keen to introduce, in English, Rachel, then Claire, to his great-grandmother, Varvara Petrovna, who responded by raising her head and looking down at the guests as she silently and starkly shook their hands. Alyosha, unaware how unwelcoming his great-grandmother was, laughed excitedly, and said to Claire and Rachel, "My great-grandmother don't speak English." His mother, coming into the room, said to him, "Doesn't." Varvara Petrovna looked as if she would refuse to speak English even if she could, but she said to

Alyosha, "I speak, I speak." "Say," Alyosha told her, " 'I am pleased to meet you.' " But the old woman, her head raised more, remained silent and stark. Sasha, in a sweater and slippers, came into the room.

Vera said to Claire and Rachel, "Please take off your coats."

When Rachel did, the Russians, even Alyosha, went still. Rachel's pregnant belly bulged her loose woolen shift. She held out her coat for a while before Vera said, taking it, "I am sorry." Sasha said to her, "Please sit," and indicated a divan, across the back of which was a folded crocheted blanket. Claire saw that Varvara Petrovna was staring at Rachel's pregnancy. Claire sat on an antique chair at an antique table, and said, "What beautiful chairs and table," but no one responded to this.

While Vera was out preparing tea, Alyosha, the only one moving about the room in which everyone else sat, pointed to a book on a shelf and said, "This is book," to which Claire said, "Yes," and "This is telephone" and "This is lamp" and "This is rug," to which Claire, smiling at him, said, "Yes." The boy looked around for something else he knew how to name in English. Claire asked him, pointing to a small painting of a sunset in a heavy gilt frame high on the papered wall, "And what is that?" The boy said, "I do not know." Claire said, "It is a painting of a sunset," but this was too much for Alyosha and he turned to his father, who told him what it was in Russian. Vera entered carrying a tray of mismatched cups and a teapot with a cracked lid. A large red rose was on the side of the teapot.

Vera said to Alyosha, "Now sit and drink your tea," and the boy did, but still excited, he spoke in Russian and seemed often to say the name Maurice, though Claire could not be sure.

Her arms wrapped around herself as if to protect herself, Rachel asked, "Maurice?"

"I am sorry," Sasha said. "Maurice has died."

This shocked Rachel, whose arms jerked away from her body and stayed out for a long moment before she brought them back again to hold herself.

Sasha said, "He went out to buy a bicycle, and died of a heart attack on the way from the shop."

"He was alone?" Claire asked.

"Claude was with him. Claude was wheeling the bicycle alongside him when he fell."

"And Claude?"

Vera said, "We don't know. We don't know where Claude is."

"We don't understand," Sasha said. "We find Westerners very difficult to understand."

"Shouldn't we get in touch with the police?" Claire asked.

"No, no, not the police," Vera said.

"Isn't there anyone we can get in touch with who will help?"

"We can only think," Sasha said, "that he was determined, after Maurice's death, to find the painting, and as you yourself said, something happened."

"Something, meaning he's got into trouble."

"I didn't use that word."

"But it's what you meant."

"I am not quite sure what I meant."

Clasping her hands together, Vera said, "It is a big business now, a big criminal business, selling paintings to foreigners for hard currency. It is not a business we would like to see yourselves involved in."

"We don't want to buy the painting," Claire said. "We want only to look at it."

Vera separated her hands.

"Once," Sasha said, "we might have helped. My grandmother would have been in a position to help. We would have been in a position even to ask the police to help, once. Now, as you know, everything has changed in our country. We can't help."

Varvara Petrovna, in a deep voice, spoke in Russian, but Sasha didn't translate.

Rachel asked him, "What did she say?"

"She said," Vera answered, "that we are still above being criminals and selling Russia."

Rachel lowered her eyes.

"Please understand us," Sasha said. "For as long as she can remember, my grandmother, for whatever ideological belief, has abided by the principles, what she believed, and still believes, are the highest principles." He removed his glasses and said, "Yes, the chairs and the table of our dining room set are beautiful. They belonged to an eye surgeon before our October Revolution. He lived in a large house in Moscow. After our civil war, many people, including my grandparents, were moved into his house, and he was reduced to living with his family in one room, then was forced out with his family to live in his dacha in the country. He sold his furniture. My grandparents bought the dining room set. My grandfather was a scientist, my grandmother a young, idealistic member of the Party. They believed it was right for the surgeon to lose his house to people who needed it, since he had a house in the country. But about the furniture they bought, they often told me they believed the surgeon would one day have his revenge, and when I, their grandson, was born almost blind and incapable of being helped by any surgery, they thought the revenge was me. But he has had a far greater revenge than that."

Sasha and Vera looked toward Varvara Petrovna, who shifted in her wooden armchair.

Rachel said, "I think I would like to go back to the hotel room." But no one moved.

Alyosha, sitting near Claire, put his cup and saucer on the table and went to her. He said, "Maurice was good." Claire hugged him.

Rachel stood. As if Varvara Petrovna had been thinking of nothing else since she had seen Rachel was pregnant, the old woman went to her as she was putting on her coat, which Vera had given to her, and she placed a hand on Rachel's bare head. She spoke to her in Russian, and Vera said to Rachel, "She is giving you her blessing." Rachel closed her eyes and tears wet her lashes. She opened her eyes when the old woman removed her hand. With a sudden, convulsive look of pain on her face, the old woman turned away, but turned back to Rachel and said, "I am sorry for your suffering," and again turned her face, convulsed, away and walked to the other side of the room. Rachel's tears ran into the corners of her eyes and down the sides of her nose.

The snow was falling more heavily. In the car back to the hotel, no one spoke, and when Sasha said goodbye to Claire and Rachel he didn't say he'd see them again. With the snow, darkness too fell.

All there was to eat in the hotel restaurant was sausages, boiled potatoes, and grated carrot salad, after which Claire and Rachel went to their room. Though it was early, they silently prepared for bed. Claire waited for Rachel to get into her bed before she shut off the light.

Waking in the darkness, Claire did not know where she was, and, panicked, she reached out to touch something. When she told herself she was in a hotel room in Moscow, she asked herself, Why?

Then she thought, Rachel, and listened for her twisting and turning, listened at least for her breathing.

She jumped out of bed, searching for the light, calling, "God." In the sudden illumination, she saw that Rachel's bed, the strange bedclothes consisting of a blanket inserted into an envelope-like sheet thrown to the side, was empty. In her desperation, Claire, pulling at the bodice of her nightgown, paced the narrow room, again calling, "God." She drew off her nightgown, dressed quickly, and opened the door to the outside corridor, but she had no idea where to go, and she shut it.

She remembered having identified Frank's body, his large, dark body, matted and swollen with the river water he had drowned in.

Once more she opened the door of the room to go out, she had no idea where to, and Rachel was there. A high whine rose involuntarily from Claire's throat, and she stepped back as Rachel entered and sat on the edge of her bed. While Claire stood before her, she rocked a little, backward and forward, on the edge of the bed. Clutching her stomach, she leaned as far over as her pregnancy would allow, about, it seemed, to vomit.

In a keening voice, Rachel said, "Over and over, over and over, over and over, you've told me something would happen so I wouldn't have to make myself do what I know I've got to do."

Claire felt her blood drain out of her, and her mind became entirely clear. The clarity startled her, revealing to her, with the force of such sudden and preemptory clarity, what was so obvious, and what she should have always known was so obvious. She seemed to shrink, to become very small, surrounded by the totally clear obviousness of the vast darkness into which she looked. The condition of humanity was to be entirely dependent on its own will.

Claire heard a thin voice, which may have been hers, say, "What I've told you won't happen."

Rachel, her hair falling forward, went still.

Immediately, the realization of what she'd said made Claire hysterical. "No, no," she said, "I didn't mean that."

Slowly, Rachel rose and sat upright, her hands, palms up, in her lap, below the curve of her stomach.

"I mean," Claire said, "I mean —" She opened her mouth again and again, about to speak, but she only licked her lips and uttered, "Ahn, ahn." I can't let this happen, she thought. She licked her lips and said, "I don't mean you should just accept the world as it is and everything will work out. I mean —"

Rachel narrowed her eyes. She was so much more intelligent than her mother. She was so much less naive than her mother. She was so much more original, and because of that so much more demanding, than her mother. What could her mother say to her, say against what Rachel knew, even more than her stupid, naive, unoriginal mother knew, was clearly obvious? Against the obvious, Claire thought. With her narrowed eyes, Rachel observed her.

As if alone, Claire walked back and forth in the room, brushing the long, tangled strands of her hair from her face, and with each pacing of the room she felt rise in her, on a mixture of resentment and anger and fear, the impulse to say anything, do anything, that could get her, even if it couldn't get Rachel, out of here, out of *this*.

Rachel couldn't get away from it, but Rachel was the cause of *this*, and each time she passed her daughter Claire felt her resentment and anger and fear turn more toward her daughter, as did the impulse to say something shocking to her. In front of Rachel, not knowing what was about to come out, she shouted, "But it happens, it happens, it happens."

Rachel's voice was as sharp as her look, and she intended it to cut her mother. "What?"

All her mixed feelings out of her control, Claire said, "What was impossible *is* possible."

Confronted by her mother's hysteria, which always made Rachel reasonable, she said, to hurt her mother into also being reasonable, "How?"

"You want an explanation?" Claire shouted.

"Yes."

A fury, beyond hysteria, and beyond resentment and anger and fear, took over Claire. She made fists of her hands and clenched them close to the sides of her contorted mouth and screamed, "By faith."

Her own fury pressed into a fine, cold edge, Rachel asked, "What is that?"

Claire let her arms drop. Turned away from Rachel, she undressed and put on her nightgown and got into bed. After a while, Rachel too got ready for bed, and shut off the light.

In the morning they got up and dressed as if they had slept and nothing else had happened during the night. At breakfast they even talked, in subdued voices, about Alyosha.

Claire left it to Rachel to decide what they would do. Rising from the breakfast table, Rachel said, "I want to go out." She said this calmly, but there was tenseness between them, however calmly they acted toward each other. In the uncertainty of their tense calm, not knowing what they expected of each other, and not wanting each other to think anything was expected, they went out into the cold, colder now than the day before, and snow, a sharper, icier snow than the day before, which, hitting them in cold blasts directly in the eyes, made seeing very difficult. As on the day before, Claire followed Rachel.

In sidelong glances, she thought she recognized some of the palaces they had seen, but she wasn't sure. Rachel seemed to know where she was going. Where she went was always in the direction of the wind, which blasted the stinging snow against their faces. To have said to Rachel, Let's go back to the hotel, would have destroyed the tense calm between them, but however much returning to the hotel was what Claire wanted to do, she could not leave Rachel on her own.

Rachel stopped at a corner that cut off the wind, and her frown showed she was wondering where to go next. Claire thought: She's lost. That should have been reason enough for returning to the hotel, but instead of turning back, they turned the corner, and a gust of wind blew the skirts of their overcoats and made them put their hands over their faces. Rachel headed into the wind.

They stood at the next corner, near a deserted wooden scaffolding from which icicles hung, out of the wind.

Claire could not stop herself from saying, "We're lost."

"We're not. I know the way."

Claire followed Rachel along a narrow street banked up on either side with snow, so it was impossible to walk on the sidewalks. Along the path in the middle of the street two women were one pulling and the other pushing a sled with a huge pail of blue paint on it. They were wearing knitted caps and dirty smocks stained with blue paint. Rachel paused to let them go by, and so did Claire, and as they passed Claire she wanted to ask them directions back to the hotel but didn't dare. If she was intimidated by them, she was more intimidated by Rachel. The paint in the pail sloshed thickly. Claire watched the women go on, then she turned to Rachel, who was walking ahead of her, and she hurried to keep up with her.

At the next corner, Claire said, "Really, darling, we must go back —"

"I told you I know the way," Rachel said.

"But —"

"I told you, I know."

A rage came over Claire, as uncontrollable as her shivering. She said, "I'm going to leave you here and go back. I can't take any more, I can't."

Rachel too was shaking. And in a rage she said, "What can't you take anymore? What?"

Claire stared at her, or tried to, as the icy flakes kept stinging her eyes. Her voice rose. "*What* can't I take?"

"Tell me. Go ahead, tell me."

"How like your father you are," Claire said.

Rachel's eyes and nose ran and made her face red and wet. Stepping back, she said, "My father?"

Claire's arms and legs were shaking so, she thought she would fall. She couldn't help herself. Her shaking impelled her. She said, "And will you kill yourself the way your father did?"

Smearing the tears and mucus across her face with the cuff of her coat, she said, "It's what I always knew about him."

No, oh no, Claire thought, and put out a hand, but Rachel walked away.

Her entire body shaking violently, Claire went to a building and leaned against it for a moment. She wanted to lie on the bank of snow. She not only shook, she from time to time shuddered. Her neck and shoulders and back ached, and when she pushed herself away from the wall to step away she thought she would step not forward but sideways, uncontrollably. At the end of the narrow street, she looked for Rachel, to follow her, just to follow her, but she couldn't see her.

In a state of horror, she stopped a big-bosomed woman in a dun overcoat and felt boots and said, over and over, the name of the hotel, and though the woman at first frowned, she finally understood, and smiled and led Claire along a street to a corner and indicated the way with left and right turnings of her mittened hand. She held by the other hand a string bag of oranges, some in green tissue.

II

I N   T H E   C O L D, Claire sweated. By the time she reached the hotel she was wet with slimy sweat. She checked to find out if the key had gone from reception; the key was still there. Claire took it but stayed in the lobby, walking back and forth, trembling, sweating in a circle of horror. Shortly after noontime, harsh lights were lit overhead.

When she thought of what Rachel might be doing right now out in this city, she felt so weak she had to sit down in one of the chairs in the stark lobby. She had never felt more helpless to do anything.

For a second Claire thought, Let her go, let her do it, and she sat up and, her overcoat open, stood again and walked up and down. There were puddles of melting snow on the floor of the lobby.

She went to the glass counter just to the side of the lobby, where she bought a bottle of sulfur-tasting mineral water. Walking back and forth, her overcoat open to her shoulders but her wide-brimmed felt hat on, she sipped at the water from a glass. The doorman watched her. That expression *to be beside oneself* she had never quite understood, but she understood it now. In her desperation, she was walking beside herself, looking at herself, stunned that there was nothing she could do to help the self she was looking at, nothing she could do to help anyone. She was frightened of her panic, which would make her do something the self looking at her wouldn't be able to stop her from doing. She put the glass of half-drunk mineral water on the counter.

She turned and saw Sasha Poliakoff coming through the glass doors of the hotel into the lobby. His large black fur hat was glistening with snow. Once inside, he removed his steamed-up spectacles and, unable to see her, seemed to stare directly at her as he wiped them with the rumpled handkerchief. When he put them on he came to her as if he had in fact seen her and, without surprise at her presence before him, asked, "Do all Americans disappear when they come to Russia?"

She said, "Yes."

"Where have you been? I've tried to telephone you all morning, and left message after message."

"No one gave me a message."

"You didn't ask. No one will give you anything in our country unless you ask, and even then you won't get it."

"Then there would have been no reason."

"No." Sasha said, "Claude is in my apartment. I wanted you to know."

Claire raised a hand to her chin.

"He has been ill," Sasha said, "with one of those fevers

Americans often get in our country. Americans get fevers and imagine a Russia that doesn't exist, a Russia that has nothing to do with our country."

"But I can't leave the hotel," Claire said. "I must wait for Rachel to come back."

"Where has she gone?"

Claire said, "I don't know."

"You don't know?"

"I don't know." She hit her chin with her knuckles. "I don't know."

"I don't understand."

"Oh, understand," Claire wailed.

Frowning, Sasha said, "Please."

"There's too much to understand."

"For me, yes. I'll leave word with the receptionist. I'll try to make sure she delivers the message by bribing her. That may work. I'll tell her to instruct Rachel that Claude is back and that she must wait."

"If she comes back."

"Why shouldn't she come back?"

Claire covered her mouth with her hand.

"Come with me now," Sasha said.

In a snow-covered vacant lot among buildings, Claire saw, from the car, a great geyser of steam rising into the wind-driven snow.

"What's that?" she asked.

"A broken steam pipe," Sasha answered.

Claude was lying on the divan in the Poliakoff apartment, dressed but covered with the crocheted blanket. He sat up when Claire came into the room. Vera was standing at one end of the divan and another woman, whom Claude introduced to Claire as Katya, was at the other end.

Claude said, "I've seen the picture."

"Oh," Claire said.

"Where is Rachel?" There was about Claude the calm of someone who has been ill and hasn't yet recovered his strength, and there was also about him the openness of someone with not quite enough strength to be anything but open.

"I think she is trying herself to find the picture," Claire said.

"She'll be pleased to know we've located it."

"She will be."

"You know Maurice died here."

"I was told."

"He died happy."

"Happy?"

"Yes, happy. I thought I was going to die too. I can hardly remember what happened, I can't even remember how the painting was located, except that it was by Katya here, and Katya's friend Viktor. I'm as happy now as Maurice." He smiled. "He got what he wanted, and I got what I wanted." Claude's hair, longish and uncombed, stood out in licks.

Claire touched her forehead.

"What's wrong?" Claude asked.

"Wrong?"

"I feel something's wrong."

Claire put her face in her hands, then she slowly ran her hands through her hair and drew herself up rigidly straight so the tendons in her neck stood out. Part of her hair had come undone and hung to a shoulder. She cried, "I don't know where she is."

Claude asked calmly, "What happened?"

"We had a fight. I told her something horrible. I told her something I had sworn I would never, ever let her know. And she left me."

Still calm, Claude said, "She will be all right."

A moan rose from Claire. "Will she?"

"She will be."

"I don't think so. What I said —"

"What did you say?"

"Please don't ask." Claire wailed faintly, "I think she is dead."

Both Vera and Katya stepped toward her, but stopped when Sasha, at the doorway, raised a hand.

Claude stood, and he held her arm. "She is all right," he said.

Claire pulled her arm away from him and said, "I know she isn't." Her jaw was shaking, and she kept opening and closing her lips. "I know she's dead."

Taking her arm again, Claude said, "We'll go to the hotel. She'll be there, waiting."

As they were leaving, Katya said, "Claude," and he turned to her. "You will not forget we found painting." He smiled at her.

On the way back to the hotel, Claire looked for the geyser of steam rising from the underground pipe, lit up by the lights of the windows of the apartment buildings.

In Russian, Sasha explained to a large-bosomed, frowning receptionist Claude's absence, and she, as suspicious as she was, gave them the key to his room, which he, he must understand, must pay for even though he hadn't occupied it. Then Sasha questioned the receptionist about Rachel. She had not been back. He questioned her until she became angry. He asked Claire if he should stay, and Claude answered that he would now stay with her. Bowing his head a little, Sasha left these Westerners to themselves. Claude, holding her by her arm as much to support her as to support himself, took Claire up to her room.

"Rachel is all right," Claude said. "I'm positive. We'll wait another hour, and you'll see, she'll come back."

"Will she?"

"You'll see."

Claire shook her head. She said, "Moscow is dark."

"She will find her way."

Again Claire shook her head, but just a little.

Weakly, Claude said, "I'll go to my room and have a bath, and then —"

"Please don't leave me," Claire cried.

"I won't, then. We'll wait together."

The room was hot. While Claire sat in the chair, Claude, in his shirtsleeves, his shirt dirty and wrinkled and smelling of body, sat on the edge of a bed. Whenever Claire moved, Claude looked at her, his eyes steady. He was calm, and Claire began to feel that he was right, and everything would be all right.

But after an hour he got up and went to the window as if to look out, though all that could be seen were their reflections in the glass and, beyond, the points of white and red lights in the darkness.

He turned around to Claire and said, "I'll telephone Viktor and ask him to come. He will help. He is good. I know he and Katya will help. They are both good."

This made Claire's body jump. She crossed her legs and pressed her arms against her breasts as if to keep herself from jumping again. "Call him," she cried, "please call him."

He dialed a number slowly, aware of Claire watching him, and he bit his lower lip while waiting for the ringing telephone to be answered at the other end.

"He's not there," Claude said, and hung up.

"Where is there?"

"Not far."

Claude again looked out the window. He dialed the telephone after what seemed to Claire a long time, and this time someone answered. "Can I see you?" Claire heard Claude ask. When he hung up he stared at the window. Claire got up and stood by Claude to stare with him. She could smell his body.

He went out of the room. She walked up and down the narrow space, pushing back again and again the lock of hair fallen over her cheek, until Claude returned.

He said quietly, "I promise you, she will be all right," and he put his arms around her and held her. Claire let herself be held. It was as though she had given in to something, and she felt again calm. Claude sat on a bed.

"Tell me," Claire asked him, "do you think that deep down, our impulse is not to save but to destroy?"

Slowly, Claude ran his fingertips across his forehead, down the side of his face, down his neck; then he let his hand drop and he said, "I think, to save." He lay back on the bed.

"What time is it?" Claire asked.

"After midnight."

"Shall we go out and look too?"

"We should wait here."

Claire unbraided the plait at her nape, then brushed her hair out and slowly replaited the braid. Claude watched her.

She said, "Close your eyes. You're tired."

"Not very," he said, but he did close his eyes. He was aware of Claire taking off his shoes and covering him with his overcoat.

He woke at dawn and saw Claire, sitting on the edge of her bed, keening silently. He sat up, dazed. The morning was clear, and sunlight was rounding out the sky. Claire stood and, as though still keening, walked back and forth in front of Claude, slowly at first, then more and more quickly, the skirt of her dress twisting and turning. She was barefoot. Her eyes were bloodshot.

Frowning, she stopped before Claude and said, "I want to see the painting."

"Now?"

"Yes, now."

"Claire —"

She said, "I have got to see the painting now. Please, please. You know where it is. I have got to see the painting now."

"We can't leave."

She was standing before him, and, her bloodshot eyes wide, she was rocking back and forth. "Please," she said, "please."

Claude clasped his hands and pressed them to his chin.

"Please," Claire said. "You understand. I know you understand. Please."

The telephone rang and jolted Claire. It rang and rang before

Claude answered it, and he said nothing into the receiver but simply listened, and then he said softly, "I will come to the lobby," and
hung up and left the room.

While he was out, Claire stood against a wall and hit her head
against it.

Claude returned and said, "Put on your coat, we will go see the
picture now."

She, hysterical, had difficulty putting on her shoes, and she
couldn't get her arms into her overcoat, so Claude had to help
her.

They got a taxi at the entrance to the hotel. The morning was
bright but cold, and the taxi, braking at red lights, skidded on the
ice, but the driver drove fast.

Claire kept her shivering lips pressed together. From time to
time her jaw jerked to the side and a muscle in her neck twitched.
Her bloodshot eyes were staring.

The taxi driver stopped by a dirty bank of melting snow and
pointed toward an archway into the courtyard of a big blank building with many windows. Pathways crisscrossed the melting snow
in the courtyard, and were muddy. Showing through the melting
snow were old brooms, newspaper-wrapped bundles, rusted pails,
and the torso of a doll. The stucco walls of the courtyard were covered with graffiti in pencil and chalk, and among them was written, in English, I WANT TO BE HAPPY. The doorways had numbers
painted crudely above them. The doors were dented and scratched,
the brown paint flaking, and some were open. The door they wanted was open.

Inside was a flight of cement stairs with an iron railing. The
plaster on the walls of the well had here and there fallen away to
the lathes, and there were graffiti, in pencil and chalk, everywhere.
Some of the treads were broken, and one was missing. On the
landings were rusted pails of sand. As they climbed higher the
smell of rot deepened. The toilets were off the landings.

Claude stopped at a doorway padded with brown vinyl, the

number painted on the wall over it. He looked at Claire before he rang. She swallowed nervously when the door opened.

Inside was an aged woman in a black dress and gray stockings and gray felt slippers and a pink crocheted bedjacket, her hair in a black hairnet. Her wide white face had moles on the cheeks and forehead. She smiled, and revealed teeth missing. Holding the door open with her back, she spoke in Russian and indicated to Claire and Claude to come in, come in. And in the little entry, where the plaster of the ceiling was crumbling with water stains, they took off their overcoats and hats, as the aged woman indicated they must.

On one side of the entry was a shut door. The woman pointed to the shut door and said, "Princess," meaning the Princess Volkanskaya was behind it. Then, pointing to her eyes, she said, "No, princess, no," meaning the princess couldn't see them. The aged woman turned to the open door on the other side of the entry and held out her hand to show Claire and Claude through into what must have been a kitchen. There was a brownish sink with one tap and a counter with a double gas ring, and black pots hanging on the wall above the counter. On the floor was a large earthenware pot filled with potatoes. Beyond the counter, against a wall, was a sofa with a crocheted blanket folded on it and a pillow with a crocheted case, and above the sofa on the cracked wall was a painting so dark it was difficult to make out from a distance what it was of. The canvas had tears in it, and in some places holes, as if a stick had been poked through it, or a gun fired at it. It had the dimensions of outstretched arms, and had no frame.

Claire faced it, with Claude a little behind her.

Claire stepped closer to the picture, her knees touching the edge of the sofa. The figures in the painting were almost absorbed into darkness, but the white face of the angel showed, and his white hands, and there was the sweep of his wings. The white face of the Virgin showed too, and her hands, raised, and through the grime Claude could see the beam of light that emanated from the white dove high at the center of the composition. The stretcher, seen about the exposed edges, looked rotten. There was a lily in a vase at the bottom of the painting.

Claire stepped back from the painting as if, as compulsively as she had come to see it, to leave it, and Claude stepped back to go with her. But he saw her kneel before the picture and lower her head. This startled Claude as much as it did the aged woman, and he reached down to hold Claire's shoulders, but she didn't move. Claude continued to hold her, and when, after a long stillness, she started to rise to her feet, he helped her up. Her face was wet with tears.

She was as if will-less, and Claude, standing behind her and holding her arm to support her, said to the aged woman, who stared at them, "*Prastytye, prastytye,*" and he helped Claire out of the kitchen and into the entry. The woman stood in the doorway, her hands to her cheeks in awe, while Claude helped Claire put on her overcoat and hat, and then put on his own.

Claude opened the door to the flat with one hand, always supporting Claire, and led her, one arm under hers, out onto the landing, and as he turned to her once they were out he saw the doom in her face. He said quietly, "Be careful of the first step."

Rachel was coming up.

III

SASHA CAME UP behind her, and he rushed ahead of her to meet Claire and Claude coming down as if he had something to tell them before Rachel reached them, but all he said was "Here she is."

Rachel's pregnancy, bulging her overcoat, made her move slowly. As she climbed, her hat hid most of her face.

As if Sasha thought that what had happened must be made fun of, he laughed and said, "We are finding it more and more difficult to understand Westerners."

Rachel paused on the stairs below, and Claude, still holding Claire by the arm, looked down at her. She seemed to be down a very, very long staircase, very far from him, looking up at him.

The aged woman in the black dress appeared. Her hands still on her cheeks, her expression one of bewilderment, if no longer awe, she spoke to Sasha in a hoarse voice.

He said to Claire and Claude and Rachel, "She told me the princess would like to see you all."

On a landing, a young man came out of a toilet, and he studied the solemn procession as it passed him.

In the entry, the elderly woman helped Rachel take off her overcoat, and she hung it. Claire and Claude hung their coats, and Sasha, who had stopped finding what was going on funny, his padded coat. The door that had been shut in the entry was now open, and the woman in the black dress led Rachel, who, moving slowly in her uncertainty, made those behind her go slowly, into a room with water-stained ceiling and wallpaper. A very old woman was sitting on a sofa, at the foot of which were folded blankets. Her face was long and white and bony, and her hair, yellow-white, was braided and coiled above her large ears. She wore what looked like a long, grayish woolen robe with long sleeves. She had no teeth, but she smiled as the elderly woman in the black dress brought Rachel to her to introduce her.

The old woman asked with a high, trembling voice, "*Vous parlez français?*"

Rachel said faintly, "*Oui.*"

The old woman said that only a little was needed, and smiled so her gums showed.

Then Claire and Claude were introduced to her, and they shook her thin hand. Sasha kissed her hand.

"*Il n'y a pas beaucoup de place,*" the princess said, "*mais assayez vous —*"

The room was very small, a large part of it taken up by a big wardrobe with an oval mirror on the front. The mirror was cracked, and some of the inlaid veneer was missing. There were suitcases piled on top. A floorboard was up, so a joist was visible below. A grayish light came through the grimy window. There were no pictures of any kind on the walls.

The princess patted the sofa next to her and told Rachel to sit there, and Claire sat on a wooden chair and Claude on a stool. Sasha stood. The woman in the black dress went out.

"*Comment vous appellez-vous?*" the princess asked Rachel.

Rachel gave her name.

The princess reached out a gnarled hand and touched her head. She said, with a French pronunciation, "Rachel," then she lowered her hand and went silent.

Rachel closed her eyes for a moment.

Then the princess asked Claire, "*Vous êtes la mère de Rachel?*"

"*Oui,*" Claire said, she was Rachel's mother.

"*Et vous, monsieur,*" the princess asked Claude, "*vous êtes—?*"

Claude said, "*Je suis le mari de Rachel.*"

He didn't look at Rachel when he said he was her husband, but at Claire.

The princess asked Claire if she was the one who had wanted to see her picture.

Yes, Claire said, she was.

The princess said her daughter had told her how Claire had been so moved by the picture.

Claire tried to smile a little, and as she did tears rose into her bloodshot eyes. "*Oui,*" she said.

Why had Madame wanted to see it?

Claire said she was devoted to the work of Pietro Testa because, because — and she couldn't think why. She said again, knowing she was getting the French wrong, "*Je me suis consacrée à son art.*"

"*Consacrée?*" the princess asked.

"*Oui,*" Claire said, "*consacrée.*"

They all sat in a circle of silence, as if waiting for something to happen.

Claire asked if her daughter Rachel, who had arrived late, could see the picture, and the princess said of course, of course.

The princess called out for her daughter, who came and helped the old woman to her feet and supported her as she walked unsteadily across the floor to the doorway through which the guests had come into the room. Her long, dirty robe swung back and forth as she lurched from time to time, and her daughter held her up. She was barefoot. Sasha remaining at a distance, they all went through the small entry hall into the kitchen. Rachel followed the old woman to the painting above the sofa. Rachel faced it, with Claire on one side and Claude on the other.

The princess said, in a voice hardly audible, that they had had to sell the frame.

IV

VERA FOUND, when she tipped the teapot to pour more tea into the cups on the table, that the pot was empty, and she went out with it. Rachel was asleep on the chaise longue. Claire slowly braided her hair into a plait at her nape, and Claude looked at Russian books in a bookcase. The room in Vera and Sasha's apartment was warm. Rachel's stomach was covered with the crocheted blanket, and her hands, which were large and red, as if she had worked hard with them, were on her breasts.

No one had, since that morning in the apartment of the

princess, mentioned the painting, as if what had happened there could only have embarrassed them.

Vera came in with a fresh pot of tea and placed it on the table.

Sighing, Rachel woke.

"Are you all right, darling?" Claire asked, going to her daughter.

A hand over her forehead, Rachel said hoarsely, "I was dreaming."

"What were you dreaming?"

"I can't remember." Rachel sat on the edge of the chaise longue and drew the blanket around her shoulders. "I would like to visit the grave of Maurice," she said. "Is that possible?"

"What do you think," Claire asked Claude, "is it possible?"

Vera said, "Sasha will be back shortly. He will take you."

Sasha said he would take them as soon as he had had a cup of tea.

In a corner of the lot where Sasha parked his car, a woman was sweeping an oriental rug on the snow. Claude watched Rachel watch the woman for a little while before she got into the back seat, and Claude got in beside her. Claire sat beside Sasha in front. Claude looked at Rachel looking out at what they passed — a wooden hut by the side of the street at the little window of which men were queuing in a long line, a shop window filled with a display of stacked cans, a dark bronze statue of a man in a uniform standing on a granite plinth — and Claude felt that she was looking around so as not to look at him.

Sasha was talking about Russia. Laughing, he said, "No, I cannot even imagine the West. Do people there sleep on sofas, eat at tables, go to work in offices and factories?"

Claire asked, "Shouldn't we bring flowers to the grave?"

"In our country," Sasha said, "that is the custom. I do not know about the West."

The crowded flower market, in a lot covered in slush and mud, was made up of long trestle tables under narrow metal roofs with icicles hanging along the edges. Yellow and russet chrysanthemums were laid in heaps across the tables, the blossoms drooping, and women behind the tables, wearing kerchiefs, overcoats, and boots, visible beneath the tables, were tearing the limp leaves from the stems.

Sasha went up to a woman and Claire followed. Still embarrassed by each other, Rachel and Claude separated in the crowd. Rachel went to look at flowers at another table, and Claude at yet another table. All the flowers were chrysanthemums, and all were yellow or russet.

When Claude turned to look for Rachel, he saw, coming straight toward him, an old woman in a torn black coat too big for her and a tight black kerchief and tennis shoes through the holes of which her toes showed. She was carrying large white chrysanthemums, the stems wrapped in brown paper. Her wrinkled face was thin and pale. As if she recognized Claude, she smiled.

Beyond the old woman he saw Rachel. Quickly, Claude passed the old woman to go to her, and he put his arms around her. He felt Rachel's arms around him.

In the car, Claire held in the crook of one arm a great bunch of yellow and russet flowers, and with her free hand turned one flower in her fingers and tapped her face with it. She had become, in her very dishevelment, sensual.

She saw us, Claude thought, she saw Rachel and me.

The cemetery was becoming dark under snow-heavy trees. Family plots were surrounded by fences of thin metal pickets, and within the enclosures were small, metal, snow-covered tables. Claire, Rachel, and Claude followed Sasha along the paths among the graves.

Sasha could not have understood the delicate air of celebration with which the Americans put the flowers on the grave of Maurice.

During the night, Claude thought: No, I don't believe in God, but I can imagine him. I imagine him as the darkness in which images occur, the darkness that, when I shift my attention from an image to what is around the image, I see spreading in all directions beyond my sight. That vast dark space behind the image of a sunlit glass of water is the only way I can imagine God.